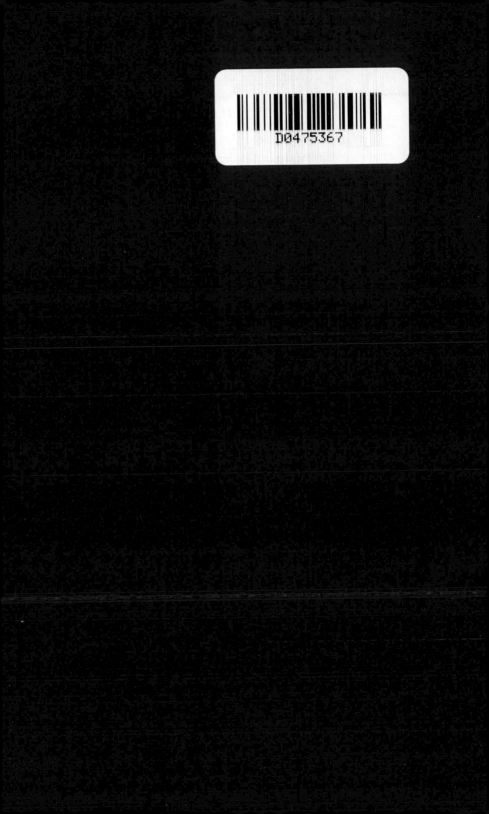

THE
COURT
OF
SHADOWS

**VAMPYRIA
BOOK I**

ALSO BY VICTOR DIXEN

11/23 ②
2/24 ck

THE COURT OF SHADOWS

VAMPYRIA
BOOK I

VICTOR DIXEN

Translated by Françoise Bui

AMAZON **CROSSING**

Text copyright © 2020 by Éditions Robert Laffont, S. A. S., Paris
Translation copyright © 2023 by Françoise Bui
All rights reserved.

Previously published as *Vampyria: La Cour des Ténèbres* by Éditions Robert Laffont in France in 2020. Translated from French by Françoise Bui. First published in English by Amazon Crossing in 2023.

Published by Amazon Crossing, Seattle
www.apub.com

Amazon, the Amazon logo, and Amazon Crossing are trademarks of Amazon.com, Inc., or its affiliates.

ISBN-13: 9781662505690 (hardcover)
ISBN-13: 9781662505706 (paperback)
ISBN-13: 9781662505683 (digital)

Cover design by Kimberly Glyder
Cover illustration and interior border illustrations by Colin Verdi
Interior maps illustrated by Misty Beee
Interior character list illustrated by © Loles Romero

Printed in the United States of America
First edition

For E.
For my parents
For my sister Lisa

We can do all we wish while alive;
afterward, we are less than the humblest.
—The words of the Sun King in his
twilight years

🦇

At last, Louis the Great is dead!
The Fates have cut his thread.
Ô Reguingué, Ô Lon La La,
They've just ended his destiny;
All of Europe is merry.
—Popular song upon the death
of the Sun King,
before his transmutation to
King of Shadows, 31 October 1715

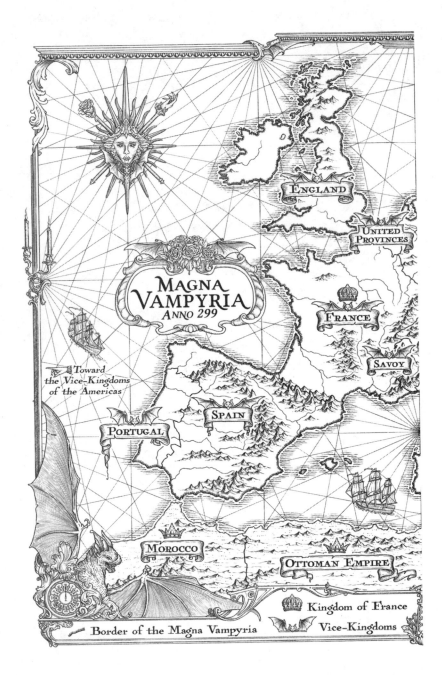

MAGNA VAMPYRIA
ANNO 299

ENGLAND

UNITED PROVINCES

FRANCE

SAVOY

Toward
the Vice-Kingdoms
of the Americas

SPAIN

PORTUGAL

MOROCCO

OTTOMAN EMPIRE

Kingdom of France

Vice-Kingdoms

Border of the Magna Vampyria

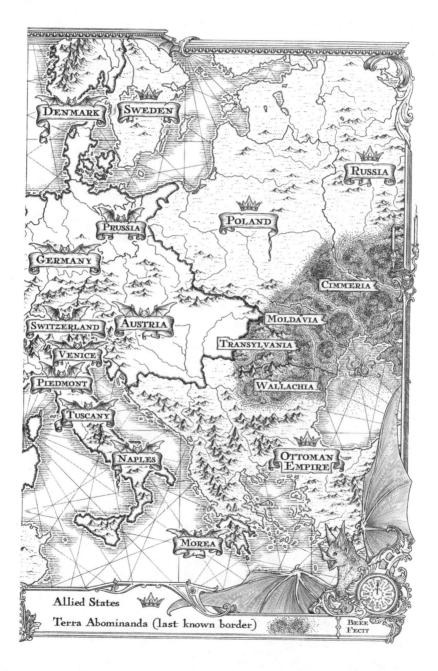

DENMARK

SWEDEN

RUSSIA

PRUSSIA

POLAND

GERMANY

CIMMERIA

MOLDAVIA

SWITZERLAND

AUSTRIA

TRANSYLVANIA

VENICE

PIEDMONT

WALLACHIA

TUSCANY

NAPLES

OTTOMAN
EMPIRE

MOREA

Allied States

Terra Abominanda (last known border)

BEEE
FECIT

MORTAL CODE
CODEX MORTALIS

Edict of
LOUIS THE IMMUTABLE,
KING OF SHADOWS
LUDOVICUS IMMUTABILIS,
REX TENEBRÆ
issued as law for governing the mortal commoners
of the fourth estate of the realm,
throughout the kingdom of France and its
vice-kingdoms of the Magna Vampyria.

HIGH NOBILITY
(Vampyres)

IMMORTALS

MORTALS

HEMATIC FACULTY
(Doctors)

LOW NOBILITY
(Feudal Lords)

FOURTH ESTATE
(Commoners)

PREAMBLE

By the grace of the Shadows, the realm of the Magna Vampyria is divided into four estates. The immortal estate: vampyres of the high aristocracy. Three mortal estates: feudal lords of the lower nobility, doctors of the Hematic Faculty, and commoners of the fourth estate. The articles below concern this last tier of mortals.

Art. 1: OBEDIENCE, *OBOEDIENTIA*
From cradle to grave, commoners remain under the protection of the vampyres, in return for which they owe total submission and the following obligations:

Art. 2: SEQUESTER, *SEQUESTRUM*
During daytime hours, for as long as the sun shines, commoners are forbidden from going farther than one league from their bell tower.

Art. 3: CURFEW, *IGNITEGIUM*
During nighttime hours, as soon as the warning bell tolls, commoners are forbidden from leaving their dwellings.

Art. 4: TITHE, *DECIMA*
Every month, commoners are required to donate one-tenth of their blood.

Art. 5: SANCTION, *SUPPLICIUM*
All who violate the above articles will be executed.

WHO WILL GAIN ENTRY TO THE COURT OF SHADOWS?

Jeanne Froidelac,
born in Auvergne, France

Proserpina Castlecliff,
born in England

Tristan de La Roncière,
born in Ardennes, France

Hélénaïs de Plumigny,
born in Beauce, France

Naoko Takagari,
born in Japan

Rafael de Montesueño,
born in Spain

AWAITING YOU AT COURT

Alexandre de Mortange,
Viscount of Clermont

Edmée de Vauvalon,
Marquise de Vauvalon

Suraj de Jaipur,
Squire to the King

Lucrèce du Crèvecœur,
Squire to the King

Raymond de Montfaucon,
Director of the Grande Écurie

Madame Thérèse,
Governess at the Grande Écurie

I

VISIT

"In the name of the king, open immediately!" a thunderous voice orders.

My parents exchange a panicked glance. We've just sat down to eat at the dining table, all five of us. My oldest brother, Valère, freezes. The second one, Bastien, drops his spoon to the floor. I grab the spoon, since I'm always picking up after Bastien—even if I'm the youngest.

"Who can that possibly be at this hour, and on a Sunday, no less?" Maman asks.

She looks at the old clock that shows it's barely past seven in the evening. The clock stands next to an almanac affixed to the wall, open to today's date: August 31 in the year 299 of the Age of Shadows.

By way of response, a fist hammers the front door, making the steaming pheasant soup shake in our bowls. My heart trembles even harder. *"In the name of the king!"* the nighttime visitor announced. He could just as easily have said, *"In the name of the devil himself!"*

I eye the framed engraving of Louis the Immutable that hangs above our fireplace, same as it does in all the hearths of France. The sovereign's long curls lost their brown coloring long ago—or, more likely, the paper itself faded over the years, since the engraving was printed ages before I was born. The king's face, however, hasn't acquired a single wrinkle. And for good reason: it's hidden behind a smooth gold mask that doesn't betray age or display any expression. Only two dark eyes emerge, eyes that callously scrutinize every person in the kingdom. The metal lips, closed and enigmatic, are far more chilling than if they revealed the sharp canines hidden beneath.

Shrugging off a shiver, I run to the window to try to see what's happening outside. Through the thick pane of glass, the main road of Butte-aux-Rats is bathed in a golden and blinding light: it's the end of summer, when the sun lingers until after eight on the plateaus of the Auvergne, the mountainous heart of the country . . . and when the vampyres rise late. It's the happiest season of the year, the few weeks when it's warm enough to go coatless. It's the time when the villagers nearly forget about the Mortal Code that for generations has crushed the Magna Vampyria, the broad coalition comprising the kingdom of France and its vice-kingdoms.

"Get away from the window, Jeanne," Maman orders me. "Don't take unnecessary risks."

She anxiously tucks a strand of her long brown hair behind her ear. My own hair, which is cut above my shoulders, has always been gray. Only my mother finds this anomaly charming.

"The rays won't burn my skin," I tell her with a shrug. "I'm not a bloodsucker."

"Don't say such things!" Papa snaps as he pounds the table.

As a good citizen who's been under the thumb of the regime, he's always the first to get upset when we don't show proper respect to the vampyres. Reverently, he's installed some dried chrysanthemums—the flowers of the undead—under the royal portrait. Next year the kingdom will celebrate the despot's jubilee. Nearly three centuries have passed since his transmutation; it happened in the year 1715 of the old calendar, the night he should have died of old age at the end of an interminable reign marked by war and famine. Instead of drifting off to eternal sleep, the Sun King took part in a heinous secret medical rite. The procedure granted him immortality but also mutilated his face. Louis XIV became Louis the Immutable, King of Shadows: the first vampyre in history. Immortal and disfigured. Soon thereafter, every monarch on the continent pledged their allegiance to him so that they, too, could transmute into immortals, ensnaring Europe in an iron yoke. The climate itself froze, and an ice age spread over the land.

"Open now or we'll smash down the door!" the person outside shouts more menacingly than before.

The fist starts banging again on the door of the apothecary that's attached to our living quarters, the entrance of which faces the village square.

My brothers get up now. Valère rushes over to the sideboard and takes out a long knife, the one our father used to carve the pheasant that I poached from the forest this very morning. Bastien just looks around, seemingly alarmed. And our old tomcat, Tibert, abandons his plate of giblets and takes refuge in a corner. As for me, I instinctively stand firmly on my legs, my thighs taut under my lambskin breeches. I may be small for my seventeen years, but my body is nimble and primed to run.

"Sounds like the militia," Valère whispers as he blinks behind eyeglasses that make him look years older. He's always been the nervous one in the family.

"Calm down," Maman says in a gentle, commanding voice. "Let go of the knife. Nothing's going to happen to us."

Valère does as he's told: in front of our mother, my big brothers toe the line. In the shop, she's the one who holds the purse strings, and at home, she has the final word.

"Maman's right: nothing will happen to us," I say. "Since when has anything interesting occurred here? And that's not about to change today. Right, Bastien?"

Despite the joking tone I take to get a smile out of him, I do feel somewhat anxious. Who could possibly find blame with my parents, the Froidelacs, the honorable apothecaries of a forsaken village way out in the depths of one of the most hemmed-in provinces of France? We're twenty miles from Clermont, the nearest city. My parents have always paid the tax, in both gold and blood. Twelve times a year, my father even helps Dr. Boniface bleed each and every villager. He starts with himself, his wife, and his children. Under the Mortal Code, an apothecary is charged not only with providing village folk with remedies but also with draining them of the precious red liquid. Such is the tithe collected by the Hematic Faculty—from the Greek *haimatos*, meaning "blood"—a religious order founded by the priest-doctors who transmuted the king.

"We have nothing to reproach ourselves for, right, aside from being deadly boring?" I say, giving Bastien a wink. He's my favorite brother, the only one in the family who appreciates my sense of humor.

Papa nods, the way he always does to reassure his patients, but his forehead is creased with fear. I've never seen him like this—or rather I have: he looked exactly the same on that frigid December night some five years ago when a group of militiamen dragged a stranger in a snow-laden coat to the apothecary. The poor fellow had defied the curfew that forbids commoners from traveling on the roads after sunset and fallen victim to a vampyre who happened by, a vampyre whose name we'll never know. The lords of the night have the right to feed as they wish on those who dare go out after the warning bell tolls. The only signs the predator had left on his victim's neck were two purplish perforations from which he'd nearly drained the prey of all his blood. I was twelve years old, and it was my first time seeing a vampyre bite. It imprinted its mark deep in my soul, as it did on that poor man's flesh, though I haven't seen another bite since. Here, in the depths of the Auvergne, where there are twice as many sheep as humans and ten times as many rats, the lords of the night hardly venture near.

I take a deep breath, trying to gather my thoughts.

On that long-ago winter night, when my father held the freezing man in his arms, he had a look of despair. But today, in summer and daylight, why does he appear in such a state?

"Apothecary, mark my words, it's my final warning!" shouts the angry voice from out on the village square.

My parents exchange a harrowed look.

Papa heads toward the door that separates the dining area from the shop.

The room reveals shelves covered with neatly aligned terra-cotta jars on which Bastien carefully hand-painted the names of various ointments and potions. The sun shines on the wooden countertop. So many times when I had to tend to the cashbox, I felt suffocated by the cramped space, filled with dread that my life was slipping through my fingers. I only feel like myself when I'm in my lambskin breeches, my hair hidden under a shepherd's hat, running through the woods to gather medicinal plants . . . and flushing out wild game when the occasion presents itself.

Suddenly, I'm gripped with worry: What if the militia has come to arrest me for the pheasant we were about to eat? Commoners are forbidden to hunt, but until now Captain Martin has always turned a blind eye to my indiscretions. He's thankful that my parents generously provide him with sage herbal tea to treat his bouts of gout.

I twist my neck to get a better look, filtering the blinding light between my lashes. At last, I can make out the visitor standing in front of the glass-paned door that opens onto the town square. It isn't Captain Martin, the small, good-natured fellow who oversees the three-man militia of Butte-aux-Rats. The visitor threatening to smash the glass of the door with his gloved fist stands tall and lean like a gibbet. His body is shrouded in a long black robe that falls to the ground. A large white pleated ruff is fitted around his neck, the frilly adornment worn by members of the Faculty.

"An inquisitor . . . ," I whisper as I recognize the bat-shaped iron-ring claw attached to his conical hat.

I've never seen an inquisitor except in the engravings of novels. But I know they're the only members of the Faculty who wear the bat claw, ready to crush the state's religious enemies anywhere they hide. The presence of such a high-ranking dignitary in Butte-aux-Rats is unheard of. The Faculty's only representative is Dr. Boniface, whose own ruff is a modest and simple flattened version.

This time I'm sure of it: There's been a mistake. A terrible error that my father will clear up in a few words.

"Children, go upstairs," Maman orders us.

"Why?" Valère wants to know.

"Don't argue."

Begrudgingly, we obey. But at the top of the stairs that lead to the bedrooms, I speak to my brothers in a hushed tone.

"Stay here, in the dark. I'm going to eavesdrop on what's happening below."

It's the advantage of being the smallest in the family—I can hide anywhere. Tightly, I hug the railing, just like when I'm in the forest, lying in wait for prey.

The lock on the door turns with a clang.

Boots pound against the tiles of the shop. The inquisitor clearly didn't come alone.

From my perch, I see him enter the dining room, followed by one . . . two . . . three soldiers dressed in dark leather, shod in thigh-high boots, all heavily armed. Atop their heads are gray cloth hats lined with fur, the long tips of which fall down to their shoulders. In horror, I recognize the headgear of the king's cavalry. These fierce dragoons are charged with eliminating anyone who threatens the ruthless mandate of the Vampyria.

Why have they come here tonight?

Papa tries to appear confident.

"Welcome to my humble dwelling, Your Reverence. My wife and I are honored by your visit. We were just about to have supper, a chicken soup."

Chicken soup, a small lie to pass off the poached pheasant for poultry purchased at the market. A stranger like the inquisitor is no doubt clueless that at Butte-aux-Rats, where it freezes two-thirds of the year, humans and animals must snatch their meager sustenance from the sterile land. Here, even a respected apothecary cannot afford a weekly chicken.

"We'd be delighted to share our modest meal with you . . . ," Papa continues as if nothing were amiss.

He points to the chipped soup tureen, the pitcher filled with watered-down wine, and the breadbasket that we always cover with a dishcloth so the rats don't take nibbles. It's a very simple setting, but the bouquet of flowers that Maman gathered adds a touch of color and grace—no, not dried chrysanthemums like those that decorate the altar to the king but fresh-cut flowers from the fields.

"In his time, didn't good King Henri wish that the royal subjects in his kingdom could put a chicken in every pot on Sundays?" Papa persists, smiling.

"Leave old King Henri in his tomb, where his bones have been moldering for centuries!" The inquisitor's guttural voice is as sharp as the razor-thin face that emerges above the ruff.

Behind me, I hear Valère swear under his breath. Henri IV was the next-to-last mortal who reigned over the land. A faraway past when monarchs were just and the sun shone brighter, a past that has always seemed to me like a fairy tale. Every Sunday, Dr. Boniface recites the Faculty's sermons—that the transmutation of the high aristocracy installed a lasting peace in France and Europe: the *pax vampyrica*, putting an end to past wars. The dogma also explains that the vampyres protect mortals from nighttime abominations when these creatures leave their lairs after sunset. I don't know if these horrors really exist, since I've never seen any. Finally, the hematic credo claims that there has been a continuous dynasty since Henri IV, founder of the Bourbons and a king who genuinely loved his people, right up to Louis the Immutable, his grandson who rules over us today. But sovereigns of the past went about with uncovered faces, like each of their subjects, whereas for three hundred years, the Immutable has been hiding behind an impenetrable mask. The kings of old lived and died like humans, while the King of Shadows bathes his immortal body in the blood of the French.

Gripped by a fear that the inquisitor detects my presence and can read my thoughts, I flatten myself even closer to the second-floor railing. Who knows what powers the eminent members of the clergy who sold out to the Vampyria are endowed with?

But the visitor's attention stays focused on my poor papa.

"Sedition has taken root in these walls, I sense it . . . ," he growls, sniffing the air as if he can discern an aroma of guilt. He points an accusing finger at the tureen. "And I detect the whiff of garlic in that broth."

"We'd never allow that," Papa objects. "We know full well that garlic is an irritant for our lords. We know it's forbidden in the kingdom! It's only chives that you smell, Your Reverence."

Losing interest in the tureen, the inquisitor moves along the length of a wall where heaps of logs are stacked. My brothers chopped the wood to get us through the upcoming six months of bitter winter. His footsteps make for the library at the rear of the room. Accusingly, he points at the shelves.

"So many books in a commoner's household. This reeks of heresy."

"These are only classic essays on herbal medicine, along with a few innocent novels," Maman snaps back, standing firm.

She's right. There's nothing unusual in our library except for an adventure series in English that I've read a dozen times out of boredom. My mother inherited the books from an obscure great-uncle whom she never knew. She learned English before she taught me, but she's never stepped foot across the Channel due to the sequester that forbids commoners from traveling more than a league farther than their village bell tower.

The inquisitor hasn't come to discuss literature. Brusquely, he turns away from the library and swoops down on my father, his long black robe whipping the air like a cape.

"Take me to your laboratory," he orders.

"My laboratory? That dark cellar is rank with toxic fumes. It's the rat poison I've been forced to produce in large quantities. Such a place isn't worthy of a visit by a man of your stature."

"Now, or I'll have your throat slit."

The dragoons draw their swords menacingly.

Papa hesitates a second, an instant of doubt.

I, too, doubt. For the first time, *I doubt him*.

Why is he reluctant to show his lab to these intruders?

A room filled with old chipped beakers and dented stills that's of absolutely no interest.

Unless . . .

"What's going on, weasel?" Bastien whispers behind me, his voice anxious.

Weasel, his affectionate nickname for me. Bastien's an artist who spends his days drawing, his eye quick to pinpoint the animal features that hide behind those of people.

"Papa's heading toward the cellar hatch," I whisper.

My father's only forty-five years old, but suddenly he looks as hunched as an old man. Quickly, he glances toward the top of the stairs and catches my eyes.

I have the wrenching suspicion that he wants to tell me so many things that he's been silent about, but now it's too late. An awful feeling tells me that the unspoken words will never leave his lips.

"Let's go!" the inquisitor thunders, giving my father a rough shove.

"I'm the only one who uses the lab," Papa says, though it's untrue.

After the chicken soup, it's his second lie: Maman, an herbal specialist, helps him to prepare medicinal potions and ointments in the lab every day; Valère studied alongside them for many years; even Bastien spends a lot of time there grinding rock pigments for his paintings. I'm the only one in the family who never ventures into the cellar. What if I'm completely unaware of the experiments that take place down there, like forbidden practices that could attract the attention of an inquisitor?

Papa rushes through the trapdoor, the inquisitor and one of the dragoons close on his heels. Meanwhile, the other two position themselves on each side of my mother.

Soon, a racket can be heard coming from the cellar—the sound of shattering glass and metal bashing against metal.

I can feel Valère simmering with anger behind me. He's glued to my back.

"We have to do something," he whispers.

"Do what?" Bastien snaps, sounding panicked. "Except hope they don't discover the secret passage?"

I look at my brothers.

In the dimness of the hallway, their faces seem to belong to strangers. It's not only their brown hair, so unlike my pale strands, nor their brown eyes, where mine are a muted blue-gray.

All three of us were born a year apart, but we're each so different. Valère inherited our father's hard work ethic; he's supposed to take over the shop one day. Bastien has our mother's refinement; when he's not busy drawing or daydreaming, his beautiful penmanship makes him the unofficial scribe of the village. As for me, I don't take after anyone. No trade awaits me. And tonight, I don't feel part of my own family.

"What are you talking about?" I whisper. "What secret passage?"

"Better that you don't know," Valère says. He looks stern behind his eyeglasses. "Papa and Maman say you're too unpredictable."

"What secret passage?" I say again, grabbing hold of his wrist.

Valère clenches his jaw and tries to pull his arm away, but I'm not inclined to let go before I get an answer.

Bastien intervenes, fearing that the tussle will attract the attention of the dragoons in the room below.

"I didn't know about it either before my eighteenth birthday last year," he tells me softly. "And you, weasel, you'd have been told too. I'm sure Maman was just waiting for you to come of age."

"Tell me what?" I ask, my stomach in knots.

I'm hurt that my favorite brother—the person I'm closest to in the world, my only friend—kept something from me. As for my mother, I can't help but glance down the stairs and into the dining room, where the destruction in the cellar echoes loud and clear.

Maman stands stoically between the two dragoons, her face unreadable. She's always had a strong personality, and so do I, which often sparked fireworks between us. All during my childhood, she was my role model: she taught me so much, giving me a love of books and awakening my curiosity about the world. Then, in adolescence, I started to resent her. Why stir up my desire for the unknown if it was only to cruelly remind me about the laws of the curfew and sequester? As I got older, Butte-aux-Rats seemed to get more and more confining, the idea of being trapped here for life only fueling my frustration.

"There's a hidden door in the cellar," Bastien whispers so softly that his voice is barely audible. "It leads to a secret room behind the lab. A workshop where Papa and Maman practice alchemic experiments for some Fronde rebels in the region."

I'd like to respond that it's impossible. My shopkeeper parents are stuck in the humdrum of the day-to-day. They're not conspirators who'll risk their lives for a lost cause. Everyone knows the science of alchemy is officially banned by the Faculty. Everyone also knows that the Fronde rebels are nuts, mere mortals who dare to revolt against the king. Rumor has it that those fools use the same energy as the one that runs in the blood of vampyres—the mysterious Shadows—to fashion the wicked arms meant to overthrow the Vampyria. It's just gossip, of course; after all, the Vampyria is indestructible.

"Papa and Maman would never have gotten swept up in such madness," I whisper, outraged. I struggle to keep my voice down. "They'd never . . ."

A terrible blast swallows the rest of my sentence and makes the house shake all the way down to its foundations.

2

SECRET

Deafened by the explosion, I let go of Valère's wrist.

Immediately, he rushes headlong down the stairs.

"Papa! Maman!" he shouts.

Thick smoke from the blast rises from the open cellar trapdoor.

My ears are ringing.

My eyes sting.

But most of all, I'm jolted by a dire feeling: My brothers were right. The cellar was full of banned explosive substances, and my father just blew himself up alongside the inquisitor so that we stood a chance of getting out alive.

Cursing and coughing, the two surviving dragoons draw their swords as they look for my mother, who's vanished in the smoke.

Quick as lightning, Valère dashes toward the kitchen knife he left on the corner of the sideboard and turns around with surprising agility. He plunges the knife into the ribs of the first dragoon, right up to the handle. But this master stroke is a fluke. He stumbles under his own weight, exposing his neck to the second dragoon.

My heart skips a beat. I take my sling out of my lambskin breeches. It's the same weapon I used to bring down the pheasant earlier. I push in a pointy stone I picked up in the forest and, in a frenzy, turn the sling round and round above my head . . . but not fast enough.

The soldier's sharp sword comes down like a cleaver on Valère's neck.

Blood spurts from the sectioned artery all the way to the fireplace, splattering the portrait of the golden-masked king.

My hand flinches, and my projectile misses the killer by a few feet, instead hitting the vase on the dining table. The sound of shattering glass fills the house.

Valère's severed head falls off his body and rolls onto the bloodied floor tiles.

I howl in horror.

The soldier looks up at me with burning hate.

I thrust my hand into my pocket, searching for a new stone, but my fingers come up empty.

Already the dragoon is heading toward the stairs, brandishing his sword.

At that instant, my mother pops out from behind the log pile in the corner of the library. Her face is marred with pain. She kneels down to pick up a fragment of the broken vase that's beside Valère and plants it into the dragoon's shoulder.

"For my son!" she yells.

The soldier freezes on the spot.

Maman snatches the fragment back and holds it so tight it could sever her fingers. Then she brings it down with all her might.

"For my husband!"

The soldier turns around at the same time and slashes my mother's neck with the edge of his sword.

"Maman!" I scream.

My mother has just enough strength for a third stab. She plunges the fragment right into her adversary's heart. Then she collapses against his chest.

The dragoon's pointy hat falls to the floor.

Leaning one against the other, the dragoon and Maman remain stock still, like two lovers fused in a monstrous embrace.

I escape from the grip of Bastien's trembling hands and hurtle down the stairs.

"Maman!" I yell again as I grab her by the shoulders. The dragoon's lifeless body crumples behind me.

My mother's own body is as limp as a rag doll between my tensed fingers. Just like the doll my parents insisted on giving me when I was young, before they understood that the only thing of interest to me was using my sling to help Tibert hunt rats.

"Talk to me . . . say something . . . anything . . . ," I manage to say between sobs.

Tell me everything you and Papa never mentioned.

Tell me who you really were.

Tell me stories like when I was young—Aesop's fables or Perrault's tales or one of your own made-up legends.

But no sound comes from her pale lips.

Her face is a blur in my tear-filled eyes.

Above her shoulders, the Immutable glares down at me from behind his frozen mask, his cheeks dabbed with red from Valère's splattered blood.

I can't stand the sight of the king anymore, so I bend over to rest my mother's body on the ground. The wildflowers she gathered are scattered around us. As I lay her head down on the tiles, my fingers come in contact with the chain of the small bronze medallion she always wore around her neck. It's broken; the killer's sword severed the links.

"They're all . . . ," Bastien says softly behind me. I can feel his ragged breathing on my neck. "They're all dead."

All dead?

In the time it takes for this unfathomable information to register in my brain, I hear the sound of a piercing whistle. It's coming from the dragoon that Valère stabbed before he died. The brute is lying in a puddle where his blood mingles with that of my loved ones. With his last breath, he blows his whistle to sound the alarm. And then he expires.

Did the inquisitor come with other henchmen? Are they waiting outside, ready to finish what he started?

"We . . . we have to go," Bastien stammers.

"Go . . . ," I echo as I look at my mother's hair—hair she was so proud of—as it floats like algae in the reddening puddle of water from the flowers.

"Don't let me down, weasel."

Bastien shakes my shoulders, forcing me to regain my wits.

In a pitiful attempt to gather a memory of my mother, I grab the medallion and slide it into my pocket.

"The forest," I say in a whisper as I get up.

The woods are where I exiled myself all through my childhood so I could flee the boredom of Butte-aux-Rats and everything about it that poisoned my soul. It's where my instincts tell me to seek refuge now.

The moment Bastien and I step across the shop with its neatly aligned jars—a space that smells of disinfectant and fresh wax, where I spent so many dull hours dreaming of escaping to the other end of the world—I'm hit with the certainty that I'll never set foot here again.

I grab my old felt hat hanging on the wall and plop it over my hair. We tumble out into the village square, engulfed in silence.

The sun that was so blinding only a short while ago has nearly disappeared behind the roofs of the thatched cottages, their shutters now all closed.

As I feared, there are more dragoons around. Across the clay-dirt square, three men armed with long spears stand guard in front of a dark wooden stagecoach hitched to glossy-coated horses. Thick black velvet curtains obscure the carriage windows.

I tilt my head to better hide my face under the large brim of my hat. Why aren't these men racing after us, after hearing the whistle?

It seems like it's more important for them to safeguard the carriage . . . and its occupant.

"A . . . a vampyre carriage," Bastien stammers.

I swallow painfully as I recall my nighttime reading, novels where I discovered the garb worn by inquisitors. Certain engravings showed carriages made of precious ebony wood, aboard which the lords of the night travel around, sealed off from the light of day.

In all my life, I've never encountered a vampyre. Even if the portrait of their creator has spied on me from the fireplace since childhood. Even if, every month, I've given them a tenth of my blood in a hematic flask labeled with my birth year. Now, for the very first time, I'm only yards away from one of those creatures. Creatures that at the same time terrify and disgust . . . and fascinate me.

"Night will fall soon, and then we won't stand a chance of getting away from whoever's inside that carriage," Bastien laments, tearing me from my thoughts.

He drags me into the semidarkness of an alley, out of the dragoons' sight.

"A vampyre has a keen sense of smell. Better even than the finest bloodhound," he tells me. "He'll easily detect our scent in the forest. We have to . . . have to hide somewhere else."

"Somewhere else? But where? There are only about twenty muddy streets, the forest all around, and the castle at the top of the hill."

"Exactly," Bastien snaps back as he grips my arm.

He eyes the crumbling castle at the top of the steep and craggy hill, the one that gave Butte-aux-Rats its name. In truth, it's more like a manor than a castle, an old fortified structure that's been gnawed at by the centuries. It's where old Baron Gontran de Gastefriche lives, the overlord of Butte-aux-Rats and the few neighboring hamlets. Since his wife's death from the fevers years ago, he and his daughter are the only nobility in the region. They're exempt from the blood tithe, same as the parish doctor. But they see to it that two hundred flasks filled with their subjects' blood are sent every month to the archiater of Clermont, the vampyric prelate who replaced the bishop of former times.

"Follow me," Bastien says, suddenly full of confidence, something I've never known him to possess.

There's a glimmer in his big sensitive eyes, the same determined, wild spark that I often saw in the eyes of our mother. In this instant, my brother is her spitting image.

He pulls me toward the path that winds its way to the hilltop, the last place I would ever have thought of as a safe haven.

The thatched roofs vanish behind the treetops. Soon we can't even see the bat-shaped weather vane that for three centuries has replaced the cross atop the village bell tower. The path continues to rise as we go around the hill.

My thoughts, too, are swirling. Obsessively.

I keep hearing the same words, a horrible refrain that crushes me. *They're all dead.*

The pain is so great that even if I wanted to scream, I'd no longer have the strength. And though tears come to my eyes, our rapid ascent dries them before they spill onto my cheeks.

We can't see the village anymore. Which means that no one there can see us. Not the villagers behind their shuttered windows, and not the soldiers assigned to the carriage. The latter have no means of knowing what direction we took. Only their master's olfactory power stands a chance when he awakens at nightfall . . .

"Why the castle?" I manage to say between two intakes of breath.

"Because . . . I know someone," Bastien answers, out of breath.

He may be a head taller than I am, but all the days spent painting on his canvases haven't prepared him for the climb, not the way running in the forest has prepared me. I have to slow down so I don't leave him behind.

"You know someone?" I say. "What does that mean? Is it a secret you've all been keeping from me, that and the one about the cellar?"

Yet again I realize that I didn't know my family, even though I considered myself perceptive. I was so focused on getting away from home that I was blind to what was happening under my own roof.

"No," Bastien pants, struggling to utter his words. "This secret is entirely mine . . . Maman and Papa and Valère . . . didn't know about it . . ."

Seeing how my questions make him short of breath and slow him down, I decide not to ask anything else. At least for now.

Once we finally arrive at the castle's tall portcullis, the sun casts its last rays over the forest.

"There's a padlock!" I cry out as I place my hands on the chain that hangs from the bars like a dozing garden snake.

"Not quite," Bastien says, sweaty.

He leads me through some thickets to the left of the sharply pointed portcullis.

My lambskin breeches protect my legs from the thorns and brambles, but the sleeves of my blouse catch and tear.

Suddenly, I see a hole in the iron fortification. It wasn't visible before. Time and rust have worn down three bars, creating an opening large enough for a person to squeeze through.

Bastien easily glides in. It's obviously not the first time he's done this. I follow in his footsteps and enter grounds filled with twisted shrubs and misshapen bushes. The manor has fallen into a state of neglect, if it ever even knew a golden age in this arid landscape where nothing grows. The name of the fiefdom itself—Gastefriche, meaning "wasteland"—seems cursed. There's no one left in Butte-aux-Rats or the neighboring villages who knows how to trim hedges in the style of Versailles. We make our way under this disheveled cover where nature has gone wild. We dart from bush to bush, escaping the attention of the guard who's daydreaming in front of the castle courtyard.

As we go around a statue of a nymph half-consumed by moss, we reach the rear of the building. The tall stone wall is perforated with dark arrow slits; the highest, largest one comes outfitted with a small balcony that's been invaded by ivy. A flicker of candlelight dances behind sheer curtains.

"The service door is never locked," Bastien assures me. He's gotten his breath back.

"What about the servants?" I ask, worried.

"The baron dines early and sends his staff off to the outbuildings before nightfall."

How does Bastien know so much about the castle? I have no idea, but I'm in a hurry to find shelter. My brother pushes the worm-eaten wooden door and lets me enter the ancestral dwelling of the barons of Gastefriche.

The door shuts silently behind us, and we're instantly plunged into total darkness.

"Do you have a light?" Bastien whispers.

I take out my shepherd's tinderbox lighter. Along with my pocketknife, it never leaves my side. I activate the wheel of the flint. Soon the sparks create an incandescent glow at the tip of the wick. Bastien retrieves an oil lamp that seems to have been waiting just for him.

"Follow me, weasel," he says.

"Where to?"

Bastien raises the lamp to shed light on his face.

He's eighteen, a year older than me, but I've generally thought of him as my little brother. Of delicate constitution, he always took days to recover from the monthly tithe bleedings. Papa had to give him a tonic of bitterroot, while I was back on my feet within the hour. According to the humoral theories preached by the Hematic Faculty, each person has a different dominant humor. The choleric, like Valère, produce an excess of yellow bile that predisposes them to anger. The phlegmatic, like Bastien, have an excess of phlegm that disconnects them from the world and plunges them into endless daydreams. As for me, I'm an exception since, according to my father's diagnosis, I have a mixed humoral makeup—melancholic and sanguine. When I'm inactive, my excess of black bile plunges me more quickly toward boredom and depressive thoughts; but when I'm fully active, my excess blood takes over and I'm impulsive, even volcanic. Bastien's soothing company often allowed me to channel my contradictory emotions, particularly useful when I needed to hunt.

The two of us spent so many hours lying in the fields, gazing up at the clouds. My imagination often made out menacing monsters and gruesome scenes of slaughter, but Bastien helped me to see bright winged horses and magical celebrations. The other village children called him "the nut," because his mind wandered. And they called me "the witch," because of my gray hair. When we were young, I defended Bastien against anyone who made fun of him because everyone knew better than to mess with the witch. As we got older, I was still the one who went searching for him when he got lost in the woods, unable to find his way home after traipsing through the landscape for a scene to paint. But tonight, he's the one who guides me through dusk.

"Let's go up to Diane's room," he says softly.

"The baron's daughter?"

She must be my age or just a few years older, but I've never spoken to her. I see her only once a year, at the church, on December 21, the Night of Shadows. It's the longest night of the year and has replaced Christmas of old. I can't fathom how my brother and the baronette are connected. He's a mere commoner, treated like livestock, while she's a mortal noble allied to the vampyres.

Unless . . . suddenly I remember that Bastien was called to the castle last summer. The baron wanted him to paint his daughter's portrait. She's now of marrying age, and like in bygone days, a successful portrait is the best way to secure a good match in another province. It doesn't make sense to travel and meet before there's a strong prospect. As with horticulturists, there aren't many artists running around in Butte-aux-Rats. My brother was the only one capable of the task. So he spent two weeks at the baron's castle, painting the aristocrat's heir.

"Diane and I . . . we're in love," Bastien says, confirming my suspicions. "I swore I'd save her from an arranged marriage—the one her father expects will come about because of the portrait." A slight smile lights up his perspiring face. "One of these days we're going to escape together."

Escape? Escape where? Suddenly I want to grab hold of Bastien and shake him hard. All my life I've dreamed of fleeing. To defy the sequester law that forbids travel, that roots commoners to their villages until death. But I'm not a dreamer like he is. I know that's impossible.

"For now, Diane will save our necks," Bastien says, his voice full of hope. He starts up a creaky staircase. "There's a deep closet in her bedroom. I've hidden there many times when a servant came knocking on her door."

"You mean you saw her again, after she sat for her portrait?" I ask, horrified.

"I've been visiting her every week, for a year," he admits. "We have no secrets from each other."

Climbing the last step of the staircase, I abruptly think back to all the afternoons when Bastien disappeared for hours at a stretch and returned to the house without having drawn even the smallest sketch. Now I know where he spent his time—in the arms of a girl whose slightest kiss could have condemned him to death if word had gotten out.

We reach a polished door, in a hallway where oil lamps glisten and their wicks flicker.

Bastien gently scratches at the door, no doubt in a pattern that's a secret code. An open sesame that will lead us to our salvation.

3

REFUGE

The door opens on the baronette. She's in a long negligee.

It's a dressing gown covered in lace, in keeping with the nobility's idea of simplicity. We've surprised her in a private moment. She was brushing her long blonde hair in front of a vanity positioned next to the balcony. Gossamer curtains hang in front of open french doors and gently sway in the evening breeze. It's nearly night now, and the only light comes from a candelabra. At the edge of the halo of light, above a marble fireplace where the embers have died out, hangs a portrait of a young smiling girl. I assume it's my brother's artwork that's come back to the fold after having traveled to who knows which noble court. The rest of the vast bedchamber is plunged in darkness.

"Diane!" Bastien exclaims as he takes her hand in his trembling fingers.

Diane, like the Roman goddess of the hunt, Diana—the old baron being a passionate hunter who doesn't hesitate to crush the wheat under his horse's hooves as he tracks deer across the fields.

"Something . . . something horrible has happened," Bastien stammers. "My mother, my father, Valère . . ."

His voice breaks in sobs. Until he reached Diane's door, he'd been spurred by crazy hope. But the memory of the dragoons snaps him back to the awful reality.

"They've been murdered," I say. "We're the only survivors."

The baronette steps aside to let us in and shuts the door without making a sound. Between the silence, the pale skin, and the spectral whiteness of her negligee . . . she looks like a ghost. Did the news of what happened to my family thrust her into this state? No, she seemed already ashen when she opened the door . . .

"An inquisitor came to the house accompanied by dragoons," Bastien says quickly, gushing. "They found my parents' secret lab, the one I told you about . . ."

His every word is like a dagger being sunk into my stomach. Not only did Bastien endanger his life by courting a girl far above his station—baron being the highest rank of the mortal nobility—but he also endangered all our lives by confiding this terrible secret to his sweetheart. A secret that I learned about not even an hour ago. He confided in *her*, the daughter of the man charged with enforcing the royal edict in Butte-aux-Rats, that our family was mixed up with the Fronde!

"The inquisitor came with an ebony stagecoach," he continues, breathlessly. "But the vampyre inside won't think to look for us here in the castle. My sister and I will be safe in your closet. The perfumes that imbue your clothes will mask the scent of our trail. And when the carriage departs at sunrise, we'll leave as well. You and me, just like I promised. With my dear Jeanne. All three of us will cross the oceans to get to the Antipodes!"

The Antipodes? The imaginary land that supposedly escaped the yoke of the vampyres?

"But the Antipodes don't exist, Bastien," I tell him, getting frustrated.

"How do you know?" he spits out. "You spent hours with your head buried in your novels, dreaming you were crisscrossing the seven seas to get to the end of the world. To America. To Africa. Even to Japan. So why not the Antipodes, huh, weasel?"

"Like you said, I was dreaming! It was only a game, just like when we looked up at the clouds. Well, clouds are nothing but water vapor, Bastien—mirages!" I yell. "And I'm not a weasel; I'm a commoner who must obey the sequester law. There's no way out. The Shadows are everywhere. Across the entire Vampyria and beyond."

He's not listening to me anymore. After living in his dreamworld for so long, he's clearly lost his mind.

Already he's making his way toward the closet. He knows just where to go.

At that instant, and for the first time since we came in, Diane de Gastefriche finally speaks up. Her voice matches her appearance—spectral, like a draft of air.

"I'm so sorry, my love," she says softly.

"Courage, my muse," says Bastien. "We need it, all three of us. You must act as if nothing's wrong and lie to your father until we're able to escape. As for Jeanne and me, we'll grieve for our loved ones when we can."

I have the awful impression that Bastien misunderstood Diane's words, not picking up on the guilt in his beloved's voice.

"Why are you sorry, Diane?" I ask the baronette, beset by a feeling of dread.

She turns her worried, misty eyes on me.

"It's not my fault," she laments. "I didn't betray your brother's secret. I swear. But . . ."

She hiccups, and tears stream down her pale cheeks.

"But . . . ," I repeat, my heartbeat accelerating.

"But Père had someone eavesdrop outside my bedchamber last time Bastien was here. Now he knows about the two of us. He knows everything: our courtship, our plans to flee, your family's secret. He could have surprised us then and there, Bastien and me, but he preferred to let him leave so that he could strike all five of you later on. I wanted to run and warn you. But I couldn't. I was locked in the castle, where Père watches me like a hawk."

In a dizzying rush, I understand what brought the inquisitor to Butte-aux-Rats. It had nothing to do with a routine check, not at all. It was because of a tip-off.

Bastien's eyes go wide, like those of a sleepwalker awaking on the edge of a precipice.

He lets go of the closet handle.

I grab the one to the bedchamber—but it twists in my fingers before I can make it turn. Someone's there, on the other side, someone who's pushing with all their might.

"Bastien!" I yelp as I jump back.

The door rattles open, and the guard who I'd thought was woolgathering in the courtyard is now totally awake, brandishing his sword. As for the angry shadow looming behind him, it belongs to the old baron himself.

"I knew it!" he shouts. "The rogue who's dared touch my daughter now wants to hide under her skirts."

The baron's heavy, dusty wig, much like the hide of a dead sheep, trembles with indignation atop his wrinkled forehead. The yellowed curls spill onto his hunched shoulders and skinny chest.

He points to Bastien.

"The inquisitor may have let you escape, but your pathetic flight ends here, you miserable scoundrel. Mathurin, skewer him like the repugnant swine he is."

The guard rushes toward my brother, his sword drawn.

"Père, have pity!" Diane shouts.

The blade sinks into my beloved brother's stomach. He bends in two without making a sound.

The shock leaves me breathless. Diane screams as loudly as if the sword had pierced her own body.

"No. *No!*"

"Shut up!" orders her father. "Focus on the upside—by exterminating this rebellious vermin, I may finally get the transmutation I've been waiting for forever."

Wild with pain, eyes filled with tears, I try to catch my breath. My beautiful Bastien, dead. And the vile baron is rejoicing because it will buy him his transmutation—the holy grail of all the mortal lords who aspire to elevate themselves to the high vampyric aristocracy!

Staggering from despair, I make my way to the balcony.

The guard pulls his blade from Bastien's body and looks quizzically at his master.

"Well, what are you waiting for, you idiot?" roars the baron. "Finish her off too."

The brute charges toward me, headfirst, like one of those wild boars I sometimes had to escape during my solitary hunts.

Swallowing my tears, I lift the curtains, disappear in their folds, and leap to the side just as my assailant makes a stab at me. Since there's no resistance from my body to counter his massive weight, he stumbles onto the balcony, ripping the curtains . . . and topples into the void before crashing dozens of feet below.

Frantically, I untangle myself from the torn curtains and step back into the bedroom, where the last representatives of the Gastefriche clan are standing over the lifeless body of my brother. The baronette is weeping loudly, and the baron draws his gold-handled gentleman's rapier.

He's a frail old man, well into his sixties, weighed down by his outdated wig, but he's armed with a long blade. I have only the small pocketknife that I use to skin jackrabbits. Standing at the end of the baron's blade, I know he could pierce me with the tip before I could ever graze him.

I leap onto Diane and grab hold of her, placing the point of my knife against her throat.

"One more step and I'll kill her!" I warn, trying to master the anguish derailing my voice.

A look of disgust distorts the baron's wrinkled face. "I know you. The Froidelac girl. The one I'm told poaches on my lands. That good-for-nothing Captain Martin has never been able to catch you in the act. Well, forget about proof. Tonight I'm going to render justice myself—by the power granted me as a nobleman. And I condemn you to death, right here, right now."

He advances toward me, moving the tip of his sword in complicated loops. I'm forced to step back with my hostage. No doubt the baron's fencing instructor taught him countless thrusts and parries in his youth. No one has ever taught me to fence. But after spending so much time with wild animals in the forest, I've honed my instincts. Like the partridge pitted against the fox, like the doe pitted against the wolf, I know that a split second separates life from death.

As soon as my heels meet up with the edge that separates the room from the balcony, I push Diane with all my might toward the baron's whirling blade. Not one moment of hesitation for the careless girl who let us fall into this trap. Not one bit of remorse for the traitor who caused the death of my family.

The tip of the sword plunges into the delicate lace of the negligee, which instantly turns poppy red.

The baron, who moments before came at me with the agility of a young man, quickly reverts to a feeble geezer.

"My . . . my daughter . . . ," he says in a quivering, disbelieving voice.

Brandishing my knife, I leap toward him and sink the short blade between the faded curls of his wig, right into his brow bone.

"Here it is, your transmutation!" I yell. "The only one you deserve."

A purple shower spurts all over me as the baron crumples, like being caught in a downpour—drenched in the blood of all those who died one after the other in the span of less than an hour.

Suddenly, the gong of a bell echoes through the open bedroom window. The sound comes from the church in the village, but it's not the gentle ringing that chimes the passing hours of the day. No, it's the strident ringing that signals nightfall and the start of curfew.

An eerie terror rips at my gut, sweeping everything else away.

I have an inkling that down below, on the village square, the door of the ebony carriage just opened—liberating a passenger with supernatural abilities.

I know it's only a matter of minutes before he arrives at the castle, drawn by the scent of blood that nothing can mask. And I know that when he does, my trusty pocketknife and hunting instincts won't be able to save me.

My arms fall to my side, suddenly as limp as the three dead bodies on the floor. A feeling of total powerlessness descends on my shoulders like a leaden weight. I can't stand anymore, so I crumple to my knees on the rug, whose worn weave becomes slowly drenched in blood.

I'm done for. And I sense that my death will be horribly slow.

The most painful torture is reserved for those who dare to raise a hand against the nobility. The vampyre won't be satisfied in killing me with just one blow once he finds me here, in this room, with the corpses of the resident baron and his daughter . . .

An idea bursts into my head—a crazy idea.

Hurriedly, I untie my lambskin breeches, pop the buttons of my shirt, and rush over to Diane so that I can take off her long-sleeved negligee. The ribbons, sticky with blood, slip between my trembling fingers, but I manage to undo them. I put on the perfumed garment, which fits me like a glove. In turn, the baronette's slim body easily glides into my hunting outfit. I keep only my tinderbox lighter and Maman's small medallion, sliding both into the pocket of the gown.

Then I take off the signet ring from the corpse's ring finger and place it on my own. It bears the Gastefriche coat of arms, a blackbird with outstretched wings.

To complete the deceit, I toss my felt hat in a corner and let my midlength hair fall on either side of my face. Then I raise my knife above the baronette's face and bring it down again and again, all the while closing my eyes so as not to see the delicate features that my brother painted turn into unrecognizable pulp.

Finally, I pierce the baronette's arm repeatedly with one of her hairpins in order to simulate the punctures of the tithe, and I open her lifeless hand and slide the bloody pocketknife into it.

I'm panting as I get up, my stomach in knots over the butchery I've just committed.

I happen to look toward the vanity mirror. My eyes are like two bottomless wells. My loose hair resembles a metal helmet that frames my dazed face. Beneath the white silk linen gown, my chest rises and falls haphazardly, racked with panicked sobs and hiccuped laughter. Yes, I'm *laughing*. Laughing nervously, crazily; I can't help it. Seeing myself disguised as a noble maiden is a sinister masquerade. A grotesque farce.

Suddenly, an icy draft lifts the torn curtains of the balcony, and all the flames of the candelabra blow out. A gale of frost hits my face.

My insane laughter stops, instantly.

Slowly, I turn around.

A shadow stands in the window frame, a tall human silhouette whose contours come into hazy focus in the dimness of the coming night.

The vampyre.

I don't need to see him to know.

Even if I've never been in the presence of one of the undead, having only read their descriptions in books, all the cells in my body cry out that I'm face to face with one now. The cold is a trademark of the Shadows, in keeping with the ice age that began with the coming of the lords of the night.

It took mere minutes since the bell tolled for this one to realize that two rebels had escaped the massacre at the apothecary and to make his way up the hill that my brother and I spent a good quarter of an hour climbing. As for how he scaled the wall and hoisted himself up onto the balcony, I prefer not to think about it.

"This . . . this boy and this girl . . . ," I stammer as I gesture to Bastien's and Diane's bodies, "they're assassins who came to slit our throats."

I'm the pheasant I killed this morning, seconds before my sling brought him down; I'm the jackrabbit caught off guard last week, the moment my snare crushed his neck.

"I was getting ready for bed when the killers appeared," I say, raising a trembling hand to my hair. "My father managed to dispatch them after a fierce struggle that ended with the loss of his own life. I'm soaked in blood . . . his blood."

"His Majesty will be grateful for his sacrifice, mademoiselle."

The creature's voice is calm, deep. Melodious. And yet it makes the hair on my skin stand on end.

Nervously, I pull at the sleeves of the negligee to make sure they're covering the bends of my arms, where the monthly tithe bleedings have left purplish marks that label me a commoner. They're the marks I hurriedly reproduced on the baronette's corpse.

"These miserable miscreants were dangerous Fronde rebels," the vampyre explains as he slowly comes closer to me. "Fearsome enough for me to come all the way from Clermont after receiving your late father's letter. They got the better of an inquisitor and three dragoons before they wreaked havoc in your home. But these traitors won't harm anyone else now."

A white hand with long, elegant fingers emerges from the obscurity, draped in a sleeve of fine silk.

The marble-like palm seems to invite mine.

When my trembling fingers reach his, I have the impression I'm touching the surface of an ice-cold statue. The weak sliver of moonlight streaming through the gossamer curtains lights up the signet ring I stole from Diane. The gold glistens on my finger.

"You are the baron's only daughter, are you not?" the vampyre asks me.

I nod, my throat too tight to utter even a word. My strategy is working: the visitor has never met the girl whose identity I've usurped. My scent of commoner seems masked by the perfume that lingers on the negligee. But the creature has only to turn and look around the room to discover the portrait above the fireplace. A portrait that is not of me! Will I have the guts to pretend it's a close relative? Will he be curious enough to inspect the corpse to see if there's a resemblance?

For now, all his attention seems directed at me.

"At present, I fear that you've become an orphan, mademoiselle . . . mademoiselle?"

"Diane," I say in a whisper.

It's the last thing I have to appropriate from my victim: her given name. It sounds strangely as if it were my own, as if it had been predestined. The baronette borrowed it from the greatest of female hunters, and it now becomes mine—the name for the girl who poached on her father's lands.

"Don't torment yourself, Diane," the vampyre says. "His Majesty is always generous toward mortals who sacrifice themselves on his behalf."

He bows. His richly brocaded blue frock coat catches the moonlight; then so, too, does his frilled shirt, on which is pinned a large sapphire; and finally his entire head. It reminds me of a statue as well. His luminous complexion contrasts with his long, silky red hair, nothing like the lumpy dust trap that sat atop the baron's head. I'm struck by the youthful beauty radiating from this perfectly symmetrical face, by skin so fine the pores are undetectable, by the full lips and thick scarlet eyebrows that look as if they were painted on porcelain. He appears as if he could be my age and no doubt probably was on the night that he became a vampyre, but who can say how far back his transmutation goes? If it happened at the same time as the king's, that means he's plagued the earth for three hundred years. In spite of his illusion of youth and angelic appearance, a small detail betrays his monstrous nature: his pupils are two black disks, so completely dilated that they swallow up almost all the white of his eyeballs. Like those of cats and owls, the eyes of vampyres supposedly adapt to darkness and see just as well as during the day . . .

"My respects," he says, bending over to kiss my hand. "I am Alexandre de Mortange, Viscount of Clermont."

I avert my eyes so I don't scream when his soft, cold lips brush against the back of my hand. Distraught, I look again toward the vanity mirror. My reflection stares back at me in the sullied negligee, the color darkening as the blood oxidizes. The face of the undead, however, is invisible. Same for his hands. It's as if his brocaded coat were filled only with air.

So it's not a myth: the skin of vampyres, of these demonic immortals, doesn't cast a reflection in mirrors . . .

"Tonight I will take you to Versailles, where I'll testify before the court about the success of this mission against the Fronde," he says, straightening up. His pale lips stretch to reveal teeth even whiter than his skin, ending in two pointy canines that gleam like agates. "And in a few days, Diane de Gastefriche, by the good grace of the Shadows, you will have the honor of becoming a ward of the king."

4

DEPARTURE

I'm paralyzed with fear.

My body feels like it's sewn to the black leather lining the inside of the ebony carriage, its vibrations reverberating right through to the hollows of my bones.

On the bench opposite mine, the vampyre sits, immobile. His chiseled face is turned toward the nocturnal landscape passing by the window. The dark night obscures his fixed gaze. There's not the slightest breath to make his nostrils quiver. It's hard to believe that one hour ago I held his arm to go down the hill until the carriage met up with us. We didn't cross paths with anyone. As with the villagers, the baron's staff stayed cloistered in the outbuildings, in keeping with curfew. Perhaps they sensed that a lord of the night was prowling about the castle . . .

Just as in the baronette's bedchamber, I have the impression of being in front of a statue. The only thing that's moving is his magnificent red hair, which gently vibrates in rhythm with the carriage. On occasion, I saw my father prepare the dead bodies of villagers for burial. Supposedly, after one's demise, the nails and hair continue to grow. In the case of vampyres, that's certainly true, as Dr. Boniface explained in his sermons celebrating the magical beauty of the lords of the night. Whereas mortal noblemen, along with many noblewomen, adorn themselves with wigs and hairpieces in order to appear more impressive, the immortals don't need such artifice. Having gorged on the blood of all those on whom they feed, their hair is supernaturally dazzling and vibrant.

I grind my teeth to stifle a groan.

I'm face to face with an undead brimming with life. It's the paradox of vampyres, a notion that was always an abstraction for me until now. But tonight it's become horribly concrete. A living death is just that: a total petrification, after which comes the ability of supernatural speed; a coldness that seems to emanate from the passenger and latches on to me in spite of the blanket he threw over my shoulders; and most of all, this awful silence that no intake of breath disrupts. The two dragoons aboard the rear of the vehicle don't say a word. I can hear only the creaking of the axle, the trotting of the horses, and the brief snap of the coachman's tongue encouraging them at the front of the carriage.

And so I'm swept off into the unknown night, traveling farther than my steps ever took me, my body chilled and my mind numb, too shocked to mourn all those I've lost.

"Would you like to eat, mam'zelle?"

Slowly, I open my eyes.

A flood of dazzling light washes over me. I promptly close my eyelids.

I have to blink several times in order to banish blinding tears. As my eyes clear, I take in the padded interior of the carriage, its black leather glistening in the sunlight. Across from the bench where I dozed off, the space is empty.

As if the vampyre simply faded come morning.

As if everything had been a bad dream.

"Mam'zelle, are you hungry?" the dragoon asks again as he opens the carriage door to speak to me.

He holds out a wicker basket filled with warm bread and lard.

My muscles, which all night were paralyzed by the presence of the vampyre, recover a little of their suppleness. My mind regains its pluck.

An idea forms: I must escape.

As soon as possible and by any means.

Although the dragoon speaks to me courteously, no doubt under strict orders, his lips do not smile, and his eyes watch me attentively. A gun is slung over his shoulder, and a sword hangs from his belt. It's a brutal reminder of the sword that decapitated Valère. The vision of Maman's slit throat stops my breathing.

Swallowing my pain, I pretend to grab the basket when I'm really trying to assess my chances of fleeing. I pop my head outside the door and notice the rear of the carriage: two large iron trunks are strapped under a black leather canopy, where the two other dragoons must have traveled during the night. At present, they're eating on the grass, taking big, hurried mouthfuls before we set off again.

As for the carriage's fifth passenger . . .

"The vamp . . . the viscount," I whisper, only just correcting myself. "Is he gone?"

A flicker of fear crosses the dragoon's eyes.

"The viscount is here," he answers lugubriously.

I absorb his words and tone, but I don't see the viscount anywhere in the carriage. I open my mouth to question him further, but the mere mention of his employer has sent him into a feverish state.

"Well, I'll let you eat, in case you're hungry," he says, tossing the basket onto the bench. "We have to leave soon if we want to reach Versailles the day after tomorrow."

"Wait!" I yell, completely disoriented.

Versailles, the day after tomorrow? I thought it took a week to go from the Auvergne to the Île-de-France, the region around Paris.

The door shuts with a loud bang on my protests, and then the lock turns with a click.

So much for my window to escape.

As the carriage sets off again, I lower my eyes to the floor.

There's an iron ring in the center that I hadn't noticed until now. The handle of a trapdoor.

In horror, I realize that the creature is most definitely here—protected from the sun's rays as he rests in the obscurity of the luggage hold beneath my feet, closer to me than ever before.

🦇

I spend all day in the same exhausted state as the previous night, immobile in the fine silk linen negligee that dried sweat and blood has stiffened.

The fact that I know the vampyre is resting under my heels petrifies me. But doubt is even more paralyzing than fear.

Like everyone else, I've heard that there are only two ways to permanently annihilate a vampyre—by driving a wooden stake into their heart before cutting off their head, or by exposing them to the sun long enough that they burn.

Should I lift the iron ring? Should I try to open the luggage hold and deliver its sleeping occupant to the sun that's pouring into the cabin? I'm itching to do this, but I fear I won't be able to hold the monster in the light for more than a few seconds. If he was able to get to the castle with the speed of a hawk yesterday, he'll surely succeed in closing the curtains before he's charred. Instead of burning him, I risk blowing my cover . . . and dying, stupidly.

I feel black bile rise up to my brain, bringing on one of my usual migraines. A leaden weight presses against my forehead, heavy like the clouds crushing the dreary landscape on the other side of the window. The oppressive warmth of the short summer lingers on the flat land. We're already at autumn's doorstep, and I know that in a few weeks, the frost will make the ground crack. Once in a while a hamlet crops up at a bend of the road, a hamlet as isolated as Butte-aux-Rats, where the lives of the villagers are as confined as mine was.

As the hours go by, the sun sinks inevitably lower.

My reflection becomes increasingly distinct on the darkening window: a face with fine features and gray eyes squinting from a migraine, topped by a thick head of pale hair. A small weasel face, like poor Bastien used to say affectionately. A caged weasel.

The day ends, veering into twilight, twilight into evening, and then it's nighttime.

Only then does the trapdoor that I've spent all day observing, not daring to take action, begin to lift open. A glacial blast of air whooshes out.

A white hand emerges from the gaping hole, the very palm in which I placed my fingers the evening before.

The vampyre's entire body extricates itself from the hold in one swift, supernatural motion, as if an invisible force had come to set him upright.

The jabot of his blouse swells like a funeral flower.

As he brushes off the blue velvet of his frock coat, a cloud of dust shimmers in the moonlight that filters through the window. He moves his long fingers as if playing on a phantom piano to loosen them up.

"Good evening, mademoiselle," he says, bowing to me.

He straightens up and stares at me, his black eyes lacking dark circles or other telltale signs that usually mark the sleep of the living.

"Good evening, monsieur . . . ," I say feebly, the prickle of danger dissipating the migraine.

It feels strange to call this creature who seems so young "monsieur," especially as he looks even more youthful than he did yesterday at the castle. I realize that he's pulled his thick red hair back into a ponytail, which makes the beauty of his face all the more dazzling.

"You may remove your wig if it's more comfortable for you," he says, seeing me stare at his smooth forehead. "I won't take offense. I've actually never seen one like yours, a blend of real hair with silver threads. Quite daring."

I shudder at his words. Silver is forbidden in all of Vampyria. If garlic irritates the immortals, silver metal is far more toxic for them.

"It's not a wig. It's my real hair, with not a strand of silver," I hurry to clarify.

"Really?" He looks at me anew, much like an entomologist examines the carapace of an insect, then adds, "Your hair is splendid."

Not knowing how to respond, I force myself to smile but only succeed in producing a distorted grin that bounces with the rhythmic jolts of the road.

"I'm not like the other vampyres of the Auvergne that you may have come in contact with," he continues, not guessing that he's the first vampyre I've ever met. "For pity's sake, please don't lump me in with the old fossils who reek of mothballs, like the Marquis de Riom or the Count d'Issoire. Those scarecrows are still wearing the same garments from a hundred years ago. Mine are delivered from Paris every season, ensuring I'm attired in the latest style of the day." He proudly smooths the lapel of his fitted coat, which does indeed look brand new and perfectly cut to hug his athletic frame. "Believe me, my place is not at Clermont. And for the longest time I've dreamed of only one thing: flying the coop."

Alexandre de Mortange's words leave me perplexed.

He expresses himself like a present-day young man, even using the same slang as my brothers. Most of all, the way in which he refers to the other vampyres of the Auvergne. How many times did Papa scold me when I spoke lightly of the lords of the night, not showing them the proper respect?

"I'm different," my host tells me as he fluffs the jabot of his blouse. "Resolutely modern. Even, dare I say, ahead of the times that refuse to evolve. Probably too avant garde for the court of Versailles, from which I was banished years ago. But this rebellion by the agitators will be a game changer." A frustrated shadow flickers across his face. "Of course, I would have preferred that things unfold differently, as I hate gratuitous violence and unnecessary suffering. As the king's representative, I only accompanied the inquisitor. It's the archiater of Clermont who sent him. Under his respectable clerical robe, that man is a brutish thug. He and his men butchered those Fronde rebels. Just thinking of it makes me shudder. Still, I hope to enter into the good graces of His Majesty. What do you think?"

"Uh . . . yes, of course," I stammer, my throat tight.

Remembering how my loved ones were slaughtered overwhelms me.

The fact that an immortal is confiding in me so that I can reassure him unsettles me all the more.

It's because he takes me for a noble maiden, not a commoner. Even if he's a vampyre and I'm a mortal, the privilege of nobility brings us closer in his eyes.

"But here I am rambling, talking of nothing but myself, like always. I forget the tragedy that you've just been through!" he cries out. "What an oaf I am. You're still under the shock of having lost your father, and now you're being rattled in this ancient carriage. Do you know that you fell asleep straightaway last night, even before we stopped at Clermont?"

"We stopped at Clermont?" I repeat, my voice flat.

"Just long enough for me to pack my suitcases. I've left Clermont for good. Adieu. Bye-bye. Adios. Arrivederci. Next stop: Versailles."

I dig my fingers into the leather of the bench and remember the enormous trunks at the rear of the carriage; it must have taken a while to fill them. I'm mad at myself for not having seized the chance to flee then.

"I wish we had time to stop at an inn every night," the viscount goes on. "I know that mortals prefer sleeping in a bed rather than on a bench. Believe me, I appreciate the padded silk cushion of my casket a lot more than this dusty baggage hold. But I'm eager to get to the court; it's been so long since I was banished. His Majesty gave me a choice: the Auvergne or the Bastille. At the time, I was sure I was choosing the least boring option, but in hindsight I'm not so sure anymore. Ha ha!"

This is the first time I've met someone who's rubbed shoulders with the King of Shadows. In a way, the sovereign has always been a part of my life, but only as a print above the fireplace, as a masked profile on coins, or as a semilegendary figure in the tales told around the hearth at night. And now we're galloping at breakneck speed toward him.

"I asked my men to change horses at each stopover, every seven leagues," the vampyre says. "In spite of the jolts, I hope you're enjoying the journey."

"Immensely," I lie.

"I'm glad to hear it. But tell me . . . is the food not to your liking?" He points to the wicker basket that I've left untouched.

"I . . . yes, it looks delicious," I say, not wanting to offend him. "I just have a bit of a stomachache. Because of my father's death, as you said . . ."

And the deaths of my mother and brothers, I think, stifling a sob.

"I understand," Alexandre de Mortange says with a nod. "Even though it's been a while since I was transmuted, I remember how intense the feelings of mortals can be. But you know, vampyre hearts can also be deeply touched, even if they no longer beat. It's just that our perspective of events is . . . different. Our lives aren't as ephemeral as yours. It takes so little, really, so very little, for you to go from emotional peaks to valleys. You lose one person you love, and your entire world crumbles. You find comfort in a single friend, and you're revived. Let me be that friend, Diane. May I call you Diane?"

"Of course, please do, uh, Alexandre," I answer, feeling both uncomfortable at his familiarity and relieved that he's none the wiser.

"Just Alex will suffice."

"All right . . . Alex."

He extends an open palm.

"High five, Diane! I hate formality. I'll always be nineteen at heart."

I slap my palm against his cold one, shaken to see how in just one sentence he can go from polished language to slang. At least I've gathered an important piece of information: Alexandre was nineteen years old when he was transmuted.

He takes a gold lighter from his fitted coat and brings it to the overhead lantern. A golden glow spills into the cabin, dancing in rhythm with the jolts.

"And voilà: *fiat lux*, let there be light," he declares. "There's nothing like the heat and the brilliance of a flame to revive the beating heart of mortals. Certain vampyres have forgotten this after living perpetually at night, but I know it only too well."

His smile widens slightly. Still, he takes care not to raise his lips too much. It's as if he wants to spare me the sight of his canines. As for the pupils of his eyes, they shrink under the effect of the ambient glow, and his previously invisible irises emerge—a bright blue.

I have to admit that the viscount possesses the supernatural beauty of an angel. But as his lugubrious family name implies, this angel has been dead a long time. *Mortange* . . . meaning "dead angel." Beneath the radiance of his eternal nineteen years, his insides are those of a mummy.

"You must eat, Diane," he says encouragingly. "You must gain strength for the exciting life that awaits you at Versailles. You'll see—it's splendid."

I remove the dishcloth that covers the basket, grab a slice of bread with my fingertips, and start to nibble.

"Hmmm . . . the smell of fresh bread . . . ," Alexandre says, sniffing the air. "I remember how much I loved it in the old days."

"It's good," I say between bites, even though everything tastes like ash on my tongue.

"Maybe it's a little dry like that, all by itself?"

"No, I assure you, monsieur . . . Alex," I say, finding it so unnatural to be on a first-name basis with this creature. "The bread is very fresh."

"Go on, you can be truthful. Who likes bread without a topping?"

The commoners who can't afford anything more, that's who, I want to snap back at him.

"It's true that at the castle I always had fresh butter and jam at breakfast," I lie.

A fleeting frown passes across Alexandre's face, momentarily marring its perfection.

"Those dumb dragoons didn't have the presence of mind to think of it," he grumbles. "We're so badly served out in the countryside. An added reason why I'm eager to return to civilization. Versailles may be a little stuffy, and with all the marble, the wine freezes in the pitchers come November. But any self-respecting aristocrat must have lodgings there." He sighs, as if all the constraints of the court he's rushing toward are already weighing him down. "The king is *not* a jolly fellow. He spends his nights shut in his observatory, where he looks at the stars with the graybeards of the Faculty. Rumor has it that behind his solar mask, he's never smiled . . ."

Alexandre lowers his voice as he says these last words. The topic of the king's real face is taboo, banned by the Faculty. What abhorrent metamorphosis did his transmutation wreak on his flesh? The doctors pretend it's too deep a mystery—or too terrible a sight—for mere mortals to grapple with. It seems even vampyres can't talk about it without trembling . . . nonetheless, Alexandre has let a word slip, piquing my curiosity.

"A *solar* mask, really?" I repeat, appearing to be taken aback by this paradox. "For the King of Shadows?"

"Before he was the King of Shadows, the Immutable was the Sun King," Alexandre reminds me. "He's never abandoned the idea of reconquering daylight. It's the reason he wears the mask of Apollo, god of the sun."

The lords of the night reconquering daylight? Vampyres coming and going freely before the toll of the warning bell? The very thought gives me goose bumps.

But my frivolous travel companion has already moved on to another subject.

"Whatever he may be, and despite his heavy-handedness, the king has a sense of grandeur," he goes on. "Every year in December, for the celebrations marking the Night of Shadows, I assure you that you get an eyeful. And Paris is a stone's throw away. In the capital, it's always a rave. Splendid, I tell you. I'm going to get intoxicated on the new music from England; sure beats listening to the same sleep-inducing concertos played by the Clermont musicians. I'm dying to go to the Odéon Theater and applaud the latest scandalous plays. Then I'll have a blast at the Opéra Ball."

"It's quite funny to hear a vampyre say that they're 'dying to go' somewhere . . . ," I say with a squeak.

Alexandre's blue eyes sparkle with excitement in the glow of the lantern.

"You've got wit, Diane," he says. "Excellent. I love it. Just wait and see. You, too, will create sparks at Versailles and Paris."

This strange character, who claims to hate violence, doesn't cease to surprise me. His bubbly enthusiasm matches his young physique. And his title of viscount is the lowest in the vampyric aristocracy, just above the human title of baron. But what about his real age?

"Thank you for taking such good care of me," I tell him, cracking a fake smile.

"Stop it, I tell you. No standing on ceremony between us. It's only right after the ordeal you've been through. And it's only natural for the king to welcome you to the school of the Grande Écurie. The semester just got underway, so you'll be able to fit in with no trouble. I sent a crow ahead to inform them of your arrival; he precedes us ever so swiftly."

A crow, yes. I've heard tell that vampyres command those winged creatures.

"In fact, I'm a little nervous about what awaits me," I say. "Until now, I've never left my poor father's castle. The court intimidates me. And everything is so rushed. You had time to pack your bags in Clermont, but I didn't have the chance to bring any personal items . . ." I lower my eyes on the silk linen gown stained with dried blood. "Never has a *negligee* looked so neglected and been so aptly named."

"On my honor, I'm embarrassed that I didn't give you the chance to change," Alexandre exclaims. "But don't worry—as the king's ward, he'll provide for you as he's supposed to upon your arrival. His Majesty is magnanimous and will take pity on a poor orphan, just as he'll pardon a sincere repentant like me."

My tongue is burning to ask Alexandre what offense he committed to incur the sovereign's wrath. But I hold back. It would be stupid to upset my sole source of information regarding the hornet's nest I'm about to throw myself into.

"As for the habits and customs of Versailles, you can rely on me for guidance," he says, affably. "I know the palace like the back of my hand. You'll blossom there into a magnificent wildflower and outshine all the flowers of the city. The court goes bonkers for anything out of the ordinary. Your stunning, moonlight-colored hair alone is the very definition of splendid. I'm certain it will turn quite a few heads."

"Thank you," I say, forcing a smile. "I'm lucky to have a . . ." My tongue stumbles on the word, the last word I would have ever associated with a lord of the night. "A *friend* like you."

5

"FRIEND"

Once again I awake long after sunrise. It's as if the motion of the ebony carriage lulls me.

Same as yesterday, the bench opposite mine is empty.

The door to the trap is closed under my feet, only now I know what lies beneath . . .

Yet again, I'm tempted to lift the iron ring, but I hold back. As exasperating, boastful, and vain as he is, Alexandre also showed himself to be thoughtful during our conversations. Of course, he remains a lord of the night, a sworn enemy, and I pretended to be his friend solely to win his favor. But he's probably not the worst of his kind. After all, didn't he claim to be different from the others? More modern, maybe also more human? Besides, he's not the one who ordered that my family be killed. As he said, he just accompanied the inquisitor as a representative of the royal authority. Maybe if he had surfaced in time, he would have put a stop to the slaughter and been content to take them prisoner. Didn't he say that he hated gratuitous violence and unnecessary suffering? My heart flip-flops. I'm now an orphan, and I'll stay that way for the rest of my life. My parents are gone, same for my brothers, and my grandparents died long ago.

I'm alone in the world.

I don't know what I'm good for anymore. Probably nothing.

Needing to connect with something—*anything*—that belonged to my family, I take Maman's small medallion out of my gown pocket to look at it in the light of day.

It's a modest piece of bronze jewelry no bigger than a walnut, lacking embellishments except for a small clasp. As far as I can remember, I always saw it around my mother's neck but never asked her what was inside.

I press on the clasp. The medallion opens like a shell.

Inside I see a small white time dial that's protected by a glass crystal. What I had taken to be a humble piece of jewelry is really a pocket watch that Maman wore on a chain around her neck. The hands have stopped at 7:38. Maybe the mechanism broke during the struggle, unless it was already broken.

On the case lid's inner side is an engraved motto: **LIBERTY OR DEATH**. And in the locket rests a blue ribbon wound around a lock of silver hair.

My throat tightens.

My eyes tear up.

Maman, who I so often opposed just to be contrary and whose lectures I fled in favor of the forest, kept a lock of my hair against her heart. I made fun of her when she cautioned me not to take mindless risks, but she, more than anyone, knew what she was talking about; she was living life on the razor's edge. I thought I was being so rebellious when I pretended I wanted to go to the fair at Bellerive, three leagues from Butte-aux-Rats—in brazen defiance of the sequester law. I thought I was being wildly courageous when I said I wanted to hunt at night, in contempt of the curfew law and with the excuse that abominations were rare in our landlocked region.

I feel shame weighing down on my shoulders, compressing my chest, making my breath all the more painful now that my mother has ceased to exist. I ache, ashamed that I nagged at her all those years for making sure I respected the Mortal Code. She only did it so that my escapades wouldn't attract attention to our family.

I remember Valère saying, *"Papa and Maman say you're too unpredictable."* Is that why Maman didn't take me into her confidence? Would she have told me everything when I turned eighteen, like Bastien said? Does the presence of my hair in the locket mean that she believed in me?

As I'm about to put away the pocket watch, my eyes fall on the wicker basket that's resting next to me.

It's been replenished.

I lift the dishcloth and find a new loaf of sliced bread, the crust nice and golden, as well as a clod of fresh butter that's been carefully wrapped in paper and three little pots of jam.

This time I devour my daily ration with a ferocious appetite.

❦

I spend the rest of the day observing the landscape outside the window.

Soon, the hamlets grow closer together, becoming cities with rooftops that have a metallic gleam. Gray ramparts block off these projects—or should I say these prisons, where most of the commoners from the fourth estate are penned in like cattle.

As soon as the sun vanishes, I hear a warning bell toll outside the carriage. The sound is soon multiplied by all the bells in all the cities of the Île-de-France, each ringing one after the other in a menacing concert.

The trap opens with a squeak, and Alexandre appears in a burst of cold air.

"At your service, my dear," he says after lighting the lantern and pompously bowing to me. "Was it a good day?"

"Yes, even if a little lonely," I say, coyly, acting like a grateful maiden in distress. "I missed our conversation."

Putting on an act is easier than I thought. Of course, I have the supreme motivation to be convincing: survival. A faint smile crosses the viscount's lips.

"I'm here now, ready to resume our talk," he exclaims. "But first, tell me what you think of these new pumps that I put on especially for you."

He proudly shows off his new footwear: elegant shoes covered in a pine-green, scaly kind of leather.

"They're Talaria, the latest fashion. Pure Louisiana crocodile," he informs me since I don't respond. "Classy, no?"

"They're very beautiful."

"They also make women's styles that are to die for," he tells me. "The king will surely give you a few pairs since you'll be his ward. Without the red heel, of course, since those are reserved exclusively for vampyres. *Étiquette oblige*."

I look at Alexandre's vermilion heels and make a mental note of this tidbit of information. It might come in handy later on, when I need to identify the bloodsuckers at the court. The glacial aura of their presence may not be enough.

"You seem to know so much that I'm ignorant of," I say, stroking his ego. "You talk of Versailles like you've lived there a lifetime."

"But that's exactly right, Diane," he says, laughing, and this time I notice the sharp points of his canines. "One lifetime . . . even several, in fact."

Like yesterday, the impression of being in front of a nineteen-year-old boy becomes blurred.

"It was just two nights ago that I was thinking about my past," he goes on. "I was gathering all my memories so I could put them in the right order before we reach Versailles. It won't do for me to confuse one person with another, to kiss the hand of the wrong marquise, or to speak to the wrong duke. The Court of Shadows has its codes, its deadly snares, and the slightest misstep must be paid in blood . . ."

I now remember how Alexandre spent hours in total stillness on the first night of our journey. He was just lost in memories . . . and I have to draw out as many as possible.

"This school that awaits me in Versailles, the Grande Écurie—what is it exactly?" I ask.

"The Grande Écurie—or Great Stables—is an institution that was created three centuries ago by Louis XIV himself, before his transmutation. The best riders in the kingdom have trained there. Nowadays you still learn to be an equestrian, but that's not all. It's where the finest among the mortal nobility receive an education. The crème de la crème, if you see what I mean. Every year come mid-August, girls and boys from the top aristocratic families of the Magna Vampyria join the boarding school before making their official entrance at the court. The best among them are admitted into the service of the king himself, as squires. Every October thirty-first, the anniversary night of his transmutation, His Majesty selects two of the third-years." He chuckles. "I was talking about the court as if it were a nest of vipers, but it's nothing next to the fistfights that take place every year among those who seek the king's favor. Every detail matters. You, you'd already be disqualified . . ."

He points at my negligee with his finger.

Along with the streaks of brown blood on my gown, there's a trace of orange—a small apricot jam stain.

"You'll have to learn how to eat without getting food everywhere," he scolds me playfully. "Or you'll suffer the wrath of Madame Étiquette, the hydra who oversees manners and decorum at the court."

"Don't tell me you've never stained yourself during one of your . . . uh . . . *meals*," I say, trying to muster my bravery. "It's well known that blood stains horribly."

He bursts out laughing, his mirth mingling with the grinding of the fast-spinning wheels.

"I *love* your outspokenness. And the court will appreciate it as well." He stretches his lean body back against the bench and places his red heels next to mine. "You're right; I've spoiled more than one lace jabot, and they're so hard to recover once soiled."

He sighs deeply.

"Blood. More blood, always blood. We constantly come back to it, the most annoying part of our vampyre nature. We're called the lords of the night. But in reality we're slaves, slaves to blood."

I sense that he's serious, no longer making pleasant banter.

We hear only the groans of the carriage as the lantern swings on the ceiling.

"If you only knew how I long to be freed of this debilitating thirst," he continues. "Of all the shackles of the past that weigh on our kind, it's the heaviest to bear. Me, I told you, I want to fly into the future. I want to fiercely embrace everything that's modern. With every fiber of my gut, mind, and . . . soul. Secretly, I dream of a world where vampyres no longer have to drink human blood to survive."

What Alexandre tells me troubles me more than anything else he's said since we met. I would never have imagined that a vampyre would speak of his *soul* and, still less, disparage blood, the supreme asset that gives structure to the state.

"Maybe your dream will come true," I whisper, goading him on, needing to learn more of his desires. "I mean, maybe one day vampyres will discover another way of surviving."

Alexandre leans forward and takes my hand in his.

It feels a little less cold than before.

"I see that you're an incorrigible idealist like me. You'll have to be careful at Versailles—there are many who want to crush any hint of progressive thought."

"Thank you for the warning, Alex. I'll remember it."

He smiles, then leans back onto his bench.

"For the time being, one must unfortunately conform to the curse of the Shadows. Despite all the fine words and all the best hopes, it's still the order of the day."

He slides his hand into his fitted coat and takes out a glass receptacle that I immediately recognize: a hematic flask, specially designed by the Faculty to preserve the tithe. It's filled to the brim with a red, viscous liquid.

"I apologize for taking my sustenance in front of you," he says. "I usually do this in private. But given how narrow this carriage is, I don't have a choice."

He opens the flask and brings it up to his nose.

For the first time I see his nostrils quiver—yes, quiver with pleasure!

"What a delicate aroma," he says joyfully. "This blood is still fresh, unlike the half-coagulated flasks the archiater of Clermont sent me every month, damned be the Faculty. I confess that I myself drew this beverage from the carotid of my victim. Can you believe it, Diane, that one of those stupid Fronde rebels was still alive when I woke up two nights ago? A woman."

I'm now rooted to the bench, devastated by what he just said, what it means.

No.

No, it's impossible.

Maman was dead when Bastien and I left the house. I'm sure of it.

"That bitch was dragging herself along the floor of the dining room, one hand plastered to her neck to try and stop the bleeding," Alexandre continues. "It's crazy how vermin clings to life. If those rebels had let themselves be captured, all five of them, we'd have been able to properly decapitate them in order to collect their blood without losing a drop. Do you remember I told you I hate unnecessary suffering? Well, if you're going to suffer, it might as well prove useful. As the Faculty affirms, there's no worse crime than wasted blood. So I lifted that hag's fingers one by one so that what was left of her warm blood could drain from her wound. I collected enough to fill three flasks."

"Enough . . . be . . . be quiet," I stammer, seized by a violent urge to regurgitate the jam-covered toast that this piece of trash whom I dared call a "friend" offered me.

"Goodness, Diane, don't get all bent out of shape," he huffs. "I'm speaking about an enemy of the Vampyria. A vile criminal, someone mixed up with those cowards who murdered your father. She begged me to spare her. If you'd heard the way her grotesque pleas mingled with the blood gurgling from her slit throat, split open like a smile . . . it was comical. You should savor your revenge the way I'm about to savor this nectar."

He raises the flask to his pale lips, sucking up in one long gulp all that remains of my mother.

6

HATE

Only a few hours ago, I asked myself what I was still good for. Now I know—to make sure Alexandre disappears from the face of the earth.

Vengeance, that's why I'm still alive.

I stupidly let my chance to accomplish my destiny slip by. Or at least the chance to try. Twice I hesitated to lift the trapdoor under which my revolting enemy slept, defenseless.

He's presently sitting on the bench in front of me, merrily talking after having swallowed a flask filled with my dear mother's blood.

She was still alive.

She could have been saved.

In the dead of night, I know that the monster in front of me is invincible. So I'm condemned to listen to him go on for the hundredth time about how bored he was in the Auvergne and how happy he is to be returning to Versailles. Which is getting closer. That's the price I pay for being a coward. I hate him so much for killing my mother I could die. But even more, I hate myself for listening to his delusions of redemption, his hopes of being liberated from the curse of blood, for believing him for even one minute. A pulsing, savage migraine grinds my brain, as if punishing me for my stupidity.

"These are the banlieues of Paris: fortified outskirts aimed at housing herds of commoners," he says with a gesture. "We're nearly there."

Behind the carriage window, the urban areas are now so close together that they're separated only by empty lots overgrown with weeds. The moon drools on ever-higher ramparts that confine the increasingly dense housing projects. Sentry paths go around the ramparts. Tiny silhouettes armed with halberds patrol the area, keeping watch over the streets, on the lookout for anyone who would defy the curfew. Immense cathedral towers capped with iron bats dominate these open-air prisons. I don't dare think about the size of the tanks enclosed in these gigantic buildings and the tons of blood that the Faculty preserves there . . .

"I admit it, these banlieues aren't exactly cheerful," Alexandre says. "But they're necessary to warehouse the tens of thousands of the toothless needed to nourish the court. Their blood in exchange for our protection—that's the very foundation of the Mortal Code."

With every word this demon utters, my stomach contracts more tightly, and my migraine ratchets up. I'm repulsed by how the meek, subjected to the fangs of the powerful, have been labeled "toothless." As for the "protection" provided by the vampyres, it's never seemed so hypocritical. Dr. Boniface's sermons pretend that the immortals were sent to save mortals from their warmonger instincts—same as if we were quarrelsome children who needed to be penned up so as not to hurt ourselves. The lords of the night are also supposed to be protecting banlieue inhabitants from the abominations inflicted by the Shadows, but in truth the lords are the worst among them. All the inequity of the *pax vampyrica* explodes in my face like never before.

"The rest of us, we immortals of the Magna Vampyria, have renounced our feral instincts in favor of drinking from a flask," Alexandre continues pensively, oblivious to the repulsion he inspires in me. "But no flask, however fresh it may be, can replace the thrill of bleeding a live prey legally. That only happens when we're lucky enough to chance upon a commoner who's defied the curfew . . . or when we corner an enemy of the state. I have to confess that after I filled my three flasks, I finished off the rebel by gorging on her throat. Pure gluttony."

He gives me an odious, knowing smile. I have an almost irrepressible urge to jump at his throat and tear off his smile with my bare hands. But he covers his face with a lace handkerchief.

"Pew, what a foul odor," he exclaims as we pass by a housing project even more massive than the previous ones. "That's how the lower class smells when we cram them together. It must be teeming with bodies, just like the caged hens at the bleeding houses of Plumigny. I bet that project doesn't provide a premier vintage, just a cheap jug variety destined for impoverished vampyres. Questionable hygiene and diseases galore—hello, stench. Don't you smell it?"

I shake my head, the jolts from the uneven paving stones hammering as many iron nails into my brain. The only thing I smell is the sharp odor of my sweat in this damned silk linen gown that I haven't taken off in three days.

The sinister banlieue-prisons finally give way to white-stoned buildings adorned with moldings. Given the late hour, many windows are brilliantly lit with chandeliers, the summer-evening breeze stirring the curtains. The languid cries of violins float down through some windows, sprightly minuets from others. I hate to think of exactly who's frolicking in those apartments—vampyres, mortals, or worse yet, a mix of both.

"At last, some air we can breathe," Alexandre cries out as he opens the window slightly.

The nocturnal breeze flows into the carriage, lifting his red locks like flames around his face, a face that seems modeled on the beauty of the devil.

"I smell the scent of gunpowder from fireworks and the trail of perfumed gloves," he exclaims, his pupil-dilated eyes widening. "I smell the excitement of party animals who're dancing the never-ending jig. I smell the sweet aroma of vampyric roses and the spicy aroma of blood oranges wafting from the palace orangery."

Nonstop jig? Vampyric roses? Blood oranges? My head can't conjure up the horrors that Alexandre mentioned with shivers of pleasure. Under the carriage wheels, the regular sound of the neatly aligned paving stones replaces the jolts of the country. We cover the last league as if in a dream, or rather a nightmare.

The carriage stops in front of a giant iron gate. The bars are four times taller than me, with sharp lancelike pointed tips.

"Here we are," Alexandre says. "The Grande Écurie."

He opens the door before one of the dragoons has time to help him and leaps into the night.

"Mademoiselle?" he says invitingly, as he breaks into an enticing smile.

I overcome my disgust and take hold of the arm that he extends so I can exit the carriage. As we brush against one another, I'm once again gripped by the wild desire to lacerate his face with my bare hands.

"We'll have to part now, but my promise still holds," he says. "When the school at the Grande Écurie deems you ready to make your entrance at the court, be it in a month or a year, I'll be here to help you. Cross my heart and hope to die, stick a needle in my eye—oops, so much for old superstitions since I'm already dead and glad to be. Ha ha!"

I'd forgotten that repulsive promise.

But it serves me equally well.

The voice of reason supersedes the voice of rage.

I need to be better armed to attack.

I need to strike when I have the upper hand.

I need to put every chance in my corner to eliminate my mother's killer—it's worth the wait.

"I'll remember," I manage to say in spite of my pounding migraine and the disgust tearing at my guts.

"I'm counting on it. But the hour's late, and you must get to bed. You're deadly pale, and I know what I'm talking about, right? Ha ha."

Already I see the outline of a woman hurrying toward us. She's wrapped in a long navy cape and holds a lantern in her outstretched hand. She crosses the huge horseshoe-shaped courtyard that's just beyond the gate. Ferocious barking starts up in her wake, coming from unseen kennels.

"Good evening, madame," Alexandre tells her. "This is Diane de Gastefriche, the young orphan I said would be arriving. I sent a homing crow with the message."

"Very good, Viscount," says the woman. "You can entrust her to me; everything's been taken care of."

Alexandre places his hands—his claws—on my shoulders.

"And so I take my leave of you now," he says to me. "I'm off to plead my rehabilitation at the palace. I sent some homing crows there as well, and I think I'll be heard with a friendly ear." He climbs back into the carriage. "Especially as I bring tangible proof of the aborted rebellion."

"What proof?" I mutter, trying to gather another morsel of information about my family.

He points with his chin toward the luggage at the rear.

"One of the trunks contains all the debris we could collect after the explosion in the secret lab. The inquisitors will be able to gather enough information to understand what was going on over there. But the courtiers couldn't care less about science; they leave those kinds of tedious subjects to the Faculty. So for them, I brought back trophies that are a little more . . . how best to say this . . . a little more splendid—the heads of the five Fronde rebels. I had my men section them off with their swords. It's certainly not as neat as with an ax, but the dragoons made do with what they had."

He slams the door shut, and the carriage immediately starts up, taking him into the night, along with his hideous laughter.

Don't throw up.

Don't listen to the carriage as it grinds off behind me.

Don't trip on the courtyard paving stones in front of me.

Lean on my guide with all my weight.

And most of all, chase out of my mind the thought that for the past three days I traveled next to the severed heads of my loved ones.

"I am Madame Thérèse, governess of the girls' wing," the woman tells me once we've reached the imposing semicircular building whose dark mass wraps around the courtyard. "I'm in charge of organizing day-to-day life for the young ladies at the school of the Grande Écurie."

I raise my eyes and look at the governess for the first time. Under a ribboned mobcap that matches her cape, her face looks mature and austere, steeped in principles. She didn't use an aristocratic surname to introduce herself, which means that she's a commoner like me . . . for now, she observes me rather unkindly; the dark circles under her eyes indicate that she stayed up late for my arrival.

"The boys are housed in the second wing," she says, pointing toward the other half of the semicircle. "But you'll only mingle with them at suppertime. Lessons are strictly segregated by gender so as to avoid wantonness. I prefer to warn you straightaway that this is an elite establishment—lessons are held seven days out of seven. Raymond de Montfaucon, director of the school and grand equerry of France, coordinates everything." She brings the lantern close to my face to get a better look at me. "I didn't find your family papers in the archives, since we only maintain those of families presently at the court. Tell me, how old are you, Mademoiselle de Gastefriche?"

"Eighteen," I answer, remembering that the baronette was the same age as Bastien, one year older than me.

I'm a little relieved to know that the governess doesn't have access to the papers pertaining to my subterfuge. It seems the Gastefriches haven't been to the court in ages, if they ever set foot here at all. There's probably no one at Versailles who remembers the real Diane—at least I hope not . . .

"Then you'll follow the lessons for the third-years, and you'll sleep in their dormitory," Madame Thérèse says. "The school year began two weeks ago, but don't misunderstand: you'll have to make up for a great deal of lost time. Most of your classmates have already been studying here for some time as part of our three-year program. You'll have to work twice as hard if you want to be able to make your entrance at the court come the end of the school year in June. Tell me, did you learn anything worthwhile in your province?"

"I know how to read and write," I rush to tell her, worried about the delay she's just mentioned.

Ten months before my entrance at the court—that means ten months before I can get the revenge that's smoldering within me.

The governess rolls her eyes.

"Lucky that you know how to read and write," she says with an exasperated sigh.

"I also know English."

She furrows her brow.

"Really? That's unusual, coming from the provinces. I must tell you that English is not as commonly used as before at the court due to the folly of the vice-queen Anne and the events that took place in New York . . ."

I vaguely heard talk of the vice-queen vampyre who sits on the throne on the other side of the Channel. Her allegiance to the Immutable might be shaky, but I don't know anything more. As for the events in New York, I haven't the slightest idea what that's all about.

"And what else?" she follows up. "Can you sing, dance, play an instrument?"

"Uh, no . . ."

"We teach the five noble arts here: art of courtly manners, art of conversation, art of equestrianism, art of weaponry . . . and art of vampyrism, strictly reserved for third-years. Is there one you excel at?"

"I . . . I know how to wield a sling," I stammer.

Madame Thérèse's frown dissuades me from revealing any more. A sling is likely not a weapon that the dignified young lady I've become would ever use.

"Enough talking," she says dryly. "For now, it's advisable that you rest. You must be very tired, and so am I, as the Shadows are my witness."

Lighting the path with the halo of her lantern, she leads me to a large stone staircase that gives off a hollow echo as we make our way up to the fifth floor.

She pushes on a double door that opens onto a vast room. A main aisle runs down the center. On each side are four-poster beds with canopies, all curtains drawn.

"On your tiptoes, please," the governess orders me in a whisper. "Your classmates are in bed."

In bed, maybe. Asleep, I'm not so sure . . . I have the impression that several pairs of eyes are watching me from under the edges of the curtains, eyes more menacing than those of the guard dogs in the courtyard kennels.

7

NEWCOMER

"Hey there, newbie, still sleeping? I thought hicks from the sticks rose with the rooster at the crack of dawn."

A sheet of water falls on my face.

I bolt upright from my soaked pillow, my hair dripping wet, my thoughts still haunted by nightmares of decapitated heads.

In contrast, the head that's bent over my bed is very much alive. It belongs to a girl whose startling beauty is tarnished by a cruel smile.

"That'll get your toilette going, little gray mouse," she says, roaring with laughter. She puts the glass she just emptied on my head on my night table. "But seeing how covered in mud you are, I'm afraid you'll need an entire bucket to wash up."

Her laughter makes her iron-curled chestnut hair shake, hair that falls in serpentine fashion on either side of a face that looks as if it were painted by an Italian Renaissance master.

She probably thinks she's dealing with an easy target. But I didn't brave village insults my entire life and witness my family being murdered in order to be squashed by a bitch who looks like a Madonna putting on a show.

"It's not mud," I say, grabbing hold of the canopy bedpost to get up.

"Oh, really?" she answers, turning to the other girls who've witnessed my rude awakening. "What is it then? Dung?"

"Dried blood."

The beautiful girl's laughter dies out.

Her eyelids open wide, her amber-colored eyes flashing as brightly as pure gold.

"B-b-blood?" she stammers, furrowing her perfectly painted brows.

"Would you like to touch it and make sure?"

I march straight toward her in my filthy, water-soaked negligee.

The impudent girl steps back, tripping in her high heels . . . and falls backward onto her petticoats. Everyone can see the wicker hoop that gives her bright-yellow damask dress its structure.

The last of the girls who were still laughing rush to her rescue, crying out in alarm.

"Are you all right, Hélé?"

One girl takes advantage of the diversion and gently grabs hold of my arm.

"Come, I'll show you where to bathe . . . ," she says softly with a hint of an accent.

Her attire is a lot simpler than my rival's, a pale-mauve silk robe that wraps over the chest held by a wide matching belt. Exotic white flowers, a variety that Maman didn't teach me about, are embroidered along the hem. Her smooth, abundant black hair is gathered at the nape of her neck in a thick bun. A red wooden lacquered hair stick holds it in place. Under bangs cut level with her eyelids, a face with high cheekbones and eyes with slightly dark circles appears. I once read an account of a voyage to the Far East, the etchings showing graceful inhabitants of the region who looked like this girl.

I let her lead me outside the dormitory and across a hallway with shiny tiles. The light enters freely through the high windows despite the cloudy sky. The immaculate walls, adorned with delicate moldings, are at least three times as tall as the walls in our house in Butte-aux-Rats.

Suddenly, I freeze in front of a window. A hundred yards beyond the glass lies a vast space that extends toward colossal ramparts. Whereas the high walls that hemmed in the banlieues were dark and dreary and stained with the droppings of scavenging birds, this wall is made of the brightest cut stone with giant, exquisitely sculpted motifs. But as I look more closely, fear overtakes wonder—those high reliefs aren't of nymphs and gods like in the old Baron de Gastefriche's garden. They depict gigantic vampyres in all their savagery, baring their sharp teeth in broad daylight, plunging their fangs in the necks of defenseless, swooning mortals who've completely surrendered to them. In the middle of this frozen pandemonium that seems to proclaim the bloodsuckers' omnipotence, packs of wolves, ravens, and bats swirl around huge baroque columns.

"What you're seeing, at the other end of the Parade Grounds, is the Hunting Wall," my guide whispers in my ear, her calm voice a contrast to the surrounding horror. "That's the name of the walled enclosure of the Palace of Versailles, which was built during the first century of the Magna Vampyria. It's a completely sealed defense—totally impenetrable—that shuts in the palace and its occupants during the day. At night, the wall opens, driven by a hydraulic system connected to the same aqueducts that supply the fountains at Versailles. The structure is the work of Jules Hardouin-Mansart, the king's personal architect, and the sculptures are the masterpiece of François Girardon, his favorite sculptor. Both of them were transmuted so they could continue their work over the centuries. The tens of thousands of mortal laborers who died on the construction site didn't get that chance." My guide pauses. I'm taken aback by the depth of her knowledge. "It's always shocking when you see the Hunting Wall for the first time," she adds.

When she sees me shudder, she touches my shoulder.

It's not the sculptures that make me tremble; it's the growing awareness that the wall stands between the Grande Écurie and Alexandre's apartments . . . between me and my vengeance.

"You'll end up getting used to the view," my guide assures me.

She pulls me away from the window.

"By the way, my name is Naoko Takagari. I'm the daughter of the Japanese ambassador. The daytime ambassador, of course, as the nighttime ambassador is a vampyre."

My intuition was right. Naoko comes from faraway lands where the sun rises, faraway lands that I dreamed about in my room at Butte-aux-Rats. Even if Japan isn't part of the Magna Vampyria, the emperor who rules there has also been transmuted, so he's represented at the Court of Shadows.

"Yesterday, Madame Thérèse asked for a volunteer who'd make sure the newcomer integrated well," Naoko tells me as she starts on her way again. "I offered. I know it's not easy to fit in at the Grande Écurie. When I arrived here two years ago as a first-year, I bore the brunt of Hélénaïs's viciousness."

"Hélénaïs?"

"Hélénaïs de Plumigny," Naoko specifies. "The youngest daughter of Anacréon de Plumigny, lowly lord of Beauce and the kingdom's principal purveyor of guinea fowls, capons, and chickens."

I lower my eyes, remembering how just yesterday Alexandre compared the project dwellers to fowl crammed into cages at Plumigny.

"The lords of Plumigny are known to take grand names from antiquity as a way to compensate for their recent claims to nobility," Naoko tells me. "They were ennobled less than a century ago for their service to the Crown."

"I see . . ."

I try to avoid making eye contact with the girl for fear that she'll guess my claims to nobility go back a mere three days. Despite the kindness she's showing the "newcomer," Naoko must be like all the other boarders at the Grande Écurie. She's privileged and living in her bubble. She's well to do and exempt from the tithe, avoiding the Mortal Code that oppresses the fourth estate. She's an ally of the vampyres and no doubt aspires to join their ranks as soon as the opportunity to be transmuted presents itself. I won't make the same mistake I made with

Alexandre. I'll never consider her my friend, and she must never suspect that I'm a usurper.

"My name is Diane de Gastefriche," I say hurriedly. "Something . . . something horrible happened to my family back in the Auvergne. Hence my presence here."

My voice breaks. I can't say the word *family* without thinking of my parents and brothers.

Naoko smiles sadly.

"Yes, I know, we were warned. Your poor father was killed by Fronde rebels. But you're safe now."

As she says this, the hallway turns off, and we find ourselves face to face with an armed man standing at attention in front of a window. Nothing like the black-uniformed dragoons of Clermont. This soldier wears a sumptuous ruby-red uniform with gold-braided trim on the shoulders.

"He's a Swiss Guard," Naoko explains, going round him without a glance, as if he were a statue. "The Crown's most loyal warriors, ready to lay down their lives in a heartbeat."

I take a quick, nervous look at the soldier. What with the guards and the ferocious hounds out in the courtyard, Versailles is decidedly under close monitoring and surveillance. I'll have to be clever to carry out my revenge. And even if I succeed in killing Alexandre, I'm under no illusions—my death will be instantly sealed. I'll quickly follow him to the grave. But at least I'll have the satisfaction that the monster will be destroyed, never again to rise from his coffin.

"You're safe here," Naoko goes on, totally out of sync with my thoughts. "The king appointed an entire regiment of Swiss Guards to protect the Grande Écurie. So there's no chance of Fronde rebels infiltrating the premises."

Her last words hit me like a ton of bricks.

"The king fears the rebels?" I ask.

She gives me a look from under her thick bangs.

"Hard to believe, right, that the most powerful monarch in Europe has to worry about such a threat, in his own palace no less?"

"Hard, indeed," I say, trying to slow down my quickening breath. Only last week I thought the Fronde was just a rumor. Now, after having discovered that it's for real and that everyone in my family was part of the resistance, I'm learning that this secret network extends all the way to Versailles.

"Rumor has it that there are always attempted attacks," Naoko tells me. "His Majesty's secret service thwarts them every time."

She stops in front of a door painted with a mermaid surrounded by seashells.

"This is one of the bathing rooms," she says.

She pushes the door and invites me inside a room completely tiled in white, clean and spacious and immaculate. I blink. I've never seen anything like it before.

"The bathtub is here," she tells me, gesturing toward a deep, shiny copper vessel decorated with a bronze swan-shaped spout.

"The bathtub?"

Naoko looks at me, in surprise.

"Well, yes, to wash yourself," she replies. "The hot water is here, on this side of the faucet." She turns a handle to the left of the swan, and it spits out a jet of steaming hot water; then she turns a second handle on the right. "And the cold water, here. I'll let it run. Don't you have a bathtub in your castle?"

"Uh . . . yes, of course," I hurry to answer, trying to save face. "But it looks different."

I have to remember that I'm no longer Jeanne, the wild girl of the woods, but Diane, the little darling brought up in silks. Even if I only ever washed myself with a damp cloth over a basin filled with cold water drawn from a well, I must pretend I'm used to luxury.

"I'll leave you," Naoko says. "Help yourself to the perfumed bath salts. The linens to dry off and the new clothes that Madame Thérèse assembled for you are here, on the dresser. They should be your size,

but the seamstresses can always make alterations later on if needed."
She motions toward a stack of neatly folded fabrics, next to which rests
a tray with food. "I took the liberty of adding a few cookies to your
breakfast, as well as a cup of café au lait. As soon as you're refreshed, pull
on the velvet cord, and I'll come back. You have to hurry—this morning, we're studying the art of conversation with Madame de Chantilly."

She heads toward the door and then stops on the threshold.

"By the way, even if Hélénaïs called you a gray mouse, I wanted to
tell you that I think your hair dye is very stylish."

"Oh, thank you . . ."

No need to correct her.

"I'm so glad I was chosen to be your guide," she adds. "You seem
nice and without malice. Maybe we can even be . . . friends?"

"Uh . . . but of course, Naoko."

She gives me a radiant smile, one that momentarily lights up her
tired eyes and makes her pale cheeks blush. Then she leaves.

I take off the negligee that's now like a starched carapace from the
dried blood and rancid sweat.

Once naked, I enter the tub that's been filled with heated water by
who knows what means of witchcraft.

The steam relaxes my tense muscles. The noise of the jet that's still
spilling out from the faucet dissolves my thoughts. My body and my
mind unwind all at once. Here, curled up in the tub, surrounded by all
this incredible opulence, I finally let myself go for the first time since
leaving Butte-aux-Rats.

With no one to see me, neither vampyre nor mortal, I give myself
permission to weep.

The marble staircase click-clacks under my new shoes, sporting the
highest heels I've ever worn. The thick beige brocaded skirt hinders my
legs. Under the three-quarter-sleeved bustier, my corset leaves me short

of breath. As for my unruly hair, Naoko tied it up in no time into a bun that I'll never be able to do myself.

"Let's go," she says. "We're late for the lesson."

I hold on to the polished railing so that I don't take a tumble as I glance nervously at the Swiss Guards posted on each landing. When we reach the second floor, we head toward a door painted with a muse holding a lyre between her hands.

Naoko knocks gently three times, then turns the doorknob.

The entire class of third-years turns to look at us, a good fifteen girls seated at individual desks. Hélénaïs is in the first row, sitting in all her glory.

"Ah, Naoko, we were waiting for you," exclaims a lady seated in an armchair that faces the desks.

She's wearing a creamy organdy dress, her white hair puffed up by hairpieces, atop which rests a lacy kerchief. Her eyeglasses remind me of Valère's, though hers are rimmed with gold instead of iron.

"And you, you must be Diane de Gastefriche," she adds.

"At your service, Madame de Chantilly."

I try my best to imitate the curtsy that Naoko executes with such grace, but I almost get tangled up in my petticoats, which elicits stifled laughter from some of the others.

"A little indulgence, mesdemoiselles," the teacher orders. "Diane can work on her courtly gestures with General Barvók. May I remind you that this morning's lesson is the art of conversation, not the art of courtly manners."

She nods, inviting us to sit at the last two remaining desks that are free.

"If the newbie isn't able to curtsy properly, I don't see how she'll be able to string together two interesting words," Hélénaïs scoffs.

"Mademoiselle de Plumigny!" the teacher scolds her.

I feel my heart beating fast, anger lashing at my temples. I have to show this girl that I'm her equal—an impetuous noble maiden, arrogant and cruel.

"Pardon me, Madame, but does she belong in this class?" Hélénaïs persists, designating me with her graceful chin. "From the looks of it, she's never stepped foot beyond her miserable countryside. What can she possibly converse about beyond cows and pigs?"

"Sheep," I correct her.

"Excuse me?"

"In my miserable countryside, as you say, the soil isn't rich enough to allow the breeding of cattle and swine. We make do with sheep. In fact, your magnificent curls remind me of Pâquerette's, the most famous ewe in the herd of my father's estates."

"But . . . but my hairstyle, à la hurly-burly, is the latest rage at the court," Hélénaïs chokes out.

"Really? In any case, Pâquerette won first prize at the agricultural fair in 294. You should sign up this year. You might have a chance of winning the blue ribbon."

Stunned and hiccuping, Hélénaïs turns to Madame de Chantilly. A few girls giggle.

"I hope you'll be punishing her for her insolence," she says.

"And why would I do that, Hélénaïs?" the teacher responds. "It seems to me we're fully demonstrating the art of conversation—a full-on battle of wits, to be exact. It's an indispensable skill at the court. Your charms, worthy of the beautiful Helen of antiquity, won't be enough to make you shine there if you remain mute. So counterattack. Let's see what you're capable of."

My rival turns her delicate, flushed face toward me, all eyes riveted to her.

A supporter whispers hushed words of encouragement: "Go on, Hélé, show her what you've got!"

She searches for words, obviously used to letting her beauty do the intimidating, unleashing Trojan War with one bat of her eyelashes.

"I . . . I won't allow it," she finally stammers. "First, you . . . you're the one who's a ewe. Or even worse—a gray mouse, just like I told you this morning." A smile reappears on her curled lips; she's clearly happy with her comeback. "Yes, that's it: you're a stupid, insignificant mouse."

"If you think a mouse is stupid, I can tell you you're wrong, because the ones in my castle dodge every trap. On the other hand, it takes a lot of patience to converse with a turkey, even if she's the daughter of the emperor of chickens. I believe our exchange just proved that."

Hélénaïs is speechless.

The other girls hold their breath, not knowing whose side to take now that the queen bee has been dethroned. Even Naoko lowers her tired eyes. I imagine she remembers the painful bullying Hélénaïs inflicted on her in the past.

Applause breaks the silence. It's the girl seated at the desk next to mine; she's clapping at the same time that she's chewing I-don't-know-what. She's clad in a navy fitted dress, cut from a seemingly rough and elastic fabric that contrasts with the shimmering silks favored by the other girls. I catch a glimpse of some lacy undergarment that daringly juts out in the low cleavage of her bodice. Deliberately, I'm sure. Under her high bun of brown hair, swept forward at the top of her head and attached with knots made from the same frayed fabric, her dark makeup—charcoal eyes and midnight-blue lips—strikes a note of defiance. Her complexion is so wan that I almost think she's a vampyre . . . until I remember that's not possible since we're in broad daylight.

She stops chewing to address me in a slightly hoarse voice, marked by an English accent, the language my mother taught me.

"Checkmate, *darling*! Sheep or turkey, you fleeced her and then plucked her."

Hélénaïs shoots daggers of rage at the pale-skinned girl but doesn't dare say anything. She's demonstrated to all the class that clever repartee is not her forte.

Madame de Chantilly clears her throat.

"Calm down, Proserpina," she says. "It's not becoming to pick on those who lose. And stop with that insufferable chewing gum. I've already told you I do *not* want that nasty American habit in my class."

A habit from America? Could this boarder also have been born as far away as Naoko? As for her name—Proserpina—I know it refers to the queen of the underworld in Roman mythology, the wife of Pluto, god of the dead. It fits this ash-complexioned girl like a glove.

She unfolds a handkerchief and spits out a piece of chewed gum, then shoots me a complicit wink out of a blackened eyelid.

"Thank you, Proserpina," I whisper.

"Poppy," she corrects me.

"Well, mesdemoiselles, after this pleasant interlude, let's get back to the lesson at hand," Madame de Chantilly says, putting an end to our brief exchange. "We were speaking about the gods of Mount Olympus and their romances, a topic of conversation that comes in very handy in society since it's a way to broach matters of the heart with tact and delicacy. The day before yesterday we discussed Adonis and Venus, Cupid and Psyche, and Orpheus and Eurydice, and I assigned you some chapters from Ovid's *Metamorphoses* to read for today . . . since we're welcoming someone who bears the name of a Roman goddess, can anyone tell me who Diane's lovers were?"

The girls exchange dubious looks.

One of them, a petite brunette, wearing a lime-green dress and pointy eyeglasses that resemble the teacher's, raises her hand.

"Yes, Mademoiselle des Escailles?" the teacher says.

"It's a trick question, Madame. Diana had no lovers. She's a huntress who took a vow of chastity."

"Very good, Françoise. And who can name the suitors she gave the cold shoulder to?"

I raise my hand in turn, determined to play the game to the end. I, too, have read Ovid. He had a prominent place on my parents' bookshelves.

"Diana poisoned the giant Orion with a scorpion," I say. "She killed the Titans Otus and Ephialtes with her arrows. And she transformed the hunter Actaeon into a stag so that his own dogs devoured him."

Madame de Chantilly looks at me approvingly above her eyeglasses.

"Impressive, Mademoiselle de Gastefriche," she declares. "You add erudition to your wit, two major qualities for the art of conversation. I confess that when Madame Thérèse told me a new student was coming from the middle of nowhere, I had my doubts. I thought we were taking on a charity case by welcoming a poor orphan girl within our walls. But now that I see and hear you, I've changed my mind. Perhaps you can compete in the Sip of the King this October."

I'm startled by the teacher's words. I've supposedly just lost my father, and *this* is how she speaks to me? But then I notice a murmur starting up among the girls. For the first time since I woke up, there's no hint of contempt, no menace, only admiration.

8

COMPETITION

"What's the Sip of the King?" I ask Naoko.

She and I are both sitting off to the side in the small dining hall in the girls' wing. A large nocturnal portrait of the King of Shadows towers majestically above the fireplace. It's a sooty canvas, quite sinister. The monarch sits astride a dark stallion whose coat is barely distinct against the blackish forest. The king wears a burgundy hunting outfit and a big three-cornered hat, bedecked with pheasant feathers, that's pushed down onto his cascading hair. The only vaguely luminous thing in all this dullness: the sovereign's gold mask, pierced with black holes.

Under the king's gaze, the room rustles with the servants' ballet and with the conversation of the girls who've come to lunch—fifteen third-years who are around seventeen years old, but also sixteen-year-old second-years and fifteen-year-old first-years. Fifty girls total, all from families of the highest nobility.

Naoko looks up from the fillet of sole that she hasn't touched, preferring to pick at the small vegetables that accompany it.

"The ritual of the Sip is the ceremony whereby the king selects two new recruits to be his mortal guards," she explains. "Traditionally, a boy and a girl."

"His mortal guards?" I repeat, thinking back to what Alexandre said. He had mentioned that the King of Shadows chose two students from the school every October 31, but he hadn't said anything about a military role. "I thought the king simply appointed a male and female squire . . ."

"Precisely. Whoever's chosen has the privilege of joining the innermost circle of mortals in whom the king has complete confidence—three boys and three girls who serve as his bodyguards. The six squires aren't just tasked with accompanying the king during the night. They're also responsible for ensuring his personal safety and keeping watch over his coffin during the day."

I glance furtively out the window that overlooks the courtyard of the Grande Écurie, right up to the tall bars and above to the Hunting Wall. Behind the brilliant whiteness of that colossal rampart, a secret palace lies hidden. A palace in the depths of which rest the black coffins of all the immortals at the court . . .

"Aren't the king's Swiss Guards enough to defend his coffin?" I whisper.

"No, they're not enough," Naoko tells me. "The guards will always be attached to the palace. But once the king's squires have served for several consecutive years, they're called to a higher status at the court. They enter into prestigious marriages and go off to the provinces, or even to foreign lands. They become His Majesty's eyes and ears, the strongest pillars of the French kingdom throughout all the Magna Vampyria and beyond."

For a few moments, I contemplate what Naoko's just told me, and I take in the almanac that hangs on the wall, open to today's date: September 3. It's an eternity until the third-years will be presented at court—next summer, at the end of June.

And what if I was lucky enough to be chosen by the king, just as Madame de Chantilly stated this morning? Not to serve him, never that. But the idea that I could enter the palace as soon as October 31, in two months, suddenly makes the prospect of my vengeance against Alexandre far closer and more tangible.

"I see . . . ," I say. "But that doesn't explain why the ceremony is called the Sip of the King."

Naoko leans in a little nearer.

"Because that's how the king seals the unique bond that links him to his squires," she whispers. "He lets them drink one sip of his own blood."

I gently place my fork on the edge of my plate, incapable of eating another bite. My knowledge of vampyres is more than limited; still, I know that drinking an immortal's blood is required for transmutation.

"The king transmutes his followers into vampyres?" I ask, instinctively lowering my voice as if the imposing portrait above the fireplace could hear me. Seeing Naoko's astonished expression, I instantly add, "Forgive my ignorance, but in the remote region where I come from, the lords of the night are not plentiful."

"Transmutation is a complex ritual, dangerous and highly regulated. It can legally be achieved only with the consent of the Hematic Faculty," she explains patiently. "The number of vampyres roaming the Magna Vampyria is strictly limited, *numerus clausus*, in order to ensure that the immortals constitute a tiny minority in relation to the mortal livestock destined to feed them."

I nod. That explains why we never saw any lords of the night in my backwater village.

"The transmutation ceremony requires that a powerful vampyre give a large quantity of his blood to a mortal who's been drained of their own blood beforehand," Naoko goes on. "While the ritual of the Sip, as the name implies, only involves a small amount of royal blood, it's enough to endow those who take the sip with extraordinary powers, but it doesn't transmute them completely. Thus, every year, the king offers a sip to all his followers so they can maintain the full force of these powers."

A young redheaded servant comes to clear the table. The crooks of her elbows are covered in purple scars from the bleedings reserved for commoners. The sight ruins my appetite. Under the long sleeves of my dress, my skin bears similar scars, hollowed out since childhood by hundreds of needles. Right arm and left arm, alternately punctured each month, shameful scars that will likely never fade.

"Toinette, please wait," Naoko says to the servant who's about to clear my plate. She turns to me. "Aren't you going to finish your vegetables, Diane?"

I shake my head, and Naoko transfers my leftovers onto her own plate.

"I'm a vegetarian," she explains.

"Vege-what?"

"I don't eat fish or meat." I give her a puzzled look, and she adds, "The consumption of animal flesh . . . uh . . . gives me insomnia. I'm a light sleeper, and heavy meals prevent me from having a proper slumber. The kitchens seem to have forgotten that today, but it's no big deal; I'll finish your portion."

I nod, intrigued. In the countryside, meat wasn't abundant, and fish even less so. At home, my few hunting successes improved the ordinary fare. As for Naoko's insomnia, the dark circles under her eyes indicate that her diet hasn't resolved the problem . . .

"The powers conferred by the Sip of the King, what are they?" I ask.

"Supposedly they differ, because everyone reacts differently to the Shadows. I heard talk of nocturnal visions, enhanced senses, even telepathy. The only thing that's certain is that the king's followers cease to grow old as long as they drink the royal blood. After many years, most of them end up completely transmuted. In recompense for their good and loyal service, the Faculty makes room for them in the *numerus clausus*. They forever join the ranks of the high aristocracy of immortal vampyres. Under these conditions, you can imagine how tough it is to get chosen."

"Yes, someone told me that the selection process every autumn turns into a fistfight."

Naoko nods, all the while delicately nibbling peas at the tip of her fork.

"Well, this autumn, the fistfight comes down to a duel in the girls' wing," she tells me. "You met the two rivals. Last year, they already shared first place in all the arts. Hélénaïs de Plumigny has no equal in fencing and courtly manners. And Proserpina Castlecliff tops everyone with her biting wit and good seat in a saddle."

I follow Naoko's gaze across the dining hall. The third-years are gathered around two mostly equal tables. One headed by the girl with curly chestnut hair, the other by the pale-skinned brunette. Now I understand why the latter was so pleased that I put Hélénaïs in her place earlier, and in front of everyone to boot. It wasn't out of support, as I naively thought, but fierce competition.

"Proserpina comes from one of the oldest families in England, the legendary lords of Castlecliff," Naoko whispers. "Their claim to nobility goes back to William the Conqueror, but today they're impoverished."

"I heard there were tensions between France and the vice-kingdom of England," I whisper back, recalling what Madame Thérèse said.

"That's precisely why Proserpina was admitted to the school free of charge: to strengthen the diplomatic ties between the two countries, especially during these turbulent times. If she became one of the king's squires, it would send a powerful signal. She speaks fluent French, as you may have noticed."

"So do you," I hasten to assure her.

Naoko shakes her head, revealing a lack of confidence that I've already detected.

"I may speak correct French, but I'm unable to come up with word-plays like you did this morning. My courtly manners are far from rivaling those of Hélénaïs, whose beauty lights up every room she enters.

And I don't have Proserpina's poise and way of imposing a personal style in clear disdain of prevailing etiquette." She points with her chin in the direction of the caustic brunette. "Who else besides her would dare wear denim to school?"

"Denim?"

"Yes, *toile de Nîmes*, named after the city in southern France where it was invented. It's a new and inexpensive elastic fabric that young commoners wear next to the skin. You've got to admit that on Poppy it's gorgeous. She even tops Séraphine de La Pattebise, with her short-fringed capes and frilly dresses, in elegance."

I nod, taking stock of how I know nothing of these fashion styles that never penetrated the distant Auvergne.

A new servant comes over with something she calls a "guava-and-pine-apple mousse," fruits as unknown to me as the exotic fabrics of Versailles. I try the concoction, a little wary . . . and discover it's delicious.

"Poppy and Hélé, it's the old aristocracy facing off against the new nobility," Naoko concludes pensively, all while eating her mousse. "They share the teachers' high grades and the attention from the boys in the other wing. They dominate the game, unless they end up canceling each other out."

"What do you mean?"

"At the end of last year, the tension between them was so palpable that Monsieur de Montfaucon called them to his office and threatened them with expulsion."

Naoko shivers in her silk robe at the mention of the school director, whom I've yet to meet.

"The grand equerry is really that fearsome?" I ask.

"He descends from a long dynasty of torturers ennobled by the king—the executioners of the Gibbet of Montfaucon. We're talking about the biggest gallows in Paris, in the French kingdom, even all of the Magna Vampyria. Supposedly up to a thousand convicted victims can be hanged there at one time."

I open my mouth to ask a new question, but at that instant, the sound of a chime comes from the entrance of the dining hall. It's Madame Thérèse, ringing the bell to call us back to our lessons.

If mornings are devoted to activities of the salon—alternatively, conversation and manners—afternoons are consecrated to physical activities such as horseback riding and weapons training. In fact, today the third-years repair to the weapons room, which is in the basement of the Grande Écurie.

It's a large vaulted room, lit with enormous wrought iron chandeliers. All sorts of weapons hang on the walls: swords, sabers, lances, but also pointed and blunt shapes that I've never seen before, even in books. I can't help but think of the long hours I spent in my parents' library, wondering about the vast outside world. I used to imagine its dangers from the warm comfort of my home. But now I have to face them for real, utterly alone.

"Gastefriche, en garde!" a voice suddenly thunders, increased tenfold by the cavernous room.

I turn around.

A woman of about thirty stands in the room's entrance. In contrast to all the others I've met till now at the Grande Écurie, she's wearing not a dress but men's breeches similar to the ones I wore at Butte-aux-Rats, with thigh-high boots. Above her fitted shirt, her auburn hair is knotted in a ponytail, setting off her oval face and piercing eyes—which are turned on me.

She throws me one of two swords she's brought.

Taken by surprise, I nearly hurt myself as I catch the weapon.

In the time it takes me to grip the hilt, the fencer comes at me in quick steps.

I see myself three days ago, in the old baron's castle, but today I'm not holding his daughter to create a distraction, and there are no drapes to get lost in. I have only the trembling sword at the end of my fist.

"Madame, I . . . I don't understand—" I stammer.

Before I can finish my sentence, the combatant lunges with feline agility.

I don't manage to evade the thrust, restricted as I am in my unwieldy dress. The blade rips off the brocaded bow decorating my left shoulder.

"Had I wanted it, you'd no longer have a left arm," the fencer says, easily recovering from her sudden thrust with not a hair out of place. "Let's see if you can better defend your right arm."

Again, she lunges at me, and this time, I instinctively raise my sword. Her blade slides against mine, making a sharp screeching sound. But just as I think I've parried her, she zeroes in on her intended target. The bow on my right shoulder falls to the ground like a dead leaf.

"You've been transformed into Venus de Milo," the she-devil says mockingly, referring to the statue without arms whose reproduction I admired in a book at home. "Am I also going to morph you into Victory of Samothrace?"

I saw that statue in the book too—she doesn't have a head!

The instant the fencer brandishes her weapon again, I bend my legs so suddenly that I tear my skirt.

The sword misses my forehead . . . but slices right through the ribbon that held my hair in place, and it falls freely on both sides of my face.

"Voilà, no more head," the fencer says, her mocking voice resonating above my nape.

My thighs, now liberated from the layer of fabric that encased them, are back to being agile. Still squatting on the ground in front of my adversary, who thought she'd finished me off, I strike her boots in a leg swipe.

"And now you have no feet!" I cry out.

Mowed down by surprise as much as shock, the fencer loses her balance.

She falls to the ground and rolls into a ball with the suppleness of a cat, and straightaway rises to her feet. Now, a slight sweat makes her forehead shine, and some strands of hair have escaped from her ponytail.

Instinctively, I raise my sword in anticipation of another blow.

Instead, the fencer extends her hand to help me up.

"Nice move," she tells me. "Unexpected. I'm Adrienne, Knight of Saint-Loup, and mistress of weapons at the Grande Écurie."

"I . . . I'm sorry about the new dress," I say, lowering my eyes to the skirt torn during my fight with the lady knight. "It was a gift from the king."

"The king will get over it," the knight says with such assurance that I'm stunned. "Better to lose a dress than to lose your life. If I'd been an assassin bent on killing you, you wouldn't have thought twice about sacrificing those clothes, and you'd be right." She turns to the rest of the class. "That said, mesdemoiselles, grooming and finery aren't necessarily inconveniences. The heavy fabrics slow us down, but they also make us seem more innocent than we are, useful to trick the enemy. Not to mention all the weapons we can hide in the folds of a wicker-hooped dress or an elevated bustle. So much for the artifices that are inaccessible to men and that give us an advantage over them, as if we needed any."

A girl with a long swanlike neck raises her hand.

"But is it gracious to use underhanded tricks, Madame," she asks, "especially for young ladies of our standing?"

The knight sweeps aside her scruples with a flick of her hand.

"There's no such thing as an underhanded trick, Séraphine de La Pattebise. Only two blows exist, successful ones and unsuccessful ones. As for the proper grace that ladies are supposed to exhibit, that's an invention of men so that they can subdue us." She lifts her chin with bravado. "You're known as the best dancer at school, Pattebise, but in my weapons room, I teach the moves that allow you to survive, not artistic fencing. Save your good manners for the balls and Barvók's fine dinners. Here, I forbid curtsies and simpering affectations. Boy or girl, only the determination to win is permitted!"

9
BOYS

"The mixed-company suppers are General Barvók's idea," Naoko tells me as she brushes my hair.

It's nearly seven o'clock, and after a full day we're getting ready for dinner. While I was tending to my evening toilette, the seamstresses in the bowels of the school worked their magic and fixed my dress.

"Our teacher for the art of courtly manners doubles as quartermaster for the boys' wing," Naoko continues to explain. "He requires that the girls and boys dine together so that we can practice gallantry and proper manners under conditions that reflect the court's."

I'm only listening to her with one ear as I replay in my head the events of my first day at the Grande Écurie. Despite my apprehensions, it went fairly well. I showed the girls who wanted to walk all over me that I wouldn't be bullied. I gained the admiration of two teachers. But most importantly, no one doubts my identity. For now, the illusion is working like a charm.

The only question is the timing of my revenge.

Waiting till June to make my entrance at the court with the other third-years?

Or pushing my luck and applying for the Sip of the King, and maybe entering the palace as soon as October 31—in only eight weeks?

Each of those possibilities presents dangers. If I wait until June, I multiply the risk of being exposed. And if I'm recruited to be one of the king's squires, I'll have to play it close to the vest in order to kill Alexandre without having to drink the monarch's blood . . . because it's out of the question that my lips will touch that evil liquid!

"Voilà, that's perfect," Naoko declares.

I raise my eyes to the mirror I'm sitting in front of in a new bathing room. There are several on each floor.

Whereas Naoko was pressed for time this morning and knotted my hair into a quick bun, tonight she has surpassed herself. The bulk of my hair is brushed upward at the top of my head, forming a sophisticated quiff that adds a good four inches to my height and shows off the curve of my neck. My oval face looks all the finer.

"You look lovely," she says. "I chose a pale-pink ribbon to bring out the cold sheen of your hair. You're blessed with such wonderful nuances and a shine like no other. Your hair looks like it's woven from pure silver."

"I don't know if I have silver hair, but you have a golden touch," I say, a little embarrassed by her compliments. "Who taught you how to style hair like this?"

"No one. I taught myself. Just like I learned how to paint on silk so that I could decorate my dresses with lotuses and orchids."

I turn toward Naoko, intrigued by her terse answer. Above her white rice-powdered face, her hair is in a magnificent bun. She's added diverse brooches, pins, and ornaments to her long wooden red-lacquered hair stick. As for her robe, it's decorated with hand-painted flowers that are even more exquisite than the ones on her daytime garment.

For a brief instant, I feel a swell of sympathy for Naoko, a solitary girl plagued with persistent insomnia who still hasn't really found her place at the Grande Écurie. She reminds me of Bastien, disconnected from the world, making me want to protect her from herself and others.

I quickly check that misplaced—dangerous—sentiment. If she found out what I really am, I'm certain she wouldn't be smiling at me. She'd be frowning in disgust.

Still, it will be useful to have a confidante at school . . . even if our attachment is based on a one-way lie.

"I'm so glad you asked me to be your friend this morning," I tell her. I place my hand on her wrist. "True friends."

"I . . . yes," Naoko says, blushing a little beneath the powder.

A vague shame overtakes me for being so familiar with her, much in the way my worst enemy behaved with me in his vile carriage. But I sweep away all feelings of guilt. I'll do whatever it takes to avenge those I loved.

While lunch took place in the small dining hall on the second floor, dinner is held in the large banquet hall on the ground floor, where the girls' wing connects with the boys'. We go down, escorted by Madame Thérèse. Entering this majestic room lit up with chandeliers takes my breath away. Ten round tables sit atop the polished parquet floor, all dressed in an abundance of crystal glasses and gleaming cutlery. I guess that it's made of pewter, not silver, which is banned, but it sparkles just the same.

"Here come the boys," Naoko whispers into my ear, snapping me back to reality.

A door opens opposite the one through which the girls arrived.

Around forty boys enter in turn, first the first-years, then the second-years, and finally the third-years. They're dressed in long bespoke jackets and immaculate shirts, with matching breeches that clench at the knee and silk tights below. The only exception to this proper attire: at the Grande Écurie, students are permitted to go bareheaded, their hair left to its natural state, instead of sporting heavy wigs as befits the gentlemen at the court. There's even a boy with short hair, a tall student with chiseled features and brown skin.

"Boarders come from all over the Magna Vampyria," Naoko says, again whispering into my ear. "Even from the other side of the Atlantic, as does Zacharie de Grand-Domaine. He was born in Louisiana to an African mother and a French father."

I take my eyes off the handsome boy to look at the imposing person who brings up the rear. He, on the other hand, wears a wig, and I take him to be the famous teacher of the art of courtly manners, quartermaster to the boys' wing. In the middle of his dense gray curls emerges a ruddy face with a full mustache trimmed just so. His greenish-blue frock coat is topped with an iron brace that holds his neck and chin perfectly still. There's something jerky in his gait and robotic in his movements. He crosses the room to join Madame Thérèse. As he gets closer, I'm startled to see that his hands are missing. Both his arms have been replaced with metallic prostheses. Pincers emerge from his lace sleeves.

"What happened to him?" I ask in a low voice.

"Rumor has it that General Barvók was one of the bravest officers in the Hungarian army, and that he guarded the eastern rim of the Vampyria, on the borders of Transylvania," Naoko whispers. "He was dismembered in a battle against the stryges. And once he was maimed, he could no longer fight, so he was called to Versailles, where the Faculty attached those prosthetics. Supposedly he can never remove his iron brace, even at night; otherwise his vertebrae would dislocate."

The stryges . . . according to the Faculty, they're the most fearsome of all the abominations that infest the nighttime. Dr. Boniface often spoke about them in his sermons. He would ask us to praise the lords of the night for their protection against these demons threatening to invade Europe. I thought it was only legend, an added argument to justify the Mortal Code. It's believed they're mutant vampyres who escaped the control of the Vampyria and became deformed and deranged under the influence of the Shadows. The dogma claims that the Immutable's armies have waged battle against them for close to three centuries. All the way over on the eastern front, on the threshold of the Terra Abominanda—the Abominable Land, thus named because the abominations reign there, absolute.

I'd like to ask Naoko more questions on the subject, but just then the teacher of courtly manners clinks his pincers together to demand silence.

"Mesdemoiselles and messieurs, greetings," he says forcefully, his voice deep and accent guttural.

Immediately, the forty girls execute a coordinated curtsy, while on the other side of the room, the boys bow their chests as one. I manage as best I can to follow the others.

"Mesdemoiselles and messieurs, to your positions," he then orders as if he were leading his troops to attack.

The girls begin to walk toward the tables, as do the boys.

"The third-years sit in the center of the room," Naoko whispers. "But the seating arrangement changes every night so that we learn how to mingle graciously in polite society. Sit where you see your name."

Indeed, I notice that a small card is arranged in front of each plate, displaying family names in elegant calligraphy. Already, Naoko heads to the table where she spotted hers, leaving me to manage on my own.

"Oh, pardon!" I say as I collide with a girl.

"No harm done."

I raise my eyes. It isn't a girl but a boy in a handsome light raw silk jacket. His hands are resting on the back of a chair, so he's obviously found the spot he's been assigned this evening.

Under his ash-blond hair, his harmonious face is blemished by a long scar that extends from the corner of his right eyebrow all the way down to his cheek. The old wound runs a mere inch from his eye, which is deep blue; he came close to being half-blind.

"I'm looking for my place," I say.

"Princes are like valets. Aren't we all looking for our *place* in this world?" he comes back at me.

I freeze, seized with anxiety. Is he speaking to me about valets because he's found me out?

No, it's the word *place* that he stressed, and a glimmer of defiance in his eyes seems to call for a response. The four other girls and boys standing around the table are also scrutinizing me. I recognize Séraphine de

La Pattebise, the one who took offense at my lack of grace in fencing—and she's staring at me pointedly, waiting for me to gather my wits.

"Indeed, monsieur," I answer, trying to get in the game. "Except it can be difficult for those of us who, as the saying goes, are *caught between a rock and a hard place*. But let's stop philosophizing. You've found yours; now let me hurry to find mine."

I'm about to go around him, but he doesn't give me a chance.

"And what if we dined in the kitchens, *in place* of the tables?"

I'm aware of drawing the attention of everyone presently in the room, including the general and the governess from their vantage point by the entrance. The other boarders have stopped talking to better hear the newcomer and see how she handles herself.

"I fear we'd be a bit *out of place*," I snap back.

"We could always get ourselves *replaced*," responds the boy with the scar, continuing his ridiculous variations on the same word.

"Good grief, I'm just looking for my place," I say, sighing and out of comebacks.

"You already said that," he tells me. "Seems to me you're *all over the place*, mademoiselle . . . mademoiselle . . ."

"De Gastefriche," I say.

My neighbor to my right gives me a discreet nudge with his elbow. He's not very tall, with a head of tousled brown hair. His all-black velvet outfit, with tights up to his chest, is in stark contrast with the colors worn by the other boarders. Even his fingernails are polished black. But above his stiff collar, his dark-green eyes are full of concern.

"Your seat is here, mademoiselle," he whispers in a husky voice with a slight foreign accent.

I follow his gaze toward the card on the table—where my name appears.

Finally, I've found my seat, but it doesn't get me anywhere. How can I sit in the middle of a joust when everyone is waiting for my brilliant response? As I rack my brain, my eyes desperately fixed on the tablecloth, I catch a glimpse of a strangely shaped pewter knife . . . it's probably a fish knife, based on the scales decorating the handle.

Gripped by a sudden flash of inspiration, I raise my head up high and reply to the blond boy: "Even if you were the *highest-placed* count, fishing for approval from your betters only makes you look like battered *plaice*, Your Grace."

The guests sharing our table applaud softly, including Séraphine de La Pattebise, her elegant white hands decorated with small diamonds. Her neighbor, too, applauds, a shy brunette whose place card reads *Marie-Ornella de Lorenzi.*

I hurry to sit down, relieved that muffled conversations start up again around the room. Even Barvók withdraws, limping away behind the door, leading Madame Thérèse with him to discuss who-knows-what.

"You crucified me with your last retort," the boy with the scar says as he sits beside me. "*Place* and *plaice*, who would have thought of that. High art! Plaice is not the usual flatfish at Versailles—here they prefer to serve sole, which is supposed to be even finer."

"I like both," I lie, as I've never tasted any of this seafood, only having gazed upon engravings of them in a book at home.

A glimmer of defiance lights up in the boy's eyes again, as if he still wants to spar despite the compliments.

"Nonetheless, you addressed me inaccurately," he says. "I'm not a count, a title reserved for immortals, but merely a chevalier. A simple knight."

I glance at his place card: *Tristan de La Roncière.*

"No one's perfect, Tristan," I say, smiling my sweetest smile so as to make it clear that the joust is decidedly over, and that he lost.

I conspicuously turn my back to him and address the boy in all-black velvet seated to my right. The one who kindly showed me my seat. His place card reads *Rafael de Montesueño*, a name with Spanish consonances.

"Thank you," I tell him.

"You're welcome. I know what it's like to be a foreigner at the Grande Écurie."

Foreigner. Like Naoko, this boarder comes from elsewhere, and his integration at the school must not have been easy. There's something sad in his voice, in his eyes. I'm about to ask him questions when the servants enter the room, their arms full.

A porcelain plate lands in front of me, filled with a white opaque soup that gives off a subtle aroma.

Out of the corner of my eye, I study Séraphine's delicate gestures. She's facing me, and I'm trying to determine which spoon, among the six that are laid out around the plate, to use.

"Diane, how do you like this cream-of-white-truffle soup?" she asks me. "The truffles are from Piedmont. Isn't it delicious?"

She smiles above her plate. I'm unable to determine if her cordiality is sincere or calculated.

"Let . . . let me taste it."

Taking note of what the others do, I dip the appropriate spoon in the steaming soup. I can't help but think with nostalgia about going mushroom picking with Maman every autumn when I was little, before I decided that I didn't need anyone to go with me into the forest. There weren't any white truffles in Butte-aux-Rats, only ordinary mushrooms, but nothing will ever replace the taste of my mother's soups. This memory catches me off guard, causing me to tremble.

"Hmmm, you're right, Séraphine. Delicious," I say anyway.

The truth is that I'm hungry as a bear after everything that went on today.

I plunge my spoon into the soup again, where it butts against something.

Is it a mushroom that didn't get minced?

I lift my spoon to get a better look at the morsel under the light of the chandelier. It's of a tacky and furry consistency, with hairs that catch the cream soup . . . an oval shape with clear fragments that resemble bone . . . and long yellowed teeth that poke out in front.

It looks like . . .

. . . the head of a dead mouse.

Wanting to retch, I let my sinister discovery drop onto the plate. The splattering of cream lands on my newly repaired dress, triggering exclamations from my table companions.

My stomach heaves, and I spit up my spoonful of soup.

Hélénaïs's light laughter echoes across the room as everyone stares at me.

"Is that how you were taught to dine at your castle?" she scoffs from her table. She's taking advantage of the teacher of courtly manners' absence to raise her voice so that everyone can hear her. "I'm surprised. At the same time, what manners can you expect from a gray mouse?"

The way Hélénaïs stresses the word—*mouse*—I surmise she's the one who slipped that filth into my soup.

I get up under gales of laughter, shaking with shame in my soup-stained dress. The servants themselves have stopped the dinner service to look at me disapprovingly.

"You . . . you're the one who put that thing in my soup," I stammer.

"What thing?" Hélénaïs says, looking startled from the other side of the room.

"Don't play innocent!"

"I don't know what you're talking about. First your mess at the table, then this ridiculous outburst—pull yourself together, for goodness' sake. Did your mother die before she could instill good manners in you?"

It's the straw that breaks the camel's back. Even if Hélénaïs is alluding to the real Diane's mother, the baroness who died of the fevers years ago, it's the image of my own mother that shoots up in my mind. Killed only days before, just to maintain order in the Vampyria, just so that the well heeled like Hélénaïs can savor their cream-of-truffle soup.

Rage prevails over shame.

I grab the sharpest knife resting next to my plate, but at the last moment, I hold back from throwing it; with my other hand, I snatch the saltshaker and hurl it with all my might across the room. My years of practice with the sling have taught me how to aim. The saltshaker lands right in Hélénaïs's soup plate, splashing her chest and face.

She lets out a screeching howl.

"Enough!" a deep, thunderous voice scolds.

It's the general, his face peony red above his iron neck brace.

In my fury, I hadn't seen him reenter with the governess.

He stands there, his metallic prosthetics knocking together as if he's lost control.

I start stammering an excuse as I slip the knife in the pocket of my dress.

"I'm burned to a crisp!" Hélénaïs wails as she applies a napkin to her long, milky neck. "My renowned beauty has been destroyed, forever!"

It's all an act, of course. But at the Grande Écurie, as at the court, every hypocrisy seems to be permitted.

"Gastefriche! In the office of the grand equerry, right now," Madame Thérèse orders.

🦇

The governess dashes through the hallways, leading me along on her clicking heels. Night has nearly fallen, and sconces have been lit along the walls. The Swiss Guards have not budged an inch.

Try as I might to explain what happened to Madame Thérèse, she doesn't want to hear it.

She stops only when she reaches a large door padded in leather and flanked by two motionless guards.

She gives three short knocks.

"Come in," says a hollow voice on the other side.

Madame Thérèse opens the door and pushes me ahead of her.

In front of us stands a tall wooden secretary, atop of which are heavy candelabras with rearing horses cast in bronze. The glow of the candles sheds light on imposing shoulders wrapped in a riding coat with a large collar. A face with a waxy complexion emerges, seeming at once harsh and sickly. The sharp features look as if they're chiseled out of rock, the broad cheeks two dark holes, the protruding jawline highlighted by a small bristly patch below the lower lip. A long black wig, its curls limp and greasy, hangs heavily on either side of a frightening yellowed face.

But more alarming than the grand equerry's head are the jars on the shelves behind him. Strange shapes float in the translucent liquid. In the twilight, I can hardly make them out, and I can't determine if it might be a collection of animal organs . . . or human ones.

Monsieur de Montfaucon, the feared director of the school, has the physique of his ancestors. He looks like an executioner in his lair.

"The new boarder savagely attacked Mademoiselle de Plumigny," the governess accuses me. "I saw her throw a saltshaker with the fury of a wild animal. She was aiming for the head."

"No, I was not aiming for the head," I say, trying to plead my case, ashamed that I let my emotions get the better of me.

"Silence!" the grand equerry orders, his voice making the formaldehyde slosh in the sinister jars.

Under his bushy brows, his feverish eyes glow like two embers ready to consume me.

"Do you know what fee the parents of the other boarders pay for their children's education at the Grande Écurie?" he asks me.

"No . . . I . . . I don't . . . ," I stammer.

"Evidently, since you're not spending a penny to be here. You are the king's guest. As such, your behavior should be above reproach."

"I promise that it won't happen again," I say, feeling crucified that I have to bear the responsibility of a quarrel I didn't provoke.

The grand equerry strokes his patch with the tips of his executioner's hands, his huge fingers bedecked in heavy rings that knock against one another in alarming clicks.

"Indeed, it won't happen again," he repeats. "There were enough arguments last year at school between Plumigny and Castlecliff. Last thing I need is another outsize ego. You will spend the following days locked up in one of the servants' rooms, in the attic. By week's end, we'll find you a spot in one of the Faculty's convents in Paris."

"But I'm the king's ward!" I protest.

What abject irony to invoke the king's name to save the day.

The grand equerry looks at me hard.

"The king doesn't even know who you are, you impertinent girl. How would he be aware of your pitiful existence? His staff organized your arrival out of consideration for your father's sacrifice. You've had your chance. You'll remain a ward, but within four walls. You'll cost the Crown a lot less once you've been cloistered."

A deluge of chimes beats down on me. It's the warning bell that rings from every church tower of Versailles, signaling the arrival of nighttime.

I've ruined everything.

Only two hours ago I was making plans to enter the palace, and now I'll never step foot inside.

For the hundredth time since I've been locked in this tiny room at the top of the school, I pummel my pillow. This pathetic outburst of rage manages only to aggravate the migraine that's drilling into my brain.

My sullied brocade clothes were taken from me; in their place, I was given a crude coarse linen dress. No need for frills for the life that awaits me at the convent. Madame Thérèse prepared a bag with modest effects: brush, undergarments, austere shawl to cover my head and shoulders. I was able to keep only my pocket watch, my tinderbox lighter, and the meat knife I stole at dinner. But of what use will it be to me now? A carriage will come for me at week's end, when I'll have been accepted into a convent.

A low rumbling can suddenly be heard, making the walls shake and my head throb.

At first I think a thunderstorm has erupted after having simmered for days.

But no, behind the dormer window of my attic room, the clouds aren't being ripped apart. They're still whole, full and menacing, obscuring the moon and stars.

Yet the rumbling continues.

A nervous wreck, I cross the dark room and press my aching forehead against the vibrating window.

The daunting high wall of the palace appears even more monstrous than by day, as if the nighttime had shortened the two hundred yards of the Parade Grounds. Under the dancing glow of torchlights, the huge vampyres sculpted into the wall seem to come alive to chase their mortal prey.

But . . .

. . . it looks like they're really moving.

On closer inspection, it's the Hunting Wall itself that's opening, sliding on invisible tracks and creating a seismic rumble. As Naoko explained to me, when night falls, the force of the rivers upstream from Versailles is used to move thousands of tons of stone.

When the rumbling finally stops, an enormous portal has opened in the middle of the fortifications, tall and at least dozens of feet wide. Carriages enter and exit the royal enclosure, all under the watch of Swiss Guards brandishing torches. Some of the light-colored wood carriages transport the living, and others, in ebony, convey the immortals.

Knowing that I'll never be able to cross through that gaping opening kills me. I break out in a cold sweat, my hand trembling on the window frame.

Oblivious to my distress, a vehicle larger than the others tears away from the funereal traffic. Drawn by six horses, it's entirely shielded in iron and engraved with a large bat, its wings outstretched, the insignia of the Hematic Faculty. I shiver as I think about the amount of fresh blood contained in that traveling tank, which must have left the banlieues of Paris right at nightfall to come feed the court . . .

While the evil convoy stops to abide by the necessary checkpoints, a sudden movement attracts my attention just off to the side of the Parade Grounds. I plaster my face a little more against the glass, convulsively erasing the steam of my breath so I can better see. Three figures are hurrying toward the portal: two Swiss Guards who frame a third man clothed in rags and putting up a struggle. They're too far away for me to see their faces or hear their voices, but the prisoner's contortions, the way his body rears up in terror, give me chills. I think about the solitary traveler back in the Auvergne, the one who had the misfortune of walking after the curfew, and whom a vampyre bled to death. Tonight this poor beggar stayed out after the start of the curfew, probably because he had nowhere to go. Presently, the soldiers are leading him into the densest nest of vampyres in the kingdom . . . where he'll be subjected to his punishment.

I'm just like that vagabond: distraught and powerless.

How did I think, for one instant, that I'd be capable of fighting against the lords of the night?

Exhausted and desperate, my head filled with black bile and my cheeks overflowing with tears, I let myself topple onto my bed.

10

ESCAPE

I'm like that vagabond.

As I wake up, that thought goes off in my head, which is finally free from the shackles of my migraine.

I'm like that vagabond.

Last night, black bile drowned my thoughts, but this morning everything is clear.

I'm like that vagabond!

I've hit on the way, the only way, to enter the palace: allow myself to be captured like a lamb being brought to slaughter!

I toss aside the sheets, under which I slept fully dressed, and run to the window.

Under the gray morning, where clouds hang more heavily than ever, the Hunting Wall is closed. But unlike yesterday, the sight of the most impenetrable fortress in the kingdom doesn't dismay me. On the contrary, I'm inspired. If I manage to penetrate the enclosure as a prisoner, maybe once inside, I'll find a way to escape my guards and find that monster of an Alexandre. Maybe I'll have time to mutilate him, even kill him, before I'm sent to my own death.

A great calm comes over me. My mind is perfectly focused. Whereas yesterday I was distraught, in the grip of a deep melancholy because I didn't see a way out, now that I have a plan, however crazy and suicidal it may be, the huntress in me has returned.

Monsieur de Montfaucon said that a place would be found for me in a convent by the end of the week. That means I can expect to be at the Grande Écurie tonight, and I can try to escape from this bedroom. But how?

On one side, there's the double-locked door, behind which are five floors infested with highly trained Swiss Guards; on the other side, there's the narrow dormer window that opens onto the roofs, gutters, and courtyard full of big ferocious hounds. My instinct leans toward the window. In my forests, I confronted fierce animals a lot more often than I did soldiers.

Now, weapons . . . I need a stake to drive into Alexandre's chest and a blade to cut off his head. For the decapitation, I've got the meat knife. It will be total butchery to section off the head of a vampyre with this kind of utensil, but I'll derive all the more pleasure since Alexandre didn't think twice before mutilating the dead bodies of my family.

As for the stake, the one chair in the small bedroom will do. I'll wait until tonight, after the guards' last rounds, to craft the fatal weapon.

Feeling emboldened by my plan, I spend the day motionless, just sitting on the edge of my bed.

The hours have never seemed longer.

Every time that the key turns in the lock of the door, I'm gripped with anxiety. *Don't let it be anyone taking me away to the convent.* But no, it's just the guards bringing my meals or emptying my chamber pot.

The day finally begins to wane, my excitement increasing as the light dims.

I wait until the warning bell rings before I go into action. Now I'm certain no one will disturb me for the rest of the night.

First, I turn over the chair. I take advantage of the noise the Hunting Wall makes as it opens again outside, and I kick repeatedly at one of the wooden chair legs with my heel. It finally breaks and detaches from the frame without attracting the attention of the guards. I grab the wood and feverishly begin to cut the tip with the blade of my knife. Shaving after shaving, a point starts to take shape. Once I think it's sharp enough, I weigh the foot-long stake in my hand, now sore from an hour's worth of labor. It's perfectly balanced.

I remove my dress and tear a portion of the bottom off so that it ends midthigh, allowing my legs to move more easily. I make a band from the large piece of torn cloth and wrap it in an X across my chest so that it acts as a sheath behind my back. I slide in the stake and the knife, one weapon against each of my shoulder blades, both within reach. I put on the shortened dress over everything, minus the corset, and I tie my hair with a ribbon. Last of all, I kick off my pumps, liberating my bare feet.

At that very instant, the church bells of Versailles ring out ten times. It's ten o'clock at night.

The most dangerous time has arrived: my escape over the rooftops. I turn the handle of the dormer window.

The night air caresses my cheeks while the racket from the carriages converging onto the Parade Grounds rises to the window.

I take a deep breath and, without a backward glance, hoist myself through the narrow opening.

I scan the rooftop, searching for a place to begin my descent. The clouds that hide the moon conceal me, but they also make it hard for me to see clearly. So I grope my way on all fours, trying to find a descending pipe. I do my best not to look down into the black abyss of the courtyard below, hoping that the watchdogs in their kennels are securely fastened.

While I listen to the nighttime sounds, paying close attention to any growls coming from the hounds, something cracks behind me.

I turn around slowly, poised on the edge of the roof, all my senses on high alert . . .

. . . but I don't see anything.

It must have been a nocturnal bird.

My stomach filled with fear, I resume my labored search until my fingers meet a welded joint that's connected to a pipe going down toward the courtyard. I grip it firmly and give it a good shake to test its strength. The pipe doesn't give way. I'm hoping it'll be as strong as the tree trunks I used to climb when I stole pigeon eggs from their nests.

I let my legs dangle in the void until my toes touch a welded joint along the vertical pipe that can bear weight. I press the balls of my feet on each side of the pipe, not thinking about how cold the metal is against my bare skin.

With my right hand, I let go of the roof and dig my fingers between the iron pipe and the stone wall to secure my grip. Finally, I remove my other hand and join it to the first.

Voilà. My descent begins.

I've already gone down a few feet.

My rough guess is that I have twenty more yards of emptiness before I reach the ground.

I lower one leg along the pipe in search of another welding where I can put my foot.

Lower . . .

Lower still . . .

When I finally feel a knurl-like protuberance under the tip of my big toe, my body stretched between my extended leg and my hands still extended above my head, a bright white light tears at the sky. My fractured shadow is momentarily flashed against the wall. A second later, a fearsome rumbling of thunder answers the lightning bolt. A storm has just broken out.

I give a frantic look at the sky.

A warm drop of rain lands on my forehead.

Another lightning bolt blinds me.

By the time I bring my wandering leg back up, the shower has turned into a downpour. The sky rips open. The gallons of water I'd sensed accumulating during my journey to Versailles gush down on me.

I try to move my hands up along the pipe to reach the gutter, but it's already overflowing with rainwater. The drenched drainpipe is slippery under my palms. The downpour hurtles down the plumbing, sending vibrations up to my inner thighs.

Thunder roars in my ears, the deluge hitting me hard.

The furious wind tears off my ribbon and plasters my hair over my eyes.

Inch by inch, I feel my fingers slide.

As hard as I try to grab the metal, to the point of breaking nails, nothing helps.

I'm about to fall . . .

I . . . I'm . . . falling!

A viselike grip suddenly takes hold of my left arm, the last to let go.

For a second, I'm floating over the gaping void, suspended by one arm.

Then whatever grabbed me raises me up with phenomenal force.

I land in a ball on the rooftop, panting, with a battered shoulder.

The sheets of rain are so thick, so dense, that I can't see anything around me . . . nothing but a shadow bent over my bruised body.

"Who—who are you?" I stammer.

Rainwater rushes into my mouth, and the storm swallows my words.

The person who saved me takes my arm again and raises me up.

I stifle a pained cry . . . then suddenly, as if by magic, I'm being lifted from the roof tiles.

The roof starts to go by in a flash before me: I'm in the creature's arms.

The feel of his drenched chest against mine is unusually cold, like the skin of a . . . vampyre?

No, it's impossible. A deafening noise booms against my ear, louder and deeper than the cracks of thunder. It's the sound of a beating heart.

I raise my eyes to try and see my abductor's face, but it's hidden under a large leather hood, battered by rain. His body gives off a soft scent of autumn undergrowth, a fragrance of decaying leaves.

"Where are you taking me?" I shout.

No answer.

"Let go of me!" I cry as I reach behind my back to take out my knife. "Let go of me or I swear I'll kill you!"

I bring the blade up to the bottom of the creature's hood, but that doesn't stop him. In fact, as he reaches the middle of the roof, he leaps onto the biggest chimney stack and slides into the large shaft. Holding on to the bars of a rusted chimney sweep ladder with one hand, still holding me with his other arm, the creature goes downward with extraordinary agility.

The fury of the elements becomes progressively muffled the farther we go into the well of darkness and ashes.

The weak light goes out completely.

Soon, I hear nothing other than the beating heart that I could easily stab with a jab of my knife.

By the time we hit the ground, the sounds of the storm have hushed.

I guess that we've reached the bowels of the Grande Écurie—lower than the classroom floors, lower than the banquet hall on the ground floor, lower even than the weapons-training room in the basement.

My mysterious kidnapper finally puts me down.

We're in a crypt, its size hard to make out in the weak light coming from a small iron lantern that rests on a wobbly table. In the trembling halo, I notice a large mantelpiece over an extinguished fire—our point of entry.

The stranger stands at the edge of the halo as if afraid to come into the light. I can make out only the coarse leather shoes that envelop his feet and the bottom of his cloth pants, dripping with rainwater. The rest of him, his chest and hood, disappears in the dark.

For a few seconds, we remain face to face in total silence.

As my eyes adjust to the dimness, I still can't make out my abductor's features, but I can see the various objects laid out on the small table. There's a clay jar, an iron goblet, and the last thing I would ever have imagined finding here: a harmonica. And behind these modest items lies a pile of something white . . . a heap of hideously familiar shapes.

In a horrible aha moment, I make the connection between the pile and my father's anatomy books.

Half-gnawed tibias.

Femurs broken to suck up the marrow.

And skulls fractured like coconut shells to devour the brains.

I brandish the knife that I imprudently lowered.

"The exit," I croak in a voice full of fear, realizing that my host might have dined on human remains.

He moves slightly toward me, extending a hand that briefly appears in the light.

"Stop!" I yell, raising my weapon. "The exit, I said!"

He quickly turns on his heel.

I just have time to grab the ring of the lantern before I follow him.

"If you try to ditch me or make me lose my way, I'll stab you," I warn him, shivering and trembling down to my bones.

The recluse of the depths moves just as quickly down below as he did on the rooftop. I run to keep up. The shaky halo of my lantern never reaches beyond his fleeing heels.

A narrow staircase suddenly appears, spiraling upward. I hurry to keep up with my horrible guide. The balls of my bare feet strike steps that have been worn down by the centuries. With each step I climb, I think I feel fresh air.

It's more than just the frenzied dash—a breath from above caresses my face!

Stronger and stronger.

Nearer and nearer.

Nearer still!

Suddenly, the light goes out, snuffed by a gust from above.

Surprised, I miss a step and let go of the lantern ring. It tumbles down the stairs in a metallic din, then smashes a little ways below.

I'm now plunged in total obscurity just when I thought I'd finally reached the exit.

I clutch my knife with both hands as I plaster my back against the staircase wall.

An autumnal scent fills my nostrils. Instantly, I recognize that it belongs to the recluse, who's approaching me. Even if I can't see him, I smell him. His scent reminds me of death and decomposition. Of fear itself.

"Don't touch me!" I scream as I wield the knife.

The blade slides into a rough surface of cloth, then into soft flesh beneath.

Immediately, a sickly sweet discharge oozes forth, followed by muffled steps.

I don't know what's more horrible—having felt the creature so close to me or the fact that he ran off without a pained cry, without even a word, after I stabbed him.

Out of breath, my back still to the wall, I ready myself to strike again.

But I don't detect another whiff of dead leaves, just the mineral scent from the old stones.

Suddenly, I hear hinges creaking at the top of the staircase.

A stream of faint light falls onto the steps above me.

I dash up the remaining flight of steps and rush out the door that just opened.

I burst onto a deserted alley, the ground splattered with large puddles where I see the reflection of the three-quarter-full moon.

I raise my eyes. High above, the thunderstorm has passed. In the newly washed sky, the stars shine bright again. A crisp freshness has replaced the heavy end-of-summer warmth. Autumn is on its way.

I hear a creaking sound behind me.

I barely have time to turn and see the iron door close in the facade of the Grande Écurie. The cannibalistic recluse who hides inside the school shut it. I didn't see his face. I glimpsed only his hand earlier, in the halo of the lantern. I remember it now because it imprinted itself on my eyes and memory: a hand with long olive-colored fingers, its palm crisscrossed with black stitches.

11

VAGABOND

"Can I help you?" a voice growls in the distance.

I turn around. It's a police officer, and he's coming toward me from the other end of the alley, his black uniform blending with the night.

Taking advantage of the darkness, I slide my knife behind my back and under my bodice, next to the stake.

The officer approaches, his eyes narrowing under the rim of his three-cornered hat as he looks me up and down. He sees my bare feet, my torn skirt, and my sopping-wet hair.

"Do you have your aristocratic identification papers?" he asks menacingly.

With my rags, he can't possibly imagine that I'm a boarder who escaped from the Grande Écurie right behind me. I look a lot more like a hobo. Good. That means he'll arrest me and toss me like a snack to the vampyres at the palace. Just as I planned.

"I . . . I don't have my papers," I stammer, making my voice tremble. "Have pity, monsieur officer, I'm just a poor beggar."

My appeal for the officer's leniency is purely rhetorical, part of my plan. I know only too well that officers of the Vampyria show no mercy for those who violate the Mortal Code.

But contrary to expectations, this man doesn't arrest me.

"Haven't you heard of the curfew, you little ditz?" he says. "Hurry and go take shelter in the hospice at the end of the boulevard before you lose your life." He points toward a wide avenue, perpendicular to the alley where I tumbled out of the Grande Écurie. "The nuns of the Faculty will draw a syringe of blood in exchange for your overnight stay, but it's better than being bled dry if you remain outside. Go, I tell you. I'll pretend I never laid eyes on you."

Under normal circumstances, his show of humanity would warm my heart, but tonight it interferes with my plan.

"No!" I cry at the top of my lungs as if I'm crazy. "Not the hospice! It's full of roaches and spiders."

The commotion attracts the attention of another man, who emerges from the archways of a nearby street now that the rain has stopped. His uniform isn't black but red: a Swiss Guard.

"What's going on?" he asks, coming closer.

The brave policeman heaves a sincerely regretful sigh.

"You missed your chance to flee, poor child . . . may God have mercy on your soul."

The mention of God explains this man's charitable behavior. Even though the Christian religion was banished from the French kingdom when the Shadows arrived, many still practice it in secret. The churches may have all been requisitioned by the Hematic Faculty, the crucifixes melted down and reshaped into bats, but the old faith lives on in people's hearts.

"It's just a vagabond who's lost her reason," the policeman explains to the Swiss Guard. "Let me take her to the hospice, my friend."

"Friend?" he says sternly. "Do you know that such familiarity could cost you your job? The vagabond has broken the curfew. The Mortal Code is clear: she must pay a price."

He grabs my arm and pushes me in front of him, in the direction of the Parade Grounds.

I pretend to resist a little, squealing and tripping into puddles.

The Hunting Wall is getting closer by the minute, its menacing sculptures growing bigger with every step. Each detail becomes vividly real: the gaping jaws, the ferocious eyes, the hooked claws. Even if it's my intended destination, I can't help but shiver as I see the ecstatic expressions of the vampyre statues and the desperation of their victims, forever carved in stone.

"Here's another prey for this evening's gallant hunt," the Swiss Guard tells his associates manning the portal.

I look so weak that they don't bother to search me. They part their halberds to let us enter into the vast tunnel that goes across the wall. It's a good fifteen yards thick.

"The gallant hunt?" I repeat, unsure of what the guard said. "You're not taking me to the chopping block?"

"Chopping block or not, what do you care, you beggar?" he replies, his hard face half-lit by the torches that burn in the rock face of the tunnel. "Either way, you won't be seeing the sunrise. We've got to keep those hard-to-satisfy courtiers entertained. Every evening, on the stroke of midnight, fifty delinquents and lowlifes of your sort are released in the gardens of Versailles for the fun of the aristocrats. See, here are yesterday's prey that we're getting rid of—at least what's left of them."

He gestures toward a huge cart coming in our direction on grinding wheels. It's being driven by coachmen whose faces are hidden behind leather masks. In the torchlight, I can make out corpses stacked on the cart, all white, drained of blood. A putrid smell wafts from the bodies, suffocating my nostrils.

I barely have time to process this grisly scene before we arrive in front of a majestic iron gate at the end of the tunnel. A finely gilded effigy—a mask resembling the one on the engraving of the king at my parents' home, but ten times bigger and ten times more intimidating—crowns the main entrance. The gate is wide open. I deduce that I'm facing Apollo, the sun god whom the Immutable claims to be, but reversed. This sun is a black star radiating an evil power. Its mouth isn't sealed like the masked one in the engraving but partially open, revealing canines covered in blood. Beams of light sharper than blades surround eyes as dark as nothingness. The outstretched wings of a bat frame this terrifying face, while two nightmarish insignia spring out from the head of hair billowing in a supernatural wind: to the left, a huge petrified rose; to the right, a hand of justice with sharp claws.

I shiver as I step across the fateful gate, as if I were crossing the very threshold of hell, only to be taken aback by a breathtaking view.

The Palace of Versailles.

Even more magnificent than I'd imagined.

At the end of an immense cobblestone courtyard stands a majestic main building flanked by two gigantic wings. The facades are embellished with columns and hundreds of windows that sparkle like stars, rising upward, the very top decorated with cornices in the shape of shields. Two big fires burn in marble basins, illuminating everything and bringing out the glistening white of the stone. Against the light of the flames, I'm able to distinguish dozens of bewigged figures: the courtiers.

The splendor of the place overwhelms me.

The vastness of it all crushes me even more.

I hesitate to flee from the grasp of the Swiss Guard now. How could I possibly find Alexandre in all this?

"This way," the guard growls as he pulls me by the arm. "You didn't really think you'd be going all the way to the gardens through the Court of Honor, did you? We'll use the gardeners' entryway."

He takes me far from the chatter of the courtiers and the melodies of the harpsichord coming from the windows. We make our way to the end of the left wing of the palace.

"Enter here. It leads to the gardens," he orders as he pushes me under an archway where a large metal basin with burning coals reddens. I realize it's a brasero.

When we're halfway through the archway that leads to the other side of the palace, he stops me.

"My pretty, why not have a good time before confronting death? You're not curvy, but I'm sure you've got hidden charms under those rags."

He plants his hands on my hips and pulls me toward him.

"Let go of me!" I cry.

His breath, reeking of tobacco, assails my nostrils.

"A kiss, just one kiss . . ."

Suddenly, he freezes.

I'm guessing that his groping hands have met up with my dorsal sheath.

"What is that?" he growls. He takes out the stake from its cloth case. "Damn you! If someone finds out that I allowed a stake to enter the heart of the palace, it would be the end of me."

He tosses the piece of wood into the brasero, where it instantly catches fire.

"No!" I shout, rushing to retrieve it.

But the guard savagely grabs the long sleeve of my bodice.

"Just a minute: I asked for a kiss and you're going to give me one, whether you want to or not!"

I pretend to raise my hand to stroke his cheek, but I prolong the gesture so that I can grab the handle of the knife still hidden at my back. The bastard thought he'd disarmed me when he took the stake and didn't notice I had a second hidden weapon.

As he brings his lips closer to mine, I ram the blade into his jugular with all my might.

I only have time to take one leap backward to avoid having his blood spurt all over my soaking-wet dress.

He slumps against the wall with a groan.

"Little . . . bitch . . . ," he gasps. "You . . . you . . ."

I don't give him a chance to finish his sentence. I deal him a second blow on his bent neck, right where I used to strike jackrabbits to finish them off so they wouldn't suffer.

He crumples completely, dead.

I stay still an instant, catching my breath under the archway where the flames of the coal heater dance. My improvised stake is burning and, with it, my only chance of overcoming Alexandre tonight.

Along with the sting of frustration, I'm disgusted by what I've just done. After the old Baron de Gastefriche, this is the second man I've slain. They were both full of malice, but it still turns my stomach.

Already I hear footsteps approaching from the Court of Honor. There's only one way out—toward the gardens.

I put the knife back in its sheath, bolt across the gallery, and arrive at an esplanade of white gravel that has a 180-degree unobstructed view.

If I thought the palace was monumental, it's nothing compared to the immensity of the gardens of Versailles. They extend to the end of the night, decorated with groves, symmetrical flower beds, pedestal statues, and fountains that reflect the moonlight. All the way at the extremity, I can make out a gigantic canal with what look to be gondolas, lit by tiny lanterns, floating on the water.

I cross the pathways like a shadow, terrified by the increasingly loud echoes at my back: the sounds of the courtiers amusing themselves in the gardens after the rain. A cry comes from the archways—the guard's body must have been discovered. My frantic running ends in front of a large square bushy hedge. At the farthest end, almost one hundred yards off, stands an octagonal tower topped with a dome. It's entirely obscured, with no torchlights or lit windows, which is why I didn't see it from the esplanade. I don't have time to hesitate, and I step through the green archway.

I'm now in the middle of a corridor of dense foliage that muffles all sounds. In just a few steps, the chatter from the gardens vanishes. Here, there are no torchlights or violins. There's only the crunching of white gravel under my feet and the stars above my head. I turn right at the bend of a hedge, then left at another, becoming aware that I'm plunging deeper into a maze.

I suddenly collide with a fountain decorated with two sculptures, a jackrabbit and a turtle, each animal spitting out a long jet of water toward the shimmering sky. My heart tightens in my chest as I recognize two of the protagonists from Aesop's Fables, the first stories that my mother read to me when I was little. Instinctively, I touch the watch in the pocket of my dress.

Then I take off running again, going round the fountain so that I can go down another path that ends at yet another body of water. This time a stone fox is eyeing a bunch of grapes.

The scenes follow one another as I run madly, bringing back childhood memories. They all seem jarring in the midst of this nightmare: "The Roosters and the Partridge," "The Dolphin and the Monkey," "The Peacock and the Magpie" . . . until I reach a large wrought iron pergola covered in fragrant honeysuckle. The most spectacular fountain of all is here. The circumference of the basin is decorated with sculptures of dogs, wolves, and ferrets, their gaping mouths turned upward toward suspended birds. The stone beaks spurt jets of water whose splashing sounds resemble furious chirping. At the top of the baroque structure is a sculpture of a bat, its wings outstretched. I recognize the fable "The Birds, the Beasts, and the Bat." It's about how the bat, a hybrid creature of both terrestrial and aerial animals, couldn't choose sides when war broke out between the two camps and so was thereafter condemned to fly at night to hide its shame.

As I catch my breath, I decipher the little marble plaque at the front of the fountain. In an odious perversion, the moral of the fable has been reversed so that the bat is the hero of the story: a lord of the night who ranks above the other animals, just like the aristocratic vampyres sit prominently at the apex of the pyramid of the four estates.

> War between beasts of the land and birds of the sky,
> That none wanted to deny;
> But the bat, transcending either side,
> Established its reign beyond the light.

As I read the last verse, footsteps echo behind me.

Gasping, I look for a way out, seeing none, and the fountain basin isn't deep enough to dive into. I'm trapped at the pergola. With no other recourse, I hide behind the animal statues. The already cool temperature seems to lower instantly by several degrees.

Vampyres are definitely approaching.

I hunch down a little more, making myself as small as possible, while snippets of conversation reach my ears.

". . . the king may be celebrating his jubilee with great pomp next year, but the political situation is growing more tense," says a female voice. "It's been centuries since the *pax vampyrica* was under such threat. Every day the chances of war with England increase."

"And this truly worries you?" a male voice replies in a harsh, minced fashion. "The French kingdom enjoys the best army in the world, not to mention those of the vice-kingdoms. If England turns its back on the king, it will pay a price. Nothing can resist the power of the Magna Vampyria, Princess des Ursins. I guarantee you."

Princess des Ursins. I'd heard that name mentioned back home. The minister of foreign affairs. The fact that I'm just feet away from one of the most influential immortals in the kingdom makes me shiver even more. As for this possibility of war . . . I was aware of the faraway altercations with the stryges of the East, but this is the first time I'm hearing about a conflict that would pit one vampyric kingdom against another.

"Precisely, Monsieur de Mélac," answers the Princess des Ursins. "Your soldiers cannot mount a charge against England, at least not before landing on its shores."

If the Princess des Ursins's name cooled me off, Mélac's leaves me frozen in terror. Everyone fears his name: Ézéchiel de Mélac is none other than the cruel minister of the armies, master of the soldiers and dragoons who killed my family.

The two strollers stop in front of the fountain, not far from me.

I dare not breathe, and I pray that the honeysuckle masks my scent.

"Look at this fountain, Mélac," says the Princess des Ursins. "It's always instructive to lean on the wisdom of the ancients. See that tiger brought down by an eagle, this bear with its eyes poked out by an owl. On Earth, predators are indestructible, but they lose the battle against the birds who attack from above. The same goes for the Magna Vampyria: almighty on the continent but vulnerable out on the open seas. If war breaks out, the first battles will be by sea, and the continental navy is far from the equal of the English."

I plaster myself a little more against the trellis, numb with fear.

"What could push Vice-Queen Anne to attack?" Mélac asks.

"Thirst, Mélac . . . ," the princess says, lowering her voice. "Thirst for blood. Vice-Queen Anne wants to appropriate the vast mortal populations on the European continent, and no doubt those of the Americas, merely to feed the English vampyres. Don't tell me you haven't felt your own thirst increase these last few months. A need for blood that's more and more urgent . . . more and more difficult to satisfy."

"Indeed, but I thought it was just me," Mélac says.

"In truth, we're all affected. My spies in the diverse courts of Europe have confirmed this. Everywhere, the Shadows get stronger. Uncontrollable. In the châteaus and palaces, the thirst of immortals increases; in the countryside and slums of cities, the abominations grow restless. The stryges are in the grips of a never-before-seen frenzy, if I'm to believe the reports of massacres coming from the Transylvanian front. In Wallachia . . . Moldavia . . . Cimmeria, our Ottoman and Polish allies have a great deal of trouble containing them. To the east of the Black Sea, it's even worse: the stryges have continued their chaotic expansion over the vast Kazakh Steppe. At present, they're threatening the foothills of the Indian subcontinent."

The diplomat's words bring back memories. I can see the atlas that I spent so many hours poring over at home. The Kazakh Steppe spread out over thousands of leagues. Is that entire territory now part of the . . . Terra Abominanda?

The Princess des Ursins heaves a long sigh. She sounds anxious.

"To quench the thirst of the immortals of the Magna Vampyria, the Faculty is thinking of doubling the tithe. If the decree is passed, many commoners will perish from exhaustion, and those who survive will be considerably weakened, especially as the winters have become increasingly harsh. I don't see you going off to war with an army of mortals drained of blood, anemic and malnourished, whether it be against England to the west or the stryges to the east."

Double the tithe? In Butte-aux-Rats, the youngest and oldest already took days to recover from the monthly bleeding, so I can't imagine what would happen if they were drained of twice as much blood. It would be carnage! What the Princess des Ursins is saying amounts to genocide, pure and simple.

She clears her throat.

"As if the foreign situation wasn't difficult enough," she adds, "the intelligence services have noted a resurgence in acts of sabotage by the Fronde, everywhere in the kingdom." She starts walking alongside her companion again, talking about everything as they head off through the maze. "Why, just yesterday, a vampyre from Clermont came up to Versailles with the heads of five dangerous rebels . . . who were preparing . . . a revolt . . . king . . ."

The rippling water of the fountain swallows the last of the sentence and covers up the sounds of their diminishing footsteps. Whereas for many long minutes I was imploring the sky to make the vampyres leave, now I'd like to keep them near to hear the end of their conversation. My family was preparing a revolt? Did Bastien reveal this to his love when the baron was listening at the door? And what else did he tell her?

I come out of hiding, spurred by a pressing need to know more, which overcomes my fear. I often followed dangerous animals in the forest, so I know how to walk without making a sound. And since there's a wind coming from the direction of the two vampyres, I surmise that my scent is undetectable.

If only I could get close enough to hear a few more words . . .

As I lend an ear, a gleeful voice rings out behind me in the maze.

"Look what I found, Marcantonio. The king is spoiling us. It's not even midnight, and they've already released the game for the gallant hunt!"

12

PREY

I pivot on my heel.

I see the silhouettes of two courtiers behind me in the middle of the boxwood path.

Two vampyres, one male, one female.

I was so intent on catching the last bit of conversation between Des Ursins and Mélac that I didn't hear them coming, no more than I paid attention to the drop in temperature signaling their approach. But there they are, shadowy figures with opalescent faces of a startling spectral whiteness.

"This prey is in sorry shape, Edmée," the male vampyre says in an Italian accent. "*Che peccato!* Usually the stewards overseeing the royal amusements dress the offerings in a more appetizing package."

He himself is attired in a gold jacket with pleats that glimmer under the moonlight. Between the curls of his imposing mahogany lion's-mane hair, his face pegs him as a thirtysomething. His skin looks like the marble all vampyres are chiseled from, a smooth surface without flaws, except in the case of this specific immortal, a small beauty mark rests on his cheek. His big black eyes, the pupils completely dilated, seem even more enormous.

"I find those rags mouthwatering, Marcantonio," the female vampyre replies. "It's more—how shall I say?—bohemian. It makes me feel as if I'm on a safari in one of those sordid banlieues populated by mortals rather than being in the palace gardens."

She seems to be the same eternally fixed age as her companion. And she smiles wide, stretching her vermilion-stained lips to reveal sharp canines. Then she lifts the folds of her large mauve taffeta skirt, showing off a graceful milky-white ankle, in order to step over a puddle.

On the surface of the dark water, the reflection of the moon is briefly eclipsed by the dress, which seems to be moving by itself: the vampyre's face isn't reflected there.

"I'm not who you take me for!" I cry out, my stomach knotted in panic. "I'm not prey!"

"Tsk-tsk-tsk," the vampyre clucks as she shakes her head. It's piled high with enormous coils of brown tresses that are studded with a myriad of pearls. "They all say that. But no use in talking, little one. You must be swift now."

"I would even add: *To win a race, the swiftness of a dart availeth not without a timely start*," says her sidekick, citing the lesson from the "Tortoise and the Hare" sculpture I saw earlier.

The two vampyres burst out in laughter.

"You don't understand," I shout. "I'm one of the king's wards."

The one whose name is Edmée points at me with an incredibly long, red-polished nail.

"Do you hear that, Marcantonio? She's quite amusing. The king's ward, no less. This prey certainly has gumption."

I'm suddenly reminded of the reason that brought me here.

"Take me to Viscount Alexandre de Mortange if you don't believe me," I declare.

The crystal-clear laughter of the female vampyre ceases abruptly.

"Mortange?" she asks her companion. "Isn't he that prig who set fire to the opera twenty years ago?"

"I believe so," the other answers. "A horrible cad, so they say, and recently back in the court's good graces. I bet he already planted his fangs into this prey and she somehow managed to escape before he was done." He gives me a predatory smile, then adds, "And you think yelping his name will save your life, you silly little chatterbox?"

"What a shame," Edmée says with a grimace. "It's totally against etiquette to drink from the neck of another's prey."

I open my mouth to plead my case, but the ringing of a bell can be heard beyond the maze. It's coming from the palace chapel: the twelve strokes of midnight.

"My dear Edmée, *bellissima*, I assure you that this prey is now ours and ours alone," Marcantonio says with ferocity. "I don't know who started with her, but we're going to finish her off. The hunt is open. *Salute!*"

He jumps over the puddles more briskly than the deer of my faraway forests.

I feverishly search for the knife stored at my back.

As I take it out, the vampyre is already on top of me.

I raise my wrist and strike with all my might, aiming for his chest . . .

. . . in vain: the tip of the knife misses his stomach.

My adversary avoided the blow easily.

"Careful, Edmée, this prey has claws," he hisses behind my back.

I turn around, brandishing the knife, and again he effortlessly dodges the attack.

"I have claws too," Edmée says, clear voiced. She leaps next to me, as if by magic, before I can see her coming.

With one hand, she grabs my puny weapon and tosses it over the hedge. With her other hand, she slashes my cheek.

The shock and pain are such that my vision fogs up.

When I get a grip on myself again, I see the vampyre lick her long manicured nails, now dripping with my glistening blood.

"Yum, fresh and velvety, rich in red blood cells," she says. "Smells of the forest and open fields." She opens her large mouth, revealing ghastly canines primed in anticipation of the feast to come. "This prey doesn't come from the battery cages of the banlieues. She must have been reared in the fresh air of the countryside. You should have a taste, Marcantonio."

My gut tells me that I've got only one last hope: fleeing.

I run headlong into the maze, running faster than I've ever run before.

The sharp gravel scrapes my bare feet with every stride.

However loudly my beating heart throbs in my head, however fast my breathing, it's not enough to mask the giggles of the vampyres in hot pursuit.

That sardonic laughter is the only sign that they're after me. Their hearts no longer beat. Their breath no longer catches. Even their shoes make no sound on the pathway, as if they were floating along more than running.

"She's scampering off faster than a rabbit," says Marcantonio with a chuckle that sounds frighteningly close.

"All the better," Edmée responds. "Her blood will be that much more oxygenated."

They're playing with me.

Like my cat, Tibert, toyed with the rats.

And when they tire of the game, they'll break me. They'll bleed me and toss me aside.

Feeling dizzy, I turn around the corner of an umpteenth hedge—is it the same one, is it another?—and crash into the obstacle that lies behind it.

My skull reverberates like the warning bell.

My ribs throb as if they are all broken.

And most of all, a painful cold chills my skin.

I've collided head-on with a vampyre.

Shivering, I raise my eyes. A shadowy figure is there, just inches away from me.

I ready myself to feel a painful bite on my neck . . .

"Diane? Diane de Gastefriche?"

I scrunch my eyelids, flabbergasted, clinging to the blue silk jacket I've hurtled into.

The features of the stranger come into focus under the moonbeams. The shape of his scornful mouth . . . the elegant arch of his eyebrows . . . and his magnificent red hair pulled back in a ponytail . . .

"But yes, it's you, Diane," exclaims Alexandre de Mortange.

His eyes look away from mine, drawn to the gash on my cheek. His pupils instantly contract at the sight of blood.

My first reflex is to feel for the stake at my back, the one that was meant for him. But my fingers grope the void.

"Alex . . . Alexandre," I croak.

At the same time, I hear Edmée's wrathful voice behind me.

"Speaking of the devil," she says. "Look, Marcantonio, it's him. Mortange. I recognize him. Just as shameless as twenty years ago. Not only did he have the nerve to start on this prey before midnight, but here he is trying to steal it from under our noses."

The vampyre growls savagely.

Her animal cry transforms her face into a horrid scowl. Her pupils contract until they nearly disappear. Her painted lips curl back, exposing her gums. Her entire face is now no more than a snapping jaw, hideous and bent toward me.

But just as she surges onto Alexandre to snatch me away, he growls, opening his mouth wide. His canines stretch outrageously, shooting out from the pale gums, where they were partially retracted.

He . . . he's defending me, the monster!

Edmée's nails—the claws that slashed my cheek—shine under the moonlight.

Alexandre throws me behind him against the hedge and uses his body as a shield.

His attacker tears off the tie of his ponytail, liberating his fire-like hair.

From behind my protector's shoulders, I see Marcantonio transform into a savage brute, his lips rolled back onto razor-sharp teeth.

"She's ours!" he snarls, his voice inhuman.

"It's our turn. Our turn!" Edmée repeats, her crystal voice becoming a hoot.

The two vampyres rush at Alexandre. He steps back in shock, pressing me into the protruding branches of the hedge, which dig into my skin like a thousand needles.

Blinded by the fight, I see nothing else.

I'm suffocating, crushed under three creatures who are tearing at each other.

But just as I think I'm going to be smothered, the combatants unexpectedly pull apart.

I sense a palpable coldness, just like when the high plains of the Auvergne turn blue in deep winter. A fourth immortal is approaching, I can feel it, one who's more powerful than all those I've encountered so far. The aura that precedes him possesses the chill of death itself.

Panting, semiasphyxiated, I open my eyes wide: the white gravel path is visible in the moonlight. The three vampyres have their backs turned to me, as motionless as the statues of the fountains. Edmée is leaning forward in a curtsy, Marcantonio and Alexandre in deep bows.

With each passing second the chill increases. The silence is disturbed only by the nighttime breeze, the rustling of small nocturnal animals foraging under the bushes, and the distant cries of human prey released in the gardens.

Then suddenly, he appears around the curve of a hedge.

The king.

Despite the weak light that transforms him into a shadow puppet, I know it's him. That haughty bearing and leonine hair that cascades in thick curls—I saw it every day of my life on the official engraving in Butte-aux-Rats. In the dark, I can make out the opalescent outline of a sumptuous white velvet jerkin decorated with gold embroidery and pale gemstones that glisten under the moon rays. The ostrich feathers that festoon the monarch's hat quiver with his every step. Under the large light-colored satin brim, his head is a mere black hole.

"What is this ruckus?" he demands. "How dare we be disturbed on the way to our observatory."

Even though he's only whispering in the midst of the silence, his voice tears my soul. It's deep, like a horn, brimming with authority.

The observatory must be the octagonal tower I noticed at the end of the maze, the spot where, according to Alexandre, the Immutable spends his nights contemplating the stars, dreaming of reconquering daylight.

As for the *we* he used, it isn't just the royal *we*: the monarch is accompanied. The outlines of two magnificent dogs huddle close to his red heels, and the figure of a man in a long coat appears behind him.

"It's . . . it's Mortange, Your Majesty," Marcantonio stammers, bowing even lower. "He robbed us of our prey. He violated the rules of the gallant hunt."

The king roots himself like a sculpture in the middle of the path.

Under his imposing hat, which seems crowned by the moon, his face remains a gaping hole.

"This brawl was not particularly gallant either," he asserts in a scathing, weary tone, sounding like a god who's lowered himself from the sky to observe a battle between insects. "Marquise de Vauvalon, Count Tarella, we shall not tolerate such manners at our court, especially as we set an example for the entire world. And all this disorder for what—mere prey?"

Even if I can't make out the sovereign's eyes, I have the impression he's eyeing me through and through. And what if he detects a whiff of my commoner scent, reared in the haystacks and forests, instead of the perfumed salts I've recently bathed in?

I move slightly to disengage myself from the hedge. At the same time, the two dogs start to growl. Six figures emerge from behind the king and the courtier accompanying him, three men and three women who were always there but whom I hadn't noticed until now, too hypnotized by the monarch. They're dressed in black, as if to better merge with the night. As swift as quicksilver, the guards slalom between me and the stock-still vampyres.

Hands clasp my body. Warm hands, not cold. Their breath on my forehead is warm too. As for the faces bent over me, they look youthful, like the young vampyres I met at Versailles, but not with the grave pallor that's the privilege of the living dead.

I'm in the grips of the king's most loyal subjects, his squires.

"Stop," he orders in a whisper. "This terrorized prey presents no danger."

The hands release me as quickly as they encircled me, and the six squires return to being specters at the rear of their sovereign.

"You are absolutely right, as always, Your Majesty," Alexandre says, now choosing to intervene. His head is still lowered, his red hair hanging in the void. "Not only does this young girl present no danger, but she's not even prey."

The courtier accompanying the king clicks his tongue, a sound as sharp as an axe on a chopping block.

In the drab moonlight, I see the color of his coat: scarlet red, held closed by a bat-shaped clasp worn by those belonging to the Faculty.

"Look, sire, it's Mortange," he says in a voice as velvety as the garment that completely envelops him. "Always up to no good, that one. These last twenty years of banishment don't seem to have changed a thing."

I can feel Marcantonio and Edmée quivering with pleasure.

"Pardon me, Your Eminence, but it's precisely in my banishment that I met this young lady," Alexandre replies, lifting his head. "Like you in former times," he dares add, "I put my exile to good use."

Your Eminence . . . a title reserved for the highest religious dignitaries. As for his allusion to the prelate's exile, it's very clear. I'm in the presence of the grand archiater, Exili, chief of the Hematic Faculty of

France, and the king's closest adviser. I heard that he got his name by leading a life of exile throughout all the courts and prisons of Europe some three hundred years ago before he presided over the demonic ritual that transmuted Louis XIV. Soon afterward, he himself became one of the very first vampyres, his Machiavellian reputation even having reached Butte-aux-Rats. After having come close to Mélac, master of all the dragoons of France, I'm now a few steps away from the demon who commands all the inquisitors of the kingdom.

Alexandre turns again toward the king.

"Diane is none other than the only child of the Baron de Gastefriche—your ward, sire," he says. "I brought her all the way from the Auvergne to Versailles. I don't know why she's here tonight, but she's harmless, by my word."

The irony of this plea in my defense throws me for a loop.

"Don't listen to him, sire," Edmée yelps. "This little savage is *not* harmless. She tried to attack me with a knife!"

"A knife?" the king repeats, still in semidarkness. "Well, Mademoiselle de Gastefriche, what do you say to that?"

He's addressing me directly.

Him, the greatest monarch in the world, who was the ruler before my father's birth, before my father's father's birth, and before their forebears, going back six generations.

Him, the Bogeyman-King, whose terrifying umbra scares children into not going outside after the warning bell rings.

I'm overwhelmed by childhood fears that well up from the depths of my memories.

"I . . . I lost my way . . . ," I stammer, suddenly becoming a little girl who's caught doing something wrong.

The king advances toward me, striking the ground with his walking stick with each solemn step.

The two guard dogs advance with him in perfect unison. They come into the moonlight, and I see that they aren't dogs: they're two big white wolves whose coats match the jerkin of their master.

The sovereign's head finally emerges from the night.

I have the crazy, nauseous sensation that I'm seeing the engraving above the fireplace come to life. Like in a delirious dream. Like in a living nightmare. The gold mask of Louis the Immutable shines in the middle of an amazing head of hair. That long straight nose, that smooth high forehead, those thin lips frozen without expression: an artificial face that's wholly inscrutable, like time itself. History says that Louis was seventy-six when he was transmuted, but what does he really look like beneath that ageless mask? Did his flesh benefit from the malevolent rejuvenation that the other vampyres enjoy? Or has it preserved the appearance of his advanced age? Or worse, what unspeakable mutilation was it subjected to?

By way of response to the questions that are boring into my brain, the Immutable interrogates me in turn.

"You lost your way, did you? And in your wanderings, did you inadvertently stab one of our Swiss Guards, whose body was found barely one hour ago at the edge of the gardens?"

Through the slits in his mask, I'm able to discern his pupils, which are largely dilated by the dark. His inscrutable gaze, blacker than even the night, frightens me. It reminds me of my insignificance, my total vulnerability.

My teeth start to chatter. Not just from fear but also from the cold. The air is so glacial that it penetrates to the hollows of my bones, and deeper still, to the depths of my soul. I have to catch hold of Alexandre so I don't stumble.

There's no way out.

There's no acceptable explanation for my presence in the gardens, clinging as I am to the arm of a vampyre whom I hate . . . unless this pathetic tableau is my salvation?

"Not only did I . . . did I lose my way, sire," I sputter, "I also lost all reason as I tried to find my eternal love."

I raise my eyes toward Alexandre, whose head I swore to myself I would cut off.

"Diane?" he whispers, furrowing his reddish brows. "What are you saying?"

"I've fallen for you, Alexandre. Ever since our journey in the carriage. When I first laid eyes on you, in fact."

My voice trembles in disgust as I make this foul, totally false declaration. But what do those who are listening to me know? In their eyes, I'm trembling not from fear but from passion, and that's all that matters.

"Spending one more hour without you was unbearable," I continue. "I ran away from the Grande Écurie to find you . . . my love."

I cling to his silk jacket as if I'm a baby bird seeking shelter, and I break into sobs.

"As for that Swiss Guard . . . he . . . he acted as if he was bringing me to you, but the louse merely wanted to take advantage of me. I simply tried to defend my honor the only way I could and took a knife from his belt. I've never wielded a weapon before. I . . . I didn't realize he died of his wound."

The tears flow abundantly down my cheeks, but not out of pity for the vile Swiss Guard. It's the accumulated stress building since the beginning of the night that suddenly erupts like the explosion of the clouds when I was up on the rooftops.

"Mortange!" the king thunders as quickly as the lightning that streaked the sky.

It's the first time that he abandons his distant and vaguely bored tone to raise his voice. The effect is all the more terrifying as the metallic lips of the mask haven't moved one iota. His roar is enough to quiet everything in the gardens, even the nocturnal animals in the hedges. Alexandre, too, is rendered speechless, struck down by the royal wrath.

"You turned this young mortal's head in order to seduce her," the king accuses him, striking the ground so hard with his walking stick that I feel a seismic tremor all the way up from my legs. "You have obviously not learned any lessons from the past."

Alexandre's chest shudders against my cheek—yes, shudders in fear. My guess is that these "lessons from the past" hearken back to the reason why he was banished twenty years ago. Was it because of the fire at the opera that Edmée mentioned? Doesn't matter: the only thing that counts is that the king is now focused on Alexandre instead of me.

"You are back to playing the Don Juan again, without any thought of the consequences, you miserable creature. Always embroiled in the thick of human passions," the terrifying voice behind the mask goes on. "And here is the result. You will be deprived of the court's privileges for two months: no balls and no festivities for you until further notice."

"Your Majesty—" Alexandre manages to utter.

"Silence! If you had not managed to crush those vile vermin rebels, I would be exiling you again—and this time for forty years."

Hearing my family mentioned tears my guts.

The way the king refers to them as vermin breaks my heart.

I dare glance in his direction. My eyes happen to look right into his, and they're completely dilated. I have the impression I'm drowning, body and soul, in a bottomless chasm, as if the thousands of nights the king has spent observing the universe from the top of his tower have filled his mind with a cosmic void, infinite and glacial like the universe itself.

I lower my head, my eyes brimming with tears, my soul in shreds. I'm incapable of putting up with this scene for another second without going mad. My attention wanders to the white wolves, who peer at me with smoldering black pupils. Their eyes are also dilated in an abhorrent, supernatural manner: I'm sure these animals have vampyre blood coursing through their veins.

"As for you, mademoiselle, you are a fool," the king hurls at me, his voice oozing with contempt over my bent neck. "You are besotted with a vampyre like a vulgar commoner from the banlieues. What were you hoping, that he would transmute you? Not only is it illegal to transmute someone without the accord of the Faculty, as per the *numerus clausus*, but this pipsqueak is far from having the power to carry out such a procedure. He would succeed only in bleeding you dry. Your error in judgment alone should merit that we expel you from our school."

My eyes are riveted to my bare scraped feet. I swallow to wash down the bitter taste of my survival, a survival I snatched in place of a lost chance at vengeance.

"But your courage, however muddled it may be, demands that we keep you on," the king continues. "You escaped from the clutches of a lout who wanted your virtue and from two vampyres who chased you. That is quite something for a little gray mouse like you."

Gray mouse, the same words Hélénaïs used to insult me.

But coming from the king's mouth, they sound strangely like a compliment.

"Suraj, accompany Mademoiselle de Gastefriche to the Grande Écurie," the king orders. "And make sure she is provided with a wardrobe worthy of her name. Not this coarse clothing. Let it not be said that the king dresses his wards in rags. At present, the stars are calling to us: the empyrean is never more limpid than after it rains . . . come, Exili. Let us take our leave of these base and frivolous quarrels among courtiers. We must go contemplate the infinity of space and time."

I lift my head and see the masked king turn on his red heel, his grand archiater, his vampyric dogs, and his silent escorts trailing after him toward the mysterious observatory. The cold ebbs like a receding tide. From among the six squires, only one has stayed behind: a statuesque, copper-skinned young man with a proud demeanor. Under his ocher-colored turban that matches the leather of his breastplate, his severe eyes study me carefully. The strange dagger attached to his belt evokes the mysterious East of my adventure novels: two curving blades, one deploying on each side of an engraved handle.

"Mademoiselle . . . ," he says, extending his hand.

There's something serious in his deep voice.

I take hold of his arm to detach myself from Alexandre, who's still mute after the king's rebuke. He gives me a passionate glance, as if to promise me that we will see each other again soon. He really believed my desperate declaration of burning love, and now his eyes burn too.

Supported by the squire, I head toward the exit of the maze, toward the outside world, toward life.

13
RETURN

Astonished whispers start up as soon as I push open the classroom door, along with muffled exclamations.

"She's back!"

"Apparently something happened between her and a lord of the night."

"Her lover promised to transmute her despite the *numerus clausus*."

"I heard that the king himself gave her a second chance."

I spent the previous day sleeping in the dormered bedroom to recover from the ordeals of my wild night. Everyone stared at me, the girl who was destined for the convent. After all, by royal order, I was readmitted to the school from which I'd been expelled. Madame Thérèse herself dressed my wounds without daring to berate me for running off. In turn, I didn't dare look her in the eyes, fearing she might be able to guess the real reason I'd tried to infiltrate the palace. Goodbye coarse convent fabrics; I was given a brand-new brocaded dress. And here I am, back after a forty-eight-hour absence, for the day's lesson on courtly manners.

"Hurry, Mademoiselle de Gastefriche," General Barvók hurls from the rostrum. "You're just in time to practice parlor games." Since his metallic neck brace prevents him from turning his head toward me, his big eyes roll in their orbits as an invitation to enter. "I hope you'll be better behaved than you were at the dinner three nights ago. Nothing is more discourteous than losing one's cool when playing cards."

Today, the girls are seated not at their own desks but in groups of four at small round tables. Each one is covered in a green feltlike fabric, where decks of cards and chips are set out.

"Have a seat here," the general says as he gestures to a table with the tip of an iron pincer.

The table accommodates Proserpina Castlecliff, Hélénaïs de Plumigny, and a third girl I had dinner with on the first night: Marie-Ornella de Lorenzi, one of Hélé's closest friends.

I take a seat, doing my best to ignore the curious stares of my classmates around the room as well as the venomous looks I'm getting from Hélénaïs and Marie-Ornella right next to me. I prefer to focus on Proserpina, who gives me a complicit smile. Today, yet again, she's wearing a denim dress, not blue but acid-washed gray, with frayed bits for decoration.

"*Welcome back!*" she tosses out at me, using her native English language with her raspy voice. She shoots me a wink with her kohl-blackened eyelid.

"*Thank you . . . Poppy,*" I answer, my English rather stilted because of my French accent.

"No foreign languages in my classroom," the general immediately reprimands.

We spend the morning learning the rules of brelan, a game involving a good amount of luck and bluff that seems to be very popular among the courtiers with nothing better to do.

"When a player has three identical cards in their hand, that's brelan," Barvók explains in his Central European accent, rolling the *r* in *brelan.* "You simply have to keep smiling as you charge forward, but don't be fooled, mesdemoiselles: some fortunes have been won and others lost on the green carpet."

While the former soldier from the eastern front explains the way to bet and outbid with ever-increasing sums of money, I think bitterly about the gobs of cash that my classmates must possess. Not fortunes won at card tables but fortunes snatched from the peasants of the fourth estate. Neither they nor their families are vampyres in the proper sense, but they are in the figurative one: instead of blood, it's the sweat and tears of the people that quench their thirst.

"Why are we playing with chips rather than gold this morning?" Hélénaïs asks the general, echoing my thoughts. "It would be a lot more fun."

"This is a learning exercise, Mademoiselle de Plumigny," Barvók replies harshly. "When soldiers are in training, they use blunted swords and fire with blanks. Just as it's never a good idea to go off to war with an army of cripples, I do not wish for you to make your entrance at the court already bankrupt."

Hélénaïs shrugs. The peacock feathers that adorn her hurly-burly hairdo sway, giving off shimmering glints that match her eye shadow.

"Pfff, a few hundred crowns less won't ruin us, isn't that right, Marie-O?"

She winks at her friend, whose hair is even more laden with pearls than Edmée's was. Over these last few days, I learned that the Lorenzis are a family of wealthy bankers, as rich as the Plumignys, who hail from Florence and who've been in Versailles for generations.

"You're right, Hélé," the Florentine responds. "What's a few coins less?"

The two friends look treacherously at Poppy and me. They must sense that the daughter of an obscure baron from the Auvergne isn't rolling in dough. As for the acerbic English girl, Naoko told me that her family has been impoverished for generations.

I keep my mouth shut. I'd rather swallow glass than get myself expelled again over a stupid angry outburst. Stick it out till the end, gain entry into the palace, and this time, kill Alexandre: that's all that counts.

But Poppy doesn't seem to see it that way.

"No, Hélénaïs, I don't have a few hundred crowns to place on the table," she says, staring pointedly at her rival with her charcoal eyes. "In truth, I'm not even able to bet one copper coin . . ."

Hélénaïs's smile widens. She's ready to keep piling it on, but Poppy isn't finished.

". . . no more than my ancestors had to fork over a single penny for their aristocratic titles. Those were hard won on the battlefields. Contrary to *your* forebears."

Hélénaïs's sarcasm dies in her white throat.

"I'd really like to know which battlefields you're talking about," she says in a hollow voice. She narrows her lids over her bronze eyes. "The battlefields of the Hundred Years' War, when the English massacred the French?"

Barvók strikes the table with his iron pincer in a frenzied hammering. Every time he becomes agitated, his artificial limbs shake uncontrollably, as if his body wants to reject the grafts he was given courtesy of the mysterious Faculty laboratories.

"Enough!" he thunders, puffing up in his neck brace. "It's extremely rude to talk politics in polite society. And the time for old quarrels is in the past. Today England is united with France, just like all the vice-kingdoms of the Magna Vampyria."

Thus silenced, Hélénaïs grabs the nearest deck of cards and starts dealing them out furiously with her delicate hands. Like most of the boarders, she must have gotten wind of the tensions between the two officially united vampyric kingdoms. But she doesn't suspect how imminent the conflict may be.

After three hours of tense and nervous card playing, it's finally time for lunch. I look for Naoko in the dining hall. She's there, at the corner of a table in the rear. Her trademark bun is tightly wound at the back of her neck.

I sit in front of her, relieved. But instead of starting up a comforting and friendly conversation, she glares at me with her tired eyes from above her plate of vegetables.

"You're not getting any congratulations from me," she says coldly by way of a welcome.

"I was scared, but I'm unharmed," I say, forcing myself to smile. "I'm safe and sound."

"I'm not talking about that. I'm talking about my trust, which you betrayed. You pretended you wanted to be my friend, but you never said a word about your romance with a vampyre—yes, Madame Thérèse told us about it. You never mentioned you planned on running away. I thought I had finally found a *true friend*, the very term you used. Someone I could talk frankly to. But I realize that I don't really know you."

Naoko's accusations affect me more than I'd like.

I sensed her solitude when we first met, her visceral need for a friendly ear, but it's blowing up in my face.

The lies that I answer with burn my tongue.

"I'm exactly as you see me. I'm Diane, your true friend," I say. "I don't want to have any secrets from you. If I didn't tell you about Alexandre, it's because I didn't have time. And it felt like too much to share. But now, I'll tell you everything."

Naoko stares at me with her black eyes.

"You swear?" she asks me.

"I swear."

She nods and gives a hint of a smile.

"You're crazy, you know," she says.

"Because I ran off?"

"Because you fell in love with a bloodsucker."

Those words, coming from Naoko's usually refined speech, shock me. Commoners can talk about vampyres like that, but not aristocratic young ladies. Was it a translation error, an expression that she mangled in her otherwise excellent French?

But no, Naoko goes one better.

"Those creatures aren't like us," she says, lowering her voice. "And in their eyes, we'll never be like them. Just toys to be played with."

"But . . . some aristocratic mortals are sometimes transmuted," I say. "Starting with the king's squires, after they've completed several years of service. You told me that yourself."

"Honestly, I don't wish that upon anyone."

Another shock. Until now, I assumed every aristocrat aspired to one thing: getting ahead, moving on up to the other side of the glass ceiling that separates the lower nobility of mortals from the higher nobility of vampyres. But apparently that's not the case.

Naoko seems to pick up on my bewilderment.

"I'm opening up to you because we just swore that we'd tell each other everything," she says. "I can understand that you want to enter the court—but do you really wish to compete for the Sip of the King?"

The question catches me off guard, reviving a dilemma that I haven't yet resolved.

"The royal favor would probably constitute a unique opportunity for an orphan like me. I could rebuild my life . . . ," I babble.

"I understand, and I won't try to talk you out of it. To drink a sip of vampyric blood won't turn you into a living dead. But tell me: Would you eventually agree to be transmuted into a vampyre, whether by the king or by your lover from the Shadows?"

No! I shout inwardly. *I'd rather die a thousand deaths.*

"I've never asked myself that question," I pretend, since I don't know what answer the real Diane de Gastefriche would give.

"Well, now's the time to be asking yourself that question. After all, you're in the heart of the Vampyria," Naoko whispers. "It's time for you to realize that beneath their bewitching beauty, the lords of the night are dried-up cadavers who forgot what it means to be mortal and who've lost every ounce of humanity. It might be hard to imagine that when you look at your handsome Alexandre, but those heads out there reveal the true face of their cruel beauty."

For the first time since entering the dining hall, I glance out the window overlooking the courtyard. At the other end of the cobblestones, spherical shapes are planted onto the five central spikes of the main gate.

Despite the distance, I can make out human features, bloated by putrefaction.

They're five impaled heads, the ones Alexandre brought back from the Auvergne.

My vision blurs.

My breathing stops.

With all my might I fight the urge to regurgitate what little bit of the rabbit dish I've eaten as a migraine begins to throb behind my forehead.

Keep control over your body.

Keep up appearances.

Stay at the Grande Écurie.

Kill, kill, kill Alexandre!

He must be the one responsible for this grisly scene.

"The king asked his people to install those trophies on the spikes, in your honor," Naoko says.

"The . . . the king?" I manage to squeak out.

"Those heads belonged to your father's assassins. The Immutable takes pleasure in humiliating those who dare revolt against him. He's offering you this spectacle for your jubilation: he must have thought you'd rejoice to see the remains decompose and get pecked at by scavengers."

Echoing Naoko's words, a raven descends from the sky and perches on one of the heads—the one with the long brown hair that hangs in the void. My mother's hair.

I suppress a whimper at the back of my throat . . . *Ah, Maman. My dear maman.*

The winged creature begins to poke at her hair, searching for shreds of skin to tear. Its sharp beak ends up plunging into the eye socket . . .

I'm incapable of looking away from the gruesome scene, and it feels like the bird's beak is pecking at me. My pewter fork collides with my porcelain plate and rattles in my shaking hand until Naoko places her own hand on my wrist to make it stop trembling.

Finally, I find the strength to tear myself away from the atrocity.

"Judging by how pale you are, I'm guessing that that spectacle disgusts you as much as it does me," she says. "Even if those people killed your father, they're still human beings whose remains don't warrant such desecration."

I nod, my throat too tight to utter a single word or swallow the smallest morsel.

On an empty stomach churning from horror, I enter the vast indoor riding school, where the last lesson I haven't yet attended is underway: the art of equestrianism. For the occasion, we were allowed to change out of our dresses and into riding pants made of thick material. Today, we're riding astride.

"I like this better than riding sidesaddle," Naoko whispers to me. "Even if it's less elegant, it's more practical. What about you?"

She stuck additional pins into her hair to secure it during the lesson. Her bun now looks more like a black helmet.

"I'll never transmute into a vampyre," I say, my throat tight, holding back tears. A decoction of cyclamen may have calmed my headache, but nothing can erase the sight of the impaled heads on the spikes from my brain.

Naoko stares at me from under her bangs.

"That's my answer to the question you asked me earlier," I tell her. "Whatever happens, I'll never transmute. I swear it."

Before I can say anything else, a loud voice booms from the center of the ring.

"Mesdemoiselles, to your horses!"

In the middle of the rectangular room, I see Monsieur de Montfaucon standing in a black leather jacket. His arms crossed over his large chest, his heavy boots rooted to the sawdust spread out on the ground, the grand equerry sizes us up from his full height. In the glimmer of the chandeliers, his waxy skin looks even sicklier, as if saturated with an excess of yellow bile—the humor of bitterness and anger. Behind him are five grooms, each one leading three harnessed horses.

My classmates head over to their mounts. Obviously, the horses were assigned at the beginning of the school year, before my arrival at the Grande Écurie. That leaves me with the fifteenth: a dark-bay stallion with quivering nostrils that stands above the rest of the pack.

Even though my hands are still shaking after I saw the decapitated heads of my family, I take hold of the reins that the groom offers me.

"His name is Typhon, mademoiselle," he tells me. "People say he's difficult, but he's just hypersensitive. Be gentle with him."

"Saddle up!" the grand equerry shouts.

The groom releases the reins. He and his fellow grooms step back behind the kickboard of the ring.

I've never gotten on a horse in my life. At Butte-aux-Rats, laborers had only donkeys. I look around feverishly at my classmates. They each know exactly what to do, lifting their left legs onto the left stirrups, leaning in for support, and hoisting themselves up onto the saddles.

I try to imitate them as best I can, but as soon as my right foot leaves the floor of the ring, the horse nervously paws the ground.

Thrown off balance, I topple backward onto the sawdust.

"Gastefriche, who gave you permission to dismount?" Montfaucon yells, pointing at me with his long riding crop.

I get up with difficulty, aware of the muffled jeers coming from some of the riders.

Again, I grab hold of the pommel of the saddle and try to lift myself over it. Just when I'm about to sit down, Typhon rears up, sending me flying to the ground.

My shoulder aching, my mouth full of sawdust, I get back on my feet as the grand equerry showers me with abuse.

"Well then, looks like we'll be here all day. I knew you belonged in the convent. If it were up to me, you'd already be there, if only to protect you from yourself and your starry-eyed-girl heart."

Given the contempt dripping from Montfaucon's words, I gather that he's aware of the excuse I gave for breaking into the palace grounds, aware of my made-up love for a vampyre and everything else that denotes a weak fortitude.

"One must bend to His Majesty's wishes," he concludes with a sigh. "All the same, I wager that you'll not last long at the court."

I hate him. I hate this man who's taking his petty revenge for having lost face.

I hate the jeering girls who feel so superior astride their saddles.

I hate the entire blasted court for getting its laughs at the expense of the people.

But most of all, I hate *him*, the one this whole bloody empire rests on: the king.

Humiliated and covered in sawdust, I start to glimpse a bigger revenge, crazier than anything I previously imagined.

One must bend to His Majesty's wishes, Montfaucon said.

And what if I made him—Louis the Immutable, master of the Magna Vampyria—bend? What if I made him bend in two when my stake drives through his ice-cold heart?

Just imagining this ultimate vengeance gives me the shivers, like having a mystical revelation. If I succeeded in dragging the King of Shadows down into the void with me, my sacrifice would be an apotheosis.

"Go on," Montfaucon orders. "How do you pretend to be ready to enter the court if you're not even capable of staying in the saddle?"

I grab hold of Typhon's bridle with my clammy hands, my heart enraged.

I have to mount him. I have to. The stirrup is the first step that will take me to the palace . . . right up to the king.

The stallion pulls on his bit, his black eye rolling furiously between the long hairs of his flowing mane. Half a ton of muscles versus my 110 pounds . . .

I'm no match. With a swipe at my neck, he sends me down a third time.

"I think it's useless to insist," the grand equerry lashes out.

"Give her my horse, instead."

That accent belongs to only one boarder: Proserpina, who's riding a large sorrel.

"Myrmidon is easy to lead, monsieur, and you know quite well that Typhon has an indomitable reputation," she goes on.

"Enough with the insolence, Castlecliff," he yells, cracking his whip against the leather of his boot.

"It isn't fair to give the stallion to the newcomer," Naoko says from atop her small gray-dappled horse. "I can lend her my mare. Calypso is very docile."

"Enough, I said!" roars the director of the Grande Écurie. "Castlecliff, Takagari, you're not the ones leading the class. I am. Gastefriche will mount Typhon or not at all. End of discussion."

For the fourth time, I walk over to the stallion. His shimmering coat trembles nervously under the flames of the chandelier. As I look at his quivering skin, I remember what the groom told me. *He's just hypersensitive. Be gentle with him.*

"Now, now," I whisper so softly that only he can hear me. I place my hand on his neck. "I'm just as terrified as you are."

The fact that I can feel his brute force under my fingers is strangely soothing.

As my heartbeats slow down, little by little, I can also feel Typhon's heart grow calmer in his large chest.

He stands still, not budging as I put my foot in the stirrup and hoist myself into the saddle.

No one in the ring is laughing anymore. I may have been outdone by the other riders for a while, but now I outshine them all. And though

I'm holding tight to Typhon's mane with both hands, I'm not really scared of falling. The heat from his flanks under my calves reassures me. The power in his muscles perks me up.

The grand equerry gives me a perplexed stare, as if he can't understand how the indomitable stallion could accept such a poor rider on his back.

"Voilà, I'm ready now," I toss out at him. "For the court. And for the Sip of the King. I want to enter the competition."

My public announcement elicits stifled cries. I think I hear Poppy's raspy voice and Hélénaïs's indignant oaths. But I look only at Naoko, forcing myself to smile at her as a reminder of what I pledged: even if I become a squire, I will never transmute into a vampyre.

"Your candidacy is noted," Montfaucon grumbles menacingly. "But I warn you, Gastefriche, it's not just about *wanting*. His Majesty will give his precious blood only to those who can prove that they possess at least ten quarters of nobility. Can your official papers attest to that?"

"You know the circumstances of my arrival at Versailles, monsieur," I reply. "I wasn't able to take anything from my castle, not even a decent dress, much less official papers. But I assure you that the nobility of the Gastefriches dates back at least to the Crusades."

The grand equerry grimaces.

"You'll excuse me if I don't take your word for it. As I told you the other night, over the course of the years I've seen more than one outsize ego parade within these walls." He clears his throat and spits into the sawdust of the ring. "Tonight, I'll dispatch a crow to the Cathedral of Clermont. I'll ask the archiater to pull the complete extract of your aristocratic papers from the archives and send them back by said crow. Everything will be documented—lineage, noble ascendency, coat of arms, right up to your portrait—with no possibility of forgery."

14

PAPERS

"How long will it take the crow to come back with my papers?" I ask flatly.

"I'd say three days, four max," Poppy responds, twirling a long strand of brown hair that escaped from her messy bun. "Come on, Gastefriche, relax. I assure you that the director will receive your papers well before the Sip of the King."

My new "friend" pushes away her finished plate and puts some chewing gum in her mouth. The random seating arrangements brought us together for dinner. I'm sharing the evening meal with her, Rafael de Montesueño, and three other boarders I haven't met until now. Poppy is addressing me informally, but I don't know if it's out of real sympathy or just to keep a close eye on one of her rivals for the Sip of the King.

Right now, her intentions are the least of my worries. I'll never take part in the competition if the crow returns with papers showing a portrait that isn't mine. With her large, aloof eyes; upturned nose; and high, curved forehead, Diane de Gastefriche doesn't look like me at all. In the blink of an eye, Montfaucon will out me as a usurper.

"I'm worried that the crow will lose his way, especially with the autumn storms that are about to start," I lie. "How can I be sure that he arrives back safely? And . . . where is he even supposed to land?"

"Directly in Montfaucon's room," Poppy answers as she stops chewing her gum for a second. "That horrid fleapit under the roofs, the one he shares with the owls and crows."

I feel myself go pale. There's no way I'll be able to intercept the mail before he reads it.

"I'm kidding, darling," Poppy exclaims in that English accent I used to find charming and that I now want to make her swallow. "If you could see your face."

She bursts out in genuine laughter, as do the others. One among them chuckles loudest of all, as if to attract the attention of the brown-haired beauty: a boy named Thomas de Longuedune whose eyes gleam each time he looks at Poppy. Only Rafael remains stone faced.

But the English girl's laughter soon turns into a coughing fit. She presses a handkerchief against her mouth while she gets her breath back.

"Even if Montfaucon is a boor, he has to maintain his rank," she goes on after putting her handkerchief back into the pocket of her denim dress. "He sleeps on the second floor, in one of the master bedrooms. Did you really imagine him holed up in the attic like a recluse from some sensational novel?"

"No, of course not," I shoot back, trying to laugh too.

Proserpina Castlecliff is being clever to amuse present company, but she doesn't know that a real recluse haunts the bowels of the Grande Écurie without anyone being aware . . . a monstrous hermit with stitched hands who eats mangled bones, who would instantly put an end to her joking banter if she ever brushed against him.

"Carrier crows arrive by way of the aviary," Rafael says, putting an end to Poppy's teasing.

Like every time that I've seen him, he's dressed in all black, the style at the court of Spain, which I learned is where he comes from. Over there, the Faculty is even more severe in its inquisition than in France, and the Shadows are celebrated in a more funereal manner. As for Rafael's past, it's a mystery. He seems just as solitary in the boys' wing as Naoko is in the girls', two foreigners having trouble finding their place at the Grande Écurie.

He points toward the window with his black-polished index finger. Taking care to avoid looking at the evil gate and its sinister trophies, my eyes follow the direction he's indicating, toward a straight stone turret at the other end of the second wing. In the evening air, crows come and go through round openings clustered under the conical roof.

"The aviary connects to the mail room," Rafael explains in his accent. "Every morning, a page collects the missives that arrived during the night and takes them to the grand equerry. The crows come from all over Europe and beyond: the Netherlands, Austria, from my Castile . . . and even from India." His green eyes seem to glaze over. "If the crows can cover the thousands of leagues that separate us from the Orient, they can easily come from the Auvergne to Versailles. Lady Castlecliff is correct. You shouldn't worry. Your papers will soon be on the grand equerry's desk."

I give a false relieved smile.

But inwardly, I'm processing all the information I've just learned: this mail room is where I must gain entry. But when exactly will the crow return, and how will I recognize it?

I endure a restless night with little sleep.

Each time I'm about to doze off, the nightmarish vision of the severed heads jolts me awake.

In the morning, I get out of my sweat-drenched sheets. The bruises from the many horse falls I took are more painful than the day before.

The hours go by slowly. I follow Madame Chantilly's art-of-conversation lesson with a distant ear and limit myself to dodging during the heated fencing bouts orchestrated by the Knight of Saint-Loup. At last, in the evening, the moment I've been waiting for arrives: we have one free hour at the end of classes to get ready for dinner.

I escape from Naoko's care under the pretext of wanting to be alone in the ground-floor bathing room to shave my legs. In reality, I take off to explore the hallways of the Grande Écurie. In theory, boarders are free to come and go within the walls of the school, but the aviary turret and the adjoining mail room are located in the boys' wing. Will a girl be allowed to wander over?

My steps lead me to the vast central staircase we routinely take to go to the banquet hall for dinner. I dash swiftly to the other side and enter unknown territory. I walk by several Swiss Guards, making sure to look busy and avoid eye contact. None of them stop me. I imagine that the boys are occupied with their evening grooming too.

Just then, a door opens to my right, liberating a cloud of steam.

A bare-chested boy emerges, a bath towel tied around his hips. He's holding a bundle of clothes in his finely muscled arms.

Startled, I recognize Tristan de La Roncière. His cheeks are ruddy from the heat of his bath, his hair still damp.

"Diane de Gastefriche?" he says. "What are you doing here?"

"I . . . uh . . . I'm looking for the mail room," I stammer, averting my eyes from his well-defined abdomen. "Madame Thérèse asked me to retrieve a letter."

"Really? Wait here. I'll put my day clothes back on and take you there," he offers.

Without leaving me time to say that I can get there on my own, he goes back into the bathing room and soon comes out wearing a shirt, breeches, and tights.

"Is it because you're from the countryside that Madame Thérèse sent you on this errand instead of a servant?" he asks me as he starts walking.

He smiles mockingly, and I instantly want to wipe it off his face with a slap.

Instead, I giggle.

"Very funny. But you've got it all wrong. I offered to go since I'm expecting mail from the Auvergne that concerns me directly. I'm eager to open it."

As we walk, Tristan scrutinizes me with his light lynxlike eyes, as if he's trying to read my thoughts. Between his strands of wet blond hair, I notice the long scar across his right cheek.

"I understand," he says. "You're homesick."

"No, not at all," I say.

But it wasn't a challenge. We're not engaged in an oratory joust anymore. Barvók isn't watching us: it's only Tristan and me in the deserted hallway.

"You're very strong if you've managed to forget your province only days after having left," he says, nostalgically. His mocking tone is gone. "A lot stronger than I am. I've been at the Grande Écurie two years, and I still miss the large forests of my countryside. They will always be in my heart . . . and bones."

He touches his scar, not as if he wants to hide a flaw that he's ashamed of but as a gesture that seems to bring back memories.

"One night when I was coming back from hunting, I came face to face with a bear. Fought him with my bare hands. I've never been so close to death. And strangely, I've never felt as alive." He sighs. "The Faculty diagnosed me half-sanguine, half-melancholic. In my forests, it was the sanguine that dominated. My heart raced at full speed during my solitary rides. But here in Versailles, black bile pumps its poison into me. I feel like I'm in a prison. On certain nights, I even cry when I think about the Ardennes."

The unexpected confession unsettles me more than the complicated wordplays and sharp zingers. It takes courage to fight a bear unarmed. It takes even more to admit to crying, especially in this school, where any admission of weakness is immediately punished.

This strange aristocrat may come from the northeast of France, far from my central Auvergne, but he, too, was raised in wild woodlands.

He's a solitary hunter, with the same humoral profile as mine. Do we have anything else in common? I don't want to think about it.

"Don't tell anyone, but I don't think I'll ever feel at home at the court," he tells me as he turns the corner of a hallway. "My mother sent me here to represent the La Roncières. Ever since my father's death, she's been in charge of our fiefdom, a force to be reckoned with. She's fair and just, and I'll do my best to obey her. But my soul will always remain in the forests."

"Just like mine," I assure him, anxious to reinforce the link that he sees between us. "I admit that I lied about not being homesick. You and I are the same: countryfolk, like you said. We need to stick together."

The smile that flashes across his face again is genuine. Good, I scored a point.

"Here we are," he says, stopping in front of a raw wooden door with no decorations.

He knocks three times.

"Come in," says a gruff voice on the other side.

The door opens onto a room with walls covered in shelves, where carefully labeled drawers are piled high. An elderly valet in a taupe-colored uniform stands behind a writing desk. He's busy jotting down figures in a big ledger.

"Diane, this is Fulbert, first valet in the boys' wing," Tristan says.

"Good day, monsieur," I say. "Madame Thérèse sent me. I'd like to know if a crow arrived from the Auvergne . . . from Clermont, precisely."

The old valet looks at me over his thick eyeglasses, then pulls a different ledger from his desk and starts to consult it.

"Clermont . . . Clermont . . . ," he says. "No, I don't see anything. There's only mail hailing from Plumigny, as there is every day. Would you like me to alert you if we receive something?"

"I'd be grateful. You could just send a guard directly to me."

No need to loop in Madame Thérèse. I curtsy, which seems to amuse Tristan.

"You're an odd demoiselle to be curtsying in front of a valet," he says once we've left the mail room. "You decidedly don't do anything like everyone else."

"I get a kick out of curtsying in front of menials," I bluster, playing the insufferable snob to make up for my blunder. "I enjoy doing things my way."

"That's what I've heard people say. Your escapade three nights ago is a fiery example. A real vampyre huntress."

My breathing catches.

"What . . . what do you mean?" I sputter.

"Only that you seem to chase your lovers among the immortals," he answers.

"You shouldn't believe all the chatter you hear, Chevalier de La Roncière," I toss out at him as we come to the main staircase, relieved that he knows nothing of my real intentions. But the gossip has obviously reached the boys' wing.

"No, of course not," he says. "I always prefer to have a firsthand account. I hope the seating arrangements at dinner will reunite us soon. Your company enchants me, and I hope you don't find mine too unpleasant"—his smile widens ever so slightly, colored by a new emotion—"even if I don't possess the sulfurous attractions of the lords of the night."

I merely smile back at him. Without saying anything more, I dash back to the girls' wing.

The following day unfolds in anxious waiting.

I have a hard time concentrating on Barvók's boring lecture about the length of dress trains and how they correspond to one's rank at the court. The only thing that soothes my nerves is being reunited with Typhon during the art-of-equestrianism class. He follows the movements of the other horses in the ring, going at a relaxed trot as if he wants to handle me with care. I whisper words of thanks in his ear as I hold on to his mane.

"Your seat is deplorable, Gastefriche," the grand equerry proclaims, looking for the slightest reason to harass me. "You look like a toad on top of a tobacco box. And stop that awful whispering. Where do you think you are? Only cart drivers talk to their horses."

Come dinnertime, I don't participate in the conversations of my table companions. I stare out the window of the banquet hall, on the lookout for any movement of crows at the top of the aviary. As night falls, I can't make out anything.

When it's time to turn in, still no one has alerted me to any mail having arrived from the Auvergne. Like the previous night, it's hard for me to sleep; all I do is twist and turn on my mattress. Anxiety grips my chest, and I feel like I'm suffocating in the alcove of my canopy bed. Was it wise to ask Fulbert to keep me informed? What if my brazen behavior got back to Montfaucon's ears?

As the twelve strokes of midnight ring out in a distant tower, I can't lie still anymore. I climb out of my sheets. I part the heavy curtain of my bed and make my way across the dormitory on tiptoes. Dressed in my nightgown, I go out into the hallway. It's deserted: at night, the Swiss Guards are instructed to leave the girls' dorm floor and stand watch on the lower levels. I reach the closest bathing room without running into anyone and open the window.

At last, I can breathe.

A fresh breeze caresses my face, carrying the distant sounds of the palace's nocturnal parties.

Little by little, my eyes adjust to the darkness, and for the first time in days, I dare look in the direction of the gate.

The five heads are still impaled there—the heads of my family and the real Diane de Gastefriche. But instead of the sun that cruelly revealed the horrible details, the soft moonlight gives them a powdery aura that's almost magical. I can't really make out my loved ones' martyred skin anymore. Their features have been as savagely hollowed out by the pecking birds as the baronette's was by my knife. Only their hair remains, floating gently in the breeze.

"I love you . . . ," I whisper in a strangled, ravaged voice. "I'll never forget you. And don't forget me, wherever you may be. I'll join you in death before long, as soon as I've avenged you. Behind the mask of Diane, I will always be your Jeanne—your daughter, your sister, forever."

I'm gripped with the desire to talk to them like never before. I could really use Maman's and Papa's good advice. I'd give anything to hear one of Bastien's jokes again . . . or even Valère's lectures.

"I swear to you that I'll see this vengeance through till the end," I say again, trembling with emotion. "I know I'll only have time to deal one blow before I'm killed. Until today, I wanted to murder the one who beheaded you. But now, I want to strike the one who ordered that your heads be placed on the spikes."

As I state my plan for regicide out loud, I realize just how huge my task is. There's what, one chance in a thousand that I'll succeed in killing the tyrant who rules over the Vampyria? One chance in a million?

I take out my mother's watch from the pocket of my nightgown. I'm never without it, and I stroke it with my fingertips like a good luck charm. In the nocturnal light, its bronze surface glistens a little. I've never been superstitious, but I need a visceral sign.

"My dear departed: everyone pretends that the Immutable put your heads on those spikes to humiliate you," I go on. "But I know that's false. You came here to watch over me from the gate, to make sure I'm all right. If only I could hug you! But you're out of my reach, just as the crow from Clermont will be when he flies above to bring my downfall. Alas, I will never be able to catch it."

I lend a close ear in spite of myself, in the delirious hope of hearing voices that have been forever extinguished.

Of course, I hear nothing but the whistling wind, the creaking of carriages, and the sound of muffled violins coming from the palace . . .

. . . nothing else, really?

Isn't there a second melody overlaying the sprightly minuet of the party?

A simpler tune, sadder . . . closer.

Yes, I hear it coming from the rooftop, a melancholy tune on the harmonica.

I'm suddenly reminded of the recluse's lair in the bowels of the Grande Écurie. There was a lantern; a pile of human bones, half-gnawed . . . and a harmonica that seemed so out of place.

Seized with panic, I quickly shut the bathing room window and flee down the hall to my bed.

The recluse still roams the Grande Écurie.

I wake up with this frightening notion in my head.

In the sunbathed dormitory, the thought seems unreal. It's difficult to imagine that such a monstrous presence haunts these immaculate walls.

"You're so pale," Naoko says at breakfast. "Are you all right?"

It's kind of her to worry about my health when, judging by her haggard appearance, she had another difficult night.

"It's just indigestion from yesterday," I pretend.

"Same for me," Poppy chimes in. She now sticks with us most of the time, apparently enjoying our company. "A mere whiff of your coffee turns my stomach. I've always found that beverage disgusting, but today it's worse than ever . . . I think last night's lobster pie wasn't exactly fresh. Blagh. I was bloated all night long."

"Charming, what elegance from an English lady," Naoko says, rolling her eyes.

Poppy bursts out laughing.

"Don't be an old poke, you Levantine. It proves that I'm still alive and haven't yet been transmuted into a vampyre. But that won't be for long, girls, I promise you."

Naoko refrains from commenting. She already gave me her thoughts on transmutation. Poppy doesn't seem to have the same reservations. Like the majority of the mortal aristocracy, she obviously aspires to gain entry into a higher rank . . . and her ascension means going through the royal path to get there: the Sip of the King.

A new morning of torture begins. Each time the floor squeaks behind the art-of-conversation class's door, my heart tightens: Is it a valet who's come to tell me about the arrival of the letter? Or the grand equerry himself, who, having already read the letter, is on the verge of unmasking me as an imposter? But the door stays closed, and the footsteps wander down the hallway. The rest of the day unfolds like the one before it—from the dining hall to the weapons room, then the banquet hall. Once again, I go to bed playing a waiting game, unable to fall asleep. Same as yesterday, I listen for the twelve strokes of midnight before escaping the stifling prison of the canopy bed. I need fresh air or I'm going to suffocate.

But just as I enter the bathing room, I'm met with a surprise: the window is already open.

I freeze in the doorway, on high alert, searching the semidarkness of the room.

A rustling sound attracts my attention. There's a large overturned wicker basket on the tiled floor. Something is flapping inside. Gently, I shut the door behind me and rub my tinderbox lighter to start the oil lamp resting on the rim of the bathtub. Then I cautiously approach the basket. In this very place last night, I asked for a sign; has it arrived? I kneel down slowly and place the lamp on the tiles. Between the strands of woven wicker, I think I see shiny black feathers . . . yes, the feathers of a crow.

"Easy, easy . . . ," I whisper softly, as calmly as I spoke to Typhon in the ring.

The bird caught in the trap stops moving; his legs stop hitting the wicker.

Only then do I lift a corner of the basket. The tamed crow lets me take him out without trying to flee: a slim leather cartouche is attached to his left leg. I gently remove it and place the calmed bird back in the basket. I open the small cartouche cover and take out the thin paper document rolled up inside. It's a parchment no bigger than my little finger, yet it unfurls to almost a foot in length. Diane de Gastefriche's entire life is recorded in fine print—her birth date of May 5, 281; her hematic baptismal; the titles and medals passed down to her—as well as her parents' family tree, going back over twenty generations. The parchment ends with a vignette on fresh paper that was glued to the document, a recent addition. It's an etched likeness of the baronette. I instantly recognize the reproduction of the portrait painted by my brother, the one that I saw at the manor on that fateful night when he met his death. An ethereal face, embellished by the amorous brush-strokes of an artist.

"Did you bring me the crow, Bastien?" I ask, raising my eyes toward the window and the gate outside.

My mind tells me it's impossible, but my heart would like to believe that my dear brother reached out from the beyond, hearing my prayers.

I scan the night, searching for his impaled head.

It's not there anymore.

Not his, not Valère's or our parents', not even the baronette's: the five funereal trophies have vanished from the sharp spikes.

Above the gate, the stars shine vividly—those different celestial bodies that have always existed and that the King of Shadows spends his nights observing suddenly seem to be looking back at me. As if the spider-night were ready to eat me alive, spying on me with its thousands of shining eyes.

I shake off the sensation before it chills my brain and try to think. Could the heads have fallen into the courtyard? Did the ferocious hounds devour them—the ultimate outrage? I get up slowly, raising the lamp above my forehead to shed light on the immense darkness outside. Of course, the little flickering flame doesn't reach there; its halo illuminates only the shiny tiles, the dresser full of towels . . . and the external window ledge where five round shapes are resting. In the darkness, I thought they were flowerpots like the ones that line the sills of many windows at the Grande Écurie. But now, I see what they are.

The heads.

Lined up by the same hands that captured the crow . . . hands that are stitched every which way . . . I'm sure of it.

Short of breath, I pivot on my heel, brandishing the lamp.

"Recluse, if you're here, show yourself," I whisper, torn between the desire to scream and the need to stay calm so as not to awaken the entire dormitory.

Nothing steps into the light, but I know the recluse is close by . . . I know it by the autumnal scent that I previously detected in his presence.

"You're an abject creature," I tell him. "Are you going to feast on those remains? Did you bring them here to devour in front of me? I'll stop you, you filthy monster."

As I utter these words, I'm not expecting a response. The human-shaped beast stayed mute when we first met, so he must not be gifted with speech. But he's gifted with intelligence, I have to admit. For he heard me last night and understood when I prayed in front of the window, when I thought no one could hear me. It's the only possible explanation. I expressed my longing to catch the crow from Clermont, and the recluse brought it to me. I wished that I could embrace my loved ones one last time, and the recluse brought me their heads.

Could he be an unlikely ally? Or is there a price to pay, as there usually is when one makes a pact with a demon?

Try as I might to avoid looking at the heads, I can't help myself. Their eye sockets are hollow, empty of the ocular globes that the birds swallowed. The missing eyes have been replaced by white pebbles, polished and round, giving the heads a surreal, almost serene look. Even their skin looks as if it's been sewn up with care where bird beaks tore it apart, and any traces of blood have been carefully washed away. Two days ago these remains appeared before me in all the horror of decomposition, whereas tonight they seem as if they've received the most respectful mortuary care. That includes Diane de Gastefriche's head, which, even if unrecognizable, no longer elicits disgust but has more of a worrisome strangeness: the embalmer gathered the slashed skin and gave it three long sutures—one for a mouth, two for the eyelids—thus giving the baronette the face of a hand-sewn doll.

As if echoing my thoughts, a few long notes from the harmonica scatter into the night.

I lean over the heads and notice a dark figure hanging on the nearest gutter. But before the halo of light from the lamp can illuminate it, the figure runs off into the heights with the agility of a monkey.

"Wait!" I cry.

Realizing that I've raised my voice, I clamp my hand over my mouth.

I hear the door handle to the bathing room turn, the noise of hinges creaking.

Was someone already drawn by my cries?

The door opens, creating a draft.

The wind lifts the parchment that I left on the ground next to the wicker basket.

The note blows right over to the doorway, where a hand grabs hold of it.

Naoko's hand. She's wearing a black robe, one of her kimonos.

"Diane, what's going on?" she asks, raising the candlestick she's holding in her other hand in order to see. "I woke up in the middle of the night and saw that your bed was empty. So I came to find you."

Naoko and her wretched insomnia. I should have been more careful. And I should have barricaded the door to the bathing room.

"Are you ill again, like last night?" she asks.

"I . . . I'm fine," I stammer, closing the window so she doesn't see the heads on the outside sill. "I just needed a little fresh air. You can go back to bed . . . after you hand me the paper."

I rush over to her.

Her eyes are puffier than ever, and the bun she quickly attached at the back of her head indicates that she's still half-asleep, sufficiently groggy that I can take the parchment from her before she has time to examine it.

"I jotted down a few things," I hurry to say. "Some ideas for the next art-of-conversation class."

"Oh, really?" she says, narrowing her eyes and lowering the candlestick to the parchment. "This portrait is beautifully drawn. You didn't tell me you were an artist. Who's the girl?"

"Give it to me!"

I try to grab it from her, but she snaps it back.

"You don't want to tell me? It can't be a secret since the name is written right here . . ." Her heavy eyelids draw back in shock as she sees the name on the aristocratic papers. "Diane de Gastefriche?"

15

TRUTH

"It's not what you think," I croak, my throat in knots.

But despite all my denials, I know it's useless. Naoko is totally awake now. The way she's looking at me confirms that she's figured out my secret.

"And what am I supposed to think?" she asks, bitterly. "Can you tell me, you, my *true friend*?"

The expression I've used on several occasions hits me like a blow.

I don't even try to take the parchment from her again. There's no point anymore.

I'm completely at her mercy. As soon as she leaves the bathing room, she'll be able to expose me . . .

. . . unless she doesn't leave.

An image rears up in my crazed mind: my hands around her graceful throat, squeezing until she can no longer speak. I grab hold of the bathtub to steady myself. Only a few days ago I would have said that every obstacle between me and my vengeance had to be swept away, scruples be damned. But Naoko has been nothing but kindness itself since my arrival at the Grande Écurie. She took me under her wing. She forgave me for my lies of omission. She deplored the inhumane treatment vampyres subject their enemies to. She's effectively shattered my prejudice that lumped all aristocrats in the same basket.

"I . . . I can explain," I say.

"I don't want explanations," she shoots back. "I want the truth. Who are you really?"

I'm caught with my back against the wall, the moment I've most dreaded, where I toss my mask aside.

Either I kill Naoko, or I tell her everything.

There's no other choice.

"My name is Jeanne . . . ," I say reluctantly. "Jeanne Froidelac."

As I utter these words, I feel like I'm tearing my skin, like I'm ripping a mask sewn to my face.

"I'm not an aristocrat," I continue in one breath, dismembering the lie piece by piece. "I'm a commoner. I'm the daughter of the ones whose heads you saw attached to the spikes."

Naoko's eyes go wide with incredulity.

Under her black bangs, her shadowed face flinches.

"That's why you were so pale when you saw the heads the other day," she says. "And your ignorance of courtly manners, all the questions you asked me about things that seemed so evident, right up to how nervous you've been about receiving your aristocratic papers . . . I . . . I should've known."

Panic grips my stomach: she's going to turn around now and rush directly to the grand equerry.

Like an animal pinned in a corner, I grab her wrist to prevent her from leaving. She lets go of her candlestick, which goes out. I quickly grab it in midair before it smashes onto the tiles.

We stay frozen in the silent dimness, each gripping the other as if suspended in time: one more second and the sound of metal hitting the floor would have woken everyone in the dormitory.

"Don't tell anyone about this, or else," I threaten.

"Or else what? You'll get rid of me?" she snaps.

Her coolness is the opposite of my panic.

The way she states out loud the murderous impulse that raced through my brain seconds ago petrifies me.

Words gush out of my trembling lips, a mush of incomprehensibility.

"I . . . I . . . I don't . . ."

"You'll kill me the same way your family killed the real Diane de Gastefriche?"

"Shut up."

A bolt of lightning goes off in Naoko's eyes.

"It's you, isn't it?" she accuses me. "You're the one who killed her."

I clamp my hand over her mouth to make her stop talking, pressing so hard she could suffocate.

In one gesture, she reverses my grip, grabs my arm, and throws me to the floor.

I roll into a ball on the hard, cold tiles in order to soften my fall, but mostly to lessen the noise.

Did the bathing room door muffle our scuffle? Nothing disturbs the silence, no warning cries or hurried footsteps. I hear only the sound of my heart throbbing.

"What did you do to me?" I whisper, parting the hair that fell in front of my eyes.

"An aiki-jujutsu move," Naoko says. "It's about sending your adversary's force back at them. I have another dozen moves in my repertoire should you dare lay a hand on me again." She plants herself in front of the door and crosses her arms. "Go on with your story."

I get up, out of breath.

The bathing room is lit only by the oil lamp resting on the floor. The white silk of the kimono captures the light. It's decorated with cherry-tree flowers that Naoko painted by hand.

"I used Diane as a shield against her father's sword," I tell her. "It was either her or me. But I had to live. I had to usurp her identity in order to come up to Versailles. To avenge my loved ones." I take a deep breath. "I'm not in love with Alexandre de Mortange. He's the one who murdered my family. I didn't go to meet him when I ran off from the Grande Écurie the other night: I went there to plant a stake through his heart."

Voilà. I've admitted everything.

I feel drained, like the sky after the storm last week.

"What are you going to do with me now?" I ask.

Naoko's gaze has never looked more impenetrable.

She raises her hand, displaying the aristocratic papers she's still holding, the irrefutable proof of my duplicity.

"What am I going to do?" she says. "Help you falsify the document, of course. I'm told I draw rather well. But we have to be quick."

"You . . . you're going to help me?" I manage to say, amazed.

"Isn't that what you'd expect from a true friend? And you've finally been honest. It explains that unspoken something I sensed between us. Now I also understand why you want to become one of the king's squires, and I believe you when you say you'll never want to be transmuted. Now that the abscess has burst and drained, I can trust you. At last."

I feel a warmth in my belly, a surge of solar gratitude in the middle of this cold night, in this hostile school.

"Yes, Naoko, you can trust me," I say. "Totally, absolutely! You don't have to doubt me anymore."

She nods. "Wait for me here. I'm going back to the dormitory to get my pencil case, notebook, and inkpot."

She hands me the aristocratic papers and brings the candlestick to the oil lamp to light the wick again. Then she heads off silently into the dark hallway. I'm not afraid that she'll betray me—if she wanted to, she had only to scream.

Alone in the bathing room, I suddenly remember the recluse suspended from the gutter. I hastily go to the window. On the outside sill, the heads have disappeared. Spirited away, I'm sure, by the one who brought them here so that I could say my goodbyes. Where are they now? Did he take them back to his lair to . . . eat them?

Naoko returns.

"Everyone's sleeping soundly and there're no Swiss Guards on the floor," she says, sitting down on the tiles. "Let's take advantage of that and get to work."

She quickly lays out her painting supplies near the oil lamp and candlestick along with a drawing pad that she removes from the pocket of her kimono.

"Fill this container with water and boil it over the candlestick flame," she says, gesturing toward a soap dish resting on the corner of the sink. "The steam will allow us to unglue the vignette of the deceased. Meanwhile, I'll begin your portrait."

She dips the tip of her pen into her inkpot and starts to capture me with precision. As I observe her, I'm reminded of the care Bastien took with the pencil sketches he drew from life. Naoko raises her eyes in the same furtive way, as if to steal details from her subject.

"I don't know how to begin to thank you . . . ," I say, deeply touched.

"We'll talk about that later," she answers, her eyes still feverishly darting to and from my face and back to the notebook. "For now, stay still if you want the portrait to be accurate."

Accurate is a weak word. Once Naoko hands me her finished work, it's like seeing my reflection in a small mirror. In the meantime, the old vignette is now detached from the aristocratic papers. Naoko burns it in the flame of the candlestick. Then, with a few dots of glue from her pencil case, she affixes the new vignette to the blank spot. The illusion is perfect.

"Voilà, Jeanne," she says. "Or should I say, Diane, as these papers attest. Now, we have to dispatch them to the grand equerry. How to do that?"

"The crow," I say, motioning to the basket.

Naoko furrows her eyebrows.

"You managed to capture the homing crow on your own, with your small hands? Well done. My aiki-jujutsu master would be proud of you."

"I'm not the one who captured it, Naoko. There's somebody outside, or something . . . a strange creature, a sort of monster, who's either a bloodthirsty demon or a guardian angel."

Naoko gives me a small smile.

"Then let's say it's a *guardian demon*. After your immortal dandy, I think it's fair to say you have strange acquaintances. But you'll tell me about that later. We have to hurry."

She helps me lift the lid of the basket and reattach the cartouche, in which we've placed the aristocratic paper, back to the crow's leg.

Gently, I take the black bird into my hands and go to the window.

The messenger flies off into the night, heading straight for the aviary, the final destination of his journey from Clermont.

"Diane, Monsieur de Montfaucon requests your presence in his office," Madame Thérèse tells me as breakfast ends.

The moment of truth, the moment I've been waiting so anxiously for since I woke up.

I exchange a glance with Naoko; she gives me a discreet, reassuring smile. Then I follow the governess as she heads toward the grand equerry's office.

The last time I was here, it was dusk, and the visit left me with bad memories. The office isn't any more cheerful in daylight. On the contrary. This time I can clearly make out the contents of the glass jars aligned on the shelves. They're hands. Some are whole, cut off at the forearm; others are cut at the wrist, with missing fingers. The enormous nails, yellow and curved, look like the claws of ferocious beasts.

Gesturing with the tip of the shaggy goatee on his chin, Montfaucon orders me to sit in the small chair facing his desk.

"I received your papers," he says solemnly. "You certainly took me for a ride."

All my muscles tense up.

He knows!

He's discovered my deception.

"I . . . I don't know what you're talking about, monsieur," I stammer.

"Don't play innocent!" he roars.

"I mean it."

"Silence. You wanted to pass yourself off as someone you're not."

My gaze locks onto one of the big bronze statues of rearing horses on the corner of the desk. Am I strong enough to lift it and knock him out?

"Your aristocratic lineage doesn't go as far back as the Crusades, as you shamelessly claimed, only to the Great Wars of Italy!" he thunders.

His accusation leaves me speechless.

The . . . the Crusades?

"I already told you that I don't tolerate boasting," he hurls at me. "The court has enough megalomaniacs as it is, and I don't want my school adding to the nonsense. Certainly not among the king's squires."

I don't believe my ears.

"Do you mean that I can compete for the Sip of the King?" I ask.

"Isn't that your ambition?" he snaps back. "To push your way to the front row at the court? *And* to be transmuted, as your ill-advised dalliance with that questionable vampyre attests to?"

I barely squelch a burst of nervous laughter, forcing myself to maintain a poker face.

"I'll do my best to be worthy of the royal favor," I say.

"Enough, enough . . . ," Montfaucon grumbles. "Keep your boot-licking for others." He sniffles loudly, his nose scrunching in disgust. "Let's be clear, Gastefriche: I don't appreciate you and your arrogant, pushy ways. Get out of my sight. Return to your lessons and try to make yourself small."

Just as I rise to leave, my eyes are drawn again to the repugnant hands preserved in the formaldehyde. I remember the sinister reputation of Montfaucon's ancestors, a line of executioners in the pocket of the Vampyria.

The director's eyes sparkle under his limp wig.

"My collection of ghoul hands interests you?" he asks.

"Ghoul hands?" I say.

Like the stryges, here is another kind of abomination spawned by the Shadows that I thought was just a legend until today. The storybooks pretend that these cannibalistic creatures haunt cemeteries come nightfall so they can feast on human remains.

"There . . . there weren't any ghouls in the Auvergne," I stammer.

The grand equerry laughs.

"Of course not. Your village didn't have enough people to attract the scavengers. But Versailles and Paris are teeming with them. Total trash. The cemeteries and mass graves overflow with their kind."

Mesmerized by the revolting specimens, I think about the recluse at the Grande Écurie and the half-gnawed human remains I saw in his lair. I felt a corpse-like coldness emanating from his body—not as pronounced as the vampyres' but enough to denote the presence of the Shadows. Obviously, I was in the company of an abomination. Was he a ghoul . . . ? Yet his hand seemed human, even if it was all stitched up, nothing resembling the deformed appendages marinating in the jars.

"You seem captivated by everything that's morbid," Montfaucon says, snapping me from my thoughts. "The heads exhibited on the gate in your honor must have delighted you. But the show is over. I asked the Swiss Guards to remove them this morning. And now it's time for you to remove yourself and let me work in peace."

He buries his nose in his papers again without giving me another glance.

I go down the hallway to rejoin the art-of-courtly-manners class, haunted by a new mystery about this place, a place already full of mysteries. The grand equerry wants me to believe he ordered the removal of the heads, in broad daylight, but I know that's not true.

Why is Montfaucon lying?

Does he know about the monster who prowls inside the walls of his school?

Who is this creature? *Who?*

16

PROGRESS

My questions about the recluse at the Grande Écurie go unanswered in the days and weeks that follow. Ever since the strange episode with the severed heads, there's no sign of him. And the hectic pace of my classes occupies too much of my time to allow me to chase after a chimera.

In the eyes of the boarders and teachers, I'm no longer the "newcomer." Everyone knows I'm here to stay. Hélénaïs seems to have decided to ignore me as if I'm part of the furniture; instead, she's focused on classes and beating me fair and square during the competition for the Sip of the King.

I'm getting better and better at mastering my persona of provincial baronette and her way of thinking, the past I invented for her based on what I know of the real Diane de Gastefriche. Each day that I play the part, it seems a little easier than the day before . . . a little more dizzying too. Jeanne and Diane—two names that sound nearly the same, like two sides of the same coin. During the day, only the head's side exists: the mask behind which I hide. But at night, sheltered behind the thick curtains of my canopy bed, I turn back to the tail's side. Here, in total darkness where no one can see me, I'm Jeanne again. I open my silent pocket watch, forever stopped at 7:38.

Liberty or death says the motto inscribed on the backside of the hollow case lid.

I choose death.

Because liberty has no meaning in a world without my loved ones.

Because death is the price to pay for attempting to eradicate the person responsible for their disappearance: the Immutable.

I continue to throw myself headlong into my transformation. I don't have a difficult time with my classes led by Chantilly and Saint-Loup. Most of the boarders take provincials for illiterate peasants, but the education my parents gave me often allows me to eclipse them when it comes to the art of conversation. As for the art of weaponry, I'm learning how to use a saber and a sword, but hunting in the woods has already honed my warrior reflexes, and the years I spent using a sling help me to hit my target with a pistol.

Admittedly, the art of equestrianism is harder. Typhon goes easy on me and obediently follows commands, much to everyone's astonishment. But when we have to do a solo dressage exercise in the ring, just him and me, the grand equerry starts up with the taunts and barbs, criticizing the way I hold on to Typhon's mane, the poor use of my aids, and my deplorable seat. I take it all in without a peep, trying to glean bits of helpful pointers from the rebuking. It's only at the end of October that competitors in the running for the Sip of the King have to execute a carousel, a perfectly coordinated equestrian ballet.

In the end, the art of courtly manners is what gives me the most trouble. I have a hard time remembering the habits and customs of a court that horrifies me. I usually get all scrambled choosing the right cutlery, curtsying too low or too high, mixing up the correct order of rank—in short, I mangle etiquette in a thousand small ways that make Barvók wince. Thankfully, I can count on Naoko, who excels in the subject. She gives me advice, going over the mistakes I make to help me correct them. She always addresses me as Diane. Only when we're behind the locked door of a bathing room to get ready for dinner in the evening does she call me Jeanne. Away from indiscreet ears, with faucets running to mask our whispers, we talk about our lives. As she embellishes her bun with ornaments, Naoko describes her native country and its customs. Listening to her, I think the imperial court of Japan sounds just as cruel and codified as the one in Versailles. In turn, as she brushes my hair, I tell her about the Auvergne: the boredom of my monotonous days, the joy of running through the forest, and the quarrels with my mother, which now seem ridiculous considering the battle she was waging.

"Alchemy is practiced a lot more than anyone thinks, even if it's officially banned," Naoko answers me. "The emperor's doctors in Japan are devoted to it with a passion. The same is true for the doctors of the Faculty in the West."

I look at her under her black bangs.

"What *is* alchemy, exactly?" I ask.

"A manipulation of the humors," she answers, lowering her voice even though we're already whispering.

"The humors? Do you mean the ones that flow in the bodies of the living: phlegm, blood . . . yellow bile, and black bile?"

She nods. "Plus a fifth humor unique to immortals. Shadowessence."

I'm speechless for a few seconds, letting the gurgling of the water and rattling of the plumbing fill the silence.

"The Shadows are a humor?" I'm finally able to articulate.

Ever since I was little, I've lived in fear of the Shadows, but I've never been able to clearly define them.

Naoko nods again, solemnly.

"The Shadows are like energy that manifests itself in multiple ways: by chilling the climate; by giving birth to abominations; by bringing cadavers back to life. In the veins of vampyres, that mystical energy gets condensed into shadowessence, or at least that's what the Faculty claims."

I remember the feeling of cosmic horror that came over me in the gardens, when I looked into the king's eyes through the slits of his mask.

I thought I was falling into an interstellar void, but it was shadowessence saturating the royal gaze: a substance as dark as space . . .

"That's why immortals turned medicine into the new world religion, surrounding themselves with doctors who are priest-physicians," Naoko says. "Not only to draw the blood of the people but also to try and understand this supernatural humor that belongs only to them." She nervously adjusts her bun. "All right. Enough talk of horrors we don't understand. Let's finish getting ready for dinner before we turn into icicles."

She's right. If we stay much longer in this bathing room with its ice-cold tiled floor, we're going to end up sick. Night is almost here. Barvók is waiting for us downstairs, in the banquet hall. It's time for me to become the baronette.

"Today is October third, which means there's less than a month before the Sip of the King," Madame Thérèse announces the next morning at breakfast.

At this point, all the girls who want to compete have declared themselves—twelve young ladies vying to be a new squire to the king. Naoko, who is among the three who've decided not to take part, gives me a look of encouragement as she drinks her tea. Poppy's support is less subtle: she gives me a pat on the back, causing me to almost spill my café au lait.

"Who would have believed it, Belle-of-the-Fields?" she says mischievously. "Only one month ago you were still busy with livestock competitions in your countryside, and now look at you, a contender for the highest honor. If you win that ribbon, Pâquerette the sheep had better watch her back."

The way in which Poppy applies the flash of wit I used against Hélénaïs is somewhat amusing. But above her jovial smile, her kohl-underlined eyes gleam fiercely. She knows there's only one ribbon to snatch . . . only one.

"The last four days of October will be devoted to four successive disqualifying tests," Madame Thérèse reminds us, stating a rule that we all know by heart.

"On the twenty-eighth: the art-of-courtly-manners test will select the six most polished competitors.

"On the twenty-ninth: the art-of-equestrianism test will determine the top three riders.

"On the thirtieth: the art-of-conversation test will retain the two most eloquent boarders.

"On the thirty-first: the art-of-weaponry test will be a duel to decide between the finalists. At midnight that same evening, the king will proceed with the ritual of the Sip with the winning girl. He will do the same with the victor on the boy's side, thereby designating two new squires."

I smile at Naoko. The first disqualifying test involves my worst subject, and I'm going to need all her help to overcome my shortcomings in the four weeks ahead.

But Madame Thérèse isn't finished.

"I'm sure you know, mesdemoiselles, that there exists a fifth noble art—the art of vampyrism—that only the third-years are taught. This most refined art is the only subject that doesn't require a test, but it's necessary to master certain rudiments before entering the court."

I'm not exactly sure what the art of vampyrism is all about, but I assume the worst. There's something horrible in the way the governess evokes refinement. Even though she's a commoner, my guess is that her skin hasn't been jabbed in ages—her position at the Grande Écurie offers lots of privileges. I was hoping to make her an ally when I first arrived at the school, but it quickly became clear that she was completely devoted to the Vampyria.

"This evening, you will receive your first lesson. For the occasion, and in accordance with tradition at our school, we have the honor of welcoming two of the Grande Écurie's most prestigious former boarders. I am of course speaking of the two who won last year's Sip of the King: Suraj de Jaipur and Lucrèce du Crèvecœur."

I remember the squire who accompanied me back to the school the night I ran off, almost a month ago. It's a hazy memory because I was exhausted and in shock, hardly standing upright.

I'm eager to wash up for the evening, when Naoko and I are able to be alone in our bathing room and I can ask her questions.

"Since you were here last year, do you know the two squires who are coming to give us a lesson?"

She nods. "Yes, I know them. They were the most talented third-years—the toughest, too, since you don't become a squire to the king without putting up a fight . . . Hélénaïs's ruthlessness is nothing compared to Lucrèce's," she says. "After she drank the Sip of the King, the Shadows revealed her true self: a ferocious Fury. A predator as beautiful as she is merciless. As for Suraj, he's a Rajput knight, descended from an ancestral caste of Hindu warriors. He comes from Jaipur, one of the most powerful kingdoms among the many that comprise India. From what I've heard, the maharaja of Jaipur sent his best swordsman to Versailles in the hopes of getting the Immutable's support and forging a military alliance."

What Naoko tells me echoes what I heard the Princess des Ursins say in the gardens. The minister claimed that the Indian subcontinent was being threatened by stryges: I assume it's the reason the maharaja of Jaipur dispatched an emissary to the Court of Shadows.

"Suraj fought tooth and nail to become one of the king's bodyguards so that he could have the monarch's ear," Naoko says. "I don't know if he was ultimately successful. When I arrived at the Grande Écurie two years ago, our geographical roots brought us closer for a while. But I haven't spoken to him since."

By the way her carmine lips are quivering, my guess is that there was more to their closeness than she's saying.

"Suraj and you, you were . . . together?" I ask.

Naoko smiles faintly. "No, I've never been with anyone," she says.

The infinite solitude of this odd young girl breaks my heart, the same as when she told me about learning to style hair and paint all on her own the day we met.

"Besides, Suraj's heart was already taken when he lived at the Grande Écurie," she adds. "No one knows this. But I found out during one of my nightly walks last year, during my bouts of insomnia. I saw Suraj cross the courtyard from one of the hallway windows; he was headed toward the stables . . . with someone else."

"You mean Suraj had a liaison with another girl here?"

Naoko shakes her head. "Not a girl. A boy. A second-year, the caballero Rafael de Montesueño. I saw him sneak into the stable with Suraj that night. It's only one of their many nighttime rendezvous."

I've had my breath knocked out of me.

A lot of human passions beat in the heart of this conservative school. If relations between girls and boys are forbidden at the Grande Écurie, under the influence of a patriarchal court obsessed with etiquette, I can't imagine the disgrace that a romance between two lovers of the same sex would generate.

"Of course, I never said a word to anyone," Naoko says. "I'm not the sort to reveal the secrets of others." She gives me a slightly mischievous smile. "Anyway, Suraj put an end to that forbidden romance when he entered the king's service, in accordance with the wishes of the maharaja. His future is no longer his: the Immutable alone decides who his squires will marry. No doubt he'll send Suraj back to India, where he'll represent France. Unless Suraj dies beforehand, in service . . ."

I ponder what Naoko tells me. It sheds new light on the sadness I saw in Rafael's eyes when he mentioned the crows that came to Versailles from as far away as India. As for his usual black attire, I sense that it's not only the style in Spain but also the color of mourning for a lost love.

At dinner, as if to echo my conversation with Naoko, fate places Tristan and Rafael at my table, just like on the evening of my arrival.

The young Spaniard seemed immediately friendly, if a little shy, when we first spoke. Now that I know his secret, he's even more likable, forced to play a role, same as me. I'd like to talk to him, to tell him that I had a brother who also loved someone he wasn't supposed to . . . but of course, I don't. He remains silent throughout the dinner, using his utensils to fiddle with his food, lost in thought, his eyebrows furrowed. The prospect of seeing Suraj at our art-of-vampyrism lesson, probably for the first time in almost a year, must distress him.

Tristan makes up for his tablemate's muteness with pleasant conversation. Over the past month, I've gone out of my way to encourage the feelings he seems to have for me. He's become my source of information on everything that happens in the boys' wing, and I suspect that he'll be even more useful later on.

"I've heard that you yet again outshone everyone during your art-of-conversation class," he tells me, pushing his dessert plate away. "I'm glad I won't be pitted against you for the Sip of the King. I don't know anyone with a more biting wit than yours."

"That's no doubt because I'm predestined to transmute into a vampyre, hence my biting wit," I shoot back, not missing a beat. "As far as you're concerned, Saint-Loup told us that you managed to disarm three attackers at one time in your saber lesson. Impressive."

His blue eyes seem to shine a little brighter at my compliment. Just as I'm a front-runner among the girls, Tristan is well in the lead among the boys. It's all the more ironic that the court repulses us both, and that he's competing for the Sip of the King to please his mother—an assertive woman, it seems, as overbearing as my own mother.

"I may have my chances," he acknowledges modestly. "Except in the art of equestrianism, where Rafael beats us out every time. Everyone knows Spaniards are the masters of dressage, and he's the master of them all."

He nods at Rafael, but the latter doesn't cheer up. Poor soul. For him, perhaps the Sip of the King isn't about racking up honors but a last-ditch effort to hold on to a lost love . . .

"Can you imagine if on October thirty-first you and I are both named squires?" Tristan tells me. "We'd make a fine team. It would be amazing."

"Amazing, indeed," I say, fluttering my eyelashes to make him melt.

And even more amazing, my dear boy: the King of Shadows' head rolling on the ground, after I've pierced his heart and slit his throat.

As if to quiet my thoughts, the strident warning bell rings in the towers of Versailles. Night is falling, and with it comes the absolute reign of the vampyres.

"Mesdemoiselles, messieurs, it's time," Madame Thérèse announces. "Dress warmly and follow me and the general into the courtyard in orderly and silent fashion."

I slip into my fur coat, courtesy of the wardrobe the king gave me. It's very warm, so it isn't the night air that makes me shiver when I step foot into the yard: it's guilt, because I'm wearing the equivalent of a year's salary for a family of farmers in my village on my back.

In the middle of the cobblestones lit by torchlights, two figures are waiting for us. The first belongs to Suraj de Jaipur. Tall and sculptural in an ocher leather breastplate, he towers over the other boys. Next to him is a young girl, her brown hair carefully pulled back into a ponytail: Lucrèce du Crèvecœur. Her plum-colored dress lined with mink lets you guess at the curves of her athletic body. These are the Immutable's squires, each dressed in somber clothing to blend in with the night. They're only a year older than us, yet they emanate self-confidence beyond their age. I can't imagine the terrors they must have encountered during the eleven months they've been in the king's service.

"Welcome, dear former students," Barvók greets them.

He tries to lower his head, but his neck brace stops him; he doesn't fare any better when he tries to bow from atop iron legs that are stiff as poles. The doctors of the Faculty clearly did a poor job when they "fixed" him. With each of his choppy movements, I can't help but think of the stryges responsible for his condition.

"Um . . . thank you for honoring the school with your presence," he continues, straightening. He looks at the guests with pride, as if he were reviewing the best elements of his troops. "Mademoiselle du Crèvecœur, I heard that the king sent you as his representative to Normandy last summer, along with a battalion charged with subduing a peasant revolt."

"Fishermen, my general," the brunette says in a voice as clear as a chip of ice, as clear as her eyes. "Those boors dared to protest against the salt tax. They claimed to need salt to preserve their fish during the long months of winter, when the weather prevents them from fishing."

"Protest, well, that's certainly bad manners," the military man says, indignant.

"We punished them with our whips . . . and claws," Lucrèce declares.

She raises her right arm, and there's a sudden glare. For a second, I think her hand has been replaced by a metallic prosthetic, similar to Barvók's. But no. She's wearing an iron gauntlet, elongating each of her fingers with a hooked claw. They look like talons. Now I understand why Naoko described her as a "fierce Fury," the name of the ancient deities of vengeance, half-woman, half-raptor.

"I myself poured their precious salt on their open wounds," she dares boast.

Revolted by her cruelty, I stuff my fists into the pockets of my coat. But Barvók is already turning toward the second squire.

"As for you, Monsieur de Jaipur, I heard you volunteered to battle the ghouls that infest the Cemetery of the Innocents in Paris. They say these creatures are proliferating, that they don't hesitate to leave the catacombs to attack commoners and steal newborns from their cradles."

The general's nostrils scrunch in disgust, more so, it seems, over the mention of the foul-smelling creatures than the thought of what they subjected people to. I shiver as I remember the conversation I overheard in the maze, one month ago: the Princess des Ursins claimed that the nocturnal abominations were restless as never before . . .

"My haladie dagger is at the service of the Magna Vampyria," Suraj says solemnly in an accented voice. He places his hands on the long double-bladed dagger at his belt.

Unlike his teammate, he doesn't seem to rejoice over his military exploits. I remember what Naoko said: since his arrival at the court, Suraj has the reputation of being a death seeker . . . ever since he broke things off with Rafael.

"We leave you in good hands," Barvók concludes, turning toward us. "Try to follow in the glorious footsteps of your elders."

With that, he walks off, the governess at his heels.

"Good evening, friends," Suraj says unenthusiastically.

His piercing eyes, topped by furrowed brows, sweep across his audience—carefully avoiding Rafael.

If Rafael hasn't gotten over the breakup eleven months later, it looks like Suraj is also feeling aftereffects . . . which may be the reason why he's always risking his life.

"Tonight, we're going to talk about botany," he says.

He points to a box mounted on wheels that valets must have brought here. Inside is a large rosebush with white flowers.

White roses that are still in bloom in October, in this glacial cold, can't be natural; their strange vitality doesn't bode well.

"Who can tell me what a vampyric rose is?" Lucrèce asks, confirming my suspicions.

As usual, Françoise des Escailles raises her hand first.

"It's a flower that feeds on the blood of mortals," she says with such energy that the tail of her beaver hat falls onto her face, toppling her eyeglasses.

A few muffled exclamations can be heard—"Toady!" "Brownnoser!" "Four-eyes!"—along with hushed laughter. But not mine.

A blood-drinking flower. What a horrid idea.

"That's correct, but there's more," Lucrèce says. "Vampyric roses, marvels that were created by botanists of the Faculty, don't just absorb human blood: they also exhale its fragrances. Nothing smells sweeter to the noses of our masters, the immortals. Vampyric roses have no equal when it comes to whetting their appetites."

The squire's combination of servility and ferocity sickens me. With disgust, I think back to the way Alexandre's nostrils quivered with excitement aboard the carriage as we got closer to Versailles and the scent of the roses wafting from the palace.

"Let's move on to a little demonstration," Lucrèce suggests as she pulls from her cleavage a vial filled with blood.

She opens the vial, her talons clinking against the glass. Then she comes closer to one of the white roses and drips the liquid into the corolla.

Nothing happens with the first drop.

With the second, a subtle movement seems to agitate the flower, like a nocturnal breeze.

But with the third drop, the rose comes to life. Its stem bends toward the vial in Lucrèce's hand, its corolla becoming dilated to absorb more of the blood.

"What a spell . . . ," I whisper, while murmurs of fear and excitement gush around me.

I take a step back, colliding with Tristan, who's behind me.

"I never saw such evil spells in my Ardennes," he whispers, astounded. "And I gather neither did you in the Auvergne. They call this the 'marvels of botany,' but in fact these are abominations. The court is even more perverse than I thought."

Lucrèce empties the rest of the vial, letting a long stream of blood flow forth. The white petals that were previously stained turn entirely purple. They seem to be throbbing, like veins.

She extends her right index finger, its sharpened tip sparkling like a dagger. In one swift supernatural motion, which I suspect is enhanced by the Shadows, Lucrèce sections off the stem. The rose puts up a brief fight in her hand, sending drops of blood into the air. The way it writhes reminds me of a lizard's tail, one that's been cut off, an abhorrent hybrid of the vegetal and animal kingdoms.

"Smell it," Lucrèce commands as she brandishes the rose in front of us.

A powerful metallic scent fills my nostrils, bringing back the most painful memories of my life: it's as if I'm in the dining room of my home again, the floor tiles drenched in my family's blood.

Unable to stand the vile smell one second longer and sensing a migraine coming on, I bring the sleeve of my coat against my nose.

"You!" Lucrèce shouts in a voice used to giving orders. "Come here. And take that sleeve away from your face."

With everyone's eyes on me, I'm forced to do as I'm told. But I start to breathe through my mouth so as not to smell the blood.

"What's your name?" the squire asks me dryly.

"Diane de Gastefriche, at your service," I answer in a strained voice because I'm not using my nose to breathe.

"Ah yes, I recognize you . . . ," she says, lifting her pointy chin. "You're the one who broke into the royal gardens last month. The king pardoned your brash behavior, but it's not a reason to make impertinence your trademark. Didn't Barvók teach you to never manifest the slightest disgust when confronted with the customs of the vampyric aristocracy? Give me your hand."

"My hand?"

"I just finished demonstrating how to water with the vial. Now we have to show your classmates how to water in vivo, with a mortal ready to be bled."

A sadistic smile spreads over the squire's thin lips.

"Whenever you bring prey to an immortal, it's the best way to reveal its bouquet. But be careful: vampyric roses react more strongly to fresh than bottled blood, so you have to be dexterous."

Quick as lightning, she grabs my wrist through the sleeve of my fur coat and pulls me brusquely to her.

I don't have time to react before she cuts my palm with the tip of her metal nail.

"Owww!" I shout, forgetting to breathe through my mouth.

"It's only a scratch," she scolds me. "Stay still, if you don't want the rosebush to tear off one of your fingers."

I see the rosebush start to quiver, the evil flowers bending toward me, trembling in excitement. Branches covered in thorns deploy like tentacles.

In her iron grip, Lucrèce holds my hand right over the thirsty roses, aiming my dripping blood into the nearest rose.

The rose's petals snap just inches from my cut palm, like the beaks of a disgusting brood of ravenous birds.

"Enough," the squire decrees once the white rose has turned entirely purple.

She shoves me roughly back into the group. Tristan barely catches me in his arms.

Then the squire sections off the vibrating stem and displays the monstrous cut rose; it exhales a heady perfume—that of my very own blood, intense enough to make one swoon.

"Your turn now," Suraj announces, coming out of the silence that he maintained throughout the demonstration. "Pair off and water a different flower."

I make a fist to stop the bleeding, shaking with fear and anger.

"I think you've given plenty tonight," Tristan says into the back of my neck. "If you like, I'll be your partner. And after you've poured my blood into one of those diabolical roses, I'll give you the pleasure of slashing off its stem and smashing it under your foot."

17

HUNT

"La Roncière seems to be falling for you," Poppy says mockingly.

It's already October 23, five days before the tests for the Sip of the King get underway. Lately, the English beauty has been eating breakfast with Naoko and me, then going off to spend the rest of the day with her many friends. She doesn't miss an opportunity to tease me . . . to test me.

"Tristan, really?" I respond innocently even though I've done everything I could these last few weeks to fuel his interest.

"I have to admit that blondie is cute, especially with his bad-boy scar. Maybe you're not so indifferent since you seem to have forgotten your high-drama vampyre."

"I, for one, don't have time to be thinking about boys, not one week before the first test," I say.

What a ridiculous idea she's got in her head. How could I feel anything for Tristan when he's just a pawn in my game?

Poppy gives one of those big husky laughs that are hers alone, a laugh that devolves into a coughing fit.

"Are you all right?" I ask.

"I just caught a little cold the other night," she says, getting her breath back. "When I escaped the dormitory after dark to go see one of my admirers." She smiles innocently. "What can I say? Contrary to you, *I*, for one, always have time to think about boys. And I assure you that they're always thinking about me, during the day when they're supposed to be listening in class and at night, in their most *torrid* dreams. Ever since I kissed him under these damn cold archways, Thomas de Longuedune doesn't leave me alone. He even slips me poetry in secret."

She winks at me provocatively with her darkened eyelid.

"You and Thomas—" I start to say.

"There is no 'me and Thomas,'" she replies. "First, he's a horrible kisser. Second, his verses are beyond banal. I'm embarrassed for him." She sighs. "Honestly, there's only one boarder who makes my heart beat faster. Zacharie de Grand-Domaine."

"The one from Louisiana?"

She nods. "To start with, he's American, which for me is a big plus. Add to that the fact that I think he's positively sublime. I bet he's interested in me too . . . but I also get the feeling that his heart is like an armored tank. Something torments him. He's a handsome fellow with a big secret, I'm sure of it—and that makes him wildly attractive. Mystery makes me want to live life to the fullest!"

She inhales and continues:

"*Live now, I beg you, wait not till the morrow. Gather today the roses of your life!*"

"If those are vampyric roses, you can have them," Naoko pipes up, tired of our tablemate's showboating.

"Oh, you, the insomniac nun, you'd be better off if you just let loose a little," Poppy quips. "You could take advantage of your sleepless nights to experience a lot of adventures. Two years at the Grande Écurie and not one romantic tryst to your name. A crying shame considering how cute you are. You should take the advice of poets a lot more talented than Longuedune, the poets whose verses I learned in my French classes back in England: *Gather, gather your youth: since age will tarnish your beauty as it has faded this flower.* Where you're concerned, Pierre de Ronsard, the prince of poets, must be turning in his grave."

I rise from the table, wanting to spare Naoko any more teasing.

"All right, girls, that's all good, but the art of conversation awaits us," I say. "Poppy, if you're feeling poetically inspired, you could spout more verses in Chantilly's class. She's *la crème de la crème* of professors."

"Oh, nice wordplay. Your tongue is sharper and sharper, darling."

We start to make our way toward the art-of-conversation classroom. But as we exit the dining hall, we're collared by the Knight of Saint-Loup.

"What's going on?" Poppy asks. "Isn't the art-of-weaponry class this afternoon, like it always is?"

"Not today," the knight says. "The morning is supposed to be sunny, if a little chilly, and the grand equerry decided that it would be devoted to outdoor activities. He's informing the boys of his decision as we speak. Take off your dresses, mesdemoiselles, and change into your warmest breeches—we're off to tease the deer on the royal hunting grounds."

The wardrobe the king gave me includes a hunting outfit, but it's the first time I've had occasion to wear it since arriving at school. I feel instantly comfortable. Even if the thick leather breeches aren't as supple as the ones I wore back in the Auvergne, it's still a lot easier to move around in them. The knee-high boots that go with the breeches are snug and light. The three-cornered hat is decorated with a pheasant feather and is roomy enough for me to tuck my hair inside. As for the short burgundy velvet jacket lined with Russian squirrel fur, it's a lot less cumbersome than my long fur coat.

"Oooh, *sexy*! All eyes are going to be on you, Belle-of-the-Fields," Poppy says when I arrive at the stables. Myrmidon's stall is next to Typhon's.

She's wrapped her impressive head of hair in a net, showing off her graceful neck, and her breeches are made of the same fabric she's fond of wearing at school: denim.

"You don't know what you're talking about. You're the one who's going to attract all the attention," I reply, smiling.

She turns full circle so that I can admire her slender legs.

"You like? It's the latest fashion craze worn by settlers in the American colonies. Dyed with Genoa blue. They call these *blue jeans*."

"You seem fascinated by the Americas," I point out to her. "Your chewing gum. Your denim breeches. Your obsession with handsome Zacharie."

Under her extravagant hairdo, in keeping with her personality, Poppy's face lights up.

"It's a country where anything's possible, or so they say, right? I've dreamt of escaping there forever. To carve my path, far from France and England. A new life in the New World, and why not on Zach's arm."

Her dreams of escape touch a nerve. I had similar daydreams in my small bedroom in Butte-aux-Rats, but I always imagined going off on adventures alone.

"If I win the Sip of the King, after a few years of service, I'll ask to be sent over there as an ambassador," Poppy confides as she girths her horse. "But I don't know anything about *your* ambitions, Diane. What does Belle-of-the Fields dream of?"

"Serving the king. That's the only thing that matters to me," I pretend.

"Pffft! Bootlicker," she says, laughing her fractured laugh.

The girls' and boys' horses start off on the wide avenue that begins at the school and leads to the royal hunting grounds: thirty mounts advance in two neat rows, led by Montfaucon and Saint-Loup. The mistress of weaponry rides an elegant chestnut horse with a smattering of red and white hairs. The grand equerry is perched on an enormous smoky-bay steed, even bigger than Typhon. A sizable hunting horn is strapped to his back, the copper surface catching the cold rays of the autumn sun.

As we advance, trees go by on each side of the avenue, all nearly bare, exposing the white facades of the buildings.

A carpet of dead leaves muffles the sound of hooves striking the cobblestones.

The horses' quivering nostrils spray long jets of white steam into the chilly morning air.

The hunting dogs striding alongside the grand equerry emit even more vapors with their open mouths. There are about thirty ferocious hounds: big dogs with grayish-blue coats, all excited to be out of their narrow courtyard kennels to stretch their legs.

We finally arrive in front of a large coach gate bookended by a wall that extends past our view on either side: one of the entry points to the hunting grounds.

Beyond the portal the town of Versailles disappears as if by magic, and we find ourselves at the edge of a vast forest. A gamekeeper dressed in a dark uniform and wearing a thick wool cap greets us.

"Welcome, Monsieur Montfaucon. This is Ajax, our best bloodhound," he says, gesturing toward a dog with lively dark eyes that's pulling on his leash. "He'll accompany you to flush out the deer. The mating season came early this year, so it's going to be a harsh winter." He blows on his hands to warm them up. "The bucks and does are everywhere, spread across the grounds, but especially concentrated in the Vallée de la Bièvre, where the river hasn't frozen yet. That's where I recommend you go."

"We'll follow your advice," the grand equerry says. "Do you have the daggers and spears?"

"Of course."

The gamekeeper snaps his fingers. A half dozen valets bundled in thick coats emerge from the hunting lodge that adjoins the wall, next to the coach gate. They bring over long spears embellished with pennants, and glistening daggers as sharp as the swords at court.

"Today we'll be hunting with bladed weapons," Montfaucon tells us from atop his steed. "Big-game hunting is the leisure sport of kings, a necessary skill for those who want to shine at the court. Pair off: one takes a spear, the other a dagger. The duo that brings back the deer's heart will be declared the winner of the day."

I turn to Naoko, but she shakes her head from her dappled mare, not moving a hair of her heavily pinned bun.

"Don't count on me this time," she says. "Remember, I'm vegetarian. I'm just going to follow the hunt from a distance."

A familiar voice resonates in back of me.

"How about you and I team up, the countryfolk duo?"

I turn in my saddle. It's Tristan, perched on a horse with a dun coat, the yellow-sand color picking up the ash blond of his hair.

"All right, but I'm taking the dagger," I say. "I don't see myself wielding a spear that's as tall as I am. The horses, the weapons, the pennants, the horn . . . all this stuff is awfully cumbersome."

"Didn't you hunt in the Auvergne?"

"Yes, but alone. A real hunter should only rely on oneself."

"Well, I'm honored that you're making an exception for me," he answers with a big smile.

We each grab our weapon from one of the valets' outstretched hands.

"Well, well, Gastefriche and La Roncière," the grand equerry exclaims, grimacing. "The rabble join forces."

He turns his back to us and commands his mount to start walking.

"Looks like Montfaucon took a dislike to you too," I tell Tristan.

"You bet! I think that he can't stand provincials. But we're going to show him what we're made of, you and me, right?"

I nod, and then I press my calves against Typhon's flanks so that he catches up to the rest of the group.

As we make our way into the forest at a slow trot, the trees grow denser, tearing at the sky with their bare branches. Guided by Ajax, the dogs begin to pant faster as they become increasingly excited.

Suddenly, the lead bloodhound comes to a stop, pointing his nose deeper into the forest.

"Over there, steam!" the grand equerry exclaims, extending his ringed hand toward a small pile of round droppings that's still steaming. "Those are from a male. We're on the right track."

He blows the hunting horn, the sound deep and lugubrious, making the mossy tree trunks shake.

The pack of dogs hurtles forward with deafening barks.

The horses gallop behind.

Surprised by the sudden burst of speed, I nearly topple and just have time to grab hold of Typhon's mane. I press myself against his neck so that the branches whizzing by don't cut me.

The noise of the stampede, the rush of the wind, the barking of the dogs, the furious beating of my own heart—all of it makes me dizzy.

Images flash between the tree trunks like flashes of lightning.

Hélénaïs de Plumigny's ecstatic face, her chestnut curls billowing in the wind gusts like snakes adorning a magnificent Medusa.

Rafael de Montesueño's focused gaze, his somber attire blending with the coat of his jet-black thoroughbred, giving the illusion of a centaur.

Françoise des Escailles's terrified expression as she clings to her reins even more tightly than I do to my horse's mane.

Tristan's radiant joy at being in his cherished forests, urging his horse with quick clicking sounds.

Suddenly, the pack hounds freeze. The group stops. Typhon comes to an abrupt halt behind Myrmidon; I hold on fast so as not to topple headfirst over Typhon's neck. Up ahead, the dogs seem to be hesitating between two paths; they raise their damp snouts to the wind to find the scent of their prey. Near me, Poppy starts to cough, out of breath from all the effort. I've often witnessed her coughing fits, but this one is worse than ever.

"Are you all right?" I ask her, out of breath too.

She gives me a sinister look above her embroidered handkerchief. The mark she left on the fabric isn't from her lipstick. There's way too much red. It's a large stain of blood.

"You already asked me the other day. Of course everything is all right," she replies dryly as she stows away her handkerchief. "I told you it's just a cold. It'll pass. Mind your own affairs."

At that instant, a voice shouts, "Over there! The stag!"

The dogs take off straightaway, dragging us again into a frantic pace.

I narrow my eyes, which the cold and speed have misted with tears. Over in the foggy bushes, I notice the rear of a large animal in flight.

A lone buck, against thirty dogs and as many horses and riders in hot pursuit . . .

The lopsidedness of this battle is revolting.

Going after this quarry has nothing remotely similar to my forest outings. Back in Butte-aux-Rats, I was alone against the whole of nature, and I had only one chance to take down a jackrabbit with my sling—not counting the risk of being devoured by wild beasts. But today, all I'm doing is taking part in a pastime for rich town dwellers, no danger, no glory.

The cries of the hounds and riders blend into the same savage clamor, reminding me of Edmée's and Marcantonio's laughter. The only gallant thing about the hunt in the royal gardens was its name. Similarly, big-game hunting—the so-called leisurely recreation of kings—is only a barbaric killing.

This parody of combat between man and beast goes on for hours with an ignoble goal: exhaust the buck until he's too tired to go on. But the group runs up against a river that blocks the way. The completely disoriented dogs start to go crazy on the bank.

"May the Shadows take the buck!" the grand equerry yells from his smoky-coated steed. "He crossed the river to mask his scent. He's gotten away." He raises his eyes toward the sky, where gray clouds have chased away the sun. "The hunt is over. Let's go back."

But Tristan doesn't see it that way.

"Just a bit longer, monsieur!" he shouts. "You'll see what the rabble is capable of." He turns his sweat-drenched face in my direction. "Follow me."

Torn between the desire to head back and wanting to shine in the eyes of my rivals, I let Typhon spring forward on the hooves of my teammate. The two horses gallop into the river, right up to their bellies, in large sprays of icy water. They come out dripping, leaving the rest of the group on the other side of the riverbank.

"This way!" Tristan yells.

Spurring his mount, he takes off into thickets that grow ever denser, where a path of ferns has been crushed by the buck. The branches rip my hat off. I can feel my hair coming undone.

We abruptly stumble onto a clearing.

The animal is here, kneeling in the tall grasses, out of breath.

Tristan slides off his horse and goes closer to the buck. He raises his spear.

"No!" I shout, jumping from my saddle.

He turns toward me, his cheeks on fire, just like when I saw him emerge from the steam-filled bathing room half-naked.

"Do you want the honor of killing it?" he asks. "All yours if you like."

"There's nothing honorable in killing an adversary when they're on the ground," I say, panting.

He looks at me with his blue eyes, reminiscent of the already distant summer sky.

I suddenly find him irresistibly attractive—the way he stands there in the full light, in his element, in the middle of a rustling forest. He looks like a young faun who's leaped from the pages of Ovid, a halo of blondness.

His rugged good looks take my breath away. I feel slightly light headed with . . . butterflies in my stomach?

What's happening to me?

"But what about the buck's heart?" he says softly. "The grand equerry said the ones who brought it back would be the conquerors of the day. We could show him what we're worth, you and I . . ."

"I have nothing to prove to that boor," I say, coming closer to Tristan. "I have nothing to prove to the court. But you can prove to me that you're a free man, not a servile courtier. You can take the liberty to spare that beast."

Tristan's eyes look troubled.

The wind brashly lifts his blond hair.

My silver hair whips my face.

"Spare the buck for liberty . . . ," he says, "or for a date?"

I walk over to him, guided by a surge of feeling from deep in my gut. More than a feeling . . . a desire.

I stand on tiptoes and rest my hand on the gash on his face. The scar makes him more real in my eyes than all the courtiers and their smooth-powdered skin.

Then I kiss him on his partially open lips, taking my breath from his mouth, letting him take his from mine.

He tastes like tender ferns and budding flowers, a flavor of the underbrush in springtime that reminds me of the Auvergne more than ever. Yes, he tastes like life itself, in the middle of a Versailles filled with death. I bring my hands to the neckline of his open shirt, grazing his chest, which heaves from exertion, his heart drumming away. Gently, he glides his fingers under my jacket to encircle my quivering waist.

Overwhelmed by our kiss, I barely register the buck rising to his feet and slowly taking off in the bushes. Then the deep sound of the hunting horn blares, making the tall grasses in the clearing sway. It's

Montfaucon calling us back from the other side of the river. But I don't pay attention.

The only thing that matters is this boy whom I barely know and whom I actually badly need. Pressed against him, I feel totally alive one last time before I throw myself into a mission where I will die.

"Diane . . . ," he says, choked up. "I wish this could last forever . . . but you'll catch cold."

"Not in your arms."

"My arms won't be able to warm you against the approaching winter, and your jacket is torn."

I look down. It's true. The thorns from the thickets slashed my right sleeve.

"Take mine," Tristan says softly, removing his velvet jacket.

He stops just as he's ready to place it over my shoulders.

"Your blouse, it's torn too . . . ," he says.

"Doesn't matter," I reply.

But the sound of his voice puts me on alert—it sounds suddenly serious, more . . . distant?

I lower my eyes. The sleeve of my blouse is torn the whole length down, revealing the skin underneath.

In the middle of the ripped cotton, at the crook of the elbow, a purplish puncture scar is visible on my pale skin: the shameful mark of a commoner.

18

UNMASKED

"Gastefriche, La Roncière, you'll be punished for your impudence!" roars a voice behind us—the grand equerry.

I snatch the jacket from Tristan's hands so that I can put it on and hide my bare arm.

We glance at each other for a fleeting second, his sky-blue eyes suddenly blue-black with anger.

Montfaucon emerges from the thickets on his steed, dripping wet from the river water.

"Didn't you hear the horn calling you back?" he scolds us, his waxy forehead covered in sweat as if he's perspiring yellow bile. "Or were you too busy chasing the buck, who obviously got away?"

He spits on the ground, his filthy habit to show contempt. But if he could see the scar on my elbow, his face would twist in rage.

"I knew what both of you were from the first day: arrogant. You think the Sip of the King is yours by right. But I'll do everything in my power to prevent you from taking part. Do you hear me? Everything."

"Monsieur—" Tristan starts to say, making my blood freeze in fear that he'll denounce me as a commoner if only to redeem himself in the eyes of the director.

"Silence, La Roncière!" the grand equerry bellows. "One more word and I'm expelling you from the school. As for you, Gastefriche, don't think for a minute that your status as a ward offers you eternal protection against your insolence. You'll both head back without uttering another word, at the head of the convoy, just like the condemned led to the gallows."

The return trip takes place under a gloomy atmosphere marked by the weary pounding of hooves. No more neighing, no more barking: the horses, like the dogs, are exhausted. The riders have stopped talking. In this deathly silence, just feet away from the grand equerry, who's right behind us and watching us like a hawk, it's impossible for me to communicate with Tristan. Without his jacket, he's shivering on his horse. His blond hair, hanging on either side of his face, hides his scar and eyes. If Montfaucon hadn't threatened him with expulsion, I'm sure he would have already denounced me.

Back in the school courtyard, the grand equerry orders that we stay cloistered until the following day with no lunch or dinner in two rooms at opposite sides of the Grande Écurie. Madame Thérèse leads me to my cell; General Barvók, the quartermaster in the boys' wing, does the same with Tristan.

And so I return to the room with the dormer window that I was locked in two months ago. Since then, the only window in the room has been boarded up with thick wood panels to prevent anyone from escaping over the rooftops. The only source of light comes from the small fireplace, where Madame Thérèse had logs placed so I wouldn't die of cold during my punishment.

In a sickening replay of the past, I crumple on the iron bed I thought I'd never see again.

I had every chance going for me, and I messed everything up. Over the past weeks, I escaped from many close calls: being sent to a convent, being raped by a repulsive brute of a soldier, being ensnared in the clutches of vampyres out hunting, and being suspected by the king himself . . . and for what? To lower my guard in front of the dreamy eyes of a boarder I was supposed to manipulate, just days before the tests for the Sip of the King . . . I didn't have the right to lose my grip over myself.

I was weak. Cowardly.

Maman, Papa, my brothers, can you forgive me for letting you down?!

Again, I pummel the comforter with my fists until I've exhausted the last of my remaining strength.

Only then, gasping for breath, in a room barely heated by the flames in the fireplace, my body spent, I let myself think.

What if Tristan hasn't said anything?

After all, when Naoko found the real Diane's nobility papers, she didn't turn me in. On the contrary, she helped me falsify the papers. Am I crazy to hope for the same indulgence from Tristan? When he held me in his arms, I believe I felt affection . . . yes, I'm sure of it.

The thought reassures me a little, but another immediately shrouds my hopefulness: Tristan assumed he was embracing an aristocrat, not a daughter of the people, one who's been pulling the wool over everybody's eyes.

The doubt tortures me.

I don't know much about love. Aside from the slightly stiff example of my parents' devoted marriage, and the crazy, catastrophic romance between Bastien and the baronette, I have few benchmarks. I had some encounters with boys back in Butte-aux-Rats, but they were too awestruck by my gray hair, or perhaps they were intimidated by my intellect. I can't put myself in the shoes of a disappointed beau. I can't put myself in Tristan's head. The last look he gave me before we separated plays in a loop in my brain. What did I see there? Disbelief? Doubt? Hate?

I don't know.

I don't know!

Having this sword of Damocles hovering above my head is too much. I need to be certain of Tristan's silence—my dearest wish.

"My dearest wish . . . ," I say in a whisper.

The last time I made a wish, an invisible genie granted it—my *guardian demon*, as Naoko would say.

And what if I asked for his help again?

Is such a thing even possible?

Now that we're well into autumn and that winter is nearly here, I don't know if the recluse of the Grande Écurie is still running around on the rooftops. Maybe he stays away from the big chimney shaft he usually goes down, in case someone lit a fire early in the season.

The small fireplace in my bedroom crackles softly.

I toss water from the jug to kill the flames. The fire's minuscule warmth is instantly replaced by a penetrating cold. I lower my head to look under the lintel. A hard-to-see flue, about half a foot wide, goes up to a small circle of glacial daylight. It's much too narrow for me to glide through but large enough to carry my voice.

"Oh, recluse of the Grande Écurie, if you can hear me, stop Tristan de La Roncière from talking until the end of the month," I yell into the flue.

My words fly up into the chimney, awaking cavernous echoes.

Only the whistling wind answers me from above.

I remember that the recluse who haunts the school's rooftops comes out only at night. So I'll have to keep at it until nighttime and beyond, endlessly repeating my request in the hopes that he hears me . . . and that he comes through.

"Mademoiselle de Gastefriche . . . ? Oh!"

I become vaguely conscious of the panicked cries around me.

Hazy outlines of servants come and go in front of my half-closed, seemingly frozen eyelids.

My body, too, is numb, insensitive to the hands rubbing it.

Madame Thérèse's orders burst forth in the dim room, dry and sharp as always when she talks to her subordinates.

"Well, don't just stand there! Help me get her down to the fifth floor. To the room with the mare tapestries, it's the warmest one. Get the fire going again! And go make some sage herbal tea."

I'm carried through dark attic hallways until we reach a room covered in tapestries. These ancient, faded wall hangings depict horses twisted in strange postures. The thickness of the cloth retains the heat from the blaze in the fireplace. Here, ensconced in a deep armchair next to the hearth, I feel my nerve endings come back to life. The governess scrutinizes me from the stool she placed near the fire, her expression a mix of worry and anger.

"Diane, why didn't you tell the guards that your fire had gone out?" she wants to know.

"I . . . I didn't notice . . . ," I manage to stammer.

It's a lie, of course. I spent the night whispering into the unlit flue, in that icy room, until the cold numbed me and the weight of fatigue made me lose consciousness.

"First, that river you rushed into during the deer hunt, then this past night with no heat—you could have caught your death and risked my life as well," Madame Thérèse scolds me, her ribboned mobcap shaking with indignation. "What would I have told the king?"

There we have it. The governess isn't tending to me out of care or devotion; she's worried about incurring royal wrath.

"I'm better," I assure her. "It wasn't so cold in the room. The fire probably didn't go out until early morning."

Madame Thérèse heaves a sigh of relief. The king's ward is safe, and her own reputation as well.

I force myself to smile.

"I'm more worried about Tristan de La Roncière," I add. "Yesterday, he gave me his jacket and made the return trip from the hunting grounds in only his shirt. I hope he's not ill because of me . . . ?"

Madame Thérèse's face hardens again.

"Don't talk to me about that one! He ran off during the night, just as you did last month. We should have boarded up his window as well. Little savages from the countryside, that's what you both are." She swiftly gets up. "Enough chatter. You've gotten some color back. You seem warmed up. Drink your herbal tea, now. You'll find clean clothes on the dresser. I'll leave you to get changed, but be quick about it. You know as well as I do that General Barvók cannot abide tardiness where his lessons are concerned."

The art-of-courtly-manners class goes by like in a dream. I can see the general gesturing on the rostrum, moving his metal pincers to show us the appropriate glass to choose for each beverage—all from a complete assortment of crystal glassware—but I don't hear a word he's saying. It's as if there's an infinite space between him and me. Shooting pains in my legs and arms come and go, no doubt due to sore muscles from the hunt. My body feels numb, maybe because I stayed near the fire too long. As for the migraine pounding my skull, I've become used to the sensation.

The only thing that matters is that Tristan—the only person who could have incriminated me—has been taken out of the equation.

At lunch, the dining hall is buzzing with his disappearance, each girl floating her own theory. Did he run off to go back to the Ardennes that he missed so much? Did he try to enter the palace the same way I did a month ago? Some girls seem to wonder why I'm still here. Poppy, in particular, gives me dirty looks from across the room. She's been avoiding me since the deer hunt, as if she's mad at me for seeing her spit blood into her handkerchief. She had previously assured me that she had just caught a cold, but in truth it seems to be much worse than that . . . what is her secret ailment? I can't ask her, and I suspect she wouldn't answer anyway.

In the afternoon, all during the rehearsal in the ring, the grand equerry doesn't say a word to me. He seems to have decided that I'm not even deserving of his invectives. Unless he stays quiet to let the musicians play; these last few days, a half dozen Swiss Guards have been invited to the musicians' balcony that overlooks the ring. With their flutes and drums, they play the military rondo that accompanies the horses' dance. I'm content just following the general movement, carted around by Typhon like a sack of potatoes to the sound of the sprightly rondo. I try to convince myself that it's the stallion's trot that makes my teeth chatter even louder than the drums, but that's before I surrender to the evidence: I'm shivering from head to toe.

"You're so pale," Naoko tells me when we're getting ready in the bathing room that evening.

"Really? Just put some more blush on my cheeks before we go down to dinner."

"Are you sure you wouldn't rather rest in bed with a nice broth?" she persists. "You look feverish and ill."

"Out of the question," I croak. "Besides, tonight is the last lesson on the art of vampyrism before the start of the tests. Only four days away."

Over these last several weeks now, Suraj and Lucrèce taught us to discern the most precious vintages among the hematic vials; to decant the blood by pouring it into carafes before serving it to vampyres; to fluff up the padded silk pillows of a coffin so it's at its most comfortable when the lords of the night are at rest. Tonight, the squires are going to show us how to care for bats, outdoors in the icy courtyard.

"What's the point of preparing for the tests if you die of pneumonia beforehand?" Naoko says.

"You don't want to help me? No big deal."

I take the pot of blush from Naoko's hands and apply a good layer over my cheekbones. My fingers tremble uncontrollably. A guilty conscience gnaws at my feverish mind. I know that I'm being harsh with Naoko; she only wants what's best for me. But I can't let anyone compromise my chances of winning the competition.

I'm able to swallow only a few mouthfuls of bread at dinner. A horrible nauseous feeling knots my stomach. Under my brocade dress, I feel like my body is burning up and freezing at the same time. I don't know how I'm going to last through the art-of-vampyrism lesson outside. But as I'm about to get up to retrieve my fur coat, the two squires enter the dining hall.

"Tonight, the class is taking place indoors," Suraj announces.

They've brought a third person with them—a young redheaded servant who's barely older than me, someone I often cross paths with in the school hallways.

It's not a fever that's making her tremble. It's terror.

"The care of bats can wait," says Lucrèce du Crèvecœur in her taupe leather dress. "Instead, we're going to demonstrate a bleeding in front of everyone—a critical skill for those who want to serve the king." She gestures toward the servant with the tip of her index finger, the one sheathed in an iron gauntlet. "This thief was caught red-handed in the kitchens this afternoon. She was stealing a pound of flour, isn't that right, Madame Thérèse?"

The governess nods vigorously, shaking the ribbons of her mobcap.

"Toinette disappointed us," she says coldly.

The young servant moans in distress.

"I beg you, Madame Thérèse! I swear I would have paid for the flour as soon as I could!"

"Don't we feed you enough, little ingrate?"

"It wasn't for me. It was for my family. As I've said, my parents are ill, and my carpenter brother can't work right now. He broke his leg last month when he fell from the—"

"Scaffolding. You already told us repeatedly that he tumbled when he was working on the expansion project of the palace. Over and over."

Unmoved, the governess crosses her arms over her chest. More than ever, I see her as a traitor to her class, someone who raised herself from the fourth estate up to the Grande Écurie so she could treat commoners with even more contempt than if she were an aristocrat.

"Not only do you live off the king, but your brother does too," she accuses. "And this is how you thank him—by stealing his food supply. A real stab in the back."

"He who will steal an egg will steal an ox," Lucrèce states. "And whoever commits a crime must be punished. If it makes you feel better, Toinette, your punishment will serve as a lesson to the boarders of the Grande Écurie."

Unfeeling to the poor servant's pleas for mercy, she grabs Toinette's right arm with the same lightning speed I witnessed during the episode with the vampyric roses.

Brutally lifting the cotton sleeve of the dress, Lucrèce exposes the servant's puncture marks.

"The Mortal Code stipulates that every thief must pay threefold the price of their theft, in blood," Lucrèce says. "But given that this involves royal property, it will be tripled. We're talking about nine pounds of premier-quality flour, rounded up to ten. The equivalent of one full quart of commoner blood."

A savage spark gleams in the squire's icy-blue eyes while muffled gasps fill the room. Everyone must have done the same arithmetic I did: Toinette can't weigh much; she's got maybe four quarts of blood in her body. So one-quarter of her blood will be drawn—huge!

Suraj places a leather case on the nearest table and opens it to take out implements I recognize only too well—needles, vials, and rubber tubes. My father used the same implements every month to bleed his own family and the people in the village.

The squire sits the trembling servant down in a chair.

"Calm down, Toinette," he says in his deep voice. "It's just a bad moment that will soon be over."

Unlike Lucrèce, he doesn't seem to derive any pleasure from the punishment imposed on the servant. His professional demeanor reminds me of my father's when he reluctantly carried out his duty as prescribed by the Mortal Code.

"We need a volunteer to practice the bleeding," he announces, sweeping the room with his dark eyes.

Several hands go up.

But Lucrèce ignores them all and calls on Rafael, even though he didn't raise his hand. In fact, he's hiding at the back of the room, his black attire blending in with the shadowed wall.

"You, Caballero de Montesueño," she says. "We've never heard a peep from you in the art-of-vampyrism class. Tonight is your chance."

Under his ocher turban, Suraj's face becomes drawn.

"Why him?" he asks.

"And why not?" answers Lucrèce.

Judging by her venomous look, my guess is that she knows about his unhappy romance with Rafael. Worse, I sense that she's reveling in her knowledge. She wants them to confront each other, because she knows that nothing will make them suffer more.

But the former lovers have to keep their secret. If they balk, it would arouse suspicion. Rafael comes slowly out of the shade and walks over to the chair where Toinette sits. He doesn't dare look at Suraj, and Suraj doesn't look at him.

"Take this needle," the squire says. "Hook it up to this rubber tube, and connect the other end to the largest vial."

Suraj issues the orders in a cold, detached voice, treating his old lover like a stranger. Are my ears the only ones to detect a tiny tremor in his deep voice? Are my eyes the only ones to see his brows furrow as he observes the back of Rafael's neck, the latter busy with the task at hand?

Rafael does everything without saying a word, the metal and the glass knocking together.

"Now, practice a tourniquet. Swell the vein above the puncture tip. Push the needle in in one sure motion. There."

The horrible stream of blood flowing into the vial fills the silence, reminding me of all the times I had to give mine. I want to scream, run over to help this young girl, whose face turns white and whose pupils tremble in terror. Toinette could be me, my brothers, everyone I loved.

Unable to hold back any longer, overcome with fever and memories, I shout, "You have to stop the bleeding. She won't survive!"

Lucrèce glares at me.

"What do you mean, stop?" she scolds. "Do you need eyeglasses, Gastefriche? Don't you see that the vial is half-empty?"

A cold sweat trickles down my spine. But I can't let Toinette die without speaking up!

"No need for eyeglasses to see that the commoner can't take much more," I say. "If you bleed her longer, she'll die . . ." I force myself to add a derogatory remark. "It would be a shame to lose a maid in the prime of life, especially when she can still be useful for years to come."

At that very instant, the rubber snaps off. Rafael just made the tourniquet pop. He pulls the needle out from Toinette's arm, and using his hand with nails polished in black, he applies a compress on the site of the jab.

"Gastefriche, Montesueño, enough with the compassion!" Lucrèce shouts, clicking the articulated blades of her iron gauntlet to convey her impatience. "The law is the law. The vial must be filled to the brim with the culprit's blood." A nasty smile spreads over her thin lips. "Unless one of you prefers to offer their own blood to finish the bleeding?"

I stop breathing. My legs go weak.

If I reveal one of my arms, exposing the puncture scars, it's over for me and my vengeance.

"I . . . I—" I stammer, my lips trembling.

"I'll give blood to finish the bleeding," Rafael cuts in.

A murmur of astonishment swirls in the room.

"We're surely not going to bleed an aristocrat," Suraj says, livid. "It's . . . it's not possible."

"Perhaps not in India, but in the Vampyria it is," Lucrèce affirms. "The Mortal Code gives us the authority, per Article Twenty-Three." She starts to recite an extract from the horrible edict: "In case a debtor is unable to pay his debt of blood, the latter can be paid off by a mortal of equal or superior rank."

For the first time, Suraj and Rafael exchange a look. It feels like a clap of lightning went off between the black-eyed warrior and the green-eyed knight—disdain and defiance, deception and desire, bitterness and . . . love?

Lucrèce loses interest in me. Tormenting her teammate gives her far greater pleasure. She takes a new needle and a new tube from the case and hands them to the shocked squire.

"Come on, Suraj!" she says, gleefully. "You've taken down dozens of ghouls at the Innocents with your famous double-bladed dagger. Certainly you can practice a little jab."

Toinette takes off in wobbly steps, sputtering hushed thanks, and Rafael takes her place on the chair.

The shaking needle comes closer to his arm, his veins already prominent due to the tourniquet.

I no longer know if it's Suraj's fingers that are trembling or my feverish body.

As soon as the needle plunges into Rafael's skin, it's as if it's sinking into my own arm.

I remember the pain from all the bleedings I had to submit to since childhood, the shame of all the tithes poured into hundreds of vials stamped with my name.

As if I've been drained of all my blood at once, my head starts to spin . . .

The room twirls . . .

And the Shadows grab hold of me.

19

NAOKO

"Jeanne . . ."

"Maman?"

My mother's figure appears in the dark.

Her long brown hair floats around her pale face.

I feel like I'm floating, too, as if I'm weightless.

"Oh, Maman, I didn't think I'd see you again!" I cry out, my voice broken by sobs.

I glide toward her so that I can hug her.

But the more I advance, the more she seems to slip away.

Same as the passing clouds when Bastien and I distinguished ephemeral shapes that vanished in an instant.

"Jeanne . . . ," her pale, nearly transparent lips manage to say weakly.

"Yes, it's me. Don't go away! Stay with me. Stay . . ." Suddenly, I open my eyes, the cry dying in my throat. ". . . with me."

I'm once again aware of my body. I'm buried in a deep bed under many layers of blankets. Even my hair is wrapped snug in a thick night bonnet.

"Jeanne?" says a voice that isn't my mother's.

I turn my head on my sweaty pillow. It's Naoko, sitting on a stool by my bedside.

Behind her is a fireplace with roaring flames next to a window with drawn curtains.

"Where . . . where am I?" I ask.

"In the room with the mare tapestries. Madame Thérèse had a bed sent up. You've been sleeping here since last night. She wasn't about to put you back in the attic after you nearly caught your death."

I start to recognize the old tapestries hanging on the walls. The fireplace is the only source of light in the room, casting glimmering, dancing figures on the worn tapestry motifs. The herds of horses seem animated . . . but they're not alone. For the first time, I notice humans, half-faded, among the quadrupeds. Men and women fleeing at full speed, as terrorized as the statues of prey that decorate the Hunting Wall. The mares that chase them have eyes black as night and mouths foaming with bloodred saliva.

"The Mares of Diomedes . . . ," I say softly, suddenly remembering a chapter of Ovid's *Metamorphoses*, the one that tells how Diomedes, the cruel king of Thrace, tossed strangers as feed to his carnivorous mares.

"Actually, it's a myth we studied with Chantilly last year," Naoko says.

Hearing about the school and classes, a rush of memories tumbles forth: my conversation with the governess in this very room, Tristan's disappearance, my day spent ignoring how ill I was . . . my unease during the art-of-vampyrism lesson.

"Yesterday, did I . . . did I faint in front of everyone?" I ask.

Naoko nods.

Seized with panic, I touch my body under the covers. My dress was removed, and someone put me in a cotton nightgown.

"My arms!" I say, my throat tight.

"Don't worry. As your school guide, I offered to put you to bed. I'm the only one who saw your puncture marks. I slipped your watch and tinderbox lighter into the pocket of your nightgown. And I hurried over to your bedside this morning."

I breathe a sigh of relief. Once again, Naoko saved my hide.

"Thank you, from the bottom of my heart," I tell her.

"You're welcome."

"No! This time I won't let you shrug it off. You have to tell me how I can thank you."

Swept up with emotion, I'm gripped by a coughing fit that tears at my lungs.

Afterward, a pulsing migraine pierces my skull under the night bonnet placed on my head.

Naoko puts a cool compress on my forehead.

"Get better; that'll be a good start," she says. "Don't waste your energy on words."

"I won't be quiet until you tell me what I can do for you," I insist. "Why all the mystery? I told you everything about me, but I have the feeling you're still hiding something."

A shadow passes over Naoko's face.

She's often reproached me for concealing part of the truth, rightly so. But today I'm accusing her of the same thing, and I sense that it hits her hard.

"You're correct, Jeanne; I'm hiding something," she says. "I was waiting for the right time to tell you. I guess that time is now." She takes a deep breath, pauses, and in a halting voice, finally continues. "I . . . I'm not exactly who you think I am."

Naoko's face has always seemed enigmatic, but never more so than in this draft-proof room, by the sketchy light of the fire. She looks as if she belongs to the same world of legends as the ancient tapestries behind her, populated by beings rising from the depths of a mythic past.

"You're my best friend—that's what I believe," I say with all the energy I can muster. "Not only at the Grande Écurie but always. *You're the best friend I've ever had.* That's the pure and simple truth, and nothing will change my mind."

My words are heartfelt and sincere.

"Nothing will change your mind, really?" Naoko repeats.

"Nothing."

"Not even . . . this?"

As she speaks, she raises a hand to her bun at the back of her neck and takes out the long lacquered hair stick that holds it in place.

Her black hair falls densely across her shoulders and down the middle of her back—a formidable head of hair that would make Poppy green with envy. I realize that it's the first time I've seen Naoko with her hair loose. Whether in class, at mealtime, or even in the bathing room, she always has it in a bun, and I'm not allowed to brush it.

"You have the hair of a goddess. Is that what's supposed to test our friendship?" I say, not sure where she's going with this. "You . . . you think I'm jealous?"

By way of response, Naoko turns around on the stool.

Her back is completely covered by the black shroud of her mane, like a professional mourner.

Her hands go up the sides of her neck, and she grabs a fist of hair in each. Then she parts the hair laterally like two curtain panels.

I can't hold back a cry.

"Oh!"

Just inches above her neck, between the thick strands of hair, is a . . . mouth.

Two elongated lips, extending from behind one ear to behind the other, sealed, cut through Naoko's head of hair like a raised scar.

"It frightens you, doesn't it?" Naoko asks, her back still turned to me.

"I . . . uh . . . no," I sputter. "I was just taken by surprise."

"That wasn't a cry of surprise but a cry of fright. And disgust."

I want to tell Naoko to let her hair fall back so it hides this inhuman mouth, a mouth that stretches six inches from side to side. I want to beg her to turn around so that I see her face and her real mouth—smaller, delicate, stained carmine.

But I force myself to overcome my revulsion. I suffered through a lot of nasty stares when it came to my hair back in Butte-aux-Rats, so I'm not one to judge anyone's appearance. Besides, that mouth is probably not a mouth—just a fleshy outgrowth that looks like a mouth, a congenital anomaly, to use my father's words. Certainly impressive but, in the end, as harmless as the color of my hair.

"You have a small birth defect, that's all," I say, trying to minimize the situation. "Not a big deal. And this little secret is safe with me. I won't let the cat out of the bag."

"Well, my evilmouth got the neighbor's cat back in Japan. It became so worked up it gobbled up the poor animal alive."

I'm speechless.

Is she joking?

Utterly confused, I stare at Naoko's neck as a tiny movement contracts the monstrous lips. The corners quiver and stretch out more and more. A sudden chill makes the hairs on my skin stand on end. That piece of flesh that I thought was dead is very much alive, and . . . it's smiling hideously at me.

Before the lips draw back and reveal the teeth hidden there, Naoko suddenly lets the heavy curtain of hair fall down.

She turns to face me, looking ghastly white.

"The evilmouth never fails to wake up when I expose it to fresh evening air," she tells me in a strangled voice. "And I assure you that's not something you want to see."

Distress furrows Naoko's forehead.

I take a trembling hand out from under the blankets and place it on her arm. I sense that's what she needs right now, more than anything else—to be touched.

"When I was little, it was just a bump behind my head. My nanny didn't think it was worth worrying about," she says, answering the questions I don't dare ask. "But when I turned ten, I felt the bump start to tremble, to move . . . *to come alive.* Ever since, I couldn't deny the evidence. An abomination was grafted to my skin. I refused to let my nanny take care of me after that. I said I could brush my own hair. I kept all my father's servants at a distance. And I grew up alone, with my secret: the evilmouth, as I baptized it. Because to me it represents pure malice."

I swallow with difficulty.

"Do you mean that no one knows about this? Not even your family?"

"I'm an only child. My father has always been too busy with his career as a diplomat to bother with my education. And my mother, well, she died in childbirth, at the hands of the imperial doctors. She paid the price of the Shadows, and so do I."

I remember how Naoko spoke about the official doctors at the court of Japan, comparing them to the doctors of the Hematic Faculty—both shamelessly using alchemy to manipulate the Shadows . . . as for the icy shiver I felt when I sensed the monstrous mouth starting to move, of course it was the telltale sign of the Shadows.

"For many years, my parents were childless," Naoko goes on as the fire casts dancing glimmers on her cheeks. "As a last recourse, my father asked the imperial doctors to treat my mother so that she could bear a child at any cost. I don't know what treatments she was subjected to. All I know is that she lost her life in the process . . . and that I was born with this 'small birth defect,' as you called it."

"Naoko, I didn't know," I say.

"In their search for knowledge, the imperial doctors conduct experiments that often lead to living horrors," she continues, ignoring my attempt at an apology. "In Japan, we call them *yokai*: monsters. They're generally identified at birth and burned without further ceremony. In the West, the inquisitors of the Faculty apply the same law to the results of their failed experiments." She frowns. "The scholars don't encumber themselves with scruples; for them, the ends always justify the means. I've been lucky enough to slip through the net until now."

Everything is suddenly explained: Naoko's solitude, not having anyone help her with her hair, her mistrust of others . . . her desperate search for a friend she could confide in. I've been on high alert for several weeks now at the Grande Écurie, but Naoko has been keeping a fatal secret her entire life.

"You're not a *yokai*," I tell her, squeezing my hand on her arm. "The monsters are the ones who burn innocent infants."

She shakes her head, seemingly disillusioned.

"You say that because you haven't seen the evilmouth open. During the early years, I also gave it the benefit of the doubt. When I felt it move at night behind my neck, I knew it was hungry. I would discreetly gather leftovers at dinnertime and offer them to it in the privacy of my bedroom. At first, a few balls of rice and a swig of milk kept it quiet. Then, as I got older, I had to steal pieces of raw fish and leftover yakitori skewers to satisfy the thing. I tried hard to ignore the chewing, swallowing noises at the back of my neck. Until one night in May, when the neighbor's cat got into my bedroom through the open window. It must have been lured by the lingering scent of milk in a bowl I'd left lying around." Naoko looks repulsed.

"The wild yowling is what woke me up. The poor creature was screeching, howling as it tried to get away. But it couldn't, because I was holding it above my head with all my strength." Naoko grabs my wrist and holds it tight, carried by emotion. "Do you understand? I captured the animal in my sleep! Or more likely the evilmouth possessed me, plunging me into a state of sleepwalking to satisfy its appetite."

Naoko releases my wrist, her clenched fingers leaving a mark.

"I was horrified. My arms were covered in scratches. I dropped the cat," she says. "The poor creature took off, limping on three legs—because the fourth leg was nothing more than a bloody stump. Behind me, I heard the crunching of bones and cartilage. Can you imagine? I'll never forget that sound. Never!"

Naoko plasters her palms over her ears as if she wants to silence the sound of a memory that will always haunt her.

"That night, I understood that the evilmouth was hungry for fresh flesh," she goes on. "The same way vampyres thirst for blood. I decided I'd never again yield to its appetite. So I stopped feeding it at night. But it wasn't enough. Grafted as it is to my body, it seemed to benefit from what I ingested into my own mouth. So I became a vegetarian, and now it's totally deprived of meat. The first months were hard. I wasn't sleeping at all. I had to crush a pillow on my neck for hours at a time to squelch the evilmouth's furious clacking teeth, which only quieted down at dawn. Like all abominations, the one I bear within me goes to sleep in the early-morning hours."

"Oh, my poor Naoko," I say, observing the circles under her eyes in a new, dramatic light. "I'm so sorry. I can't imagine your ordeal, the war you wage every night."

She gives me a weak smile.

"It's strange that you use that word, because that's exactly how I view my relationship with the evilmouth: it's war. And as in every war, one starts to harden. The first battles were terrifying, chaotic. Come morning I'd be in tears, convinced I'd never make it through another night. But in time, I regained self-confidence. I noted that my vegetarian diet weakened the evilmouth. Little by little, those clacking teeth were less demanding, as if a certain lethargy had set in. Each night I managed to steal a few more minutes of sleep." Naoko takes a deep breath, her face finally relaxing. She's back to being herself. "If my struggle against the evilmouth is a war, then the front lines have stopped in their tracks. At night, when it starts to tremble, I meditate behind the curtains of my canopy bed until that contemptible thing goes numb. Only then do I go back to sleep."

As if to conclude her testimony, the sound of a distant bell rings behind the door from the depths of the Grande Écurie. It's the bell calling boarders to morning classes.

Naoko expertly gathers her long hair into a compact bun, burying her dozing nemesis. The lacquered hair stick seals the muzzle of hair.

"There. Now you know my secret," she says.

"I'll guard it as closely as I do my own," I assure her.

Her smile widens a little.

"I wouldn't have confided in you if I wasn't sure," she says, getting up.

I grab hold of her arm.

"Just a minute. Don't go yet. Now's the time to tell me how I can help you. Because there must be something I can do, right?"

For an instant, we hear only the crackling logs in the fireplace.

"For a long time, my father has been after me to take part in the Sip of the King, a supreme honor," she says. "Things haven't been good between us since I've refused. I said I was too shy. In truth, the idea of drinking the king's blood revolts me. I hate the Shadows with all my heart. They corrupt everything they touch. They reawaken the dead and cover the flesh of the living with monstrous tumors. They transform even the most beautiful of nature's ornaments—innocent roses—into abominations." Naoko starts to tremble. "I don't dare imagine how one sip of royal blood, saturated with shadowessence, would affect the evilmouth. It would awaken, for sure. And if anyone finds out, it'll be the end of me. The inquisitors will send me right to the butcher."

"No one will find out," I assure her.

"Maybe. But I'll have to be doubly vigilant when I enter the court in a year. Given my father's position, it's unthinkable that I won't find myself there. How will the evilmouth react when it's surrounded by immortals, by all that blood . . . by the Shadows in all their glory? At the palace, more than ever, I'll need a friend." Her eyes shine in the light of the fire. "Don't abandon me, Jeanne. Don't run away like Tristan did. The two of you seemed so close, and then, from one day to the next, he just vanished. Don't do that to me, I beg you. Stay by my side. Kill your Viscount de Mortange if that's your destiny, but stay alive—stay alive for me!"

My throat tightens.

It's the first time that Naoko, who's always provided aid without hesitation, asks something of me. And yet I can't grant her only request. I don't see how I'll survive assassinating the king in a few days. Naoko is in the dark about my crazy plan: she doesn't realize she's talking to someone who's condemned.

"Whatever happens, I'll always be your friend," I say.

She thanks me and escapes from my limp grip, heading into the hallway where Chantilly's class awaits her at the other end.

20

REMORSE

The day goes by in silence, in the warm cocoon of the old tapestries.

Every two hours the Swiss Guard posted to the room knocks on the door, then enters to deposit logs in the fireplace. At the stroke of noon, a servant brings me a tureen of steaming broth and slices of fresh bread, enough to make my insides all toasty. I'm able to raise the spoon to my lips without shaking, and soon I don't feel any more body aches.

But as my fever drops, my anxiety rises.

I'm mad at myself for not having confessed everything to Naoko. For the first time in weeks, my resolution to destroy the king wavers. Until now, I was convinced I had nothing to lose: no one was left who was counting on me down here, and I wasn't counting on anyone either. That's no longer the case. I'll never forget Naoko's eyes, trembling with friendship. But neither can I forget the blast that tore Papa to pieces, the swords that slashed Maman's throat and decapitated Valère, and the rapier that eviscerated Bastien. I must avenge them.

Another source of guilt torments me: Tristan.

Everyone at the Grande Écurie now seems to think that he fled like a coward. I'm the only one who knows the truth—I had him kidnapped, maybe even killed, by a corpse-eating monster.

I'd like to chase that thought out of my mind so I can focus entirely on my vengeance, but I can't. I can't convince myself that Tristan was just a convenient pawn I discarded, an offspring of the aristocracy belonging to the enemy camp. My pleas to the recluse turn in a loop in my head: *"Oh, recluse of the Grande Écurie, if you can hear me, stop Tristan de La Roncière from talking until the end of the month."*

And what if he stopped him from talking . . . forever?

I know nothing about that monster, only that he comes out at night and that he feeds off human remains. Maybe he doesn't scorn live prey . . . ?

I have to find Tristan. Not to free him, no, I can't afford that luxury before I avenge my loved ones. But I have to know if he's alive or dead, or the doubts will drive me crazy and keep me from my mission.

"You're not as pale," Madame Thérèse says as she comes into the room after the four o'clock bell rings behind the thick tapestries.

She puts a clean dress down on the small table by the corner of the fireplace. Then she walks over to the window and brusquely opens the curtains, letting in rays of light. After I've spent a whole day in semi-darkness, the light dazzles me.

"Tonight, you'll be able to dine with your classmates and return to the dormitory," the governess declares. "You'll be back on your feet for tomorrow's classes, and in three days you'll be able to compete for the Sip of the King. For now, you have three hours ahead of you to dress and get ready before nightfall."

And before the recluse of the Grande Écurie wakes up, I think. I absolutely have to get into his lair before dusk. If Tristan is still alive, I'm sure that's where I'll find him.

THE COURT OF SHADOWS

"I am feeling slightly better, thank you, Madame Thérèse," I say, making my voice quaver. "But I'm still weak. I think one more night by the fire would do me good. And I prefer to skip supper tonight. I'm a little bit queasy."

The governess furrows her brows. In her unyielding desire for order, she wants me to fall back into the rhythm of the school as soon as possible. But fear that she'll be accused of neglecting the health of one of the king's wards makes her tilt in my favor.

I simulate a coughing fit, fluttering my eyelids.

"*Koff . . . koff . . .* I don't want to risk a relapse."

My little act sweeps her hesitations aside.

"All right, but only one night," she concedes. "Stop talking and go back to sleep. I'll bring you an herbal tea after dinner."

She closes the curtain in one quick gesture, cutting our conversation short, then turns on her heel and bangs the door shut behind her.

The countdown gets into gear in my head. The boarders will dine at seven o'clock, like every night, and the governess will be back at the stroke of eight . . . I have to take action before then. When the Swiss Guard brings new logs, it will be my cue to leave.

A long wait begins, and to kill time, I watch the fire diminish in the hearth.

When the last log is consumed, I climb out of the sheets without making a sound, take off my nightgown, and slip it over one of the bolsters that decorates the bed. Just like I did two months ago when I put my clothes on the baronette's body . . . tonight, it's a rag doll taking my place. I coif it with my night bonnet to complete the illusion, then stuff the bolster under the covers. Only then do I get into the dress the governess brought me, taking care to put my watch and tinderbox lighter in my pocket. Finally, I flatten myself against the wall next to the door.

It doesn't take long before the town church bell rings six o'clock, soon followed by two quick, discreet knocks on the door. I don't answer. The handle turns, the panel opens with a slight creak, and the Swiss Guard enters the room with a basket full of logs. He gives a quick glance at the bed I plumped up with the bolster, which is shrouded by the dark. Satisfied that the patient is sleeping, he treads lightly over to the fireplace and feeds the fire. While his back is turned, I slip out into the hallway.

Unlike the lower levels, the fifth floor doesn't have a dormitory, bedrooms, or classrooms: it's deserted. I make my way in silence, my wool stockings sliding on the cold parquet, until I reach the staircase leading to the attic. Up there, I find a small bedroom with a dormer window that isn't boarded up.

An arctic autumn cold whips my face as I open the windowpane.

The frigid ledge freezes my fingers as I go through the opening.

But it's really seeing the Hunting Wall that chills me. In the waning light of late afternoon, the shadows of the vampyric high reliefs are especially elongated, emphasizing terrifying details. The first time I was on the rooftops, I didn't know the travesties that took place behind that rampart, but now it's as if they've been imprinted on my brain by a red-hot branding iron.

I make my way up the tiles on all fours, my stomach plastered to the roof. The dozen chimney stacks disgorge thick smoke from the fires heating the Grande Écurie . . . all except one, the largest of them all. I was right: the shaft leading to the bowels of the school hasn't been lit, providing a passageway for the thing that burrows there.

The ladder used by the creature two months ago, when he carried me down, is still there. I grab hold of the narrow rungs and descend into the dark belly of the building.

Soon, there's only the grainy texture of the rusted metal under my fingers and the echo of my breathing sent back by the chimney shaft. Now and then, my wool stockings slip on a rung, and I only just get a foothold on the next one. No time to slow down. It'll be night soon.

After a long descent, I finally touch ground. Here in the basement it's not as cold; there seems to be a regular temperature year-round.

"Who's there?" says a voice in the pitch darkness—Tristan's voice!

I lower myself under the chimney lintel, my heart beating fast, torn between fear and relief.

"It's me," I whisper. "Diane."

I take out my lighter and try desperately to get a flame going. The flint reddens, a glimmer in the infinite obscurity.

"Diane?" Tristan says.

"Don't move. Let me light the lantern."

I make my way forward in the dark, groping with my fingers until I find the edge of the table. I pat the surface, locate the lantern, and bring the incandescent flint near the wick.

A flame whooshes to life, illuminating the subterranean room.

The objects on the table are the same as on my previous visit: the clay pitcher, the metal goblet . . . a new pile of human bones, cracked open to extract the marrow.

As for Tristan, I notice that it was useless to tell him not to move. He's tied to the only chair. His ankles and wrists are bound by ropes sticking out from under the thick moth-eaten blankets thrown over his shoulders.

Our eyes meet for the first time since the deer hunt. Under his long blond hair, Tristan's eyes gleam in the light of the lantern. What does he know about me, exactly?

"The other day, in the forest . . . ," I start to say, trying to find the right words. "I don't know what you think you saw, but—"

"Stop," he interrupts. "We don't have time for games. We both know what I saw on your arm—the scar from the tithe. Proof that you're a commoner, an imposter at the Grande Écurie. Proof that you lied to me."

His avalanche of accusations overwhelms me.

"The monster who kidnapped me will be back soon," he continues, leaving me no time to breathe. "He sleeps during the day and wakes at night. That's if I can trust the faint ringing of the church bells that I just make out from the chimney shaft. I haven't seen his face under his hood. I haven't heard the sound of his voice. I've just seen those gnawed bones on the table. I was wondering if the underworld had sent him. But your presence here tells me that you're somehow involved in all this, am I right?" Tristan's eyes pierce me like daggers. "So tell me, after breaking my heart, are you going to free me or let me be devoured?"

The lantern at the end of my arm starts to shake.

"I . . . I don't think that he would devour you," I stammer. "He only seems to gnaw on cadavers. Like . . . like a ghoul."

"Well, that's reassuring. He'll wait until I croak, then savor my bones."

"I can't free you, Tristan! I can't risk having you talk. Not before the Sip of the King."

He raises his chin in defiance, tossing back his hair, exposing his scar.

"Because then you'll tell your demon to release me? You think once you're in the palace, my telling the truth won't be able to affect you? You're very naive if you imagine that the Immutable will prove indulgent toward a commoner who usurps a position of squire." He narrows his eyelids. "Unless you don't plan on sticking around at the court?"

His perceptiveness floors me.

"I don't know what you're imagining, but you leave me no choice," I reply, turning on my heel, my stomach all knotted up.

"Wait!"

I freeze.

"At least give me something to drink before you go. I've been dying of thirst for hours."

I put the lantern on the table, grab the pitcher in a trembling hand, and fill the goblet to the rim. Then I walk over to the chair and bring the cup to Tristan's dry lips, lips that only two days ago kissed me with passion.

Suddenly, the arms I thought were bound are free, sending the sheared ropes flying along with the iron goblet. Tristan grabs my waist with his left hand and pulls me brusquely toward him. With his right hand, he sticks a sharp blade against my neck.

I land on his thighs, pressed tight to his chest.

"Don't you dare cry out and warn your creature. I could accidentally cut your throat," he says into my neck. "Do you hear me, *Diane*? If that's really your name."

I try to twist and turn, but Tristan's hold is too strong, and with the slightest movement I risk impaling myself on the blade.

"The hooded monster made the mistake of leaving a spoon lying on the table," Tristan says. "It took me hours to move the chair over to get the damn thing. I had to shift my weight from one foot to the other, inch by inch, and then it took me still more hours to sharpen the metal of the spoon against the wall with my hands tied. Long, hard work, but worth it: *'A real hunter should only rely on oneself'*—isn't that true?"

Cruel irony. Tristan is spitting back at me the very words I used during the deer hunt.

"When you came down the shaft, I'd just finished cutting the ropes from the armrests," Tristan says hoarsely. "I had only my ankles left. That won't take me long once I've finished with you."

"My disappearance will raise suspicions," I say, breathing heavily. "Montfaucon will send a search party."

"If his search is as effective as the one that failed to find me, your corpse will turn to dust before it ever sees the light of day. Unless your ghoul servant gobbles it up."

"My remains might turn to dust or end up in a ghoul's stomach," I cry, finding my resolve. "But my spirit will haunt you until your dying day, bastard. Liberty or death!"

Proclaiming my mother's motto out loud for the first and last time fills me with wild joy. I swallow a gulp of air to utter a final curse before the makeshift knife silences me forever . . . but just then, Tristan's grasp loosens.

"Go," he says.

I leap off him, and he doesn't try to hold me back.

A metallic noise reverberates on the stone floor. It's the sharpened spoon, which Tristan just threw at my feet.

I grab it and turn toward him, my mind awash in confusion.

"Why . . . ?" I ask, breathing heavily.

"Because maybe I'm not the bastard you take me for. You would've never believed what I'm about to tell you, not with a blade under your throat. You'll probably listen to me more closely with that weapon in your hand."

By the glimmer of the lantern, Tristan suddenly looks transfigured by an inexplicable radiance.

"I often told you that I didn't like the court, and you told me that you didn't either," he says, his eyes sparkling with fervor. "But the truth is that you loathe it from the bottom of your heart, isn't that so? That you would do anything to destroy it? Well, the same holds true for me." He takes a deep breath to steady his voice. "Do you remember the last thing I told you before we kissed, when we were on the deer hunt?"

"I don't know what you're getting at," I say, shaken by what he's just said.

The memory of our brief escape, the happiest moment of my time in Versailles, rushes back at me with all my senses. The biting cold; the musky scent of the horses; Tristan's fiery gaze; and the sentence that I snuffed with a kiss, without truly paying attention.

"'Spare the buck . . . for liberty or for a date,'" I say softly.

The evidence hits me as the words roll off my lips.

"Liberty or *date* . . . liberty or *death* . . . it sounds so close."

I feel like I'm back at the dinner, the evening I met Tristan and we jousted with words. Our strange relationship was born out of word-play . . . so how did I miss what he said by the riverbank?

"When you arrived at the Grande Écurie, I instantly realized you were different from the other boarders," he says. "The way you held your own with Hélénaïs during dinner, then your escape over the rooftops . . . my gut told me you were cut from the same cloth as me—a rebel to the existing order who came to Versailles on a secret mission. But I couldn't ask you directly, in case I was mistaken. So I tried to get closer to you, finding occasions to be by your side and discover more about your mysterious past . . . in vain."

A bittersweet emotion grips my heart. I thought I was the one manipulating Tristan, taking advantage of his feelings, but he was playing the same game.

"In the forest the other day, I couldn't hold back anymore, so I took a risk," he goes on, his voice shaky. "I threw you a line by distorting my motto—mine, and the one used by all the rebels."

The sharpened metal at the end of my arm starts to tremble.

The Fronde?

The organization I thought I'd never encounter in my lifetime.

And here it is in the guise of Tristan de La Roncière?

My mind reels. I have a hard time matching the knight's luminous face with the obscure cabal that has sworn to put an end to the Vampyria. But only several weeks ago, I wouldn't have imagined I'd associate my mother's face with rebellion either.

"You belong to the Fronde?" I finally manage to say.

He nods, his golden hair gently swaying in the dimness.

"Yes. Same as my entire family, in secret, in the Ardennes. We can't take any more of the Immutable's oppression. The unbearable pressure that the royal tithe exerts on the people. The vile subservience the vampyric aristocracy imposes on the mortal nobility. The crimes and denunciations committed by the Faculty. France is dying from the eternal lives of the Versailles immortals." I feel like Tristan's tense face is the mirror image of my soul; I see the same hate I feel toward the bloodsuckers. "I lied to you the other night when I told you my mother sent me to the court to represent the La Roncières. The reason I absolutely have to be admitted among the tyrant's personal bodyguards is very different, not to serve him but to—"

"Plant a stake in his heart," I say, finishing his sentence.

A sunny smile spreads across his cold blue lips.

"I knew it!" he exclaims, his voice full of happy laughter. "That's why you're here too. When we were near the river and we were . . . close, I sensed you belonged to the Fronde as well. Yes, I was taken aback when I saw your puncture scars, I admit it, because I suddenly realized I was about to confide a vital secret to a girl I didn't really know anything about."

"The fact that I'm a commoner didn't reassure you?" I ask.

"Not every commoner is rebelling against the king. Far from it. Some, like Madame Thérèse, are their most servile accomplices."

I don't know how to respond to all this. I think back to how the governess treated poor Toinette only a day ago.

"But I don't doubt you anymore," Tristan continues. "A branch of the Fronde from the Auvergne sent you to the Grande Écurie, right?"

Stunned, I lower my weapon.

"I don't know anything about the Fronde," I tell him. "But the rest of my family belonged to the rebellion. They were all killed— those heads you must have seen on the courtyard gate were theirs . . . my father, mother, two older brothers. No one sent me to the Grande Écurie. Vengeance is my only motivation."

"No, it's destiny!" Tristan says with passion. "I'm sure of it. Destiny chose us, the two of us. You in the girls' wing, me in the boys'—we've doubled our chances of winning the Sip of the King. Doubled our chances of reaching the Immutable. Together, we'll put an end to the King of Shadows' tyranny."

As an echo to his words, a distant, repetitive ringing resonates from the fireplace like an alarm. The warning bell.

Snapped back to an awareness of time, I rush to help Tristan untie the knots that bind his ankles.

"Hurry," I cry. "It's almost nightfall, and the one who lives within these walls will soon return."

"Who is he exactly?" Tristan asks, untying the last ropes.

"I don't know any more than you do. He seemed like he wanted to help me several times, but . . . some of his actions remain a mystery." I think back to the heads of my family, all of them strangely embellished, not wanting to imagine what he did with them afterward. "We have to get away, now."

I throw the blankets off his back, then drag him toward the fireplace, but he collapses on my shoulder. After two days spent immobile, his legs are stiff and numb.

"Hurry, Tristan," I say, trying to encourage him as I barely hold up his weight. "You can do this."

I let him go up the ladder first so that I can be sure he keeps moving at a good clip.

"Go on."

As we climb the rungs, the air grows colder, the whistling breeze louder. I hear another type of whistling beneath us, down below, in the lair we've just left—a whistling that sounds furious and indignant.

Out of breath, we reach the darkening rooftops.

"This way," I say, leading Tristan on the slope heading to the dormer. "Hold on to me, and be careful not to slip."

The clouds hide the moon, and my stockings slide on the tiles, where a thin layer of ice has already formed. I don't care. The racket coming from the chimney shaft behind us scares me a lot more: a hulking body is climbing up fast, furiously rattling the rungs.

We finally make it to the small window I left open.

"Go in first," I say, my heart pounding.

"But you—"

"Now!"

He squeezes through the narrow opening with difficulty, his white shirt billowing in the icy wind.

I rush in after him, into the small room, and close the window so hard that the glass pane rattles in the frame.

"Was that . . . him?" Tristan asks, out of breath.

"I think so."

After the howling wind and the rattling tiles, the silence that reigns in the tiny room seems deafening.

"We can't stay under the roofs," Tristan says. "That monster has demonic strength. I was overpowered trying to grapple with him after he kidnapped me in my sleep."

We hurry into the hallway and to the staircase that goes down to the lower floors.

I freeze on the threshold of the stairs, suddenly aware that we have to go separate ways.

"Dinner must be nearly over," I say. "I have to distract the guard posted in front of the room with the mare tapestries. That's where they put a bed for me so I could recover from the fevers I caught deer hunting. I absolutely have to be under the covers before Madame Thérèse comes to check in on me."

"Like an agile ermine, you sure get into every nook," Tristan says.

"My brother Bastien used to compare me to a weasel . . . it's almost the same as an ermine, just less regal."

"Well, my mother says I'm wild like a lynx because I'd much rather roam the forests on my own than in a pack, the way my brothers do. The Faculty would probably attribute all my gallivanting to an excess of black bile. But solitude can be soothing, a lot like a clear brook can revitalize you."

"I know exactly what you mean," I say.

"We're quite a pair, you and I. Two wild animals, plucked from their forests and thrown into Versailles. Two wounded creatures—me with the scar on my face, you with your elbow punctures. But rightly so: wounded animals are the most cunning. Tonight, I'll create a diversion. I'll go down first and pretend I'm dying: the guard will take me to the boys' wing, which will clear the way for you."

In the near darkness of the hallway, I can barely make out the person who's standing just inches away from me, but I feel his warm breath on my forehead.

"How will you explain what happened to you?" I ask, mortified about the ordeal I put him through.

"I'll pretend that I fell ill after the deer hunt too," he answers. "Who knows what poisonous vapors flow in the river we crossed? I'll say I woke up in the girls' attic after several nights of delirium. I'll blame it all on fevers and sleepwalking."

"When will we talk again?"

"At dinner. It's the only time when boarders from both wings are together. We'll have to be doubly vigilant because you're joining us in the home stretch."

"Us?" I repeat. "Do you mean there are more of you?"

Tristan nods. "The Fronde has been getting ready for the assassination for months. The court is infiltrated by courtiers committed to the cause. Our accomplices at the palace have weapons hidden in the king's mortuary chamber: the room where he was transmuted three hundred years ago and where he holds the yearly Sip of the King ritual. The two successful candidates are left alone with the Immutable for several minutes—a rare opportunity when the despot is without guards or followers. There's a sliding panel to the right of the fireplace, one that has a molding of a lion's head. In that hidden alcove is a stake carved from oak—the most effective wood against vampyres—as well as a sword made of silver, the metal they dread most of all. Those weapons will be waiting for me if I'm chosen for the Sip, and now, for you as well." Tristan's eyes give off wild sparks. "Imagine, in one week, I may be plunging that stake into the despot's heart while you slash his throat. You and me, striking down the despot in one swoop. Tyranny defeated by . . . love."

It's a heroic image that fires me up.

"Getting closer to you these past few weeks, I thought I was just feeling out a potential ally," he admits. "But I've discovered a lot more than that . . ."

I nod in agreement. I, too, wanted to use him to achieve my goals. But my heart prevailed over my calculations.

I take his hand in mine. It's chilled.

"I'm sorry," I tell him. "I'm sorry I asked that . . . that creature to make sure you didn't talk."

"No need to apologize. I would have done the same thing if I'd thought another boarder was jeopardizing my plan to assassinate the king. You did what you had to do above all else. You acted nobly."

"I'm a commoner, Tristan."

He comes closer, his shadowed face obstructing my vision.

"I'm talking about a noble heart," he says. "Not one associated with titles and conventions and the slew of protocols bogged down in etiquette to shut out mortals. And so, if you let me . . . I'll love you even more for that, Diane."

"Jeanne," I correct him, because I can't stand hearing a name other than my own come out of his mouth. "Jeanne Froidelac."

He gently raises his fingers to my face and caresses a gray strand of hair that the wind ruffled.

"Jeanne . . . ," he repeats. "My silver ermine who sprints across the rooftops of the sky and who commands monsters from the underworld. My mother claims she chose me because I'm braver than my brothers— me, who fought a bear with my bare hands. I think she really chose me because I'm the most independent, the one she believes most capable of carrying out this mission. But I'm scared, you know . . . the bear got away without a scratch and left an indelible mark on my skin. And the

Immutable is a thousand times more formidable than the most ferocious predators. May I be as courageous as you are when I confront him."

Chilled to the bone at the top of the small staircase under the eaves, Tristan and I are perched on the edge of an abyss. We're like two animals on the prowl, same as the ones Tristan just mentioned—both on the verge of leaping into a vast, unknown valley. Fear makes my skin shiver. Excitement speeds up my heart. And the warmth in my belly is exactly what Tristan already declared—the spark of burgeoning love that's crept up on us.

Tristan's trembling lips part as they come closer to mine.

Only when our mouths touch does the trembling stop.

21

JIG

I belong to the Fronde, a joyous voice sings in my head when I open my eyes.

The evening before, Madame Thérèse was completely fooled, and this morning my body aches are gone.

I push back the thick blankets like a butterfly coming out of its cocoon, ready to fly. I also feel butterflies in my stomach as I think about Tristan and the kiss we shared before we parted last night. I'm emboldened by his strength and that of the many followers I imagine crawling backstage at the court.

Maman, Papa, Valère, and Bastien, look at me—I'm walking in your footsteps. I belong to the Fronde.

Until today, I never thought I would survive beyond my attempt to kill the king. I thought that the engraved word—*liberty*—on the back of my mother's pocket watch case lid was just a mirage. But now I'm starting to dream of the world that will follow: a world free of the tithe, sequester, and curfew. I dream of riding with Tristan in the vast forests of the Ardennes that he's talked about so much, and farther still, in faraway countries that I've always wanted to explore. His solitude, when joined with mine, turned everything upside down.

At breakfast, the La Roncière name is on everyone's lips. The dining hall is abuzz with the rumor that the boarder who vanished from the boys' wing is back. His story about sleepwalking seems to have been convincing, especially as there isn't any other explanation for his disappearance over the last forty-eight hours.

I'm dying to tell Naoko everything, but I stay mum. I swore to my accomplice that I would reveal nothing. It's safer for him, for me, even for Naoko. With the evilmouth, she's already burdened.

At the end of the day, after grooming for the evening, I run down the grand staircase before everyone else. I'm impatient to find Tristan in the banquet hall.

But a voice behind me makes me freeze at the bottom of the steps.

"Diane?"

I turn quickly around.

It's Poppy. She's early for dinner too . . . unless she followed me.

"I hope you're feeling better," she says.

It's the first time she's spoken to me since the deer hunt, after having pointedly snubbed me. I don't care to know why. There are only a few days left until the Sip of the King, and I have to focus entirely on my one and only goal.

"I'm fine," I tell her guardedly. "Still have a bit of a cold, but it'll go away."

"That river must be filled with lots of potent vapors to put you in such a state, you and La Roncière. When I think about his bout of sleepwalking . . . it's crazy."

"Crazy, yes. But now he's apparently better, and so am I."

I'd like to leave it at that and avoid saying anything more about Tristan. I have nothing to gain by prolonging our conversation.

But Poppy isn't finished.

"I'm sorry for the way I've acted since the hunt," she says. "When you saw me spit up blood into my handkerchief, I got scared . . ."

"Scared?" I answer, shrugging my shoulders. "I'm not a vampyre. I wasn't going to pounce on your handkerchief to swallow it greedily."

I turn to head toward the banquet hall, but she grabs the sleeve of my damask dress.

"Hey, careful," I say. "It's a gift from the king."

In truth, I couldn't care less about this dress. But I won't risk Poppy tearing my sleeve and exposing my scars from the bleedings. I let her lead me under the staircase into a dim corner where brooms and buckets are stored.

"I was afraid you'd turn me in. That's why I gave you the cold shoulder," she explains. "Did you happen to tell anyone what you saw?"

In the semidark alcove, Poppy looks anxious. She seems paler than usual, and neither the blush on her cheeks nor the black of her eye shadow adds any color to her complexion. I sense that she's consumed with deep worry.

"I didn't say anything to anyone," I assure her.

Her expression starts to relax, and she lets go of my sleeve.

Beyond the walls of the Grande Écurie, the repeated ringing of the warning bell announces the coming nightfall.

"Thank you, darling," she says with a sigh after the sound of the final bell. "I'd rather that the teachers didn't know I have tuberculosis."

She whispers the last word as if it's a shameful secret. Tuberculosis? Of course, this is Poppy's mysterious disease! How could I not see that? I know all about that terrible condition that eats away at the lungs, little by little. In Butte-aux-Rats, the villagers struck with this illness were ostracized. My father was the only one who showed them any compassion, doing all he could to relieve their symptoms with a medicinal pulmonary powder, short of treating their incurable sickness. Yet I thought tuberculosis was restricted to commoners; I never imagined that an aristocrat could suffer from the disease.

"Are you sure?" I ask as I think back to Poppy's chronic cough that she dismissed as a cold, her wan complexion, and the blood-filled saliva that she tried to hide from me.

She nods, vigorously, shaking her high bun.

"My entire family is afflicted. The Castlecliff name may sound glorious, but our crumbling estate is far from it. The castle is ridden with dampness, way out in the depths of Cumbria County, jammed in a corridor of cliffs between Scotland and the Irish Sea. It was built on marshland, so it's no wonder the stench has infected my family for generations." Her face clouds over. "That cursed disease already claimed my two older brothers . . ."

I'm speechless. The parallel with my own situation stuns me.

A thunderclap of heels explodes above our heads: the demoiselles are streaming down the grand staircase to head to dinner. The racket makes the cold marble of the alcove reverberate. Tired yawns from a long day of classes, excitement over joining the boys, anxiety about the approaching selection process . . . all of it rushes down above us like a thunderstorm, in the middle of which come Madame Thérèse's shrill reprimands.

"My parents probably didn't think I'd live long when they baptized me Proserpina," Poppy says once the group has rushed into the banquet hall, the staircase becoming silent again. "They named me after the young girl kidnapped by Pluto, the god of death, no doubt thinking that the tuberculosis would mow me down before my eighteenth birthday. If you only knew how much I hate that name." Her expression tenses up under her smoky makeup. "I much prefer being called Poppy. Do you know what it means?"

"Uh . . . isn't it a flower?" I say, memories of my mother's English lessons colliding with the emotions of the whispered confession. "A . . . daisy?"

"A *coquelicot* in French. A weed that persists in growing on the edges of fields and on wasteland, wherever it's not wanted. A flower with bloodred petals like the stains that smudge my handkerchiefs. An ephemeral plant in the colors of life." She takes my hand and squeezes it hard. "Up until now, I've mustered all my willpower to resist the god of death. My brothers visited him before me. Even though I cherished them, I don't want to join them anytime soon—because I love being alive. I love life passionately!"

Poppy's zest and verve explode in my face, tragically. Her rants; her high-pitched, vibrant voice; her provocative attire; her adventures with boys—she's racing against time . . . against death.

"That's why I was so diligent about learning French," she tells me. "Because it's the lingua franca of the Magna Vampyria and the passport to the world. That's why I volunteered to represent England in Versailles, so I could escape Castlecliff. I need to win the Sip of the King so I can be cured of my disease before I succumb to it next."

"Rumor has it that the Immutable's blood prolongs the youthfulness of mortals who drink . . . ," I say, thinking out loud as I recall what Naoko explained to me.

"And supposedly it cures every illness, like a panacea," Poppy finishes with enthusiasm. "After a few years in the king's service, I'll travel far away from Versailles and all its pomp, far from Castlecliff and its toxic vapors. I'll be at the prow of a ship bound for the Americas, breathing in ocean spray with every breath I take." Her eyes sparkle a little more as she evokes this vision of the future. "And of course, on the arm of my handsome American, Zacharie . . . it would be a real shame if I kicked the bucket before I live out my story with him, right?"

She heaves a long wheezing sigh that rises from her chest.

"For years I've been able to hide the symptoms by chewing gum laced with morphine," she says. "It calms my cough and soothes the pain. But every month I get out of breath faster, and these last few weeks, I've started spitting up blood. If the grand equerry found out about my condition, I'm afraid he would forbid me from competing for the Sip of the King, or he would ask the Faculty to treat me—and I don't want that for anything in the world. You know what they say about those serpents in lace ruffs: their lousy cures are worse than the illness."

She laughs in her unique, sardonic way, pulling herself together before it degenerates into a coughing fit.

Behind the windows, nightfall has arrived. The hallway chandeliers reflect off the frosted glass, making Poppy's feverish gaze blaze even more.

"I'm touched that you would confide in me," I tell her. "And once again, I promise to keep everything to myself. As for the Sip of the King—"

"I'm not asking you to withdraw," she cuts me off. "I know we're rivals and that we'll stay that way until October thirty-first. I didn't tell you all this to elicit your pity. I just want you to play fair and square. To face off against me in the tests like any other rival, without using my secret to stab me in the back." She stares deep into my eyes. "Contrary to that upstart Hélénaïs, I sense you have a true code of honor. The way you reacted the other night, defending the servant who was being bled beyond reason, proved it in my eyes. The values of chivalry have for centuries been inscribed in the noble blood of the Gastefriches, just as much as in the Castlecliffs."

Poppy couldn't be more wrong when she brings up the "noble blood" of my people. As for the values of chivalry that she boasts about, they in no way prevent the aristocracy from crushing the fourth estate.

"I promise that your secret is safe with me," I say, lowering my eyes. "Now let's go to the banquet hall before Madame Thérèse realizes we're missing and starts a hissy fit."

She nods and slips a small embossed-silk pouch into the palm of my hand.

"Those are gumballs laced with morphine. They're the best against a cough. If your bronchial passageways are still a little blocked, they'll help open things up. But careful: morphine is a strong sedative. Don't chew more than one gumball every four hours; otherwise you'll pass out."

I take the pouch without saying anything. As the daughter of an apothecary, I know about morphine. My father told me that it was a rare painkiller, a thousand times more effective than white willow bark . . . a thousand times more dangerous too. He kept only a few precious grams in the apothecary, which he used solely on patients most severely afflicted and always sparingly. Those who use morphine on a daily basis eventually can't do without.

Who would believe it? Poppy, the fierce Amazon everyone envies for her free spirit, is in fact a slave to the drug.

My heart bursts in my chest as soon as I spot Tristan in the middle of the room swarming with boarders. All the chairs around his table are already occupied. Tonight, chance won't bring us together. Still, just seeing him fills me with happiness.

He smiles at me too. I didn't notice it yesterday in the dusk, but under the light of the chandeliers, I can see just how much being abducted took out of him. In between his blond strands of hair, his face is even paler and hollower, making his scar all the more noticeable.

The coming and going of the servants and dishes is like a ballet that carries me off, in sync with the rhythmic conversation of my tablemates. Each one displays perfect table etiquette, showing a mastery of courtly manners and conversation. I have to suffer through the trivial chatter for an hour while my heart yearns for only one person in the world.

With a solemn gesture of his right pincer, Barvók finally gives us permission to get up. Tristan and I brush against one another before heading back to our respective dormitories. It's only a short respite from the hectic rhythm of the Grande Écurie, a handful of seconds snatched right under the noses of the teachers and students ignorant of the pact that binds us. But the fleeting moment when our hands touch is worth a whole day of waiting.

Tristan only has time to whisper a few words into my ear.

"I have news for you, my ermine beauty. Tomorrow night, during the art-of-vampyrism class, let's pair up. We'll have more time to talk."

As he says this, he's pulled along by the flow of boys heading back to their side of the building.

The following day unfolds in subdued tension. It's the last day before the start of the tests.

Despite my eagerness to see Tristan again, I concentrate on my lessons. In the classroom, a studious silence reigns with no talking or distractions. Everyone's attention is focused on the upcoming competition. More than ever, I'm determined to be selected for the ritual, and I'm resolute in absorbing whatever information I can to increase my chances. I force myself to grasp all the subtleties of the art of courtly manners, my weakest subject. For four hours, Barvók makes us review table etiquette, as tomorrow's test will be an official dinner specially attended by courtiers from the palace.

"We'll have the honor of welcoming the Countess de Villeforge, also known at the court by the nickname Madame Étiquette," Barvók says, puffing up with pride. "The ultimate arbiter of best practices, she personally drew up the seating arrangement and will select the six girls and six boys who show the most refinement. The dinner itself will not take place at your usual seven o'clock but at nine, a time that better suits the lords of the night. I strongly recommend you consume the snacks that the servants will bring to your dormitories early in the evening so that you can last until then. The coffee will be a stimulant—the beverage is a mortal courtier's best ally for staying awake all night long when in the company of immortals, and the court consumes a considerable quantity. As for the snacks, they'll take the edge off your hunger pangs. It's better not to be too hungry when you arrive at dinner." He sniffles haughtily. "Nothing is more rude than pouncing on food that's barely been served, like a vulgar starving peasant."

In the afternoon, during the art of equestrianism, I concentrate like never before on having Typhon execute the most sophisticated dressage figures. In spite of all my focus, I know my aids—pressure from my legs, hands, and seat—aren't as precise as those of the other, more experienced riders, but the stallion performs the voltes and changes of direction as if he read my mind. I can only hope that he'll be as tuned in the day after tomorrow, when we'll have to execute a perfect carousel in front of the court.

Come evening, Madame Thérèse claps her hands and orders the maids and valets to clear the banquet hall of the tables.

"Mesdemoiselles and messieurs, pair up for tonight's art-of-vampyrism class, the last one before the tests: the never-ending jig," she says exuberantly, her small eyes sparkling with excitement.

I thread my way through the crowd of boarders, all of them frantically looking for a partner, until I reach Tristan.

He's gotten some color back, and his raw silk jacket catches the light of the chandeliers. But he doesn't need luxurious clothes to shine, not with a heart that's as simple and wild as mine: a boy of the forests whom the court will never hold captive in its gilded prison.

"Dear boarders, I hope that you're in tip-top shape," Lucrèce says. "Like all the best things, the never-ending jig is both deliciously addictive and fatally dangerous. Many courtiers have lost their lives to it, but at least they perished with a smile on their lips."

I glance toward the front of the banquet hall. It's been cleared of all furniture.

Lucrèce and Suraj stand at the other end of the room on the freshly polished floor that gleams like a mirror and reflects the crystal pendants that light the ceiling. For the first time, the two squires have abandoned the somber battle outfits that blend in with the night. Lucrèce looks resplendent in a long scarlet silk chiffon dress, sporting a ruff collar trimmed with red ibis feathers. More than ever, she resembles a bird of prey, majestic and lethal. As for Suraj, he's wearing an ivory velvet knee-length coat with a straight collar that enhances his skin. His light-colored turban is decorated with a sparkling opal aigrette, a jeweled ornament fit for a maharaja. The two squires are accompanied by a group of musicians dressed like morticians with pale faces and sunken cheeks that stand out above their black uniforms.

"The never-ending jig is one of the most popular dances at Versailles," Lucrèce goes on. "Less technical than the minuet, more intimate than the courante. The two future winners of the Sip of the King will be required to dance this jig in the Hall of Mirrors at the end of the tests. So this is like a training session." She turns toward the funereal orchestra. "The Violins of the King honor us with their presence this evening. Like true artists, they're ready to sacrifice everything for their art. If the Italian castrati renounced their virility to preserve the purity of their voices, the Violins of the King sacrifice their youth for the sake of their emotionally stirring music."

Every time she reveals the refined horrors of the court, the squire seems to take pleasure in her own words, savoring them as they come out of her garnet-glossed lips. Suraj keeps his eyes riveted to the floor.

"You already know about the heady charm of vampyric roses," Lucrèce continues. "Well, vampyric violins are even more bewitching. A marvel fashioned by the Shadows. Each violin is cut from a maple tree watered daily with the blood of a particular musician, from birth to adulthood. Hence flora and fauna grow up together—and the man's life force transfers over to the tree. After twenty-five years, a violin maker certified by the Faculty carves a unique instrument out of the precious essence. The violin can be played only by the musician that nourished it with his blood. Of course, the violinist dies prematurely, within a few years. But I assure you that the sound he draws out of his instrument is worth the sacrifice. Similarly, there exists an all-female ensemble of prodigy harpists—the Harps of the King. You'll meet them another night." Lucrèce smiles as she looks at the miserable musicians destined to pay the ultimate price for such an ephemeral talent. "The never-ending jig is spellbinding. None can resist its lure. As the music plays, even the most mediocre dancers become virtuosos. They forget all about time, pushing their bodies to the limit, sometimes to the breaking point. But rest assured, tonight the violins will *not* play all night long. A short hour will suffice to give you a taste of the pleasures at the court."

Then Lucrèce joins Suraj, her partner for the evening. I'm suddenly aware that they must have danced together in front of the court, one year ago, when they both won the Sip of the King. The way Lucrèce places her hand on Suraj's shoulder—possessively, as if she were still wearing her gauntlet with the metallic claws—startles me. Could it be that she has her sights set on the brooding squire? Is that why she was picking on Rafael the other night—not only to be cruel but also out of jealousy?

"Music!" she orders.

The Violins of the King slowly raise their trembling hands to their instruments like old men with the shakes. But the bows have barely touched the strings when the musicians metamorphose. At the sound of the first notes, their hunched shoulders straighten and their long, sad faces seem to gain color. It's as if they've instantly become one with the instruments brimming with their lost youth. The musicians are reduced to being mere man-violins, hybrids of flesh, wood, and strings.

Suraj and Lucrèce open the ball, swept up by the rising music. Gliding on the glistening floor, they look at each other as if nothing else existed around them, twirling as subject and reflection, two sides of a mirror.

I feel my own legs set in motion, out of my control and swept along by an irresistible groundswell. In front of me, Tristan is livening up, his movements mirroring mine with supernatural mimicry.

"I . . . I don't know how to dance the jig," I stammer.

"I'm nowhere near to being an expert," he says, his eyebrows furrowed, in over his head the same way I am. "But it looks like the music knows it for us."

It's true. My feet aren't crushing my partner's but instead brush elegantly against his with every pirouette. My heels trace the pattern of the jig with magical ease on the polished parquet. My wrists lift into the air with grace, like the arms of a puppet pulled by invisible strings. My thighs bend under my petticoats, and I take off in an aerial leap—along with all the other third-years, thirty of us bounding in perfect unison.

For a few seconds, the room becomes weightless. The long curled coifs, the large stiff dresses, the brocaded waistcoats . . . all remain suspended in the music-filled air. Then sixty heels crash onto the floor exactly at the same time only to immediately take off again in the diabolical dance.

"It's phenomenal," I whisper to Tristan as the steps I don't control plaster me against him.

"It's abominable," he corrects me before the jig tears him violently from me.

The room begins to sway in front of my eyes—the crystal chandeliers, the velvet curtains, the gilded windows—swept up in a frenzied whirlwind. The wild dance makes my damask dress flutter. The smell of wax polish wafting from the floor gives me vertigo until the swell hurtles me against Tristan yet again.

His lips brush against my ear, whispering a few out-of-breath words that only I can hear over the music.

"If only one of us is chosen, it'll be enough to set off . . . the massacre."

"The massacre?" I repeat.

Before Tristan can answer, the jig tears him away, and I have to wait for the next pirouette to find him again.

The steps of the dance bring us together for a few precious seconds, and he seizes the opportunity to fire off whispered confidences.

"As soon as the two winners enter the king's mortuary chamber, the rebels who've infiltrated the palace will kill the squires standing guard . . . the conspirators will also kill the mortal courtiers and immortals who refuse to align themselves with our cause . . ." He huffs and puffs, struggling to keep his breath. "Everything has been planned: weapons hidden under jackets and petticoats, essence of garlic flower to disorient the vampyres . . ."

The dance separates us, making the long panels of my dress flap as my mind fills with bloody images. Kill the king's squires? Yes, of course, I should have thought of that. You can't make an omelet without breaking eggs . . . my eyes latch onto the couple dancing in the center of the room. I won't have any regrets seeing Lucrèce die; on the other hand, does Suraj deserve the same fate? I've never seen him exhibit the cruelty of his companion.

"The king will let the female victor drink his blood first," Tristan continues, his cheeks flushed and his breath labored when the jig brings us together again. "If it's you, I'll use the time to grab the weapons from behind the panel with the lion molding . . . *puff* . . . if it's someone else, I'll slash her throat after I stab the king . . ."

Our legs twirl us around one another in a leap that's as dizzying as the thoughts racing through my head.

"In case I'm not chosen and you enter the mortuary chamber on your own, you'll have to take the same course of action . . ." His breathing is intense, labored. "Once you'll have drunk the Sip of the King . . . you'll get the weapons and kill the tyrant . . . at the same time as whoever is taking a sip of his blood."

The dance reaches its apogee. My calves twirl madly under my petticoats, my thighs so taut from the effort that they give me a rush of warmth, same as when I ran through the woods. All around me, the girls' buns have come undone, and the boys' ponytails have escaped from their ribbons.

Rafael de Montesueño comes into my line of sight. He's busy jigging with Séraphine de La Pattebise, whose tall, supple body is made for dancing. Will I have the courage to slash his throat—he who's been nothing but kind to me?

Rather than think about the killings I may have to commit, I give myself totally over to the never-ending jig. The dance exhausts my body and tires my soul, erasing all guilt and future regrets.

22

THE ART OF
COURTLY MANNERS

A fuzzy dream.

That's what's inspiring me today, October 28, a day I've been both waiting for and dreading—the art-of-courtly-manners test. Since my arrival at the Grande Écurie, it's the first time that classes have been canceled. From now until the end of the month, lessons are on hold so that third-years can prepare for each evening's competition.

Some girls sleep in to look fully refreshed come dinnertime; others rise at dawn to do one last review of the lessons on proper etiquette. From deserted classrooms to steaming bathing rooms, an oppressive calm takes over. Behind windows, the cloudy gray sky bears down like a lead weight, an airtight cover that smothers all sounds. In this silence, my ears still buzz from yesterday's jig. My muscles are sore and my limbs ache from having danced too much. Maybe one of the morphine gumballs that Poppy gave me would alleviate the discomfort, but I'm not about to give in to temptation. I've got other plans for those medicinal drops.

On the pretext that I'm taking a nap, I spend the afternoon behind the curtains of my canopy bed, shaving and mincing the gumballs with a knife I pinched at breakfast. Thirty doses of morphine in total, reduced to fine white powder that I scoop into the silk pouch.

"Avoid drinking the coffee the servants bring at snack time," I tell Naoko at the end of the afternoon when she's doing my hair in the bathing room before dinner.

She looks at me in the mirror, above the gorgeous hairdo she's created: a silver bun adorned with white silk trim shaped like a lotus, something crafted especially for me. "A large artificial flower to contrast with and bring out the fine features of your face—a geisha trick," she explained with the impeccable taste she's known for.

"Don't worry about me," she says, adjusting the trim. "I don't sleep much as it is, so the caffeine won't change anything. And even if I don't sleep a wink, it doesn't matter. I'm not under the same pressure as everyone else to be in good shape since I'm not taking part in the Sip."

I swivel on the stool and grab her wrist to force her to listen to me closely.

"The coffee won't have any stimulating effect, I guarantee you," I say. "On the contrary, you risk taking a nosedive right into your plate in the middle of dinner. And competitor or not, that would look very bad."

Naoko's black eyes widen under her bangs.

"You're going to . . . poison the coffee?"

"No. Well, not really. I only want to make sure that, by the end of the evening, I end up as one of the candidates selected by Madame Étiquette. Most of the girls are more skilled at table manners than I am, it's a fact . . . unless they're not in full possession of their faculties, if you see what I mean."

Deep down, I'd like to get Naoko's absolution. But she starts to adjust my bun without saying a word, her carmine lips sealed.

"Toinette, it's you," I say the moment the young servant arrives at the end of the hallway. She's pushing a three-tiered cart full of food to nibble on.

Her face lights up, making her freckles sparkle.

She doesn't suspect that I've been waiting for her to get here for the past half hour in my pearl-gray dress, pretending I've just happened upon her.

"Yes, it's me, Mademoiselle Diane," she says happily. "I'm bringing snacks to the dormitory."

"Yummy, it all looks so delicious," I say, ogling the cart with its array of appetizers, sugar-powdered cookies, candied-fruit tarts . . . and two large steaming coffeepots. "I'm lucky I ran into you as I stretch my legs in the hallway. It means I can choose my favorite snack before the lionesses of the dormitory snatch everything up."

"But of course, mademoiselle!" Toinette exclaims, still brimming with thanks for my having come to her rescue during the art-of-vampyrism class. "What would please you?"

I pretend to hesitate.

"The gâteau de Savoie, there in the back, on the lower tray. I'd love a piece."

Toinette bends over to slice the cake.

I take advantage of her being stooped down to lift one of the coffeepot lids and empty my entire pouch of powdered morphine. Only half the boarders will be knocked out, but perhaps that will be enough to ensure my qualification.

"Here you go," Toinette says, straightening up.

She hands me a porcelain plate on which she's laid down a generous slice of cake with a golden, moist center.

"I sincerely hope you'll be chosen for the Sip of the King," she says. "You're a beautiful soul. The exact opposite of . . . Lucrèce."

Her pale cheeks flush because of her heartfelt boldness. She stammers an excuse and dashes off with the cart.

I feel my own cheeks growing hot with shame as soon as her back is turned. How can I possibly be a beautiful soul when I used that innocent girl to achieve my ends? And what if she's caught and accused of collective poisoning? I muster all my willpower to convince myself that it won't happen . . . that I, too, am ready to die in order to kill the tyrant . . . that risks have to be taken if liberty is to triumph.

Isn't that so?

The bell towers have barely rung nine times when Madame Thérèse bolts into the dormitory, her footsteps brisk, her frilly dress fitted with such a wide-hooped pannier that her false hips can't go through the door head-on.

"Hurry!" she shouts. "The guests are already here."

The demoiselles—in full makeup, powdered, tresses all curled with an iron—rush toward the grand staircase.

Out of the corner of an eye, I watch as some begin to yawn while others seem to drag their feet . . . the morphine is starting to take effect.

A blast of cold air hits my face as I enter the banquet hall despite the roaring fire in the hearth. Long tables dressed in white linen are arranged in a gigantic elbow pattern, with gleaming gold cutlery used especially for the occasion. Large vases painted with moths and filled with pale chrysanthemums rest atop the tables.

A good thirty courtiers are already seated, occupying one out of every two chairs so that boarders can be interspersed among them. These men and women are sumptuously attired, but it's their shoes that immediately attract my attention: half the guests are in red heels. I've never been in the presence of so many vampyres at one time, which explains the shiver that came over me when I entered the room.

"Dear guests, welcome to the Grande Écurie!" Barvók exclaims, walking stiffly as he arrives through the opposite door, followed by the boys, all wearing wigs.

Tonight, the Hungarian general has pulled out all the stops: his brocaded waistcoat is loaded with military medals, weighing down a man who already seems made of metal rather than flesh. Poor man, butchered by the Faculty . . .

He strains his mechanical articulations and bows in front of a tall woman. The lady is seated at the crook of the elbow where the two tables are joined.

"My compliments, Madame de Villeforge," he says obsequiously.

This must be the formidable Madame Étiquette, mistress of manners at the court. Looking as wan as her pale-fur-lined white dress, she reminds me of the face of an impenetrable moon. The gazes of all courtiers fall upon her. In the King of Shadows' absence this evening, she rules the court.

"Mesdemoiselles and messieurs, take your positions," the general commands.

He and Madame Thérèse remain standing at the back of the room, from where they'll be surveying dinner operations mapped out weeks ago, like a battle plan.

The boarders start to search for their seats, smiles screwed on their faces, eyes trembling from nerves.

Hélénaïs cuts in front of me without so much as a glance, her beautiful face so heavily coated with white-silver cream that she seems more dead than alive—which may have been intentional, resembling a vampyre so as to blend in among them.

On the other hand, Poppy has compensated for her pale, sickly skin by applying a surplus of blush. For the first time, she's tamed her voluminous brown hair, securing each stray strand in an incredible intertwining of braids that must have taken the whole day to style.

Tristan is at the other end of the room. We exchange a furtive glance. It's the first time I've seen him in a wig. His is the same color as his hair, just a little longer, a little more golden, a little more curled, a symbol of the court, where the artificial must always supplant the natural. Of course, we can't talk to each other, but his smile calms me, as if he were silently saying: *Everything is going to be fine.*

"Diane," a familiar voice says, close by. "I believe we'll be dining together."

I lower my gaze and instantly recognize the magnificent head of red hair that belongs to Alexandre de Mortange. He's seated here, in a blue velvet waistcoat that matches his eyes, right next to a plate topped with a place card bearing my name.

"The king asked Madame Étiquette to seat us side by side," he says, visibly moved to see me again. "This is my first dinner since being stripped of privileges at the court after our run-in in the gardens. His Majesty wants to test our ability to resist the desire that burns between us."

A ball of fury forms in my throat. The only desire I feel toward Alexandre is the yearning to kill him. This burning urge tickles my whole body, but I can't let it show, not now.

"I'll do my best to behave," I manage to say as I take my seat. I force my lips to stretch into a smile, my eyelids fluttering disingenuously. "I'll refrain from jumping into your arms to kiss you between the soup and dessert."

"In turn, I'll keep your other tablemate from pouncing at your throat to bleed you," he says all too seriously.

I'm suddenly aware of the courtier seated to my left. Instinctively, I flinch as I recognize the brown coils of hair studded with milky pearls. The last time I saw them glisten was in the verdant maze, during the gallant hunt.

"Don't listen to the babbling of Viscount de Mortange," Edmée says. "We're all reconciled now, since that is the king's wish. Isn't that right?"

By her squeaky voice and tense smile, I sense her frustration, even her anger. Just as with Alexandre, the king made sure she would be seated beside me, like a pawn on a chessboard. I'm starting to understand the Machiavellian game he's playing, moving enemies and lovers in complete disregard of their feelings, just to show, as Edmée said, that the only thing that counts is his all-powerful will.

From her center seat, I can see that Madame Étiquette is watching us out of the corner of her eye.

"The menu seems most appetizing, don't you think, my dear?" Edmée says as she hands me a beautifully printed Venetian paper illuminated with gold leaf.

The menu is divided in two columns: to the left, the "Mortal Dishes" intended for the boarders and nontransmuted courtiers; to the right, the "Vampyric Dishes," reserved for the lords of the night.

My stomach twists into knots as I read the second column that encapsulates all the horrors of the Vampyria.

MENU FOR THE NIGHT
OF OCTOBER 28

IN THE YEAR OF SHADOWS 299

The Art of Courtly Manners Test, for the Sip of the King

MORTAL DISHES

HORS-D'ŒUVRE
ASSIETTE DE CRUSTACÉS
Crustaceans with blue lobster from the Court of
Denmark,
imported to Versailles from the North Sea
Wine pairing: Crozes-Hermitage blanc

SOUPE
Velouté Forestier
Cream of mushroom soup,
with hazelnuts from the Court of Genoa,
seasoned with black truffles
Wine pairing: Pomerol rouge

RÔT
Dinde des Amériques
Roast turkey prepared with a Mexican sauce,
as served at the Court of Spain
*Wine pairing: Châteauneuf-du-Pape rouge,
Grand Millésime, from the year 277*

ENTREMETS
Gelée à la Menthe
Mint jelly as prepared at the Court of England
Wine pairing: Champagne from the Abbey of Dom Pérignon

FROMAGES
Assortiment de Nos Regions
A ten-cheese tour of the Kingdom of France
Wine pairing: Aged Port

DESSERT
Tarte Sacher
Chocolate delight per the Court of Austria
Wine pairing: Muscat wine

VAMPYRIC DISHES

FIRST BLOOD
SANG ROSÉ DE VERSAILLES
A premier vintage of bloody rosé,
freshly drawn from young maidens of the region
Description: Diaphanous hued, floral aromas,
fresh and thirst quenching

SECOND BLOOD
CUVÉE SYLVESTRE
Woodland vintage drawn from lumberjacks
of the Black Forest
raised in the fresh air
Description: Ruby hued, coniferous aromas, robust

THIRD BLOOD
GRAND CRU HÉMOPHILE
A Grand Cru Classé, this subtle blend combines
the blood of hemophiliacs
from the entire Vampyria
Description: Garnet hued, smooth and supple bodied
due to a lack of coagulation

ENTRESANG
Jus d'Oranges Sanguines
Juice of blood oranges harvested from the Orangery
of Versailles drizzled with blood from the prey
of the gallant hunts

FOURTH BLOOD
Sang Madérisé du Portugal
Bloody Madeira drawn from the widows of
Portuguese fishermen, mixed with their tears, and
aged in barrels from shipwrecked boats
Description: Funereal hued, gentle aromas, slight bitterness

LAST BLOOD
Sweet Liqueur from the Nuns of Brive
Specialty of the Hospice of Brive-la-Gaillarde
nuns,drawn from diabetic patients force-fed
an array of sweets
*Description: Syrupy, with tasty undertones
of honey and nougatine*

"The king is spoiling us," Edmée says, snapping me out of my morbid contemplation of the menu. "He's offering us a geographic tour of the Vampyria's specialties. I love traveling by way of food, don't you?"

I can tell she's delighted to see me distressed, but I force myself to swallow my repugnance. Tonight, the smallest faux pas, the slightest grimace of disgust, could cost me a chance at the Sip.

"It's my greatest pleasure as well," I reply. "I merely regret that I can taste only the dishes from the left column. One evening, I hope I'll have the honor of being transmuted so that I, too, can savor the dishes on the right."

The lie burns my tongue, but it's exactly what Edmée wants to hear.

She tilts her head back and erupts in crystal-clear laughter, the same that's haunted my dreams since our encounter during the gallant hunt.

"Patience, dear. The *numerus clausus* is very strict. Before you can even think about being transmuted, you must first win the Sip of the King . . . and you're far from being the only contender."

"I'm certain Diane has every chance of succeeding," Alexandre pipes up. He smiles at me like a knight who's come to the rescue of a damsel in distress. Disgusting. "She's splendid, the most intelligent, the most charming in her class—"

"And also the most appetizing, isn't that so?" Edmée says, cutting him off with her caustic voice.

Alexandre's smile vanishes. "You . . . you've no right to say that," he stammers.

"Did you tell her what happened to that squire twenty years ago? The one you seduced and bled? What was her name? Agata? Aniela?"

Alexandre's pupils contract at once, his canines lengthen, and his elegant mouth becomes a horrible sneer. He growls. He barely has time to put an embroidered napkin over his lips to stifle the outburst that, I assume, must be a display of the worst possible manners for a vampyre of the court.

I'm reminded of the words the king spoke two months ago in the maze: he accused Alexandre of not having "learned any lessons from the past" and of "playing the Don Juan again, without any thought of the consequences."

Thus the reason why the viscount with the face of an angel was exiled twenty years ago. I thought it was because of the fire incident at the opera that Edmée mentioned in the gardens, but the truth is worse: he killed a young girl like me, barely graduated from the Grande Écurie.

"My love for Aneta was pure," Alexandre says, his lips still trembling with anger. "We . . . we were consumed with passion."

"It's easy to blame passion," Edmée counters. "Passion has turned every single mortal who's had the misfortune of charming you to ashes, and the list is long. But all these fires have miraculously spared you. Every time, you escape unharmed, ready to start over again."

Alexandre gives me a distraught look.

This supposedly eternally young adolescent, who pretends to be a great romantic, is incapable of true love. He knows only how to possess and destroy. His romances are infatuations doomed to end in bloodshed. And me, I'm just his new obsession.

"It's not what you think, Diane," he says, mortified. "I'll tell you everything after the dinner, I promise, but not here . . ."

I try to hide my revulsion for this dishonorable bloodsucker by forcing myself to grin, my lips and teeth sealed tight, so that I don't spit in his face.

At that instant, the servants enter the banquet hall. They place a dish in front of each mortal, a plate garnished with shellfish and topped with half a lobster that lies on a bed of algae. Each vampyre is given a vial filled with the horrible blood rosé described on the menu. As the immortals uncork their respective vials, I feel like retching. They pour the contents into small crystal glasses, choosing the correct one from the forest of assorted stemware in front of them—each glass shaped differently to better savor a specific type of blood.

A synchronized pinging resonates across the room, the noise of the mortal guests who are picking up their gold cutlery from amid the complete array of tableware on each side of their plates. I've studied enough to recognize the little fork for hors d'oeuvres, the scissors for lobster, and the long picks for crustaceans. I deshell my lobster as elegantly as possible. The boarder seated on Alexandre's other side doesn't fare as well. Her lobster claw keeps slipping between her scissors, and she's unable to get a proper grip. My guess is that she's simply not exerting enough pressure—especially as she's barely able to keep her eyes open—so how could she possibly break the lobster's thick shell?

A vague shame grips my heart as I notice certain girls in the room struggling with their hors d'oeuvre. At least half a dozen demoiselles, those who drank the poisoned coffee before dinner. Madame Étiquette looks at them disapprovingly, which only adds to their stress and confusion. For the most part, I hardly know them. As for Poppy, who unbeknownst to her supplied me with the perfect weapon, I'm not worried. She doesn't like coffee, and her morphine addiction has probably raised her level of tolerance.

"Good gracious, be careful!" a mortal aristocrat suddenly cries out at the table across from mine. Her tablemate, Marie-Amélie de La Durance, has just sent pieces of lobster shell flying into her eye. The demoiselle has some of the best manners in our class, but she's apologizing profusely, her diction clumsy from the drug.

"This maiden blood is . . . how shall I say this? . . . a little harsh on the tongue," Edmée suddenly complains.

She's hardly placed her nearly untouched glass of blood on the table when I hear a voice behind me—it's Madame Thérèse, who's stealthily crept up to us.

"It must be a mistake, Madame la Marquise," she says. "Allow me to examine the vial, if you please."

The governess takes the small vial that Edmée emptied into her glass and reads the handwritten label out loud.

"Blood drawn October twenty-fourth, 299. Region: Versailles. Variety: Toinette Perrin, eighteen years old."

I freeze on my chair, suddenly comprehending that nothing at this diabolical dinner is happening by chance. Not my nearest vampyric seatmates nor the confounded vial.

The merciless look that Madame Thérèse gives me only confirms my suspicions.

"Oh, I believe I know what happened," she declares, feigning surprise. "The blood of that commoner was drawn right here at the school, during the art-of-vampyrism class. She is a young local girl, I assure you, so the varietal isn't in question . . . but I fear that the bleeding was a little disrupted, at least according to what I was told."

"How so, disrupted?" Edmée asks, looking at her glass with a disgusted look. "Don't tell me that commoner was sick?"

"Not at all. But the bleeding was interrupted by Mademoiselle de Gastefriche, herewith present. This generous soul was worried about the donor's health. The vial was topped with blood from another source who volunteered to take the girl's place, the Caballero de Montesueño."

Seated at the table across from mine, Rafael grows pale above his stiff collar. But tonight, the governess isn't targeting him. It's me she's after. Lucrèce must have ratted me out for insubordination.

Edmée frowns. "I thought there was something strange about this First Blood. I detest beginning a dinner with a blend. The palate hasn't had time to develop."

"You're entirely right, dear marquise," the governess says. "We must correct this annoying faux pas." She pivots on her heel and hails Toinette, who's standing on the side of the room with the other servants. "You, come here."

The poor girl looks desperately around, but no one can come to her rescue . . . not Rafael, not me. Interceding a second time on her behalf, this time in front of courtiers, would automatically disqualify us from the Sip.

Toinette walks over to the table in wobbly steps. Madame Étiquette doesn't intervene while the courtiers rejoice over this impromptu distraction. The eyes of the mortal ladies and lords widen in pleasure, as if they were taking in a show; the vampyres' pupils, on the other hand, contract with excitement, their predatory instinct sniffing out fear in the approaching prey.

"The time has come to settle the debt you neglected to pay the other night," Madame Thérèse tells the young servant. "To compensate the Marquise de Vauvalon for her unpleasant surprise, you'll fill her glass with the freshest blood of all—and dare I say, still deliciously warm."

"For . . . for pity's sake," Toinette stammers.

"Don't be a crybaby," Madame Thérèse scolds her. "You simply have to fill one small glass. I'm sure you'll feel much better afterward, basking in the satisfaction of a job well done. All the more so since your kind protector, Diane de Gastefriche, is the one who will bleed you. Let's see, it looks like your veins are more prominent on your right arm."

Under her stern grandmotherly airs, Thérèse is no more than a monster, worse than Montfaucon.

Holding Toinette's right wrist above the table, she gives me a needle connected to a rubber tube, the end of which she places into a new glass.

I take the needle in my trembling hand, using my eyes to implore the young servant to forgive me. Her gaze is filled with terror and incomprehension.

I search her skin for a spot to draw blood with the needle tip, just like I often saw my father do back in the village. But the crook of her elbow is still purplish. The jab from a few days ago clearly hasn't completely healed.

I plunge the needle next to the area, hoping I won't make Toinette suffer too much, and only succeed in eliciting a howl of pain. I missed the vein.

"Oh, I'm so sorry," I say, knowing that all eyes are on me, agonizingly aware that my clumsiness is losing me precious points on this odious test.

I push the needle in a second time. Again, I miss the thin vein—unless it's my hand that's trembling too much.

"Well, Mademoiselle de Gastefriche, do you have sand in your eyes this evening?" Thérèse squeaks over my shoulder.

"Perhaps I should try the left arm?"

"Tut-tut, you can't give up so quickly!"

Suddenly, I realize that Thérèse handed me Toinette's right arm precisely because it isn't healed, and she hasn't given me a garrote because she doesn't want the vein to protrude. This horrible woman wants to torture us, me and Toinette, for as long as possible.

The young servant's face is now ravaged with distress, overflowing with tears and racked with sobs. I'd like to hold her in my arms, tell her that this is all worth it, that her humiliation and all the years of bleeding she's endured will be erased by the tyrant's imminent death.

Overcome with anxiety and frustration, I jab the needle a third time—aiming right for the swollen puncture point of the other night, my only means of reaching the confounded vein that I'm unable to locate. Blood finally starts to flow into the rubber tube, but outside it too. In my lame attempts to bleed poor Toinette, I've mangled her arm even more. Drops of purple blood spread in a corolla on the embroidered tablecloth, raising excited growls from the vampyres' ranks.

"At last, it's done," Madame Thérèse declares smugly once the glass is filled. "Our apologies for the slow service, Madame la Marquise."

The governess leads an ashen Toinette toward the back of the room while Edmée raises the glass to her lips.

"Hmmm, delicious," she says with intense pleasure. "What a fine palate!—so to speak, at least for a maid raised in a fleapit, sleeping on nothing more than a bare pallet."

Her wit elicits peals of laughter and applause among the courtiers. Some raise their glasses, filled with either wine or blood, to offer toasts.

In my mouth, the lobster has lost its taste. Same with the cream soup and turkey that follow. Each bite is torture, but I force myself to swallow, the morsels of food falling like heavy rocks in the pit of my knotted stomach. For two hours, my face is nothing more than a mask frozen in a painful smile. I can't bring myself to be happy when I see

some of my rivals spill their wine or nod off. Madame Thérèse even has
to escort two girls back to the dormitory before they collapse. Seeing the
courtiers stuffing themselves with food makes me nauseous; the vampyres who greedily swill the vials of blood, the next vial always larger
than the last, horrify me. With their quivering nostrils and protruding
canines, I can't help but remember what I overheard the Princess des
Ursins say in the royal gardens: *"In the châteaus and palaces, the thirst of
immortals increases."*

When it's finally time to leave the table, I dodge Alexandre and his
stream of explanations that I have no interest in hearing. The guests
who had their fill of good food, alcohol, and blood return to the palace
with heavy footsteps, and the sleepy boarders go off to tuck into bed. I
take advantage of all the bustle to escape the crush and make my way
down the hallways that lead to the kitchens in the basement. Dinner is
over, my performance as well. My fate is now in the hands of Madame
Étiquette, and whatever comes next is out of my control. But I have to
find Toinette and apologize.

My frantic footsteps lead me to an area of the Grande Écurie where
I've never been before. I run down a staircase, eager to talk to Toinette,
painfully aware that I don't have much time before I have to be back in
the dormitory. I think I hear rustling and that I see silhouettes growing
larger on the walls. In these dark hallways, there are no maids and no
valets. I must have taken a wrong turn, thinking I was headed to the
kitchens. The walls, which have no moldings and look as if they're oozing from mild dampness, make me wonder if I might be lost somewhere
in the recluse's territory. But no, I don't think it's possible: there's no way
I could have gone that far below ground level. Besides, the oil lamps
suspended from the ceiling mean that this part of the basement is used.

I finally arrive at an impasse—a bare circular room, in the middle
of which is a round stone wall with a pulley system.

A well.

Probably the one the servants use in the dead of winter when the
ice freezes the pipes at the Grande Écurie.

With nowhere farther to go, I'm about to double back when I collide with a large figure.

In the feeble light of the oil lamps, it takes me a second to recognize the wide hoop pannier and mobcap dripping with ribbons.

"Madame Thérèse!" I exclaim.

She obviously followed me here, and now her huge dress blocks the only way out.

"Have you forgotten where the dormitories are?" she asks.

"I . . . I must have drunk a little too much champagne and gotten lost," I lie. "Would you please show me the way back?"

Instead of letting me pass, the governess advances toward me, forcing me to retreat to the center of the room.

"You may have had too much champagne . . . but you obviously didn't have too much coffee," she says.

My blood freezes.

"Don't play innocent. When I took Joséphine and Anne-Gaëlle back up in the middle of dinner, I noticed a snack cart tucked against a wall. Several rats had feasted on the leftovers."

"At Butte-aux-Rats, those creatures were a real nuisance too," I say, desperately trying to change the subject. "They get into every corner, impossible to trap."

The governess gives me a cold smile as she continues to draw closer.

"Oh, let me assure you that I had no problem capturing those rats. I just had to bend down to scoop them up and toss them into the fire. They were profoundly asleep, right near the spilled coffeepot, their whiskers coated with cookie crumbs soaked in coffee."

"You mean the coffee was . . . poisoned?" I ask, my voice quavering. "But by whom?"

"By the one who prepared the snacks, of course," the governess replies. "Toinette. Your protégé. Your accomplice."

My heels bump up against the stone well.

I can't back up any farther.

"You're the one who told her to commit that crime, aren't you?" the governess accuses me as she grabs my arm. "Admit it. Confess. Then we can finally send that goose to the gallows, and you, far away from these walls."

I try to disengage, but the old woman grasps my arm with a force I never would have guessed she was capable of.

Panic grips my chest. The earthy, humid smell coming off the walls fills my nostrils. I can't breathe.

"Little *conniver*," the governess hisses. "When the king finds out what you've done, you won't be sent to the convent. You'll be bled, just like those vulgar commoners you're so fond of."

"Let me remind you that you're a commoner too!" I manage to reply, my breath raspy.

Her angry face, thick with makeup, turns to pure hate.

"Little bitch!" she yells as she slaps my face. "You think you're so superior to me? I deserve to be transmuted as much as you or anyone else at this school."

Before she can slap me again, I grab her wrist, which is trembling with rage.

"Let go of me!" she shouts, a glimmer of madness in her eyes. "Let go of me or I'll . . . I'll bleed you!"

She opens her large mouth full of fillings, aims for my neck—but the way I'm holding her, her jaw only reaches my shoulder.

The vicious bite pierces my skin under the fabric of my dress, and I let out a cry of pain and fright.

Overcome with panic, I wrench off me this demented, transmutation-obsessed hag who already thinks of herself as a vampyre. I turn around and shove her with all my might into the well.

Her enormous wicker pannier gets stuck in the opening, exposing her many lace petticoats, silk stockings, and puny legs that flail in the air.

Under the thick layers of fabric, the governess's voice sounds muffled.

"Help me! Help me now, you little fool!"

I stand still next to the well, frozen in place, my shoulder bloody.

Inch by inch I watch as the governess's legs sink deeper down the well, her furious kicks only crushing the pannier, the hoops breaking one by one.

"I promise I won't say anything to the king about all your tricks," she says, her tone now pleading. Tearful. "And you'll keep quiet about that small, harmless bite that got the better of me. It'll be our secret. It'll . . . *aaaaaaaaaaaaaaah!*"

The rest of the pannier gives way.

Shoes, stockings, petticoats . . . all disappear into the dark hole, followed by a long scream that trails off, silenced by a distant plop.

23

THE ART OF
EQUESTRIANISM

"Mesdemoiselles, you are no doubt waiting for Madame Thérèse to come and announce the results of last night's test," Madame de Chantilly says when she enters the dormitory. "However, this morning, she . . . uh . . . she had to go run an errand in town."

All around me, girls exchange questioning looks.

Madame Thérèse is usually omnipresent, overseeing every aspect of the boarders' lives from morning to night—even more so during this period of tests. Her unexpected absence throws everyone for a loop, including the teaching staff.

"Your dear governess has gone to her milliner to adjust her outfit before tonight's art-of-equestrianism test," Chantilly states, getting tangled in her lie.

"Or maybe she followed your example and ran off to live out her 'big love' with a vampyre?" Poppy whispers in my ear. "We all know how she drools over immortals."

I force myself to smile at Poppy's sarcasm, my throat tight, my shoulder still hurting from the governess's bite under my new dress. I immediately burned the bloodstained bodice when I got back to the dormitory last night.

Doesn't Poppy see how pale I am?

And don't the others see my discomfort?

No. They're all hanging on Chantilly's every word, eyes riveted to the paper she takes out of her pocket.

After adjusting her round gold-rimmed spectacles, the teacher starts to read in her usual pompous tone, the same way she does whenever she recites odes and panegyrics in class.

"On this day, October twenty-ninth in the year of Shadows 299, I have the honor of announcing the six candidates hereby retained, following the art-of-courtly-manners test. These candidates were specially selected by the Countess de Villeforge, appointed by the king. They are . . .

"Hélénaïs de Plumigny."

Every head turns with envy toward my biggest rival, her face beaming with pride.

"Proserpina Castlecliff."

At the Grande Écurie, it seems that Hélé and Poppy are always in lockstep—and this morning, too, they're vying for first place.

"Françoise des Escailles."

A muffled cry of joy comes from my right side. The small, diligent brunette follows closely on the heels of the two class leaders.

"Séraphine de La Pattebise."

Only two names left, I think as I squeeze my mother's watch in my dress pocket.

"Marie-Ornella de Lorenzi."

One name . . .

"Diane de Gastefriche."

The knot in my throat loosens up all at once.

I made it.

The hushed murmurs of the girls who understand that their hopes have been dashed become a concert of groans. Some blame the late dinner hour, others the heady wine. Luckily, none of the losers point to the real culprit: the coffee that made them lose their self-control. The main witnesses have disappeared—the rats in the fire and Madame Thérèse at the bottom of a well. I can still hear the icy echo of her cries and the thump of her body hitting the water below. How many feet did she plummet? Fifty? One hundred? More? The long silence after her fall convinced me she was dead.

"Enough whining," Chantilly declares, clapping her hands to restore order. "Those who lost should be happy: you're free to rest until next Monday, when classes start up again as usual. The others must prepare for tonight's test. The grand equerry asked me to tell you that the carousel will take place in the ring as soon as night falls. You'll carry it out alongside the six boys who've been selected . . . whose names I will now read." She turns over the paper. "Messieurs de Montesueño, de Longuedune, de Grand-Domaine, de La Roncière, della Strada, and du Charlois."

My heart may have rejoiced when I heard my name, but it positively explodes when I hear Tristan's. Then Chantilly adds something that quickly dampens my joy.

"The carousel will take place in the presence of the Marquis de Mélac," she concludes. "The minister of the armies himself will choose the three best riders in each group—a true honor for you."

As the teacher turns around to head off, I think about this cruel irony. The one who ordered that my family be killed will decide if I can advance in the competition . . . or not.

"Do you know what happened to Madame Thérèse?"

Naoko's question catches me off guard.

From her seat in front of the bathing room mirror where she's brushing my hair, her inquisitive look shoots daggers at my reflection. Tonight, she's pinned my hair under a black felt dressage hat lined in satin as befits an equestrian test to be held in front of the eminent members of the court.

"How would I know?"

"You came back to the dormitory much later than the others last night. No one noticed because it was late and the other girls were sound asleep, especially the ones who drank your special home-brewed coffee. But as you know, I'm a light sleeper . . ."

My face goes pale in the mirror, paler even than Naoko's under a thin layer of powder.

"Remember what we promised each other," she says. "To never hide another secret."

"It . . . it was an accident," I stammer. "Thérèse fell into a basement well. There was nothing I could do to save her."

Naoko stares at me in silence, as if she can read my mind about everything that happened yesterday . . . as if she can see that I let the governess tumble down without trying to help in any way.

"Besides, she was a horrible woman," I say. "She deserved to die, isn't that so?"

Naoko remains stone faced, as locked as a prison door.

"I didn't like her any better than you did," she says coldly. "But who are you, Jeanne or Diane, to decide who deserves to die?"

"Thérèse was just as cruel as Lucrèce! You saw what they did to poor Toinette. I said it and I'll say it again: those two monsters deserve to die."

My lips itch to tell Naoko that Lucrèce's days are numbered. Like all the king's squires, she'll perish under the blades of the rebels lying in ambush at the palace. But I stay silent since Naoko knows nothing about the plan to assassinate the king. She still believes I want to quench my personal vengeance against Alexandre de Mortange.

"You're cruel as well," she replies. "Your thirst for vengeance has turned into a morbid obsession. Melancholy is devouring you. You talk about human life like a vampyre. Careful that you don't become like everything you hate. It would be too high a price to pay for revenge, Jeanne."

"No price is too high to avenge my loved ones, do you hear me!" I yell as I get up from the chair, exasperated by Naoko's accusations. "In fact, this conversation is giving me a headache. I'd better go off to the stable and get ready for the carousel. It'll be dusk in less than an hour, and I've primped enough as it is."

As soon as I enter the stable, the strong horse smell washes over me like a wave, dissipating my moody state, sweeping aside my nascent headache.

The quivering presence of the large equines jolts me back to my own animalistic, sanguine side, the one that took over my body whenever I went hunting in the woods. Flee or fight. Kill or be killed. In nature, the choice is reduced to simple, pure alternatives unencumbered by remorse or regrets.

I make my way through the semidarkness toward Typhon's stall, my riding boots crushing the straw on the ground.

Typhon's powerful hindquarters come into view. The garnet reflections of his long bare spine shine in the evening light streaming through the tall windows. Unexpectedly, Typhon hasn't been saddled . . . and with less than one hour to go before the carousel, I would have thought the grooms would have started to get him ready.

"I was just as surprised as you are when I came down to see Fuego," someone says behind me.

I turn around, squinting to see in the twilight.

A figure dressed in black clothing appears. Rafael de Montesueño. He's standing in front of the stall facing mine, his hand resting on the neck of his purebred.

"I don't think we're going to be riding our usual horses tonight," he says. "Actually, I know that for a fact."

"What do you mean?"

"The grooms haven't prepared any of the horses. I know this because I spent the entire afternoon in the stable with my loyal Fuego, who came with me from Spain. This is where I feel most at home here."

And also where you have the most memories, I think as I recall the nighttime trysts that Naoko witnessed.

"It seems that Mélac will be bringing horses that the king has chosen for us," he continues. "Animals we're not accustomed to. That's just like the Immutable, constantly destabilizing his subjects to better dominate them. Like last evening when Madame Thérèse forced you to bleed poor Toinette in front of everyone. I'm sure she had the king's backing."

I nod, a surge of emotion welling up for this stranger who dares criticize the implacable order of the Vampyria and who didn't hesitate to spill his own blood to spare a servant. Could it be that he, too, belongs to the Fronde? Probably not, or Tristan would have told me. But perhaps he could be recruited.

"If you only knew how awful I feel for having done that to Toinette," I confess, trying to figure him out. "No commoner deserves to be treated that way, no matter what the theft. It's vile. Unjust."

"The entire Magna Vampyria is based on injustice," Rafael answers.

His aplomb startles me.

Such a statement could get him expelled from the Grand Écurie or, at the very least, rebuked. The fact that he's so open about his convictions makes him even more likable. I suddenly remember that he's amid the lead pack in the boys' wing. If he ends up winning the Sip in two days and we find ourselves together in the mortuary chamber, will I have the courage to kill him?

"Suraj isn't worth it," I blurt out.

Rafael's eyes widen in the dim stables.

I feel my cheeks burning, ashamed of my indiscretion—but I have to say something. I have to dissuade him from risking his life for a boy who's going to die before the week is out, like every other squire.

"I know something happened between the two of you," I hurry to say, not mentioning Naoko.

He looks away, obviously uncomfortable.

"I didn't know it showed so much . . ."

"I wouldn't have guessed on my own. But I heard Suraj talking to Lucrèce after the jig the other night." I try to control my breathing, which is speeding up as I invent a lie that will perhaps save Rafael's life but also break his heart. "I forgot a ribbon in the banquet hall, so I went back down. From the doorway, I could hear the two squires talking. Romantic banter. Laced with cruel sarcasm."

Above the stiff collar that's all the style at the court of Spain, Rafael's face freezes.

"In between showering Lucrèce with kisses, he made fun of you," I tell him, painfully aware that my every word is like a dagger plunging into Rafael's chest. "He was telling his companion how much your goo-goo-eyed looks amuse him. Yes, that's the very word he used, *amuse*. That's all you were for him, an amusement, when he was a boarder in the boys' wing, deprived of girls. But now that he's with Lucrèce, you only elicit his laughter."

I take a deep breath, gathering all my strength to deal the coup de grâce.

"I wish I could have kept all this to myself, but I feel it's my duty to stop you from committing a terrible mistake. I suspect you're not competing for the Sip of the King to serve a kingdom you deem unjust. It wouldn't make sense. So you must be taking part in order to be reunited with Suraj. But you don't mean anything to him now, do you hear me? Nothing at all."

Rafael's face has remained frozen, stoically taking in everything I said without so much as flinching an eyebrow. But his black-polished fingernails grip the long wavy mane of his purebred like a drowning victim clings to a rope.

"Thank you for your honesty," he says finally.

"It's the least I can do," I say, swallowing the bitter taste of my lie. "Now you see why there's no reason to go all out for an ingrate. Don't inflict humiliation on yourself by joining him among the king's bodyguards. Forget him. Fall in love with another who'll love you the way you deserve to be loved—and live your life!"

I smile warmly at him as I think about that life and the deceitful words that may have spared it.

Rafael remains stone still.

"I'll never be able to forget him," he says so seriously that my smile instantly fades. "In India, I know that Suraj had other experiences before meeting me. He's just as sensitive to the charms of girls as he is to those of boys. Maybe he'll never be able to love me the way I love him. Maybe he truly found something that I wasn't able to give him in Lucrèce's arms. Maybe what we shared was only an 'amusement' for him." His green eyes sparkle wildly. "Or maybe he felt obliged to talk about it that way. To deny his feelings and not displease the king. As an envoy of the maharaja, his comportment must be beyond reproach. His duty is to establish diplomatic relations between the Magna Vampyria and the kingdom of Jaipur."

Rafael heaves a deep sigh, full of repressed anger.

"The Immutable looks down with an evil eye on anything that's out of the norm and that he perceives as a direct challenge to his authority—as if that three-hundred-year-old fossil should decide who I have the right to love or not.

"The Faculty condemns relations between the same sex, on the pretext that it's a 'vice' that affects the reproduction of human livestock. As if it's only possible to love in order to produce more fresh blood to feed the vampyres.

"The archiaters and inquisitors consider love between boys or between girls an abomination that deserves being burned at the stake, just like the stryges—as if the pure feelings I still have for Suraj were a horrible monster that had to be destroyed."

In the quiet of the stables, amid the heavy breathing of the horses, Rafael's voice has risen like an unstoppable Pegasus soaring to the sky.

"I don't know why I'm telling you all this," he suddenly says, regaining his self-control. "Probably because I sense that you have more empathy than a lot of other boarders. But I can't ask that you understand me."

"No, I understand," I respond, swept up with emotion.

I'd like to tell him that I understand what it's like to live a concealed life, that I understand the rage that goes with being different and the desire to upend an arbitrary society.

But of course, I don't.

I can only place my hand on his shoulder and squeeze it hard, my way of communicating that I'm on his side.

"Thank you," he says. "I'm touched. And if you really understand me, like you say you do, you'll also understand why I have to compete for the Sip. To prove to Suraj that I can do it. To prove to *myself* that I can do it. And to ask him in person, equal to equal, if there's really nothing left between us."

I waver, sensing that all my efforts to deter Rafael from this fatal competition cannot outweigh the strength of his feelings.

At that instant, a furious ringing of bells can be heard outside the thick walls of the stable. The warning bell.

"It's time for us to go to the ring," Rafael says.

He lets go of the long hairs of the horse that followed him from faraway Spain to the coldness of Versailles.

"We won't be teammates tonight, my dear Fuego," he says as he gives the horse one last stroke on the neck. "Wish us luck, Diane and me."

The purebred gives a long, gentle snort through his muzzle, releasing a little cloud of vapor.

An encouragement. Or a blessing.

"Ah, Gastefriche and Montesueño, we were waiting for the two of you," the grand equerry says as soon as we enter the riding arena.

The ten other riders are already there, standing in the sawdust. The boys all wear short jackets and riding breeches; the girls are in dresses to mount sidesaddle, with the exception of Poppy, who, like me, prefers to ride astride. Tonight she's wearing the same *blue jean* breeches she wore on the hunt.

I exchange a look with Tristan for the first time since dinner last night. He does his best to smile under his dressage hat. But by the way his eyes squint, I gather he's nagged by anxiety. The carousel is about to get underway, and there are still no horses in sight.

The grand equerry seems preoccupied too. He turns toward the bleachers that overlook the ring, facing the mezzanine, where the Swiss Guards have taken their place with their flutes and drums. About thirty spectators are seated there, among which I recognize several courtiers from last evening. However it's not Madame de Villeforge who has the place of honor as judge amid this assembly of velvet and lace. The central seat is occupied by a lanky man whose angular face is framed by a long wig with tight brown curls. The large hat he's sporting is decorated with eagle feathers, setting him further apart from the other courtiers.

Mélac.

His living-dead quality is more evident than with the other vampyres. There's no illusion of youth. There's something mummified about his emaciated face and sunken cheeks, as if the innumerable crimes committed by the dragoons over the course of the centuries have gnawed at him from inside.

"We're all accounted for, Monsieur de Mélac," the grand equerry says, his voice tense. "For the last time, I'll ask if you're certain that you want to go with the vampyric mares."

I instantly recall the room with the mare tapestries. I'd naively thought they depicted mythological scenes, pure legends . . . I had forgotten that at the Court of Shadows, the most terrifying nightmares have a tendency of becoming reality.

"I'm not the one behind this," the minister of the armies says sharply from the bleachers. "It's the king's idea. His Majesty chose to increase the difficulty of the equestrian test this year. Such is his wish."

Mélac claps his bony hands together, and Montfaucon can only bow before withdrawing behind the kickboard.

The door to the ring opens, letting in a gust of wind that chills me right down to my soul.

The dozen noblemen who enter are not the usual grooms. They're vampyres, with pale skin and heads adorned with large hats. Each one holds a bridle attached to a statuesque black mare champing at the bit, the horses' foreheads capped by quivering white feathers.

"If any among you would like to call it quits, there's still time," Mélac declares. "Of course, if you forgo the test, you will be categorically excluded from the competition for the Sip of the King, as His Majesty cannot abide poltroons."

The competitors cast glances at one another. Some, like Françoise des Escailles, seem to be looking for a way out; others, like Hélénaïs de Plumigny, seem to be challenging the others to abandon the contest. In Tristan's eyes, determination has replaced all doubt, and that's all that matters to me.

I refocus on the nobleman who's coming toward me, holding the reins in his gloved hand.

Under the shadow of his large hat, I recognize . . . Alexandre.

"I found a way to be here tonight," he whispers into my ear. "And I harnessed this mare especially for you."

I look at the mare's ebony head, enclosed in leather straps. Her dilated pupils resemble those of the king's wolves. Under bluish-veined nostrils that exhale a breath as cold as winter, the front set of teeth are normal—the incisors of an herbivore, made to cut down hay. But the long pointy canines that come after are made to tear at flesh. As for the mare's molars, they chew the bit with persistence, a long spittle of drool hanging from her foaming mouth right down to the ground.

"I switched out the iron bit for a silver one," Alexandre tells me, sliding the reins into my hands. "That should calm the mare for the duration of the carousel."

I know silver is a toxic metal that weakens immortals and no doubt all vampyric creatures with shadowessence in their veins. As a result, my mare seems quieter than the eleven others, as if she's been stunned. Instead of pawing at the ground and snorting with fury, she's content to drool abundantly.

By cheating right under the king's nose, only weeks after being back in favor, I know that Alexandre is taking a big risk. I stammer a "thank you" that repulses me.

"You can *truly* thank me once you've won the Sip, dear Diane," he says as he helps me put my foot into the stirrup. "The sooner you enter the court, the sooner we'll be together."

As I brush against him, my eyes catch his. They sparkle with blazing brilliancy . . . with passion. He's devouring me with his eyes, as if I belonged to him.

I hoist myself onto the saddle to quickly get away from him. The other riders have a harder time settling down. Their black mares fidget nervously, some kicking out, lifting clouds of sawdust that glisten under the chandeliers.

"The mares are the jewels of the royal stables," Mélac says from the bleachers, raising his voice to be heard over the whinnying of the monstrous quadrupeds. "On the battlefields, they slice the enemy's throat with one snap of their jaws. To be sure, sometimes they unsaddle a clumsy rider and tear open their stomach—but what can I say, that's the mares' warrior nature."

The minister of the armies seems to relish the competitors' distress. Big smiles spread across the faces of the courtiers around him. The bewigged gentlemen and noble ladies wriggle in the bleachers; some adjust their gold opera glasses as they would at the theater, to better see who will topple first.

The noblemen depart the ring, leaving us alone with the mares.

A bell rings, the signal for the start of the carousel.

As the first notes of the military rondo spill down from the musicians in the mezzanine, I use my aids to lead my mare to the end of the arena. Between my calves, her belly isn't warm and alive like Typhon's but cold and dead. No breathing swells her large flanks, even as I start her at a canter to execute an initial volte, a small circle. All around the ring, in equidistance, the other mares are also turning, their ostrich-feathered headgear swaying in step.

Having now changed hands, we canter alongside the ring, following the rhythm of the accelerating rondo. It's not only the rumbling of the drums that bores into my eardrums; there's also the thunder of hooves hitting the kickboard. Jumping and kicking, the furious beasts are already trying to eject their riders.

The girls who chose to mount sidesaddle, sacrificing practicality in favor of elegance, are having a rough time, their asymmetrical seat a serious disadvantage for maintaining balance. The most graceful among us, Séraphine de La Pattebise, is the first one to pay the price. She tumbles just as we're getting ready to change hands again on the diagonal.

As she hits the sawdust, the spectators whoop with delight. The mare that unseated her stops dead and turns toward her, baring all her fangs.

Séraphine gives a shrill cry.

She tries to get up as best she can but gets tangled in the folds of her moiré dress.

The first bite tears off her riding hat, as well as a tuft of hair.

Another mare becomes overly excited by Séraphine's cries and unseats her rider in turn—Marie-Ornella de Lorenzi.

Terrified, I hold tight to my mount's mane as I look frantically at my male competitors. They're too busy trying to control their own mares to think about helping the girls in distress. Besides, protocol forbids it. One must continue with the carousel.

I open a right lead to begin a large circle. The two riders on the ground, who've now managed to get up, rush toward the door at the foot of the bleachers.

"Let us out, for pity's sake!" Marie-Ornella de Lorenzi screams.

The mare in back of her violently tears off a large swath of her sumptuous gold-threaded dress, revealing the white petticoats underneath. The courtiers erupt in laughter, same as if they were attending a farcical comedy. Their raucous hooting blends in with the beating of the drums.

Laughing uproariously as well, Mélac finally raises his thumb like a Roman emperor in his tribune.

The grooms open the door partway, just enough to let the two crying girls take refuge.

They've just barely found shelter when their two mares, drunk with rage, start looking for new prey. They rush toward the two nearest riders: Giacomo della Strada and Pierre du Charlois. Up to now, the two boys had managed to control their mounts, but they suddenly go to pieces. Trying to defend themselves with their whips, they succeed only in throwing themselves off balance and are next to fall to the ground.

The orchestra, which had paused, starts a new movement, a signal to the riders still atop their saddles to begin another figure—a three-loop serpentine. At the tips of my tightly wound fingers on the reins, I can feel the toothy mouth on the silver bit. I squeeze my legs to move forward toward Tristan, who's coming from the opposite side. His face is tense, glistening with sweat. He gives me a quick look of feverish encouragement, then rides right by.

Behind him is Poppy, without doubt the best equestrian in the girls' wing, who's able to remain dignified. On the flip side, Françoise des Escailles is completely flattened against her mare, her eyes wide with fear behind her thick eyeglasses, her loose single stirrup bouncing in the air between the folds of her ruffled dress. Hélénaïs places somewhere in between these two extremes, her face tense with anxiety under an elaborate hairdo that comes a little more undone with each step. Zacharie de Grand-Domaine and Thomas de Longuedune are getting by about the same—which means with difficulty.

Rafael brings up the rear of riders coming toward me, in the last loop of the serpentine. His equestrian savoir faire is known to everyone at the Grande Écurie, but the way he controls his mare exceeds anything I could have imagined. Without either a silver bit or another similar trick, he's able to make her advance at an even trot, her *appuis* perfectly aligned, her head so completely pulled into her chest that it's hard to even see her sharp fangs. Only the furrows on Rafael's forehead betray his intense focus during this seemingly effortless routine.

"Courage!" he shouts when we brush by one another. "The hardest part is done."

I realize that we've actually completed three-quarters of the carousel.

My mare turns at the end of the ring, giving me a new perspective. Giacomo and Pierre succeeded in taking shelter at the last minute, joining Séraphine and Marie-Ornella behind the kickboard. The four mares now free of their riders wander in the center of the sawdust. They're attacking each other, tearing off their feathered headgear. For now, they seem uninterested in the eight remaining riders, leaving us hope that we'll finish the equestrian ballet more or less as we're supposed to.

I initiate one of the last voltes, my heart beating wildly.

But the courtiers, who've come to watch the circus games, don't see it that way. Shouts and whistles start up, mixing with the last bars of the rondo. A projectile suddenly launches from the bleachers, straight in my direction. I immediately react, and it just misses me . . . landing in the eye of the mare behind me.

A furious cry tears my eardrums, sounding somewhere between the whinnying of a horse and the roar of a lion. The animal that's been struck rears up, throwing off its rider, Françoise des Escailles.

The brunette lands with a brutal thud in the sawdust, losing her hat and thick eyeglasses.

"Help!" she cries.

Françoise starts to grope around for the magnifying glasses, without which she's as myopic as a mole. But she only gets entangled in the cumbersome ruffles of her satin dress, unable to see her mare returning to her at full speed.

"Watch out!" I shriek.

Françoise looks up in my direction, squinting, hair full of sawdust.

She raises a hand the way she often does in class, asking permission to speak, but tonight she's extending her hand toward me, her fingers stretching in desperation for help.

The half-blinded mare closes her monstrous mouth on the trembling arm.

A ghastly cracking of bones rings out.

The crushed humerus shatters between the pointy fangs.

A heavy rainfall of blood lands on the ring.

The orchestra strikes up the final drumroll, covering up the courtiers' exclamations and Françoise's cries of pain.

The four free mares charge toward her like big cats pouncing on a gazelle, ready to feast.

24

THE ART OF
CONVERSATION

"The fate of Françoise des Escailles is now in the hands of the Faculty surgeons," Madame de Chantilly announces soberly to all the girls.

This morning, a funereal silence fills the dormitory.

Everyone knows that the Faculty's surgical procedures are often synonymous with death. For every Barvók more or less patched together again, how many botched medical procedures end in the mass grave?

The last moments of the carousel go round in a loop in my mind: the endless minute that Françoise remained the mares' prey before their handlers were able to get control of them. An arm, crushed like a twig . . . tufts of hair torn off, along with fragments of scalp . . . and the bloody shreds of her dress that the monstrous mares furiously battled over . . . what could there possibly be left to save of the poor girl after such a mad scramble? Maybe it would have been better if she'd died instead of ending up in pieces on the operating table of the archiaters of Versailles . . .

"More bad news: Madame Thérèse is unable to join you for now," the art-of-conversation teacher goes on, tearing me from my thoughts. "She caught cold on the way back from her milliner and must stay confined to bed. That's why you didn't see her at the carousel and why you'll probably not see her tonight."

Chantilly readjusts her spectacles, a gesture that betrays her nerves. It would seem the governess still hasn't been found . . . just as well.

"Therefore it falls on me to announce the candidates selected for the third test of the competition," she continues.

She clears her throat, creating an artificial suspense—only three riders stayed in their saddles last night.

"Hélénaïs de Plumigny . . .

"Proserpina Castlecliff . . .

"Diane de Gastefriche."

After yesterday's bloodbath, no one thinks of rejoicing, not even Hélénaïs, whose chiseled face stays frozen between her serpentine curls. As for Naoko, instead of being happy for my success, she's taken refuge at the end of the dormitory. She hasn't spoken to me since our last heated conversation. There doesn't seem to be anything left of our friendship, not even the silk lotus flower that she sewed for me and I misplaced.

"And here are the names of the boys who were selected," Chantilly says as she reads a piece of paper.

"Rafael de Montesueño . . ."

Of course, it goes without saying since he's the top rider in our class. But Tristan is sure to come in second—he maintained his composure during the test.

"Zacharie de Grand-Domaine . . ."

The Louisianan? It's true that he performed well. Fine, Tristan will have to settle for third place on the podium.

"Thomas de Longuedune."

My stomach somersaults.

"Impossible!" I blurt out.

All eyes turn to me.

"Uh . . . I mean, are you sure you read correctly, madame?" I ask.

"If I wear corrective lenses, it's precisely to enable me to read, Mademoiselle de Gastefriche," the teacher shoots back, glaring at me from above the gold frame of her eyeglasses.

"Still, are you sure there isn't a mistake?"

Chantilly puts her hands on the ample hips of her dress, her imposing hairdo styled with a doily that shakes with disapproval.

"Twice asking the same question highlights the worst ineptitude when it comes to the art of conversation," she snaps at me. "I'm used to better from you. I hope you'll pull yourself together tonight."

"I . . . uh . . . please pardon me," I stammer, painfully aware of Hélénaïs's delight.

"Good. Don't embarrass me in front of the Princess des Ursins. The minister of foreign affairs, one of the best minds in the Vampyria, will do us the honor of judging the exchanges in the small theater at the Grande Écurie. The test will be in two phases: first, the demoiselles, then the messieurs. The chosen format is free conversation embellished with verse, favoring octosyllabic ones, since those are short and hard hitting. After each joust, the least eloquent girl and boy will be eliminated." She gives a small cough. "We will gather in the theater at nightfall before dinner. Conversation is always at its best on an empty stomach, when the mind isn't yet weighted down with the drowsiness of digestion."

October 30, one day before the Sip of the King, is the most solitary of all the days I've known since arriving at the Grande Écurie.

Naoko still isn't speaking to me. I don't have any news of Tristan, and I know I won't be able to see him before the test. The thought of continuing without him terrifies me. The prospect of bantering with octosyllabic verses petrifies me. Doubt creeps in like a poison. If Tristan was eliminated yesterday, who's to say it won't be my turn tonight?

I spend the afternoon prostrated in the bathing room where Naoko used to brush my hair. Behind the window, the titans of the Hunting

Wall observe me in silence with their stone eyes, their lids increasingly sunken as the sun goes down. In the hollow of my palm, I squeeze my mother's pocket watch.

Oh, Maman, if only you could be with me tonight.

"Diane?"

I stiffen and clench my fingers quickly around the watch. I was so absorbed in my thoughts that I didn't hear the door to the bathing room open behind me.

"Who is it?" I ask, turning around on the stool as I slide the watch into my dress pocket.

Poppy stands on the threshold. She's forsaken her signature denim in favor of a cream taffeta dress. The color is so light that the contrast makes her look less pale. Her long, loose hair cascades down in a brown stream onto the rose pattern that dots the fabric of her bodice.

"Everything all right, darling?" she asks me.

"Why wouldn't it be?" I answer.

"La Roncière's elimination must be a real blow."

"Not at all."

"And Naoko, the two of you thick as thieves since you came to the Grande Écurie, isn't here to get you ready tonight."

The English girl applies pressure where it hurts—a strategy to throw me off balance before the test?

"And so what?" I bark. "Don't tell me that's why you're showing up, to brush my hair."

"It is."

Her friendly smile leaves me speechless, and I'm suddenly ashamed I answered her so angrily.

"I'm in no way as gifted as Naoko, I give you that. But I can help you with your bun," she says. "And I wouldn't turn down a helping hand to put some order in all this."

She points to her imposing mass of hair.

I nod, inviting her in.

She takes a brush and starts smoothing my gray tresses as she talks.

"Tonight, our alliance can go beyond a mere combing of your hair. Let's team up against the feathered queen bee in the verbal joust. Conversation is her weak point, and we won't have trouble sinking her. And let's face off against each other in tomorrow's art-of-weaponry test. If I have to lose, I'd rather it be against you. If Plumigny triumphs for the Sip of the King, it would make me ill. But if you're the one who wins, I'll get over it."

She gives me a wan smile in the mirror, her eyes gleaming with a feverish spark, looking more ill than ever.

"It's a deal," I declare.

"Hurry!" Madame de Chantilly says, leading the way down the grand staircase.

She came to collect us soon after the warning bell rang. Hélénaïs trails closely behind her, looking more stunning than ever, the feathers of her hurly-burly hairstyle quivering with each step, while Poppy and I follow in her wake.

We arrive at a double door decorated with gilded sculptures representing two masks with hollowed orbits: the laughter of comedy to the right and the tears of tragedy to the left.

"Remember to always have a pleasant countenance, mesdemoiselles," Chantilly counsels us. "You can hurl killer digs all through the night as long as you do so with a smile."

The Swiss Guards posted on either side of the door open the two panels, which is how I enter into the theater of the Grande Écurie for the first time.

It's a fairly tiny room, seemingly all the more so because of the ornate moldings on the walls and the heavy red velvet curtains flanking the small stage. Facing the boards, the dim room is abuzz with chatter. The cramped benches seem to be packed with as many courtiers as were present in the vast bleachers of the ring last night.

Chantilly executes a sophisticated curtsy in front of an imposing lady with a refined hairdo sitting in the first row: the Princess des Ursins.

As much as Mélac appeared to be more of a mummy than an immortal, the Princess des Ursins seems more alive than she does a vampyre. Her long swan neck looks like it's throbbing from a beating heart—which is, of course, impossible. Her skin, smooth and flawless like all the lords of the night, has a rosy freshness that belongs only to the living. Cosmetic work? I couldn't say. The Princess des Ursins possesses a beauty as radiant as it is delicate. I wonder if her long diplomatic career taught her how to smile just so, in a pleasant fashion, without revealing her pointy canines.

"Mesdemoiselles, dazzle us with your marvelous wit," she gracefully implores.

We climb the few steps that lead to the stage.

From this vantage point, I can't make out faces in the audience, but I see eyes gleaming, reflecting the brightness of the boards. Is Alexandre down below? The thought that he can spy on me without my seeing him, like a predator hidden in the dark, makes me uncomfortable.

Three baton taps can suddenly be heard—the signal for the start of the hostilities.

Poppy launches into a direct attack, turning toward Hélénaïs to bombard her with octosyllabic verses that we prepared especially for her.

"If your wit be ever as short
As your family lineage,
I'll grill you before the whole court
Until you're stripped of patronage."

Enthusiastic exclamations erupt across the appreciative room. It may be despicable to attack Hélénaïs on her recent nobility, but it's exactly this kind of base attack that thrills the courtiers. It's also exactly what will hurt this arrogant girl, which is all that counts.

I follow up immediately, speaking loudly so that everyone can hear me clearly, pronouncing each of the eight syllables of every verse.

"Turkeys, capons, and farm livestock

Taught you well how to bill and coo:
You pretend to be a peacock
But you're just a hen from the coop."

Once again, shrieks of relish run through the spectators while Hélénaïs's perfect face starts to crumple under her feathered hairdo.

I'm expecting her to stammer, to dig herself into a hole, right in front of the audience.

But the words that spill out of her carefully stained mouth are perfectly articulated.

"Should I call you a lying witch,
You who fool the nobility?"

She turns brusquely toward me.

"How long, *Baroness Gastefriche*,
Must we bear your duplicity?"

A cold sweat runs down the length of my spine.

She knows! shouts a voice in my head. *I don't know how, but Hélénaïs has unmasked me.*

"I . . . I don't know what you mean," I sputter.

"You aren't a Baroness de Gastefriche; that's what I'm saying," Hélénaïs tosses out at me.

"Yes, I am a Baroness de Gastefriche!" I cry out. "Just like all my ancestors before me. I inherited my father's title when he died. My . . . nobility papers prove it."

In the first row, the beautiful Princess des Ursins stares at me in silence.

Next to her, Chantilly rolls her eyes in reproach, as there's nothing more contrary to the art of conversation than to raise one's voice.

Without abandoning her diabolical calm, Hélénaïs starts a new quatrain.

"She came from her far-off mountain
Like a mermaid out of her lake;
But gossipers in the Auvergne
Whisper that her papers are fake."

My eyes dart around the small theater, looking for a way out.

The feeling of being cornered terrifies me.

I can't breathe, and my head starts to spin.

Suddenly, I'm no longer Diane, the proud baronne in contention for the Sip of the King. Once again, I'm Jeanne, the little wild child from the forests. And this evening, the forests are filled with ferocious beasts whose dilated pupils are devouring me.

My legs shaking, I step back toward the wings, provoking muffled cries from the courtiers and Chantilly's categorical warning.

"Diane, that is unacceptable! I am warning you that if you leave the stage midjoust, you will be immediately disqualified."

From the edge of the stage, Hélénaïs points an accusing finger at me, as if she's crucifying me with her polished nail.

"You are quite a lousy actress,
Posing as a baronne and yet
The time has arrived to confess
That you are just a bannerette."

I freeze at the side of the stage, my head ringing like a bell with the last word my rival uttered.

Bannerette? I know that the title of banneret is inferior to that of baron in the hierarchy of the nobility.

"My father paid legal experts to do thorough research in the archives of the aristocracy concerning this student from nowhere," Hélénaïs says, jubilantly, breaking from the octosyllabic verses to freely spout her venom. She turns toward the audience. "I received the research results from a crow. It seems the Gastefriches were *never* elevated to the rank of baron. They assumed the title centuries ago, daring to have it written down on their nobility papers. No magistrate in their muddy province thought to check . . . until the investigators hired by my father discovered this vile abuse."

In the dimness of the wings, I'm suffocating in my tight corset.

The fact that old Gontran de Gastefriche appropriated a title superior to his own doesn't surprise me, pretentious as he was.

Relieved that my false identity hasn't been fully unmasked, I now feel shame at having lost face. I attacked Hélénaïs on her origins, and she gave as good as she got by denigrating the Gastefriche name. I ridiculed myself by my reaction, and she is now untouchable.

The feeling of having irrevocably lost drops down on me like a ton of bricks.

I've failed the joust.

Like Tristan, I won't reach the Sip of the King.

My family will never be avenged, and tyranny will continue for centuries to come.

Unless . . .

"Maybe I lied about my title," I say, struck with a sudden blinding thought. "But it was without my knowledge, as I was unaware of being only a bannerette and not a baronne. I dare say there are worse crimes within these walls. Others among us lie willingly every day, right in the teachers' faces, as well as the students'." I walk again toward the stage light, heading toward Poppy. "Lady Castlecliff would like the court to believe that she's a healthy young girl, but in reality her chest is rotten to the core."

Under the artificial blush of her cheeks, Poppy's face goes white as a sheet.

"Diane!" she snaps. "You *bitch*!"

My eyes sting and fill with tears, as if to blur her face and make her vanish from my sight since her face is proof of my felony.

My throat tight, I address the minister seated in the first row.

"A final-stage tuberculosis sufferer, is that really the type of person you want to promote to protect the king, Madame des Ursins?"

"I . . . I assure you that my sickness is *not* that advanced," stammers poor Poppy, pleading her case to the princess in turn.

I have the heartrending feeling that she's clinging to her dreams of America and, more, to the only treatment that could save her life. The only thing is this: the death of a tyrant oppressing millions of subjects is more important than a single life.

Suddenly seized with inspiration, the cruelty of which frightens even me, I crucify Poppy with an improvised quatrain.

"You drugged yourself with much morphine.

Will you yield to your affliction

Or be gnawed at by this toxin?

Death by disease or addiction."

It's too much for Poppy. Hit with an unsparing betrayal and short of breath, she's overcome with a violent coughing fit. The cavernous acoustics of the theater magnify the noise of the sputum she's bringing up her throat, along with all the courtiers' outraged cries.

Poppy feverishly plunges her hand into her pocket, searching for a handkerchief, but before she can bring it over her mouth, a large spurt of blood splatters onto her bodice, transforming the roses on the cream taffeta into bright-red poppies.

I'm nauseous when I leave the theater.

I feel like I'm going to vomit everything from my gut, just like Poppy spit up all the stuff from her lungs.

Her coughing fit put an end to the joust. Des Ursins declared Hélénaïs and me de facto winners. She forgave the Gastefriches for having appropriated a title above their own but not the Castlecliffs for being victims of an ancestral illness. Such is the iron law of the Court of Shadows, where the weak are systematically crushed.

The housekeepers were urgently summoned to bring the loser—now considered contagious—to an isolated room, far from anyone else.

"You were fabulous," Hélénaïs tells me as we walk out of the theater, an admiring smile on her scarlet lips. "As merciless as my idol, Lucrèce. I admit that until now I had a hard time seeing you as one of the king's squires, but tonight you showed another side of yourself. A side of pure brute force."

I clench my teeth. Hearing Hélénaïs say that I remind her of Lucrèce sounds too much like Naoko comparing me to vampyres. Have I become like the squire—an ancient Fury, a deity of vengeance devoured by melancholy with no trace of humanity?

"Maybe we can become friends?" Hélénaïs goes on. "Why don't you eat dinner at my table tonight, before we cross swords tomorrow?"

"I have no appetite, and my head hurts. Please excuse me."

I leave her at the door of the crowded banquet hall and hurry toward the grand staircase. I only want one thing—to head to bed without dinner and escape to sleep, as fast as possible and as far as I can get.

But as I climb the steps, a small group is coming down along the opposite banister. It's the boys, led by General Barvók, who are headed to their verbal joust.

Zacharie de Grand-Domaine, with his intense and enigmatic expression . . .

Rafael de Montesueño, dressed all in black . . .

Tristan de La Roncière and his shining mane.

I freeze in the middle of the staircase, feeling light headed.

"Tristan? But I thought you—"

"Thomas de Longuedune declared forfeit," he quickly tells me. "He went back to his domain, in Les Landes."

"Silence, messieurs!" the quartermaster of the boys' wing scolds, preventing Tristan from giving me any more details. "Save your saliva for the joust."

Tristan has time only to give me a fleeting smile before he's pulled along on the staircase. That's all it takes to carry me upward. I climb the steps four by four. My will to win is intact, perhaps even stronger than ever.

Now that I'm in the deserted dormitory, I rush over to Hélénaïs's bed. Just as she took the liberty to investigate the Gastefriches to take me down, it's my turn to poke around.

I pick her closet lock with the aid of a hairpin.

Among the outrageously expensive dresses and the precious jewelry, there's a bundle of mail—all the letters Hélénaïs receives daily.

I grab the top letter on the pile, the most recent, probably the one that turned up the title usurped by the old baron.

Flat and spidery handwriting runs the length of the fine paper.

Hélénaïs, along with this letter, you will find what you need to disqualify Diane de Gastefriche. But you'll only succeed if you can somehow string two quick-witted words together. Anyone else would already have gotten rid of that vile country bumpkin. Do not disappoint me the way your weak sister did. Be stronger than Iphigénie. Crush that Diane. Crush them all. And win the Sip of the King—so that the Plumigny name can continue to blaze at the court.

It's signed *Anacréon de Plumigny.*

Not *Père*, not *Papa.*

The rest of the correspondence is much the same. There's no hint of paternal love in these letters, merely scathing instructions from a master to a subordinate.

I suddenly understand where Hélénaïs's pitiless competitive spirit comes from. As for her sister, Iphigénie, whom she's never mentioned . . . I'm storing that bit of information to use against her in tomorrow's duel.

I close the closet carefully, my heart beating fast.

25

TORTURE

For weeks I imagined that if I made it to the end of the competition, the night before the final test would be long, sleepless, and migraine filled.

But that wasn't taking into account the last of Poppy's morphine pills, which I've kept under my pillow with that in mind. Under the effects of the drug, I sleep soundly, a long uninterrupted sleep.

"Tristan de La Roncière and Rafael de Montesueño are squaring off tonight," Chantilly tells us when we wake up. "Zacharie de Grand-Domaine also acquitted himself admirably, and the joust was very close."

The announcement is bittersweet. Of course, Tristan's selection makes me happy. But I would have preferred that Rafael not make it to the final round. I can't stand the idea of having to neutralize him if he ends up in the king's mortuary chamber with me.

My cheeks flush, my heart torn between joy at being so close to my goal and guilt at all I've done to get here. Was it worth it? Yes, of course it was, wasn't it? Why do I even question myself?

I turn toward the dormitory. The other girls stare at me, expressionless. Ever since the verbal joust, I've become persona non grata.

"The four duelists will be invited to the palace as soon as the warning bell rings," Chantilly continues. "It will be our mission—teaching staff and third-years of the Grande Écurie—to escort them there. Once at the palace, we will wait in the Salon of Apollo for the conclusion of the king's Grand Rising from his sarcophagus. At eight o'clock, the duelists will face off in front of him, in the Hall of Mirrors, the most prestigious room in the palace. Only the crème de la crème of French and European aristocracy will be invited. There simply won't be room for everyone."

The teacher's powdered cheeks turn pink at the idea of being among the elite invited to witness the show. Because that's what this is all about, for her and for the courtiers—a distraction.

"First blood will be the rule," she goes on. "It means that in each duel, the first combatant to bleed will be eliminated. However, be careful: in years past, the first blow has sometimes been fatal. After the duels, His Majesty will have the two winners brought to his mortuary chamber to offer them the precious Sip."

If yesterday I felt terribly alone, it's even worse today. True torture. Not only does Naoko continue to avoid me, but the other girls treat me with a mix of fear and disgust.

In everyone's eyes, I stabbed Poppy in the back, betraying her when I swore to team up with her for the verbal joust. The English girl is presently confined to her room, and it's even possible that she'll be sent back to the other side of the Channel to avoid any possibility of contagion. I've achieved the feat of turning the entire dormitory against me and making Hélénaïs the clear favorite in this evening's duel. Even among the most ruthless competitors, the degree of my betrayal is hard to wash down. My stomach is completely knotted just thinking about it, but I swallow my bile.

I'm not here to be a courtier.

I'm here to avenge my family.

The other girls can hate me all they like, whisper insults behind my back—the only thing that matters is winning tonight's combat!

After lunch, I escape from the horde of boarders and ditch my court dress to change into the outfit I'll be wearing for the evening: body-hugging velvet breeches to liberate my legs and a long-sleeved bodice buttoned down the length of my arms. I slide my feet into my flattest shoes and put on the lightest skirt from my wardrobe—a fine silk beige fabric from Lyon that won't hinder my movements—over everything. Last of all, I secure my hair with a multitude of barrettes. It's not as elegant as Naoko's buns, but at least it completely clears my face.

Once I'm ready, I rush down to the weapons room to train one last time. The large vaulted room is empty, the ceiling chandeliers unlit. By the light of a few oil lamps that act as night-lights, the weapons hanging on the walls look even more intimidating. Which one will be chosen for the duel? These last few days, at every test, the judges doubled down on perversity in order to destabilize us. Bleeding poor Toinette in the middle of the art-of-courtly-manners test . . . the vampyric mares during the art-of-equestrianism test . . . and adding the constraint of the octosyllabic verses at the last moment for the art-of-conversation test. Will they ask us to fight with sabers tonight? With a two-handed sword? Or with an even more baroque weapon?

I take advantage of the solitude to practice my thrusts and parries, using my rapier against an invisible enemy. The cavernous room amplifies the sound of my breathing. In the half light, I force myself to imagine the eyes of the entire court staring at me.

After an hour of this exercise, I'm out of breath and decide to pause.

I've barely placed the rapier back on its hook when I hear a noise behind me.

I turn around, my heart beating fast in the hope that Tristan has come down to train too.

A gigantic hand shoots out from the dark, smashing a rag against my face that burns my nostrils and lulls my brain to sleep.

Chloroform.

That's the first thought that pops into my head when I come to.

My father sometimes used this sweet-smelling anesthetic to make his patients sleep before making any incisions or extracting a tooth.

I open my eyes to a ceiling covered in darkness.

Solid ropes restrain my ankles and wrists, keeping me stretched out on a surface hard as wood.

"Calm down," a deep voice scolds.

I turn my head, crushing my cheek against the rough wooden plank. And there, seated on a chair, is Raymond de Montfaucon, director of the Grande Écurie and grand equerry of France. The only lantern hanging from the ceiling dispenses a weak halo of light, deepening the shadows of his bilious face.

"Where am I?" I cry out. "What do you want? The . . . the duel. What time is it?"

By way of response, Montfaucon points to an old clock that stands next to a chimney with a dying fire. The two needles are superimposed, indicating that it's six thirty.

A nervous tremor rattles my bound body.

"I'm expected at the palace for the one-on-one combat that starts at eight o'clock. Let me go right now, or I'm going to scream!"

But the director remains stone faced between the limp curls of his wig.

"You can scream till you're blue in the face," he says, pointing to the heavy iron door that seals off the room. "Here, in the belly of the Grande Écurie, no one will hear you. Many have shouted themselves hoarse before you. Always in vain."

Hearing him say this, I'm aware of the total silence that surrounds us. The same silence that prevailed in the recluse's lair. The grand equerry has dragged me deep underground.

As for the metallic shapes hanging on the walls, I can make out sharp contours as my eyes adjust to the dimness . . . instruments of torture. Pliers, vises, and saws—some of them brown from dried blood.

Montfaucon's sinister reputation comes rushing back to me. He is, after all, descended from a long line of executioners, and he still seems to be practicing the family business in secret, in this out-of-the-way torture chamber.

"Confess and you'll save me a lot of sweat, and yourself a lot of tears," he threatens me.

"Confess what?" I say, a sense of panic coming over me that I'm at the mercy of this maniac.

He heaves a deep sigh. "No point in playing that game. The torture rack will absolutely get you to confess. I just have to turn the crank here in order to tear your limbs, bit by bit, and you'll be spitting forth the words that won't come out."

I'm now horribly aware that the ropes encircling my arms and legs are connected to a wheel and that the torturer's left hand is resting on its handle.

With his right hand, he takes something out from the pocket of his black leather jacket.

At first I think it's a handkerchief to wipe the blood that's going to spill from my dislocated limbs.

But little by little, in the light of the lantern, I see a flower.

A white silk lotus.

The one Naoko made for me on the evening of the vampyric dinner.

"I saw you wearing this adornment to the art-of-courtly-manners test," the grand equerry says. "And I found it this afternoon lying in the basement. To be precise, I found it next to the well where the blood-hounds led me after they sniffed a piece of clothing belonging to Madame Thérèse. Her body was floating at the bottom of the hole. You're the one who pushed her, aren't you?"

My breathing speeds up.

My thoughts go crazy.

I might be taking my last breath here, tonight, but I won't betray Tristan or the Fronde.

"Madame Thérèse always had it in for me, bullying me for coming from the backwater countryside," I say, raising my eyes to the ceiling. "I couldn't take it anymore, not her digs nor her humiliations. After all, she was just an old cantankerous commoner at the end of her days, while I'm a young aristocrat with a promising future. Spare yourself the torture: I'm not ashamed to admit that she got exactly what she deserved!"

I heap it on, playing the part of the obnoxious boarder that Montfaucon accused me of being since the very first day, a quarrelsome girl with an "outsize ego," an aristocrat who "thinks the Sip of the King is hers by right." Those are the very words he used. So be it. Let me be that arrogant aristocrat as long as it hides the real reason I didn't help the governess.

"I thought as much," he says, his vile face deformed by a scowl that renders him even more repulsive. "Madame Thérèse was far from perfect. She was petty, a social climber, and often nasty. But you . . . you're even worse."

He lets go of the crank that controls the rack and heads toward a workbench under the instruments of torture.

"Aren't you letting me go now that I told you everything?" I toss out at him, my heart beating wildly. "Don't forget that I'm the king's ward!"

He turns to me, holding a long syringe filled with a whitish liquid.

"You're the worst of the aristocracy," he accuses me somberly. "The scum that believes anything goes, and for whom the life of others has no value. I don't doubt that the court would forgive you for killing Madame Thérèse. After all, you're an aristocrat, and she was a mere commoner, as you just reminded me with utter contempt. But I will never forgive you. I won't allow you to reach the Sip of the King. Not for anything in the world."

The way the grand equerry talks about the nobility, to which he himself belongs, throws me off. His face takes on a fierce, deadly determination. More than ever, he looks like the executioners from whom he inherited the torture instruments.

"It's public knowledge that the Sip opens a royal path toward transmutation," he says. "Yet this poor world, already dreadfully brutalized, doesn't deserve that we unleash upon it a scourge like you for centuries to come. I'm horrified that my school produced a monster like Lucrèce . . . that won't happen again." Brandishing the syringe in one hand, he starts to unbutton the sleeve of my bodice with the other. "Instead of eternal life, this injection of arsenic will give you eternal sleep."

"No!" I shout as he brusquely lifts my sleeve.

He freezes.

My cry didn't stop him. The scars from the bleedings in the crook of my elbow did.

"But . . . ," he sputters, his heavy, saggy eyes widening. "You . . . you're a commoner?!"

I struggle like a madwoman against the ropes binding me, terrified that not only have I been unmasked but I'm seconds away from death.

"Let me go!" I scream at the top of my lungs. "Let me go or the monster with the stitched hands will tear your head off! My guardian demon will avenge me, I swear it."

My cries sound like someone who's demented.

But Montfaucon's eyes widen a little more.

"You've met Orfeo?" he says.

Drenched with sweat, I stop fighting.

Because all my twisting isn't helping.

Because hearing the recluse's name for the first time is strangely calming.

"Orfeo?" I repeat, my lips trembling. "That's his name?"

The grand equerry sits down slowly, placing the arsenic-filled syringe at his feet.

"That's what *I* call him," he clarifies. "No one bothered to give him a name before I did. I found him one night, three years ago, in the courtyard of the Grande Écurie. He was drenched and terrified and about to get torn to pieces by the hounds. He was making pathetic, inarticulate moaning sounds with his tongueless mouth. He must have escaped from the secret laboratory where he saw the light of day, somewhere on the outskirts of Versailles. And he must have dragged himself all the way to the gate. Ever since, I've been sheltering him beneath the basement of the school."

"You named him after Orpheus," I say, thinking back to Ovid, the greatest poet of antiquity, and his masterpiece *Metamorphoses*. "For though Orfeo may be mute, he can draw the most heartrending sounds from his harmonica."

Now that I've stopped screaming, the silence of the torture chamber seems all the more deafening. I remember the recluse's haunting music and how it resonated over the rooftops of the Grande Écurie. I also remember how cold his chest was against my skin when he carried me in his arms into the depths of the school. It was the cold of death . . . and of the Shadows.

"What kind of creature is Orfeo?" I ask. "A ghoul?"

"Only the Shadows spawned ghouls, whereas human beings alchemically shaped the Shadows to give birth to Orfeo. Since you seem to know your myths like the back of your hand, tell me, how did the Orpheus of antiquity end up?"

"Uh . . . torn to pieces by the Bacchae, the demented followers of the god Bacchus, who were jealous of his music," I offer up.

The grand equerry nods seriously. "That's exactly what Orfeo is, a monstrous reconstruction of Orpheus. An assemblage of various cadaver parts, sewn one to the other in contempt of the most sacred laws of nature. I don't know where the different pieces that comprise him come from, nor why his creators didn't see fit to give him a tongue. But his face bears a teardrop tattoo below the corner of an eye. It's the tattoo of the Neapolitan bandits that infested the underbelly of Paris, which is why I gave him an Italian name."

"Was that monstrous hybrid created by the doctors of the Faculty?" I ask, buying time.

"No. If the inquisitors of the Faculty knew of his existence, they would immediately burn him at the stake. Alchemists belonging to the Fronde created the abomination that is Orfeo."

My breathing stops.

Hearing the word *Fronde* coming from the grand equerry's mouth suffocates me.

"But I thought the rebels were all uneducated," I say.

I may be pretending to be ignorant, but I can't help thinking about my parents' secret alchemical lab. Did they conduct activities other than the creation of homemade bombs? Did they try to manipulate the Shadows to create abominations too?

No, I can't believe it.

"The Fronde is a nebulous hydra with a thousand faces," Montfaucon mumbles, deep in thought. "A catchall of disparate people and groups—peasants and city dwellers, hicks and bougies, commoners and nobles. Their seeming cohesion is an illusion. Where the virtuous rebels want to abolish the Magna Vampyria in the true hope of establishing a better world, the perverted rebels seek only to gain power and eternal life. The latter shamelessly manipulate the Shadows in attempts to discover the secret of vampyrism so that they can appropriate it. But until now, for all their ungodly attempts to create a genuine vampyre, they've only been able to produce failures like Orfeo."

Montfaucon's words stun me. *Virtuous rebels? The true hope of establishing a better world?* Is it really the director of the Grande Écurie saying this? This man whom I've feared above all others, the very incarnation of royal authority at the school, is talking in a way that could lead him straight to the gallows.

He blinks, suddenly seeming to remember that I'm there.

"Why don't you tell me who you really are under your facade of provincial nobility?"

"If I have a facade, what about yours," I say, trembling with hope. "The grand equerry of France is on the same side as I am, the side of justice."

Montfaucon gets up brusquely, hovering above me with his full height, his angry head wreathed by the unsteady ceiling light.

"*Justice* is the most dangerous word in the world, for everyone has their own definition!" he shouts, sounding mad. "What slaughter has been perpetrated in its name! And how many rivers of blood did my ancestors allow to flow to quench its ongoing thirst! The Montfaucons, the Immutable's cursed executioners, we've decapitated . . . dismembered . . . skinned . . . *eviscerated* the people of France for centuries. In the silence of my nights, the souls of all these victims come to me, demanding accountability."

His large body begins to shake uncontrollably, as if it were buckling under the weight of the thousands of executions carried out by his lineage.

The man's frailty, the reason for the yellow bile that oozes from every pore of his skin, is guilt. I'm hoping this comes with its bright opposite side—the possibility of redemption.

"I see that you hate the Immutable," I say. "You abhor what your ancestors did to please him. Though you like to intimidate, you've probably never used these torture instruments yourself."

Montfaucon grows somber.

"Oh, I've used them . . . ," he says hoarsely. "The Montfaucon blood runs in my veins, and I bear the family curse—the irrepressible need to break bodies, to snap necks." His face twists into a tormented scowl, where hatred for his origins competes with the savage joy of wallowing in barbarism. "The difference between my ancestors and me is that I've been able to channel my murderous impulses and direct them against a precise target. You see, I hate hunting with hounds, as they draw blood from living creatures, which is why I did not appreciate that you defied me after I gave the order to stop tracking the buck. However, I'm an assiduous hunter of ghouls, those cannibalistic vermin who dig up the bones of the dead in cemeteries and attack poor beggars in the streets, who kidnap babies from their cradles. How do you think I amassed the collection of perfectly preserved hands that you saw in my office?"

I shiver as I think about the cannibalistic creatures who must have been stretched out on the torture rack before me.

"Orfeo also eats human flesh," I say. "You pretended you had the heads of those rebels from the Auvergne removed from the gate the other day. But it's a lie. I know your protégé took them . . . to eat them."

"No, not to eat them—to give them a burial."

"What?"

My mind swirls, and I recall the care with which the recluse arranged the heads that were disfigured by the ravens. He gave them dignity. I also recall that he filled their empty eye sockets with pretty pebbles and carefully stitched their wounds.

"At night, I roam the cemeteries of Versailles in search of ghouls to exterminate," Montfaucon says. "Orfeo follows me like a loyal dog, picking up the bones and skulls that the ghouls' dens are strewed with. You see, my protégé isn't capable of speaking the language of living men, but he understands the language of the dead. He hears them singing their stories . . . maybe that's because he himself was created from cadavers? When we get back from hunting, he cleans and polishes his macabre spoils, reassembling the dispersed remains of a body or of the same family. Then he buries them anew for all eternity in places only he knows of, where no ghoul can ever exhume them again.";

If Montfaucon is to be believed, the gnawed bones I saw on the recluse's table the first night we met didn't bear his teeth marks. On the contrary, he'd brought them to his room to repair the horrors inflicted by the ghouls!

"Appearances can be deceiving," I say.

"Indeed. And you played your part to perfection to infiltrate the school."

He removes the lantern from the ceiling and brings it closer to examine me, the sides of his long wig grazing my face.

"Who are you?" he asks me again. "And why are you so bent on competing for the Sip of the King?"

I take a deep breath.

"My name is Jeanne Froidelac," I say, exhaling. "The Immutable had my family killed. The heads on the school gate were those of my parents and brothers."

The grand equerry's mouth goes agape.

What have I done? Am I a fool to think I can convince this broken man that my cause is good?

In any case, it's too late. I can't take my words back.

"You . . . you're the daughter of those unfortunate souls?" A shadow of remorse clouds his pale face. "I was sure the spectacle of their heads thrilled you. What a mistake I made . . ."

"That spectacle filled me with rage!" I say with all the vehemence that my awkward position on the torture rack permits me. "That ghastly sight toughened my resolve to take my revenge on the tyrant. Yes, you heard me correctly: I came to Versailles to destroy the Immutable. So let me go to accomplish my destiny."

Mirthless laughter shakes the hunched backbone of my jailer.

"Reckless youth. Only the pain of mourning can inspire such folly. It's a stupid and suicidal mission, doomed to fail. Did you really think you could overcome the most powerful vampyre in the universe—you alone, a puny country waif with no experience at the court?"

I squeeze my lips together, torn between the desire to shout that I'm not acting alone and my duty to protect the secret.

"Even if you succeeded in destroying the Immutable, how would that improve the fate of the people?" he goes on. "Even if the king disappears, the Vampyria will live on. Another immortal will take his place on the throne." He shakes his large bewigged head with fatalism. "No, it's not at the palace that the revolution will bear fruit. Not tonight, not ever. You're going to stay tied up here until after tomorrow, when the Sip of the King is over."

"You can't do that! People will question my whereabouts. Everyone's waiting for me to attend the art-of-weaponry test."

He shrugs. "It won't be the first time you vanish unexpectedly. The courtiers will blame it on your unpredictable temperament. They'll say that you preferred to flee rather than face Hélénaïs de Plumigny in one-on-one combat."

"You're robbing me of my vengeance!" I shout.

"No. I'm saving your life. I didn't know your family or their motivations, whether virtuous or perverse. What I do know is that you can live in service to the people's cause in a useful, considered way, not by jumping into a dangerous mission doomed to fail." He straightens as if to better gauge whether I'm up to the task he has in mind. "You have energy and courage to spare, I'll give you that. You could put them to good use in the Americas."

"What? The Americas?" I ask.

He nods. "Over in the faraway colonies, the hold of the Magna Vampyria isn't as strong. The dawn will rise in the West, I'm sure of it. Not an obscure and ephemeral rebellion but a revolution that might be able to dissipate shadowessence itself." His eyes glisten between his flowing strands of hair, as if he were already contemplating that blazing horizon. "For years now, I've taken advantage of my position to act as intermediary between the rebels of the Americas and those of mainland France whom I judge to be sincere. And I can tell you that the latter are just a handful."

The Americas, land of hope . . . it's like hearing poor Poppy speak. I also remember the mysterious events Madame Thérèse mentioned in relation to New York. As for this mystical dream of a dawn that dissipates the Shadows . . . it makes my head spin.

Montfaucon hangs the lantern back on the ceiling and grabs a heavy chain that's welded to the wall. At the end of the chain is a thick iron hoop that he attaches to my right ankle, locking it with a small key from his key ring. Only then does he untie the ropes that imprison my legs and arms.

I bolt upright and sit on the edge of the wooden plank, stretching my stiff limbs.

"No use trying to break this chain," he warns. "It's made of the most solid links and can hold back the most ferocious ghouls."

He places a pitcher of water and a loaf of bread on the corner of the torture rack. Then, with the tip of his boot, he pushes a rusted pail near me.

"There, that'll restore you. You can use the pail like a chamber pot. And get some rest. Right now, I have to get to the palace in order to represent the school during the ritual of the Sip. But tomorrow, I'll arrange for a convoy to take you to the Havre, where you'll be able to board a ship."

He's about to turn on his heel, but I can't let him go like this.

I can't abandon Tristan to fight the king on his own.

"Wait!" I shout. "Free me; let me compete for the Sip like I'm supposed to. I promise I won't make waves."

"Out of the question," he answers categorically, slipping back into his role as director of the Grande Écurie.

"For pity's sake, I beg you!"

He furrows his brows. "Why the rush? The prospect of going to the Americas doesn't appeal to you?"

"I . . . uh . . . yes. But I'd like to see my friends one last time before I go."

As soon as I say this, I realize I've said too much.

Montfaucon's large creased forehead contracts.

My insistence has sparked suspicion in his mind.

"Did you lie to me?" he says. "Is there more than one of you involved in this regicide? Do you have accomplices?"

"No, I assure you that's not the case," I say, trying to disabuse him. It's too late.

"Could it be that you're allied with Takagari and Castlecliff, the two demoiselles you've been spending the most time with?" he asks himself as he feverishly strokes his goatee with the tips of his long fingers. "No, those two foreigners don't have the right connections to pull off such a plan. So that leaves the boys. Notably the one you seem to be in love with—La Roncière."

The grand equerry's eyes widen in the dim light.

"But of course!" he exclaims. "The withdrawal of Thomas de Longuedune should have been a red flag. Yesterday, a carrier crow arrived with news that his father had died, struck down in his manor in Les Landes by a heart attack. As the only son and sole heir, young Longuedune had to quit the competition, even school, in order to go take possession of his family's lands . . . hence freeing the path for La Roncière! I must go and stop him before it's too late."

"No!" I yell, pulling on the heavy chain.

"Didn't you understand what I told you, you little fool? La Roncière is just as presumptuous as you are. A hopeless romantic with no notion of political realities. A boy from the countryside who thinks he can change the world with one glorious feat. But this precipitous attack on the king won't change a thing."

"You're the one who doesn't understand, crazy old man! Like me, and like my parents, Tristan is fighting for liberty or death. Do you hear me? Liberty or death!" I repeat with hate and rage. "A fight you're too cowardly to wage, what with your foggy dreams of the Americas that are just an excuse for not risking your life. Meanwhile, the vampyric thirst is increasing, and the Faculty is about to double the tithe. I know, because I overheard Des Ursins talk about it. We don't have time to lose. The time to act is now. Now, do you hear me? Don't waste this one chance to take down the tyrant!"

But Montfaucon isn't listening to me anymore as he hurries toward the studded door of the cell.

He feverishly turns one of his keys in the lock.

Crazed with panic, I grab the first thing I lay my hands on—the pewter pitcher—and hurl it toward him with all the precision of my years handling the sling.

The receptacle strikes the back of the grand equerry's head with a deafening noise.

His giant body crumples to the ground.

Short of breath, hair covering my eyes, I notice the unlocked door opening with a creak.

A shadow appears on the threshold.

Orfeo.

26

ORFEO

"I . . . I didn't do it on purpose," I stammer.

Montfaucon's body lies on the cold tiles, completely still.

His protégé straightens in the dimness of the doorway, trembling.

Until now, the one I called "my guardian demon" mysteriously helped me. But now that I've assaulted, maybe even killed, the man who saved his life and took him in, I doubt he'll be as accommodating.

"He tripped and fell all on his own," I pretend, my lips quivering.

The creature's leather shoes advance slowly. The recluse enters into the weak light of the lantern, allowing me to see him more distinctly than ever before. The cloth breeches that encase his massive thighs and the tunic that envelops his powerful torso are stitched every which way. I'm guessing that he patched up his old clothes, just like he mended the wounds of the decapitated heads. As for his bent head, it's still hidden in the deep leather hood that falls onto his shoulders.

He kneels next to Montfaucon's body, whose wig fell off during the fall, exposing his bald pate.

The recluse extends his large hand. It looks greenish, nearly translucent, like the surface of high-altitude lakes in the Auvergne—all covered with green algae that the sun could never really penetrate.

His long fingers stroke Montfaucon's skull with unexpected respect. When he raises his hand, I see a dark, shiny substance on the pad of his index—fresh blood. He picks up the pewter pitcher; it, too, is covered in blood. His shoulders start to shake as the groans of a wounded animal come from his hood.

"I swear that it was an accident!" I shout, seized with panic.

The creature gets up with the nimbleness of a cat and pounces on me.

His scent of decaying leaves fills my nostrils.

His moans of distress—for that's what this is about—pierce my ears.

His fingers, which delicately grazed Montfaucon's head just before, close on my arm to break it.

Gripped with terror, I thrash around, grabbing hold of the hood with my free hand.

"You have to believe me!" I shout. "You have to believe me . . . Orfeo!"

As I say his name, I tear off the hood.

The recluse immediately lets go of my arm and covers his face with his enormous hands, but not fast enough to hide his eyes from me. For a second, I glimpse two large pale-green orbs.

We stay frozen an instant, face to face, the prisoner chained to the torture rack and the monster concealed behind the mask of his hands.

"Orfeo . . . ," I repeat softly, sensing all the power of this name that humanizes him, pulling him from the realm of abominations. "Look at me, Orfeo. And let me look at you."

His long blue-green fingers tremble.

Below the sleeve of his tunic, I can clearly make out the blackened stitch marks that encircle his wrists, like two bracelets. As if they've been sewn to the forearms.

I force myself to vanquish my fear.

"I know that you understand me. And I know that those hands you're hiding behind are capable of carrying out wonders. They know how to restore dignity to the dead and draw out sounds from the harmonica that move the hearts of the living."

Hesitantly, Orfeo finally draws his palms away. His eyes reappear. They look like pieces of jade, with black, vibrant pupils. The face that surrounds these strange gemstones vacillates between beauty and horror. A somber grace emanates from the strong and straight nose and the mouth with the pale lips of a drowning victim and the eyelids studded with long black lashes that resemble delicate insect legs. At the corner of the right eyelid, the tattooed teardrop that Montfaucon mentioned dribbles a little, almost as if the ink is starting to dissolve. Under these features, the neck is ringed with a long line of stitches that resembles a dotted purplish necklace. Orfeo's head was grafted onto a torso that isn't his.

"My name is Jeanne," I tell him.

The old clock suddenly chimes. Seven o'clock.

"Thank you for saving me the other night when I was about to fall from the roof," I say, trying to slow down my rushed words so that he understands me. "Thank you for allowing me to say goodbye to my loved ones. And thank you for placing their remains in a safe resting place, somewhere the ghouls can't desecrate."

I think I see a flicker of light in his jade eyes—yes, a flicker of emotion. Montfaucon was right: his strange protégé can really hear the song of bones. My family's remains must have touched him deep in the beating heart I heard pounding within his cold chest.

"Tonight, it's my turn to help you," I tell him hastily. "I'm the daughter of an apothecary. I know how to treat your master and get him back on his feet. But you'll need to unshackle me." I shake my ankle, causing the heavy chain links to clank. "Please, go get the key from your master's key ring."

Orfeo turns toward Montfaucon's still body.

I encourage him in the softest voice possible, all the while wanting to scream to vanquish his reluctance.

"Time is of the essence, Orfeo."

He shuffles over to Montfaucon's body and, with his long, powerful fingers, removes the key ring without jingling any of the keys.

With the same care, he places the smallest key on the ring into the lock of the ankle chain.

The iron hoop opens.

I'm free.

"Thank you," I say.

I extend my hand toward his. When my fingers touch his cold skin, I fight the urge to pull them back. I look him in the eyes to conquer my revulsion. There's a soul in the depth of this assemblage of dead flesh, melded one to the other, miraculously preserved by the power of the Shadows. Orfeo doesn't have the ice-cold grace of the vampyres, who seem carved out of stone, but in his very imperfection, he is more alive than they'll ever be.

My fingers gently clasp the key ring.

Orfeo lets me take it.

He moves his pale lips, as if he's trying to form words. His tongue-less mouth isn't able to emit anything other than a deep, hollow sound, same as the echoes in the mountain caves where I took refuge whenever I was caught in a downpour.

The frustration of not being able to express himself crinkles his strange face.

He slides a hand into the pocket of his tunic, taking out a slate tile he removed from a roof, along with a piece of used chalk.

He draws letters with the same precision as his stitch marks.

The bones of the master have not started to sing.
He isn't dead yet.
Thank you for helping him.

Reading the beautiful calligraphy of these words breaks my heart, for they're further proof of the sensitivity ticking in Orfeo's body. So what I'm about to do is truly cruel . . .

"Can you get me the flask of formaldehyde from that shelf?" I ask him as I pretend to stretch my stiff arms. "The strong smell should help your master get his wits back."

Orfeo has barely turned around when I grab the lantern from the ceiling, jump off the rack, and dash toward the still-open door.

My heart pounding, I run out into the hallway and slam the heavy iron door behind me.

With trembling fingers, I stick the largest key from the key ring into the lock and turn it.

A massive fist beats down on the other side, making the panel shake on its big hinges.

I turn the key a second time.

The pummeling of the recluse, trapped like a wild beast, sends furious tremors into my hand, right up to my shoulder.

I yank the key out of the lock like you would a dagger from the back of a stabbing victim, and then I lift the vacillating lantern and flee into the underground passages.

Even when there's only the pounding of my footsteps to be heard in the empty corridors, I think I still hear Orfeo groan—the last in a long series of allies I've betrayed, and certainly the most innocent of all.

The chilled air of the last October night hits me as I leave the Grande Écurie.

My feet instinctually find the path they took in early September, right up to the narrow spiral staircase that leads to the service entrance. One of Montfaucon's keys opens this final obstacle.

I'm now in the alleyway where I ended up two months ago. Even though I rebuttoned the sleeve of my bodice, I'm shivering, and my teeth are chattering.

I have to reach the palace as fast as possible before I freeze to death.

I have to find the Hall of Mirrors, before Hélénaïs is declared the winner by forfeit.

I rush toward the Parade Grounds, each breath of air stabbing my lungs with millions of frosted needles.

The vast esplanade is deserted, no carriages in sight. At this hour, all the courtiers are already at the palace for the evening's entertainment.

Six Swiss Guards, all bundled in thick fur coats, are posted in front of the gaping opening of the Hunting Wall. They cross their halberds to block my entry.

"Who goes there?" yells a seventh guard, releasing a cloud of vapor into the night. He's an officer, judging by his stripes.

"I am Diane de Gastefriche, finalist for the Sip of the King!" I shout. "His Majesty expects me."

The officer places his hand on the hilt of his sword, unsure of what course of action to take with a half-frozen ranting girl who dares invoke the name of the Immutable. Under the fur hat that comes down to the bottom of his forehead, his eyes shine with suspicion in the glare of the torchlight. He could slash my throat with one swipe of his sword.

"I recognize her gray hair, Captain," one of the men says. "It's the girl who entered the palace like a beggar last summer and left as the king's ward."

The king's ward. Those magic words are like an open sesame.

The halberds part. The captain lowers his sword and offers me his arm. Together, we make our way across the thick Hunting Wall.

The Honor Gate rises at the end of the tunnel, crowned by the gloomy nocturnal mask of Apollo.

The gigantic palace that was buzzing with courtiers at the end of summer rises up in the dead silence of night. Behind hundreds of hermetically closed windows, a myriad of chandeliers sparkle like thousands of fires.

"Faster, faster!" I yell at the captain as I start to pull him along. He seems startled by my impertinence. "Where's the Hall of Mirrors?"

He points toward the main body of the palace, at the end of a majestic checkerboard courtyard.

"The hall is on the second floor, on the garden side," he puffs. "The Ambassadors' Staircase will get us there."

I dash so fast he has to run to keep up, his heavy fur boots struggling to catch up to my lightweight shoes.

"Let her through!" he orders the surprised guards posted in front of a large entryway lit with torches.

They part, and for the first time in my life, I make my way into the Immutable's dwelling—not as I had imagined, with great pomp and surrounded by all the staff of the Grande Écurie, but alone and shivering.

After the dark of night, the whiteness of the immense walls blinds me. The blinding brilliance of the crystal chandeliers burns my eyes.

I grope my way to a huge stone staircase. It's carved out of red, green, and gray marble, a kaleidoscope that makes my head spin. The banners dangling from the gigantic guardrail are even more head spinning: Spain and Portugal, Prussia and Germany, Savoy and Piedmont, and so many others. I see dozens of flags stamped with the bat insignia that denotes allegiance to the King of Shadows. All the vice-kingdoms of the Magna Vampyria are here. I used to study their tiny emblems in the family atlas, and now they crush me with banners as large as sails. And me, "the little country girl," as Montfaucon would say, I dare to defy this invincible armada?

I burst onto the top of the stairs, the captain of the Swiss Guards still on my heels.

"Make way! Make way!" he shouts.

A new group of guards parts to let me enter a salon with an abundance of gilded moldings. Between the moldings are tall panels depicting painted scenes taken from mythology. Rich, heady perfumes hit my nostrils. Dozens of courtiers are planted here, all of them mortals if I go by the color of their heels.

"Mesdames and messieurs, if you please, I beg you to let us through . . . ," the captain implores.

He can't address these aristocrats in the commanding tone he used until now, and the courtiers don't seem predisposed to let us go by.

My gut tells me that these are the least well off among the palace dwellers, not in good graces enough to have the honor of admission to the Hall of Mirrors. As Chantilly said, only the crème de la crème of the nobility is invited to the duels. For years, maybe even generations, these ladies and gentlemen from the four corners of the Vampyria have had to abandon their vast domains to be crammed together at the palace in tiny rooms, the nearest they can get to a monarch who ignores them. Presently, their bitterness is directed at me. A disheveled guest, cold and blue, without even a coat to cover herself—finally, someone to look down upon.

"What an eccentric," squeaks a woman whose face is riddled with fake beauty spots.

"What an inconvenience," snaps a tiny man perched atop shoes with gold buckles.

"Get in line like everyone else if you want a chance of seeing the king at the end of the contest," another powdered individual barks at me.

These socialites are already talking about the end of the test.

Like an echo of their acidic words, a deafening chime suddenly resonates.

BONG! It's the first stroke of eight o'clock.

"Let me through!" I beg them, curtsying the way Barvók taught us in the hopes of softening them.

BONG! The second stroke chimes, echoed by all the bell towers in Versailles, behind the tall windows decorated with crimson velvet.

The courtiers don't budge one iota.

I look above the wigs full of ribbons and frills, searching for an exit door. My crazed eyes land on the painted murals that depict a maiden running through nocturnal forests.

Diana.

The goddess of the hunt, the one whose name I've borrowed.

But she's been transmuted into a vampyre. Instead of tossing Actaeon to her hounds, like in Ovid's *Metamorphoses*, she's the one tearing his throat with her sharp teeth. The miserable hunter crowned with antlers, already half-changed into a deer, seems to look at me with the same distress as Bastien—my poor brother!—when he died.

A surge of anger wells up within me.

"I am Diane de Gastefriche, the king's ward, and I told you to let me pass!"

BONG! As the third stroke chimes on the clocks and bell towers, I ignore all rules of courtly manners, leaving the useless captain behind, and lower my head as I force my way forward. Just like a cannonball, I crush polished shoes, shove luxurious coats, and cut through starched dresses.

I land in a second salon, this one entirely devoted to depictions of Mars. On the largest painting, the god of war with the vampyric complexion is wearing thorny armor drenched in blood. As for the room, it's twice as large as the first, with four times more people.

BONG! The fourth stroke chimes above the din of conversations.

Again, I charge into the crowd, elbowing and kneeing my way amid outraged protests until I reach another salon decorated with portraits and statues of Mercury, the dove wings of his swift sandals having been replaced by bat wings.

Will this nightmare ever end?

BONG! the relentless clocks answer.

I weave my way across the Salon of Mercury, thinking I've at last reached the Hall of Mirrors. But I arrive at another room, this one full of gold tapestries: the Salon of Apollo.

The nocturnal effigy of the sun god that I saw above the Honor Gate is reproduced on all the walls, giving me the dizzying impression that dozens of eyes are watching me.

BONG!

Frantic, I realize that many red heels are now scattered in the crowd that impatiently mills around, a sign that I'm closer to my target. The sensation of cold has increased, and it's not as easy to carve a path forward. While my hunting instincts let me weave between the cramped mortal courtiers in their ceremonial dress, it's a whole other thing with the immortals. As I go by, cruel nails grab me like claws, tearing my fine silk skirt, pulling out my barrettes, undoing my hair.

BONG!

When the next-to-last stroke of the fatal hour rings, I pull myself out of the Salon of Apollo and hurl myself into the final room. *Final,* yes, I can feel it. See it. Here, there are no courtiers. Only butlers in livery and guards armed to the teeth standing at attention beneath gigantic frescoes depicting the King of Shadows' military campaigns. Fields in ruin and dead bodies stretch out as far as the eye can see, bearing witness to the long-ago times when the Immutable unified the Magna Vampyria in order to freeze it forever under his yoke.

In the middle of these scenes of desolation, a beautifully carved door rises up. I'm sure it leads to the Hall of Mirrors.

I dash forward with all my strength . . .

BONG!

A hand descends on my shoulder at the same time that the last eight o'clock stroke chimes.

I fall to my knees on the marble tiles, out of breath.

"No trespassing allowed into the Hall of Mirrors, not without the express authorization of the king," a voice thunders.

My head pounding, I straighten up so that I can identify the person who stopped my mad dash.

That ocher-colored breastplate . . .

And that turban under which soulful eyes gleam . . .

"It's . . . it's me, Suraj," I stammer. "It's Diane."

"Diane?" he says, furrowing his thick brows.

He puts the double-bladed dagger that he'd automatically taken out back in its sheath. Then he extends a hand the way he did in the royal gardens.

But last summer his arm was firm and rigid, whereas today it's trembling.

"A thousand pardons," he apologizes. "The king put me in charge of this battalion, under strict orders to stop every unwelcome visitor. You barreled in headlong like a lunatic, and . . . I didn't recognize you."

"Well, you know who I am now," I say, rising to my feet, short of breath. "I'm sure all the third-years are here, behind the door, and that the duels are about to start."

He nods, frowning.

The anxiety I see on his face suddenly reminds me of the real Diane de Gastefriche's expression when she ushered Bastien and me into her bedroom. A prisoner of her father's horrible willpower, she let the boy she loved fall into a fatal trap without having the strength to head him off.

Tonight, Suraj is in the same powerless position as the bannerette. The lover he rejected, but whom I suspect he still has deep feelings for, is behind this door. Rafael is about to start a duel that might cost him his life. If the squire trembles, it's because he's dying to intervene but is unable to do so. He's torn between his forbidden love and his allegiance to the king, just as the baron's daughter was torn between Bastien and her father.

"Just one gesture from you and Rafael will renounce the duel," I whisper into his ear. "He's only competing for the Sip to get closer to you. If you stay silent, you risk losing him forever."

I step back.

Suraj's eyes go wide with disbelief, as if he's suddenly conscious of something he's always known about himself, something he wouldn't admit.

"Messieurs!" I say as I turn to the butlers flanking the door. "I am Diane de Gastefriche, the last third-year missing from the roll call. Open the door, for I am expected."

With a nod, Suraj orders the guards to let me pass.

The two doors open onto a flood of blinding light.

27

THE ART OF WEAPONRY

"Diane de Gastefriche, the king's ward."

The butler's voice at the entryway to the Hall of Mirrors resonates like a thunderclap, echoing tenfold.

My ears evaluate the dimensions of the room by its otherworldly acoustics, before my dazzled eyes take in the details . . .

First, I see the red marble columns that seem to be holding up the painted vault from which hang constellations of sparkling chandeliers. Then I notice the huge windows overlooking the gloom-filled gardens; hundreds of courtiers are clustered at the windows, chatting away, all in ceremonial dress. The luxurious fabrics part to let Suraj and me go by.

As we make our way forward, my heart beating fast, I observe the baroque candelabras that rise above the wigs. Gold-plated nymphs, each one holding a sparkling bouquet in her arms, mingle with crystal prisms and dripping white-wax candles. I have the impression that the eyes of these "statues" follow me with trembling looks, as if real women were imprisoned in the gilded shells.

Overwhelmed, I turn my attention to the opposite wall, where gigantic mirrors face the windows.

A new horror. Half of the courtiers have no reflection. Their embroidered coats and sequined dresses seem to be floating in the air like the clothing of disembodied ghosts. The glacial cold that pervades the hall isn't caused by a draft: I'm in the presence of the most powerful immortals, the most ferocious in the world.

I force myself to look at the other side of the hall, where my shaky footsteps are taking me. A gold throne rises on a high dais. The long armrests and the colossal back mimic the shape of tormented volutes, spiraling scrolls from which emerge a bevy of bats with gaping mouths, full of dagger-sharp teeth. It looks like a whirlwind from hell, frozen in solid gold, in the middle of which sits the ruler of the Magna Vampyria: Louis the Immutable.

On this October 31, 299, in the Age of Shadows, exactly 299 years since his transmutation, the monarch wears his coronation outfit: a shirt with a majestic black jabot, cascading sleeves of black lace, and shimmering black silk tights, all wrapped in a velvet coat lined with ermine fur that spills onto the steps of the dais. In the middle of this somber attire, under the dark head of hair, the gold mask glistens like a distant star.

A deep voice comes forth with no movement from frozen lips.

"Well, Mademoiselle de Gastefriche, you always seem to be off the beat. Last summer, you presented yourself too early to the court. Tonight, you arrive too late—and in what a state."

A hunched figure trembles in the shade of the throne, attired in a scarlet coat, above which spreads a large white ruff. A bald head with a blueish tint rests there, same as a decapitated head resting on a plate: it belongs to Exili, the grand archiater. His shrill laughter reverberates under the tall ancient vaults, as if repeating: *Too late, it's too late!*

My eyes fall on a large cleared space at the foot of the royal rostrum.

On either side are the teachers and boarders of the Grande Écurie. General Barvók and Zacharie de Grand-Domaine . . . Madame de Chantilly and Séraphine de La Pattebise . . . the Knight of Saint-Loup and Marie-Ornella de Lorenzi . . . all of them look at me quizzically, except for two third-years: Naoko and Hélénaïs. Under her bun decorated with cherry blossoms and mother-of-pearl combs, my former friend smiles at me—as if, despite our quarrels, she's happy I'm finally here. On the other hand, Hélénaïs looks at me with fury. Tonight, she swapped her voluminous hoop dresses for a tight-fitting leather dress more suited to fighting, similar to the ones Lucrèce wears. My rival already saw herself joining Mademoiselle du Crèvecœur among the king's squires, and here I am contesting her victory.

As for the two combatants in the middle of the cleared space, my arrival clearly interrupted them in full duel. I can't look at them without my heart tearing to pieces.

Tristan's dazzling smile as he sees me.

Rafael's exhilarated face at the sight of Suraj.

Sweaty in their white shirts, a short sword in each of their hands, they look like two puppets suspended from invisible strings held by the king.

"I have no excuse, Your Majesty," I say, curtsying deeply in my lacerated silk skirt, my velvet breeches visible underneath. "I know I've arrived too late. I know that eight o'clock has already chimed, confirming my defeat by default. But I also know that you are the immortal lord of the Magna Vampyria, the all-powerful master of space and time."

I straighten up as I say these last words—*space and time*—words I heard coming from the monarch's mouth when he headed toward his observatory to contemplate the cosmos.

"Are you not the Immutable?" I ask in the midst of the silent courtiers, who are horrified that I dare take the king to task. "Your limitless power bends over the course of time itself, as your reign brought an end to history. What are a few minutes for a sovereign who holds eternity in his hands? No doubt, with one word, one word alone, you could erase my tardiness."

From high up on the great throne, the king's gold mask remains impenetrable. I'm asking him to grant me a second chance, but I know that he could easily turn his thumb downward and condemn me to death.

The entire room seems to hold its breath, the seconds suspended like frozen drops.

A voice filters its way through the metallic lips.

"So be it."

Immediately, the Hall of Mirrors comes back to life. The courtiers start talking again; the valets return to their service; over the rustling of dresses, Hélénaïs begins ranting again; and Tristan resumes the en garde position.

He lunges, taking advantage of Rafael's turmoil and discomfiture.

The court cries out in excitement. The blade grazed Rafael's shoulder, drawing forth a purple gash on the white of his shirt.

"Suraj, since you are here, take the loser to the Faculty infirmary," the king orders. "My ward no longer needs you. She will be fighting on her own shortly."

The squire rushes to prop up Rafael.

In the third-year's eyes, I see neither pain from the wound nor regret at having lost—only joy at being in his lover's arms.

They leave together, taking their precious secret with them, far from the court, which has already refocused its attention on Tristan.

The Knight of Saint-Loup walks over to him and takes his arm, lifting it up high for all to see.

"The winner," she exclaims.

A thunderous applause shakes the hall. Who among the courtiers is slavishly greeting the new squire to the king? And who are the conspirators rejoicing in seeing their champion so near to their goal? The latter have a long reach, especially if it's true that they hastened the death of Thomas de Longuedune's father in order to clear the path for Tristan, as Montfaucon intimated. One more sacrifice on the path that leads to the king's mortuary chamber . . . and the destruction of the tyrant.

My head buzzing from the applause, I lose myself in Tristan's gaze. He has eyes only for me . . . until the doctors in black shirts and conical hats lead him off toward the mortuary chamber.

At that instant, I feel a hand gently rest on my wrist, a cold hand.

I quickly turn around, already guessing who it might be.

"Alexandre . . ."

"When I didn't see you arrive, I assumed you'd given up your candidacy, and I confess I was relieved," he tells me, his angelic face creased with worry.

"My mind is made up," I reply, anxious to get away from him.

"Listen to me," he insists. "The king decided that tonight's duelists would fight with vampyric swords, with blades thirsty for death, that have only one goal—drawing the most blood possible, whether the adversary's or that of the combatant who wields it. I beg you, Diane, be careful."

The knight's voice rings out, freeing me from this cumbersome suitor.

"Time for the sword, girls!"

She gives Rafael's sword to Hélénaïs and hands me Tristan's.

I lower my eyes, the Viscount de Mortange's warning still ringing in my head. From a distance, I'd thought these weapons were merely simple court swords, but I hadn't factored in the perversity of the palace. The richly decorated hilt is shaped like a bat, with semioutstretched wings to protect the duelist's hand. As my fingers close around the handle, I have the feeling I've grabbed a piece of ice. The two rubies set as the eyes of the bat seem to emit a pulsing gleam. Rafael's blood continues to redden the blade, but the reflecting steel begins to lose its sheen. I realize that the metal is *absorbing* the vital fluid, like parched land soaks up water.

"En garde, mesdemoiselles," declares the Knight of Saint-Loup.

Hélénaïs takes a sideways position in her leather dress.

I, too, raise my sword. It vibrates at the end of my hand, making my arm shake as if it wanted to escape from me.

I barely have time to firm up my grip before my opponent lunges at me.

Deciding not to parry her blow with a weapon I'm unable to control, I dodge at the last second. Hélénaïs's blade passes only inches from my face.

Delighted cries erupt among the courtiers.

Already, Hélénaïs is on the offense again, a wild expression on her face. Her weapon seems to be pulling her forward; or rather, the fencer and her blade seem to be more like one bloody entity.

This time, with my back to the courtiers, I don't have room to dodge, so I raise my sword to parry hers.

Intersecting steel clangs, an impact that reverberates to the hollows of my bones.

Hélénaïs is so close to me that I can feel her heavy breathing on my forehead, her look crazed.

"Give up, little mouse," she says. "You know I'm better at fencing, and my sword won't be satisfied with just a simple scratch. It wants to pierce your heart!"

In Hélénaïs's bronze eyes, I see her burning desire to vanquish me but also a kind of alarm—that of a rider swept along by her horse.

"You pretend to be strong," I whistle between my teeth. "But in reality, you're scared of being as weak as Iphigénie."

Hélénaïs's eyelids widen in shock at the mention of her secret sister.

Her blade quivers at the end of her arm.

I take advantage of her surprise to disengage, pointing my sword at her thigh to draw first blood.

But Hélénaïs is lightning fast. She pulls herself together as quickly as she let herself come undone and blocks my blade with the handle of her sword.

Thrown off balance, I stumble forward, forced to let go of my sword so that I can roll into a ball on the floor.

I land among the courtiers at the other end of the cleared space, crashing right into a valet, who drops his pewter tray.

A deluge of glass rains down around me, breaking like a crystal hailstorm on the floorboards.

Short of breath, my hair obstructing my vision, I frantically try to reach the handle of the sword lying a few feet away.

"Careful!" Naoko shouts behind me.

I gingerly pull back my fingers to avoid getting cut by glass. Powered by a demonic force, the treacherous sword has turned itself around, directing its bloodthirsty blade in my direction.

I'm on the ground, defenseless, my own weapon aimed against me, my opponent closing in fast. Thinking I'd destabilize her by mentioning her letter, I succeeded only in unleashing her fury.

You're done for! a voice inside me screams.

Trust your instincts! exclaims another.

I grab a piece of broken glass . . .

And with all my strength, I hurl it toward Hélénaïs's quivering feathers, the same way I used to aim my sling at pheasants in full flight.

She lets out a piercing scream. The sharp crystal cuts her cheek.

Stopping dead in her tracks, she brings her hand to her face, feeling the wound with the tips of her fingers as if she can't believe what happened.

"First blood has been drawn!" shouts the Knight of Saint-Loup.

"But . . . but . . . ," Hélénaïs stammers. "That bitch didn't use the weapon issued."

She turns toward the royal dais, trembling with rage and indignation.

"Sire, your ward cheated. You must sanction her!"

The courtiers' feverish exclamations cease like magic.

More so than the crystal fragment, Hélénaïs's words just sealed her fate.

A terrible growl comes from the royal mask, causing even the chandelier prisms to vibrate.

"*We must?* You dare give us orders, you miserable mortal?"

Realizing too late the unforgivable error she's just committed, Hélénaïs drops her sword.

"I . . . I was confused, sire. It's not what I meant to say," she stammers.

"*Out of our sight,*" the Immutable says in a hollow voice, more deadly than all the shouts.

Struck down with shame, Hélénaïs backs up among the tide of courtiers who swallow her up, hiding her from the royal wrath.

"The winner!" Saint-Loup proclaims as she helps me up.

Like with Tristan a short while ago, a flock of doctors hurries toward me, and their black shirts spirit me away in a raven whirlwind.

28

SIP

I've made it.

That obsessive thought goes round and round in my dazed head.

I've had to lie, betray, cheat, kill . . . but I've made it.

The doctors lead me through long corridors with squeaky floors. By the looks of the large ruffs and the gold crests decorating their conical hats, they belong to the most powerful dignitaries of the Faculty.

A crowd of courtiers at our heels, we arrive at a huge door bearing the royal insignia: the nocturnal mask of Apollo.

Exili, the grand archiater, is already present, looking deathlike in his scarlet coat. Which secret corridors did he take to get here so quickly? I hardly dare raise my eyes to look at his cadaver-like head, its deathly pallor contrasting with the bright white of his ruff. It's not only the cold emanating from him that makes me shiver; his entire being radiates a profound malaise, visceral, nauseating. I have the feeling of being in the presence not only of pure cruelty, same as with the other vampyres, but also of the most abject perversion.

"Keep the courtiers at a distance," he orders the king's squires in his unctuous voice.

All five of them are at hand, dressed in leather, standing guard. Only Suraj is missing, dispatched by the sovereign himself to take Rafael to the infirmary.

Lucrèce sends daggers my way with her eagle stare, as if she doesn't judge me worthy of the promotion that awaits. But she doesn't dare to express her contempt in front of Exili, the monarch's closest adviser. The crowd of courtiers itself, held back behind a purple velvet rope, is now silent. After the excitement of the duels in the Hall of Mirrors, a heavy atmosphere reigns. For most, it's the moment of reverence that precedes a mystical ritual; for the conspirators, it's the calm before the storm of a planned murder.

At last.

I'm here.

At the threshold of my destiny.

"Diane de Gastefriche, you will wait with Tristan de La Roncière in the antechamber," Exili instructs me. "The king will invite you himself into the mortuary chamber once he's ready to offer you the Sip." The grand archiater grazes my cheek with the long bluish nail of his bony index finger, sending shivers of disgust down to the marrow of my bones. "Entering the mortuary chamber is an exceptional privilege, offered to a rare few. Only the highest-ranking mortals and immortals of the court can attend the Grand Rising from the sarcophagus. That number is even smaller with regard to the intimate ritual of the Sip. This is the very room where I proceeded with the king's transmutation ceremony nearly three centuries ago. Ever since, time there has stopped. This stasis can destabilize mortals who aren't prepared, giving them a sort of . . . vertigo. Try to be worthy of the honor bestowed upon you. Try not to puke your guts out all over the king's shoes."

Hearing him talk about my "guts"—someone so used to dissecting people on the Faculty's operating tables—sickens me.

"I'll do my best not to, Your Eminence," I manage to say.

"Good. Be patient. The king takes his time to prepare for the ritual. He meditates on his infinite existence before he opens his veins, allowing a few droplets of eternity to bead up . . ."

As he says these fascinating, terrifying words, the squires open the antechamber door. A narrow and immaculate vestibule is revealed, fitted with lit sconces. Tristan is here, shivering in his shirt, his back still drenched in sweat from the duel.

The doctors' hands push me forward, and the door closes immediately on us.

"Are you all right?" I ask.

"With you, always," he whispers with emotion.

His voice sounds far away, hushed, even though I can feel his breath on my forehead. My gut tells me that this strange antechamber functions as a bridge between the outside world, where time unfolds normally, and the mortuary chamber, where Exili claimed it has stopped. The candles of the sconces shine steadily, without the tiny trembling that usually accompanies their flames.

In the middle of this frozen whiteness is the double door to the mortuary chamber. It's constructed from ebony, the dark wood that vampyre carriages are made of. A glacial aura emanates from the thick black panels, carved with skulls and bones mingled with esoteric symbols.

I shiver in my torn skirt.

Rather than being the two selected for promotion, I have the sense that we're the two about to be sacrificed, tossed as food to the Minotaur. The Shadows are almost palpable behind this closed door, more concentrated than ever.

Sensing my distress, Tristan takes my hand.

"I love you, Jeanne," he tells me. "I've never doubted that we would end up together here tonight. As I said, it's our destiny."

I glance anxiously around me, gripped with fear that someone will burst in on us.

But the vestibule is deserted. Our whispers can't penetrate the solid walls or the heavy door. Here, we really are apart from the world.

"Relax," Tristan says. "No one can hear us."

I nod, forcing myself to smile, which isn't difficult when my eyes are looking into his.

"I'd like this to be over," I tell him.

"So would I, Jeanne." He squeezes my hand a little harder. "You know, there's something I look forward to with even greater impatience than the destruction of the tyrant. I can't wait to finally tell my mother, the noble Dame de La Roncière, and our allies all about you."

Tristan's feelings warm my heart. But something in his words also worries me.

"Tell your allies about me?" I say reluctantly. "Do you mean that the rebels lying in ambush at the palace don't know about my involvement in the plot?"

"I haven't said a word to anyone, to keep you safe," he replies, smiling at me protectively. "You see, aristocrats of the highest rank in the land are part of the cabal. How do you think we've been able to conceal weapons in the mortuary chamber? Only noblemen with access to the Grand Rising of the sarcophagus were able to carry this out. What they want to achieve with the king's death is an end to the unbearable *numerus clausus* and the limits it imposes on the number of vampyres. That's the tyranny against which the Fronde of the Princes is fighting— the one that prevents us from being transmuted. You can well imagine that my allies would never have agreed to associate themselves with a mere commoner such as yourself. In their eyes, you're simply game."

My heart skips a beat.

Mere commoner . . . simply game . . . Is this really Tristan, my pure-hearted righter of wrongs?

"But . . . ," I say, "when you told me you were fighting for liberty or death . . ."

"Well, yes, liberty for the mortal aristocracy to access transmutations without any hindrances," he whispers. "Liberty for the lords to drink limitless amounts of blood from their vassals. Aristocrats worthy of that status owe it to themselves to be proud predators, not domesticated animals cooped up at Versailles. That's the natural order of the wild."

My head spins and my ears ring, as if I were punched in the face.

I cannot believe what I've just heard.

I must have misunderstood.

"When you got all worked up about the unbearable pressure the royal tithe exerts on the people . . . ," I insist, repeating the same words Tristan used to set my heart on fire.

"The *royal* tithe, indeed," he specifies. "Tons of blood that every year gets sent from the provinces to Versailles. What an intolerable dispossession." His eyes blaze with the flame of revolt, not on behalf of the people as I had thought but on behalf of his caste. "After the king is destroyed, the tithe will remain on the lands where it's produced," he decrees. "My mother will be able to find eternal youth by bleeding her sharecroppers. After all, those farmers belong to her as much as the fields they cultivate. And my brothers and sisters and cousins will be able to tap into the same reservoir of commoner blood. Their most sacred feudal right."

My legs go weak under me, and I have to grab hold of the only support available—Tristan's shoulder.

"Don't worry," he whispers. "I'm just as overwhelmed as you are. Our encounter at the Grande Écurie took me totally by surprise. Nothing prepared me for my growing feelings toward you. Who would have believed it—me, a La Roncière, crazy in love with a commoner. But though you were born in the mire, your heart is noble, I tell you. You're not prey, Jeanne; you're a predator, like me. Together we'll fill in the abyss that society dug out between us. Listen to me: As soon as we've decapitated the king in the mortuary chamber, we'll be able to drink our fill from his severed neck. We'll slash our wrists to empty ourselves of our mortal blood and replace it with the most powerful vampyric blood of all. Endowed with the power of supreme regeneration, the fluid will heal our wounds and erase the shameful scars from the tithe on your arms." He kisses my forehead, causing me to shiver in confusion. "The weasel from the countryside will transform into a noble ermine. No one will dare attack you on your dubious origins once you're transmuted. By marrying me, you'll leave the insignificant Froidelac name behind and become a La Roncière. Together we will create a new vampyric kingdom in the forest of the Ardennes . . . a new eternal dynasty."

The scar on his cheek suddenly seems to morph into a twig, bristling with thorns. It's the branch of the La Roncières, the one he wants me to join.

Tristan hugs me closer.

"I will make you my immortal queen," he says, tenderly, his blue eyes sparkling with love and pride. "You'll be feared and admired throughout the universe. Songs will be written celebrating your glorious silver-haired beauty, a beauty that will never fade. Jeanne the Magnificent, sovereign of the Ardennes and mistress of my heart for all the centuries to come."

It's the perfect declaration, the one everyone in love dreams of—the promise of literal infinite love.

It's also the chilling avowal that love is tragically blind indeed, as Tristan never saw who I am, and I, too, completely mistook who he was.

Before I can say anything, the double doors of the mortuary chamber open all by themselves. The eerie silence of the heavy ebony panels turning on their steel hinges fills my heart with a sinister awe.

The vast room before us must have been covered in gold once, but today it's completely black, as calcified as the remains of Pompeii. Doric columns, arching caryatids, carved in the shape of gods and animals— all covered with a uniform layer of ash, a deep umbra that absorbs all the light raining down from the crystal obsidian chandeliers and, so it seems, all sound itself. If the acoustics in the antechamber dulled sound, the ones in the mortuary chamber block it altogether.

Like inside an airtight box, the needles on the clock faces are frozen at midnight, thus forever marking the hour when Louis XIV became Louis the Immutable, nearly three hundred years ago.

An enormous black stone sarcophagus sits in the center of the mausoleum—the coffin where the king lies during the day.

At this hour, he stands before us, hovering over us with his full height.

Divested of his imposing coronation robe and embroidered coat, he's simply wearing a black silk shirt and the glistening gold mask. This stripped-down state renders him even more awe inspiring—the rolled-up sleeves reveal his bare, muscular arms, the white flesh swollen with bluish veins that snake around like those of ancient marble.

My animal instinct shouts at me to run from this ultimate predator, seated as he is at the apex of the food chain.

But my legs, driven by the same demonic magnetism that bewitched me during the never-ending jig, start toward the king.

My shoes don't make a sound as they strike the black floor.

No words come forth from the monarch's sphinxlike mask.

And yet, I hear his deafening voice resonate deep inside me, so powerful that it crushes my brain more cruelly than my worst migraines.

"Come to me, Diane de Gastefriche. Drink from the source of eternal life."

The absolute cold emanating from his being paralyzes me.

He raises his right hand. His nails stand erect, like the monstrous claws of a cat that have shot out from their fleshy sheaths. He places the pointy end of his index finger against his left wrist and punctures one of the veins. A thick liquid starts to bead.

Then he grabs my neck.

With the simple pressure of his clawed fingers, I sense that he could break it as easily as that of a baby rabbit.

His black pupils are completely dilated beneath the slits of his mask, taking over the whites of his eyes. Seeing his huge eyeballs so close up fills me with unspeakable terror. It's a fright coming from the depths of the ages, one that hearkens back to the nightmares of my childhood, and even before then—to the origins of human beings, so vulnerable in the face of the large beasts that populate nighttime immemorial.

I'd like to run away, but my body won't respond.

I'd like to scream, but no sound comes out of my mouth.

The King of Shadows gags me with his bloody wrist.

A deathly cold liquid, heavy like lead, spreads across my tongue. It has no flavor, and yet it's like I'm tasting death itself.

As the Immutable spills his shadowessence-filled blood into my body, I notice Tristan above his shoulder, seemingly near and terribly far, as if the enormous dimensions of this otherworldly room are exempt from laws of geometry. Having managed to move without attracting the attention of the monarch, Tristan is now close to the rear wall of the chamber, where he lifts one of the wood panels—the one with the lion's head. When he turns around, he's brandishing a stake in his right hand and a silver sword in his left.

I see him glide over to me without a sound, mouthing silent words, his blond hair lifting in this compressed atmosphere that carries no sound.

The viselike grip of the royal fingers suddenly loosens on my neck.

The king tears his wrist violently from my lips.

As the Immutable turns, Tristan throws himself on top of him with all his weight and drives the sharpened stake through his heart.

A silent scream rattles my soul, as if all the stars of the universe were crumbling on themselves.

The ashen walls of the room begin to vibrate.

The king's tapered fingers, deformed by outrageously long nails, close around the stake planted in his rib cage to pull it out. But Tristan continues to drive it in with all his might. He throws the silver sword at me so that he can push the wooden stake with both hands.

On his trembling lips, I decipher the mute cry that the mortuary chamber smothers.

"Now, decapitate him now."

His face displays the same elated expression it did back in the clearing with the buck.

Just after our crazy escape.

Just before our long kiss.

His passionate eyes reaffirm his declaration of love.

"Mistress of my heart, for all the centuries to come."

I see my reflection—what I could become—in the blue mirrors of his irises: a fearsome sovereign, the most powerful that the world has ever known, my eyes radiating with Shadows and my silver hair crowned with storms.

In my trembling hand, I raise the blade.

I thrust it into Tristan's neck, right up to the hilt.

Tristan lets go of the stake.

His legs collapse under him.

He falls to the ground on his knees, his two hands clamped around his throat, where blood gushes out in big spurts.

Between his long strands of hair, his blue eyes are wide, staring at me in disbelief.

His lips—which only days ago I kissed passionately—drip with blood, parting to say my name.

I can't allow it. That mouth must never speak again, not today, not ever.

Those eyes must close forever, taking with them the dizzying image they reflected of me.

My eyelids bathed in tears, my vision blurred, I raise my arm above Tristan's kneeling figure and bring the blade down with all my strength onto his neck. His head detaches from his shoulders, like Valère's before him, and rolls to the monarch's feet.

Already, the Immutable has pulled out the stake from his rib cage. It's dripping with a liquid black as ink. Shadowessence evaporates from the gaping wound, forming malignant spirals in the air. Under my foggy eyes, the monarch's punctured chest contracts. His broken ribs mend, the black blood flowing back into the wound like an ebbing tide, the whitish skin reweaving itself over the magically closed hole. A groan of silent suffering accompanies this abhorrent metamorphosis, sending vibrations into the gold mask and its frozen expression.

The Immutable sends Tristan's head rolling with the tip of his red-heeled shoe as if it were a piece of carrion. The door to the mortuary chamber opens on its own with a bang, followed by the door to the antechamber, activated by the supernatural willpower of the King of Shadows. The exterior sounds that the mystical room smothered explode in my ears: cries of pain, shouts of hate, gunshots, and the clashing of swords.

Through the suite of doors, I notice that the tall white walls of the corridor are splattered with red. The bodies of the Swiss Guards and squires who've been killed are heaped on the floor, bearing witness to the slaughter that started as soon as Tristan and I entered the mortuary chamber. My eyes rest on a glint of metal in the middle of this gruesome bloodbath—it's Lucrèce du Crèvecœur's iron gauntlet. She herself lies with her throat slashed, in her own blood. The decapitated heads of the immortals are mixed in with the gutted corpses of the mortal courtiers by the dozens. A pungent odor seasons the sweet scent of blood. It's the fragrance from the essence of garlic flower that the conspirators sprinkled liberally in the corridor before the killing began.

These conspirators, still busy stabbing and gutting their adversaries, suddenly stop and look in our direction. A realization comes over their faces, all of them smeared with the blood of their victims: anguish at their impending death replaces the wild joy of meting it out.

The king gives an earth-shattering roar.

Hunched over on the ground behind him, I see the long strands of his hair stand on end around his head, just like the vengeful rays of a black sun.

With his clawlike hands, he unlocks the secret mechanism that holds the mask to his neck.

The gold face covering falls to the floor, making a dull noise that sounds like an empty shell.

From where I stand, I can see neither the sovereign's face nor his vampyric jaw, now free of the metal yoke. But the conspirators see it all. An indescribable terror distorts their features—mouths agape with wails of desperation, eyes seemingly popping out of their sockets.

The king swoops down upon them like a shadowy cyclone, flying over the floor in a shirt that puffs out from a supernatural wind.

A violent gust slams the antechamber door shut behind him, burying me in a night as dark and silent as the bottom of a cave.

29
VISION

All five of us are gathered around the table.

Maman, Papa, Valère, Bastien, and me.

The pheasant soup steams in the tureen that sits in the middle of the table decorated with wildflowers.

Through the window, the warm rays of the late-afternoon sun bathe the faces of my family.

"Welcome home, Jeanne," my father says.

I want to respond, but distress knots my throat.

In spite of appearances, I know that my family is dead.

This memory seems so real but is only an illusion of the past, brought back to life by the evil power of the mortuary chamber, where time ceases to exist.

The last memory of my happy family will stay forever frozen in the golden light of seven o'clock, on the night of August 31, before the inquisitor's fist hammered on our door and shattered everything.

"I . . . I had the king's neck at the edge of my sword, but I couldn't behead him," I stammer. "The vengeance I obsessed over for weeks was within reach, but I couldn't go through with it."

Valère adjusts his thick eyeglasses, the way he does every time he gets ready to lecture me.

"Don't be so hard on yourself," he says.

Any trace of tension has vanished from his voice. My big brother seems calmer than ever, and his unexpected kindness soothes my strange dread.

"I'm proud of you, weasel," Bastien adds, touching my hand. "You did what you had to do."

His sensitive eyes sparkle as brightly as when we would gaze at the clouds.

"The creation of a new bloody reign wouldn't have served our cause," Maman concludes as she smiles at me tenderly, her long brown lashes hemming her golden eyes. "It's by undermining the current reign from the inside that you'll be able to carry our torch and, even more—accomplish what we fought so hard for." Her luminous smile widens, chasing away the remaining gloom that weighed on my heart. "Big changes don't come from vengeance, my dear girl, but from vision. Vengeance binds us to what no longer is, like a chain to the past. But vision propels us toward what is yet to come, like the breath of the future."

With these prophetic words, I realize that the ambient light got brighter. It's no longer the dying firelight of evening but the brilliant burst of morning. My mother's hair is different—shorter, interwoven with lighter strands. She isn't wearing one of her long dresses full of pockets to gather herbs but men's pants cut in the new cloth of the day—denim, which I've recently discovered. In fact, all the members of my family are attired in these strange pants. My brothers no longer wear the coarse shirts made of raw canvas but colorful, short-sleeved undershirts. Valère's has an image of a sphere decorated with black pentagons and white hexagons, on top of which it enigmatically says, *World Cup 2014*. Bastien's has a red-and-blue lightning bolt going across it, stamped with the phrase *WE CAN BE HEROES JUST FOR ONE DAY*.

Amazed, I look around. The dwelling where I spent my childhood is both similar and different, just like those who live there. Above the chimney, the framed engraving of the King of Shadows is gone. In its place is a sort of glass mirror with moving images: horseless chariots roll along on roads with no end in sight, in defiance of the sequester law; two mechanical birds fly without beating their wings in the summer night, carrying aboard women and men free of the curfew law; I even see a gigantic iron cathedral magically propelled toward the stars.

These extraordinary images seem to come straight out of the Antipodes, the imaginary land that escaped the Magna Vampyria, the one Bastien dreamed about. And like a dream, the images dissolve in the radiant morning light.

I open my eyes.

I'm lying in a bed, same as I did a week ago when I was felled by the fever. And again, Naoko is bent over my bedside.

"I'm here, Diane," she says. "You slept nearly all night long."

By her gentle voice, I sense that I've at last found my dear, long-lost friend again. But the name she calls me sounds like a warning: we are not alone.

I slowly realize I'm not at the Grande Écurie but in a room at the palace. It has gilded panels and is lit with large chandeliers. Doctors fill the room, their black shirts popping out against the colorful paintings on the walls.

"She's awake! Alert the king!" someone shouts.

Now conscious of the fine linen sheets on my skin, I lower my eyes. The scars from the tithe have vanished in the crooks of my naked elbows, just as Tristan predicted. A little shadowessence now runs in my veins, and the last stigma that pegs me as a commoner has been erased.

The door opens.

An icy wind whips my face while the doctors tilt their conical hats.

The Immutable enters the room, accompanied by his bodyguards, his ministers, and his grand archiater. A new black shirt has replaced the one Tristan's stake pierced, covering the wound that miraculously healed due to the power of the Shadows. The monarch's amazing head of hair once again falls onto his shoulders. His claws have retracted into his pale fingers. Most of all, he's wearing a new impenetrable gold mask, hiding a face that, despite all my efforts, I cannot imagine.

A deep voice booms from the metallic lips.

"You saved the Crown, Diane de Gastefriche. We saw you grab the sword from the hands of the ignoble regicide and turn it against him. Who would have believed that a little gray mouse like you could weigh so heavily on the scale of destiny?"

Not knowing how to respond, I lower my eyes, a sign of submission, assuming the role of the mouse that the sovereign assigned to me. Let him think I'm a small, familiar animal: I'll sneak more easily into the corridors of power, where I can gnaw at the strings.

"The members of this ignoble cabal decimated our squires," he goes on. "All five are dead, with the exception of our loyal Suraj. The vile rebels got to taste our royal wrath. Fifty among them were killed on the spot: their bodies will be impaled as early as tomorrow on the Hunting Wall. Let it be a warning. Fifty others are rotting in our prisons. The fate that awaits them is far worse. As we speak, Mélac's army is marching into the Ardennes. Our dragoons have been ordered to capture all traitors alive, starting with the Dame de La Roncière. They will be subjected to the longest, most painful tortures—is that not right, Montfaucon?"

Suddenly, I notice the presence of the grand equerry at the back of the room.

He must have found a way to get out of the underground torture chamber after he regained consciousness, unless Orfeo helped him force the door open. Now he's here, looking drab in his long leather coat.

"Yes, sire," he says, lowering his waxy face. "We will deal with the traitors as they deserve to be treated, in order to wrench full confessions out of them."

As he raises his head between his limp curls, his bright eyes catch mine. I see something I've never seen in them before: admiration. I succeeded in stopping the palace revolt he'd warned me about, the consequences of which would have been dramatic for the people. An anarchic proliferation of bloodsuckers, without the framework of the *numerus clausus*, would literally have finished off the fourth estate. I didn't kill Tristan to save the king, no, but to prepare for the real revolution—the one that will dissolve the Shadows and dethrone the Immutable as well as all the vampyres and Tristans of the world.

"You and Suraj are now my sole squires," the monarch says, not thinking that by naming me thus, he allies himself with the one who's sworn his defeat. "Is there something that we can do to express our gratitude? Speak without shame, mademoiselle. Jewels, exotic animals, sophisticated weapons. You are permitted every extravagance. What will satisfy you? And do not tell us that you would like to dance your never-ending jig of victory with that Alexandre de Mortange."

"The only thing that can satisfy me, sire, is your safety," I say. "You need to make haste and bring together a complete body of personal guards."

"Well, well, will that be all? Your concern is honorable. Indeed, we must assemble a new guard. But whom to choose? Would you have a name to suggest?"

"I vouch for Proserpina Castlecliff."

For a few seconds, the sparkling chandeliers silently glow on the surface of the mask.

"That girl who suffers from tuberculosis and was eliminated from the competition?" the king finally says, skeptical. "The very one supposedly at death's door?"

"She is already completely devoted to you, sire. If you offer her the Sip, thus saving her life, she will be even more loyal."

He nods, agitating the long curls of his incredible mane.

"That is clever thinking. You combine psychological insight with physical agility. We are eager to see what powers our Sip will develop in you, as you already show great potential."

I force a smile. The only powers I desire are those that would help me overthrow the tyrant in front of me.

"But the English girl placed only third in the competition," the king continues. "If we elevate her, etiquette dictates that we also promote the semifinalists. That works out well: four candidates to fill the four vacant spots. Thus, your wish will be fulfilled and our guard instantly reformed."

He turns toward his doctors, commanding them with his black-laced sleeve.

"Bring the chosen to the mortuary chamber immediately so that we may offer them our Sip. May their elevation take place without further delay. May the state resume its imperturbable course. Let it be proclaimed throughout the Vampyria that the Immutable was not shaken by that pathetic faction of rebels. Such is our implacable response to those who, having dared wish for our defeat, have sealed their own."

EPILOGUE

Tomorrow, November 1, is the day I will officially move into the palace.

In the eyes of the world, I am Diane de Gastefriche, squire to the King of Shadows.

But deep in my heart, I will always be Jeanne Froidelac, heir to my family's fight.

None of the other five squires to the king, with whom I've been called to live, suspect my true identity.

I don't know if Poppy will ever forgive me for having betrayed her, despite trying to redeem myself by pleading her case with the monarch. But I'm certain that Hélénaïs won't miss any opportunity to bring about my downfall.

Rafael and Suraj have too much going on to worry about me. They have their own secret to hide from king and court.

As for the enigmatic Zacharie, I have no idea what he thinks of me.

At the Court of Shadows, my enemies are many. The mortal conspirators whose plans I thwarted may not have all been killed or imprisoned by the king's dragoons. The immortal courtiers pose an even greater threat: Edmée and Marcantonio gave me a foretaste of their cruel games. Alexandre presents an even more formidable threat now that he's become infatuated with me—especially as twenty years ago he killed another squire. As for Exili, the grand archiater, my gut tells me to be as careful of him as I would the plague.

Yet just as every commoner is not an ally, as Madame Thérèse proved, every aristocrat is not an adversary. In the months and years to come, I'll be able to count on at least two among them: my dear Naoko and Montfaucon, accompanied by the haunting Orfeo. All of them as uprooted as I am, the damned of the Vampyria: a foreigner possessed by a demon, an executioner consumed by remorse, and a speechless monster with a golden heart. With their help, I'll have to accept enormous challenges and answer dizzying questions.

What is the secret of the Shadows?

Why are they becoming more powerful of late, unleashing a greater thirst for blood among vampyres and the fury of nocturnal abominations?

Will the wind of rebellion that blows in the Americas reach the heart of the Vampyria before the Shadows devour it from within?

And finally, what is the meaning of the strange vision that gripped me when I was alone in the mortuary chamber? A prophecy? A horizon? Or just a random mirage?

I know the path that leads to the liberation of the people will be steep.

Between the rebels in love with justice and those, like Tristan, who want power for themselves—the snares will be plentiful.

The road will be strewed with sacrifices even more painful than the ones I had to make to get here.

I don't care.

The time for a savage, self-destructive revenge is over.

Now it's about a meticulous and thorough destruction of the Vampyria.

For as long as my heart beats in my chest, I will wage my secret fight against the lords of the night—liberty or death, forevermore.

ACKNOWLEDGMENTS

The time has come to thank those who accompanied me on this perilous journey.

First off, my family, for their unwavering support during all the nights when I wandered between our calendar and the year 299 of the Age of Shadows.

Followed by my editors, Constance, Fabien, and Glenn, who trailed me in the hallways of Versailles, at the risk of being bled.

Nekro, Loles, and Tarwane, the talented artists who gave life to the baroque world that haunted me. Misty Beee, the amazing cartographer who courageously explored the most remote borders of the Magna Vampyria.

Joël, Céline, and Barbara, who fine-tuned the book you are holding in your hands. Alexandra, Laetitia, Céline, Filipa, Christiane, Benita, Alix, Isabelle, Tiffany, and the entire team at Éditions Robert Laffont.

Finally, Billie and Rasco, the companions of my nocturnal writing, who, like all cats, possess the magical ability to see through the Shadows, beyond the abyss of time and space.

AS YOU CLOSE THIS BOOK, DEAR READERS,
YOU SHUT THE DOOR TO
THE COURT OF SHADOWS.
BUT A NEW DOOR WILL SOON OPEN,
ONTO A NEW COURT . . .
JEANNE AND I INVITE YOU
TO JOIN US THERE!

FOLLOW JEANNE'S CONTINUING
ADVENTURES IN

THE COURT OF MIRACLES

BOOK 2 OF THE VAMPYRIA SAGA

FROM AMAZON CROSSING

ABOUT THE AUTHOR

Photo © 2019 Samantha Rayward

Two-time winner of the Grand Prix de l'Imaginaire, Victor Dixen stands at the forefront of French fantasy. His acclaimed series include Animale, Phobos, Cogito, Extincta, and Vampyria. A nomadic writer, he has lived in Paris, Dublin, Singapore, New York, and now Washington, DC, drawing inspiration from the promises of the future as much as the ghosts of the past.

Find out more about Dixen's universe at www.victordixen.com.

ABOUT THE TRANSLATOR

Photo © 2023 Elisabeth Bui

Françoise Bui spent twenty years as an executive editor at Delacorte Press, an imprint of Random House Children's Books, where her list of edited books included numerous novels in translation. Of these, four received the Mildred L. Batchelder Award (for most outstanding children's book initially published in a foreign language), and two were Honor titles. Originally from France, Bui lives in New York City.